Love After Regret

A Second-Chance Redemption Romance Collection

Alison Reid

Love After Regret – A Second-Chance Redemption Romance Collection

by Alison Reid

ISBN: 978-1-7645079-3-6

First edition

Independently published

Introduction to...

Love After Regret

A Second-Chance Redemption Romance Collection

Regret. Redemption. Second Chances.

Welcome to **Love After Regret**—a collection of emotionally charged romances where hearts broken by thoughtless words, betrayals, or misunderstandings are given a chance to heal. These are the stories of women who walked away, and the men who finally realize the depth of their mistakes.

From sun-drenched Italian estates to small-town streets and quiet moments of reflection, these standalone romances explore the journey from heartbreak to hope, showing that love—though tested by time, pride, and regret—can still be reclaimed.

Inside this collection, you'll find men forced to confront their flaws, women who refuse to settle, and the unforgettable moment when love proves stronger than past mistakes. Every story delivers slow-burning tension, emotional payoff, and a guaranteed happily-ever-after.

Whether you're discovering these characters for the first time or returning to beloved heroines and heroes, **Love After Regret** invites you to immerse yourself in a binge-worthy collection where love lost is never truly gone—and second chances are always worth fighting for.

Enjoy the journey.

Table of Contents

A Heart in Florence

Alison Reid

A complete standalone romance

Previously published individually

Chapter One

Isabella Moretti had just turned nineteen, and as she clutched the worn leather handle of her suitcase a little too tightly, her long, wavy dark-blonde hair tumbled over her shoulders, catching in the soft morning light that streamed through the high windows of Florence's airport. Her doe-brown eyes, wide with apprehension and glazed with grief, swept the bustling terminal, absorbing a world that felt suddenly foreign. Every detail—the language, the sunlight, even the warmth in the air—seemed to press against her like an unfamiliar weight. Just hours earlier, she had left London, the city that had always been her world, behind. Now it seemed impossibly distant, as though the familiar grey skies, the rain-soaked streets, and the laughter of her mother were shadows she could no longer reach.

Her chest tightened as memories surged forward—the sudden, brutal moment that had shattered her life. Rebecca Moretti, her mother, her entire family, had been struck by a car only weeks ago, killed instantly on a rainy London street. Isabella could still hear the echo of sirens in her mind, the suffocating silence afterward, the unbearable emptiness of returning to their flat with no one waiting for her. Every familiar corner of her home felt hollow; every photograph a reminder of everything she had lost.

Her mother had never married. It had always been just the two of them— Isabella and Rebecca, against the world. She knew her father, Marco Fioravanti. He was a kind man, she had never doubted that, but he had always been little more than a distant presence in her life. He lived in Florence, working as a chauffeur for one of Italy's wealthiest families. Years ago, he and Rebecca had shared a brief holiday romance, a fleeting connection that had left Isabella as its lasting reminder. Though he had visited her once or twice a year, their relationship had always been formal, polite—a connection of necessity and blood, but not of shared laughter or everyday closeness.

And now, impossibly, she was here. To live with him. To build a life beside a man she barely knew, in a city that pulsed with beauty and history yet felt alien to her aching heart.

The airport buzzed around her, voices colliding with the low hum of rolling luggage and the distant squeal of carts. Announcements in lilting Italian drifted from overhead speakers, melodic and foreign, carrying a rhythm she did not recognise. Warm Mediterranean air drifted in through the terminal doors, tinged with the scent of espresso, fresh pastries, and sun-warmed stone—a fragrant promise of a city that held both beauty and unfamiliarity.

Then she saw him. A man standing straight and composed, holding a simple white placard with her name neatly written: *Isabella Moretti*. Her heart clenched, a sudden, fierce ache cutting through her chest. This was him. Marco Fioravanti. Her father.

He was taller than she remembered, his frame lean yet strong, his dark hair threaded with dignified streaks of grey. His eyes—soft brown, lined with the subtle traces of years of labour and quiet patience—held a warmth that caught her off guard. In the rare moments she had glimpsed him during her childhood, she had seen a gentleness, a quiet kindness, but now it seemed deeper, steadier, tempered by time and experience.

When his gaze met hers, it softened into a smile. Not a careless smile, but a careful, reverent one, as though every moment of his absence had been stored and folded into this single gesture. It was a smile that carried years of waiting, of wishing he had been more present, and of unspoken regret.

"Isabella," he said, his voice low, slightly roughened with emotion. He stepped forward, each pace deliberate, grounding her in the moment. In that instant, she felt like a child again. "My little girl."

The words hit her with the force of memory and longing. Her throat tightened, tears pricking her eyes. She blinked hard, caught between laughter and sobs, the strange, tangled mix of relief and grief. Standing before this man—familiar yet foreign—was disorienting. "Hello… Father," she whispered, fragile, trembling like delicate glass.

She set her suitcase down, and he drew her into his arms. The hug began cautiously, as though he feared crushing her fragile heart, but it quickly deepened into something solid, protective, and profoundly comforting.

"It's alright," Marco murmured, his accent softening each syllable. "It is going to be alright now. You are here with me."

Isabella pressed her face into his shoulder, inhaling the grounding scent of leather, faint cologne, and something unmistakably him. Weeks of forced strength—through the funeral, the endless condolences, the empty rituals of packing up her mother's life—dissolved in this embrace. Beneath the golden Florence light, her grief surged forward, and she trembled as tears slipped silently down her cheeks.

Marco's hand smoothed gently down her back, steady and sure. When she finally pulled back, he lifted her chin with a careful touch, compelling her eyes to meet his.

"Come," he said softly, a faint curve of amusement lifting the corners of his lips, though it did not reach his eyes entirely. "We will get you settled at the estate. You will see—it is beautiful here. And…" He paused, a flicker of something playful in his gaze, "perhaps you'll find a few surprises along the way."

Isabella managed a small, tentative smile, the ache in her chest softening just enough for curiosity to creep in. The Caravelli estate. She had heard of it all her life—the sprawling vineyards that stretched toward the horizon, olive groves whispering in the Tuscan breeze, and the villa itself, an architectural jewel that seemed plucked from another century. Marco had devoted years of service to the Caravelli family, a world of wealth and power that had always felt just out of reach. And now, impossibly, she was stepping into that life—not as a guest, but as a part of the home he had built within its walls.

The drive from the airport unfurled like a dream—terracotta rooftops glowing under the afternoon sun, narrow cypress-lined roads stretching seemingly into infinity, and rolling Tuscan hills painted in shades of green and gold. Isabella sat quietly, her cheek pressed lightly to the cool glass of the window, her wide brown eyes tracing every curve of the landscape. The air itself seemed different here—warmer, softer, carrying with it the mingled scent of sun-warmed earth, olive groves, and wildflowers in bloom.

She drank it all in, yet beneath the quiet wonder was a tremor of unease. Each twist of the road reminded her that she was being carried further from the London streets she had known all her life, further from the echoes of her mother's laughter, and into a world whose rules she had yet to learn, a world in which she was unsure she truly belonged.

When the villa finally came into view, Isabella's breath caught in her throat. It rose from the hills like a monument sculpted from the very earth, majestic and sprawling, framed by lush gardens and orderly stone terraces. Tall windows glittered in the sunlight, reflecting the afternoon glow like sheets of molten gold. Fountains whispered in the courtyard, their delicate streams catching the breeze, while ivy crawled gracefully up the pale stone walls, as though time itself had chosen to adorn the estate.

The car came to a smooth stop before the grand entrance. Marco turned toward her, his expression soft with both reassurance and quiet pride. He extended his hand toward her.

"Ready to see your new home?" he asked gently.

Isabella hesitated only a moment before placing her hand in his. "Yes," she whispered, though her heart raced with a mixture of excitement and apprehension.

Stepping out, she felt small against the grandeur of the villa, her simple shoes brushing the smooth stone steps that led to the entrance. And yet, along with the weight of intimidation, there flickered a fragile, surprising thrill—as though this new chapter might, in time, hold the possibility of healing. Perhaps even of joy.

Marco retrieved her suitcase with practiced ease, the gesture a quiet reminder that he belonged here in a way she did not—at least, not yet. Together they ascended the steps, Isabella's eyes darting over the façade. The terracotta tiles gleamed beneath the fading sun, and the shadows stretched across the courtyard like brushstrokes on a canvas. Voices drifted faintly from within—staff at work, the subtle hum of life echoing through walls steeped in centuries of history.

"This will be your home now," Marco said quietly, studying her as though he could read the storm of emotions on her face. "The staff quarters are modest, but comfortable. You will have your own space to think, to rest…" He paused, his voice softening further, almost intimate. "And to decide what you want to do next."

Isabella clutched the strap of her small bag tighter, swallowing the lump that had risen in her throat. She had practiced her Italian for weeks, repeating phrases late into the night in her bedroom, yet the language still felt foreign, clumsy, not quite hers. Each step forward seemed heavier than the last, as though she were crossing not only a threshold but the invisible line into a new life—a life inextricably tied to the Caravelli family's legacy, a family she had only ever known through her father's stories and faded photographs.

They reached a smaller wing tucked discreetly behind the grand main building. Marco unlocked the door with a brass key, the lock clicking softly before he pushed it open. Isabella stepped inside, her breath catching as her eyes adjusted.

The room was modest, yet undeniably charming. Pale cream walls reflected the golden Tuscan light streaming through a single window, where linen curtains swayed gently in the breeze. A wrought-iron bed, neatly dressed in crisp white linens, stood against one wall. Opposite it, a small writing desk rested by the window, its surface bare but inviting, as though silently awaiting her sketches or private thoughts. A sturdy wooden wardrobe occupied the corner, promising space enough for the few belongings she had carried from London.

"It's small," Marco said softly, setting her suitcase down. "But it's yours."

Isabella ran her fingertips along the smooth edge of the desk, the grain of the wood cool beneath her skin. Her chest tightened. "It's... lovely," she murmured, almost inaudible. It wasn't much, but it felt safe—her own quiet refuge within the immensity of the Caravelli villa.

The door creaked, and she turned as a woman entered, balancing a silver tray. She was middle-aged, with kind features, dark hair swept neatly into a bun, and eyes that sparkled with warmth.

"Buongiorno, Signorina Isabella," she greeted in melodic Italian, her voice as comforting as a lullaby. "I am Rosa, the housekeeper. While you are here, I will see that you want for nothing."

Isabella offered a shy smile. "Thank you, signora," she replied, her English accent lilting over the Italian words, but her gratitude sincere.

Rosa's smile deepened before she gestured to a tall, slender man who stepped politely into the room behind her. His posture was impeccable, his expression formal yet softened by warm, dark eyes.

"This is Signor Aldo, the butler," Rosa introduced. "You will see him often. He takes care of the house and the family's needs."

"Pleased to meet you, Signor Aldo," Isabella said, attempting a small curtsy, her cheeks warming at her own awkwardness.

Aldo inclined his head with quiet grace. "You are welcome here, Signorina. If you need anything—anything at all—you need only ask."

Rosa set the tray on the desk, revealing a porcelain cup of tea, a small plate of almond biscuits, and a folded cloth embroidered delicately with Isabella's name. Isabella's throat tightened at the unexpected kindness. After London—the noise, the grief, the hollow emptiness of her mother's absence—this gentle gesture felt like a lifeline. She brushed her fingers across the embroidery, lips trembling as she whispered, "Grazie... I will try my Italian."

Rosa's eyes twinkled. "Ah, but your Italian is already very good," she encouraged warmly. "It will grow, day by day. Soon, you will speak as though you were born here."

Isabella's gaze wandered around the room again. Sunlight poured across the polished wooden floorboards, casting shifting patterns of gold and shadow, as though the villa itself was welcoming her. For the first time since her mother's death, she felt a fragile sense of calm—a quiet, tentative hope that here, in this ancient house with its gentle caretakers and the promise of new beginnings, she might finally begin to heal.

Lorenzo Caravelli stood on the balcony of his bedroom, the early morning sun spilling molten gold across the rolling Tuscan hills. A porcelain cup of espresso rested in his hands, its rich, bitter aroma curling upward like smoke, grounding him in the quiet ritual of the early day. Tall and lean, with dark hair that gleamed in the light and hazel eyes that shifted between green and amber depending on the sun, he bore every outward mark of the Caravelli heir. And yet, the title sat on his shoulders like chains, heavy and unyielding.

The weight of expectation was relentless. Even now, with Matteo Caravelli's health failing, the man still demanded perfection. Illness had slowed his body, but not his tongue, nor the sharp edge of his criticism. To be a Caravelli was to be flawless—ruthless in business, commanding in presence, unyielding in pride. Failure—or even the hint of hesitation—was not tolerated.

And yet, warmth had never existed here. Tenderness had never existed, not even a flicker of paternal affection. Lorenzo had grown up under his father's shadow, every mistake magnified, every success dismissed as never enough. Matteo's gaze had been cold, his words cutting like glass. Love was absent in that household; control was the only currency.

His mother, Elena, had been the sole softness in a house of stone. Gentle, patient, quietly defiant in the small ways she could be. She had tried to shield her son with laughter, with fleeting touches, with whispered reassurances in the quiet of night when the halls of the villa echoed with silence. Yet she had also borne the brunt of Matteo's cruelty, enduring his indifference, his biting words, and the endless parade of mistresses, as though fidelity were beneath him.

Lorenzo's jaw tightened at the memory. He had despised those women—not for taking what should have been his mother's, but because their very presence was a wound reopened each time. They were constant reminders of his father's callousness, of a marriage built on duty rather than love, of a legacy he had inherited against his will.

He lifted the espresso to his lips and drank slowly, savouring the warmth as if it might fill the emptiness his father had carved into him. Behind him, the villa loomed grand and imposing, its gilded halls silent—a palace of cold marble and colder hearts. Beautiful, yes, but beauty could not disguise the hollowness of a house without love.

And yet… one day, it would all be his. The vineyards, the estates, the family name—a kingdom built on wealth, power, and reputation. Lorenzo knew the cost of such a legacy all too well. He would not repeat his father's mistakes. He would not marry for convenience, for alliances, or for appearances. Love—true, consuming, unwavering love—would be the only reason he would bind himself to another. And if that love eluded him, he would remain unwed, and the Caravelli bloodline would end with him.

The thought would infuriate his father if Matteo ever suspected it. Lorenzo imagined the sharp rebuke, the fury, the contempt—but he did not flinch. He would never put a woman through the cold indifference, the impossible demands, the quiet cruelty that had defined his own upbringing. And his children—should he have any—would know warmth, tenderness, and the kind of love his mother had fought so desperately to protect. He would shield them from the shadow his father had cast over him.

Closing his eyes, Lorenzo let the morning wind ruffle his dark hair, wishing the air could sweep away the weight pressing on him. Tuscany was in his blood— the curve of the hills, the scent of earth after rain, the golden light of dawn. He loved it fiercely, passionately, but in this house, under his father's relentless rule, he had never truly belonged.

And perhaps he never would.

For now, the morning, the wind, the scent of Tuscany, and the espresso in his hands were enough. But Lorenzo Caravelli vowed silently—between heartbeats, between sips, and beneath the quiet hum of the estate—that one day, when he claimed the family name in full, he would do so on his own terms. And he would never, ever allow the legacy of cruelty and coldness to touch the lives of his loved ones.

Lorenzo's gaze drifted across the gardens below, and it landed on the girl again. Over the past two days, he had watched her move along the cobbled paths, sometimes crouched beneath the gnarled olive trees, pencil poised delicately, sketchbook resting on her lap. She seemed entirely absorbed in her drawings, every gesture purposeful, quiet, almost reverent, as if she were sketching not just what she saw, but what she felt. There was a rhythm to her movements, a deliberate grace that drew his attention without effort.

From what he had observed, she was striking in her own understated way. Tall and slender, with pale skin that, under the warm Tuscan sun, would surely take on a golden glow, she seemed almost otherworldly against the riot of green and terracotta that surrounded the estate. Her long, wavy dark-blonde hair shimmered with each brush of sunlight, tumbling over her shoulders and catching the light like threads of spun gold. Her large, thoughtful eyes—hesitant yet alert—gave her an air of delicate fragility, yet there was a subtle determination in the way she held herself, a quiet confidence beneath the careful, almost measured movements. Very English, he noted, polite, self-contained, slightly out of place in the vibrant chaos of Mediterranean light and colour. And yet, there was something about her that refused to be overlooked.

He recalled overhearing his father speaking to Marco, the family's longtime chauffeur, about her arrival.

"The girl has just lost her mother," Marco had said softly, the sorrow in his voice unmistakable. "I am the only family she has left."

Matteo had dismissed the comment with a sharp, clipped tone. "A father… she barely knows."

"But family nonetheless," Marco had persisted, his voice quiet but firm.

"Very well," Matteo had said finally, with an edge of finality that brooked no argument. "If she must come, she can stay in the staff quarters."

Marco had nodded with a hint of reverence, as though he had been granted a rare boon, a victory small but meaningful.

Lorenzo frowned, a strange pull stirring in his chest, one he could neither name nor ignore. He had never spoken to her, never truly met her, and yet he felt an undeniable awareness of her presence, as if she had quietly carved a niche into the rhythm of the estate, a subtle orbit he could feel but not define. She had become part of the cadence of his mornings, the unspoken harmony beneath the sprawling gardens and sun-drenched terraces.

A girl alone in a world defined by wealth, history, and unyielding expectation, tethered only by her father—the chauffeur. Something about her intrigued him. Something about the delicate combination of vulnerability and quiet strength made him ache to see her beyond the sketches, beyond the absorbed, solitary figure moving among the olive trees.

And so, he watched. Silently. Sipping his espresso, letting the warmth seep into his hands and anchor him to the moment. Every subtle tilt of her head, every careful stroke of pencil across paper, drew him further in. He did not yet know her, and perhaps he never would, yet already she had begun to claim a space in his thoughts—small at first, almost imperceptible, but undeniably hers. A place not just in the estate, but in the quiet, uncharted corners of his attention, where curiosity and something far deeper were beginning to stir.

Chapter Two

Isabella awoke to the soft, golden light of Florence spilling lazily across her bedroom. The warmth of the morning sun filtered through the tall windows, brushing her cheeks and illuminating the subtle shimmer of dust in the air. She had been at the villa for a week, and while the walls no longer felt completely foreign, a quiet sense of displacement lingered, like a shadow at the edges of her thoughts. For several long, unhurried moments, she remained in bed, listening to the distant hum of life beyond her window—the rustle of olive leaves stirred by a gentle breeze, the delicate tinkling laughter of water as it danced from the fountains in the courtyards below, and the faint, rhythmic clatter of the staff beginning their morning routines.

Each day, Rosa had brought her tea—delicate porcelain cups cradled in her hands, steam curling upward like a promise—and offered patient encouragement in broken English whenever Isabella's Italian faltered. Aldo's steady, quiet presence had become a comforting constant, a silent reassurance that the villa, despite its grandeur, could feel less intimidating, less like a world into which she had been thrust unprepared. Slowly, piece by piece, she was finding her place here.

All the staff had been kind, endlessly patient as they guided her through the rhythm of this new life. She found herself speaking Italian with more confidence each day, testing phrases on Marco, Rosa, or even Aldo, and savouring the small victories when her words were understood. These were minor triumphs, but they made her feel tethered to this place, rooted in a world that had once seemed impossibly distant.

Rising, she pulled on a simple, pale dress, letting the linen cling lightly to her shoulders as she stepped outside. The morning air was crisp and fragrant, carrying the intoxicating perfume of jasmine and roses from the gardens, mingling seamlessly with the earthy scent of the vineyards that rolled beyond the villa walls. She wandered along the cobbled paths, the uneven stones pressing beneath her feet, allowing her gaze to linger on the terraced vineyards, each neat row of grapes stretching toward the horizon, their green leaves catching the light in soft glimmers. Cypress-lined walkways swayed gently in the breeze, and stone benches sat tucked beneath arching trellises, half-hidden by flowering vines that seemed to invite her curiosity.

Every corner of the gardens held a quiet promise, a small moment of discovery waiting to be claimed. Nearby, a fountain gurgled contentedly, sunlight refracting in the droplets to form tiny, fleeting rainbows. A pair of songbirds flitted from tree to tree, their calls delicate and lively, a music all their own in the soft morning air. Isabella paused for a long moment atop a low stone wall, resting her hands on its cool surface, and felt an unexpected lightness stir in her chest—a whisper of possibility she had not dared to acknowledge in weeks. Surrounded by beauty, by order and care, perhaps here she could begin to rebuild herself. Perhaps here, she could sketch not only jewels but the life she wished to shape.

Her fingers ached for her sketchbook. Settling onto the stone wall with the sunlight dappling her lap, she opened the notebook she had brought from London, its blank pages promising a world of beginnings. Her pencil trembled slightly in her hand as she began to draw, tentative lines that slowly grew more confident with every stroke.

She sketched a delicate necklace, inspired by the curling tendrils of ivy overhead, imagining it draped across a slender neck. Then, a ring shaped like the sun dipping behind the rolling hills, its curves capturing the soft elegance of dawn. Each line was more than design—it was reclamation: a claim on her life, a gentle assertion of control over a future still fragile and uncertain, a quiet hope blooming amid the grief that had followed her from London.

And as she worked, lost in the gentle rhythm of pencil and paper, she felt something else stir—a sense that this new place, these gardens, and perhaps even the life she was beginning to imagine, might belong to her as much as she belonged here.

"You have a gift," a voice said softly, cutting through the gentle rustle of leaves and the distant murmur of fountains, startling her.

Isabella's head snapped up, her heart leaping into her throat. Across the terrace above her, a young man was walking, his movements fluid, unhurried, and yet charged with a quiet presence that made her chest tighten. Dark hair tousled by the morning breeze framed a face sculpted in sunlight, and his eyes—hazel flecked with gold—caught the light in a way that made them appear almost liquid, almost magical. He smiled, easy and confident, yet there was a gentleness beneath it that pulled at her, unbidden.

She froze, fingers twitching around her pencil, her chest fluttering in a way it hadn't since London, since before the accident, before everything had changed. The quiet rhythm of the garden—the birdsong, the fountain's chatter, the sway of the olive trees—seemed to pause for a heartbeat as she regarded him.

"I didn't mean to startle you," he said, taking a careful step closer. His voice was low, steady, rolled with an accent that was at once foreign and familiar, melodic and grounding. "I have seen you wandering the gardens—drawing. You have a rare eye for detail."

Isabella blinked, cheeks flushing as heat crept into her skin. "T-thank you," she stammered, instinctively closing her sketchbook a little, as if protecting something precious from the world. "I'm… just trying to keep busy."

He crouched slightly, tilting his head so that the sunlight struck his profile, highlighting the planes of his face in a way that made him look almost sculpted, like a figure carved from marble and gold. "Busy is good," he said softly, eyes meeting hers with a quiet intensity. "Sometimes… it helps us make sense of things."

There was something familiar in him, a pull she could not name, an echo of recognition that set her senses alight. His voice, his manner, even the slight tilt of his head—it was all magnetic. She wanted to speak, to ask his name, to reach for a connection she did not yet understand, but the grief she carried, and her innate shyness kept her words lodged stubbornly in her throat.

"I am Lorenzo Caravelli," he said finally, his voice deliberate, as if reading her unspoken thoughts.

"I'm Isabella Moretti… Marco's daughter," she murmured, her voice barely above a whisper, fragile as porcelain.

"I'm very pleased to meet you," he said, bowing his head slightly, the golden sunlight catching in his hair, making it glow. There was no arrogance in him, only a quiet warmth that made her chest flutter anew.

Isabella offered a small, tentative smile, feeling her cheeks burn under his gaze. He looked at her not with judgment, but with interest—and something softer, something curious, almost like wonder.

"Will you be spending much time in the gardens?" he asked, teasing lightly now, leaning casually against the stone railing. "I would love to see more of your work… if you will let me."

Her lips pressed together, fingers unconsciously fiddling with the pencil she still held. Her heart pounded, a mixture of excitement and caution. "Maybe… someday," she whispered, eyes lowering to her sketchbook, though she peeked at him from beneath long lashes, unwilling to fully avert her gaze.

He nodded, straightening, and for a long, suspended moment, they simply regarded each other. The villa stretched vast and sunlit around them, yet in that small garden, shaded by olive trees and curling wisteria, the world felt intimate, alive with possibility. Time seemed to slow, the ordinary sounds fading to a quiet hum, leaving only the tension of unspoken curiosity and the hint of something new and fragile.

As he walked away along the terrace, Isabella allowed herself a small, private smile, her hand lingering over the sketchbook. She traced the lines she had drawn with renewed focus, her pencil moving with a light, urgent rhythm. Something about this place, about the sun-dappled gardens, and the mysterious young man with the golden eyes, made her feel a tentative spark of hope. Perhaps amidst the grief and upheaval, she could find rhythm again. Perhaps she could reclaim the part of herself that had been paused by sorrow.

For the first time since her mother's death, Isabella felt possibility stirring—not only in her sketches but in the contours of her life. Her gaze drifted over the gardens, taking in the sun-warmed terraces, the winding cypress-lined paths, the fountains that sparkled like liquid diamonds in the morning light. Every curve of the vines, every glint of sunlight on the smooth stone, whispered inspiration.

Her dreams began to stretch beyond the villa. She imagined creating jewellery that told stories, that captured the beauty and emotion she saw in the world around her. Rings that held secrets, necklaces that shimmered with stolen sunlight, bracelets as delicate and elegant as the wind whispering through olive trees. Her mother had always believed in her talent, had nurtured and encouraged it, and Isabella carried that faith like a talisman, a quiet, protective charm against doubt.

She dreamed of Milan, the ateliers where master jewellers worked, of learning their secrets and carving a name for herself among the greatest. She imagined travelling—Paris, New York, Tokyo—finding inspiration in bustling streets, quiet squares, and hidden corners of cities she had never yet seen. She wanted to create pieces that would be cherished, treasured, worn by women across the globe, pieces that would reflect their beauty, their strength, their stories.

Beyond her craft, she longed for independence—the freedom to make her own choices, to live fully, unbound by grief, unafraid of the shadows of loss that had marked her life. Here, in the heart of the Caravelli gardens, with sunlight warming her skin and the gentle presence of life all around, Isabella felt the first tentative flutter of that freedom. Perhaps her life could be more than survival.

Perhaps it could be brilliance, passion, and a reclamation of the woman she had always dreamed of becoming.

Over the following weeks, Isabella gradually began to find her rhythm at the Caravelli estate. Each morning, she wandered through the sun-drenched gardens with her sketchbook clutched in her hands, allowing the gentle warmth of the Tuscan sun to seep into her skin, mingling with the heady fragrance of jasmine, roses, and the faint, earthy scent of the vineyards beyond. The cypress-lined paths, the graceful curve of stone terraces, and the dappled sunlight filtering through the olive trees seemed almost to guide her pencil, inspiring lines, shapes, and delicate forms that sometimes surprised even her.

Her Italian improved steadily, a triumph she owed largely to Rosa's patient and persistent instruction, Aldo's quiet, corrective nudges, and the occasional playful teasing of Marco, who delighted in her halting attempts at conversation. Words that had once stumbled awkwardly from her lips now began to flow with a gentle ease, and she laughed more freely at her own mistakes, savouring the small, precious victories of communication in a world so different from the foggy streets and grey skies of London.

And then there was Lorenzo. Over the weeks, he had begun to appear more frequently, quietly and deliberately, in the gardens or along the shaded terraces. Always there, often silent at first, but with that teasing, confident smile that made her pulse flutter, her heart stutter in ways she hadn't anticipated. At first, she had been unsure how to respond to the attention of a young man so effortlessly aristocratic, so assured in his presence, yet always careful, respectful, never presumptuous. And gradually, she discovered—almost against her own expectations—that his attention was not intimidating, but encouraging. It made her want to be seen, to be better, to stretch her talent beyond her own imagination.

Just yesterday, she had hesitated, her fingers trembling slightly, as she opened her sketchbook to reveal her latest designs. Expecting only polite interest, perhaps a nod of approval, she had been startled when Lorenzo leaned in, brow furrowed in thoughtful concentration, eyes alight with genuine admiration. His hands had hovered over the pages with care, treating each sketch as if it were a fragile treasure.

"These are… remarkable," he murmured softly, his voice low but warm, carrying a sincerity that made her stomach flutter. "You have an extraordinary eye for detail. I can see that you truly notice the world—how it moves, how it breathes—unlike most people."

Isabella had flushed, caught somewhere between embarrassment and delight. "Th-thank you," she had murmured, her voice barely above a whisper, unsure if she truly deserved such praise, yet secretly basking in the knowledge that he had seen something in her work that even she sometimes doubted.

Lorenzo's smile, disarming and quietly radiant, seemed to shift the world slightly in her favour. With each glance, each gentle, considered word, he made her heart skip, made her chest lift in unexpected delight. For the first time since her arrival at the villa, she felt not just the quiet thrill of possibility in her art but also a soft, unexpected warmth spreading through her, a comfort and exhilaration mingling together. Here was someone remarkable, someone whose attention and approval mattered in ways she had never imagined, believing in her, quietly affirming her, drawing out the best parts of her courage, her creativity, and even her heart.

And as she traced the lines in her sketchbook with renewed focus, she realised that the world beyond these gardens—the golden terraces, the olive groves, the sunlit vineyards—suddenly felt less intimidating. For the first time since London, since loss, she felt seen, understood, and, against all expectation, quietly, deeply, alive.

The afternoon sun hung warm and low over the rolling Tuscan hills, painting the landscape in soft shades of gold and amber. Isabella lingered on the terrace outside her quarters, her sketchbook open across her lap, pencil poised between her fingers. The heady scent of rosemary and jasmine drifted upward from the gardens, mingling with the earthy aroma of the olive groves. Shadows stretched long and dappled across the stone pathways, shifting gently as the breeze stirred the leaves. She was entirely absorbed in the soft scratch of her pencil when a familiar voice cut through the quiet.

"Isabella, can we talk for a moment?"

Her father's tone was gentle yet threaded with that quiet authority that always made her pause. She closed her sketchbook carefully, smoothing its pages as if to protect the thoughts she had poured onto them. Setting it aside, she rose slowly, her fingers brushing the folds of her dress, smoothing the creases from habit as she tried to steady the quickening rhythm of her heart.

Marco stood framed by the doorway of the villa, the sunlight catching the silver in his hair and outlining him in a soft halo. His expression was serious, yet softened by a faint, almost imperceptible smile—a look that reminded her of the few brief meetings they had shared before, always polite, always distant. But this moment was different. Something in his posture, in the tilt of his head, carried an intimacy she had not known she craved.

"How are you settling in, really?" he asked, his words deliberate, chosen carefully in slow, clear Italian to match her understanding.

"I… I think I am getting used to it," she replied, her voice tentative, the syllables still tripping slightly over her tongue when nerves made them stubborn. "The gardens are… beautiful. Rosa and Aldo have been so kind. And… I like having the space to draw. It… it feels… freeing, in a way I did not expect."

Marco nodded slowly, his eyes softening as they swept over her face, lingering on the gentle arch of her brows, the uncertain tilt of her lips. "I can see that. You have always had a gift for noticing things others overlook. Your mother saw it too—she believed in you, as do I, Isabella. Promise me you will not forget that, even when life feels heavy, even when it seems like the world is pressing in."

The words landed with unexpected weight, catching her off guard. Her chest tightened, and she felt the familiar ache of longing for her mother. "I won't," she whispered, her voice barely audible, though her eyes glistened with unshed tears. "I miss her so much, Father… every single day."

He stepped closer, the movement slow and deliberate, reaching out to brush a loose strand of hair from her cheek. His touch was light, tentative, yet full of a quiet tenderness that seemed to seep into her chest, filling some of the hollow space grief had carved there. "I know," he murmured softly. "And I wish I could have been there more—for both of you. But now… you are here. You and I will find our rhythm. We will learn each other's ways. I will do everything I can to make this place feel like yours too, Isabella. Every stone, every path, every corner—this can be your home."

She blinked rapidly, the sting of tears rising, threatening to spill over. "Thank you, Father," she murmured, voice trembling under the weight of everything unsaid, everything lost and now tentatively found. "I… I am glad to be here. With you. It… it feels right, somehow, even when I still miss her."

Marco's eyes softened further, glimmering with unspoken understanding. "She lives on in you, Isabella," he said quietly, voice low, intimate, a tether across the chasm of years apart. "And here, together, we will make new memories— ones she would have loved for us. I promise you that."

Isabella's lips curved into a tentative, fragile smile. The warmth in his eyes, the care in his tone, and the soft Tuscan sunlight bathing them both, made the villa feel less intimidating, less foreign. For the first time in what felt like weeks—

no, months—she allowed herself to believe that perhaps, here, she could start again.

After Marco had left to attend to matters elsewhere in the villa, Isabella made her way slowly toward the small kitchen, her sketchbook tucked carefully under her arm as if it were a treasured companion. The morning sunlight streamed generously through the wide window, catching the dust motes in a lazy, sparkling dance across the room, giving the air an almost ethereal quality. She breathed in, letting the warmth of the sun and the faint aroma of herbs from the gardens outside settle into her chest, easing the lingering tension from her talk with her father.

Rosa was already there, moving with quiet grace and deliberate precision as she arranged a small tray of teacups and prepared the morning tea. Her dark hair was pulled into a neat, elegant bun, and the soft lines of her face carried a warmth that made the kitchen feel welcoming rather than austere. When she looked up and caught sight of Isabella, a smile spread across her features, genuine and comforting.

"Ah, Signorina Isabella! Perfect timing. Tea is ready," Rosa said, setting a delicate porcelain cup before her. The steam rose in gentle spirals, carrying the sweet, soothing scent of chamomile and honey, tempting Isabella to breathe it in deeply before even taking a sip.

Isabella returned the smile, feeling a small, genuine lift in her spirits. "Grazie, Rosa. I… I was just thinking about my father. We had a nice talk," she said softly, her voice carrying a tentative warmth.

Rosa's eyes twinkled knowingly, her expression gentle yet animated. "That is good. You must speak often. And how is your Italian today? Have you been practicing diligently?"

"Si… I think it's getting better," Isabella admitted, lifting the cup with both hands and inhaling the fragrant steam before taking a tentative sip. The warmth spread through her, comforting in the way only a quiet moment of ritual could. "I still make mistakes, but everyone has been patient with me, and that helps more than you know."

"And that is the most important," Rosa said, reaching out to pat her hand lightly, a gesture both maternal and reassuring. "Patience and practice. You will learn quickly. Soon, you will speak as if you were born here, among the hills and olive trees, and it will feel like home."

Just then, Aldo appeared quietly in the doorway, carrying a tray of freshly baked biscuits. The scent of warm pastry mingled with the chamomile tea, making the kitchen feel even more alive, cozy, and welcoming. "And do not forget, Signorina," he said, bowing his head slightly with formal elegance, "we are always here if you need anything. You are part of this household now, and it is our honour to make your stay comfortable."

Isabella felt a quiet, comforting warmth bloom in her chest, a rare sense of safety and care that had been absent from her life for so long. "Thank you, Aldo. I… I feel very lucky. You and Rosa have both been so kind to me," she said, her voice soft but filled with genuine gratitude.

Aldo inclined his head with a small, formal smile, his dark eyes warm with approval. "Kindness is our way," he said. "You will find that Tuscany has much to offer—and perhaps inspiration as well, if your sketches are any indication."

She glanced down at her sketchbook, running her fingers lightly over the smooth cover, feeling the familiar comfort of its weight in her hands. A surge of pride mingled with something gentler—hope, fragile but insistent. "I hope so," she murmured. "I want to create something beautiful… something that my mother would be proud of."

Rosa reached out, squeezing her hand warmly and firmly, grounding her in the moment. "She would be very proud, Signorina. And so are we," she said, her voice gentle but unwavering.

Isabella looked around the sunlit kitchen, at the two people who had welcomed her with such quiet patience and care and felt a small but undeniable sense of belonging bloom in her chest. The tight knot of grief that had clung to her since London loosened just a little, replaced by warmth and cautious optimism. For the first time since arriving in Florence, she felt not only safe and cared for, but quietly encouraged—supported by her father, by the loyal household staff, and by the subtle, unspoken promise of the life she was slowly beginning to build, one small act of kindness at a time.

It was early morning, the sun just cresting the rolling Tuscan hills, casting a warm, golden glow across the gardens and terraces when Lorenzo first spotted her. Isabella sat perched delicately on the low stone wall beneath the olive trees, her sketchbook balanced carefully on her lap, pencil darting across the page with swift, precise movements. Her long, wavy dark blonde hair shimmered in the sunlight, cascading over her shoulders and catching the light in a way that made her seem almost ethereal, as though she belonged more to this sun-drenched landscape than to any world she had known before. Her large, thoughtful eyes were fixed intently on the paper, absorbed entirely in her own private universe, and for a long moment, Lorenzo simply watched, captivated by her quiet intensity, the way she seemed at once delicate and yet entirely present, existing wholly within her own thoughts and creations.

He stepped lightly onto the terrace, careful not to disturb the fragile magic of the scene, yet unable to resist the quiet pull he felt toward her. His voice, when he spoke, was soft, carrying across the garden like a gentle murmur: "Good morning, Isabella."

She started, her pencil slipping slightly, and looked up, cheeks blooming into a soft pink. "Oh… good morning," she murmured, hastily closing her sketchbook just enough to shield her pages, her fingers trembling slightly from the sudden awareness of being observed.

Lorenzo's chest stirred at the sight—the instinctive way she had guarded her work, the fluid grace in her movements, the quiet determination etched in the line of her jaw and the set of her shoulders. He felt a magnetic pull, a curiosity that demanded to know more of her, to see beyond the solitary figure in the olive grove, beyond the sketches she had so carefully hidden, to understand the girl who had already begun to occupy space in his thoughts, even before they had exchanged more than a few words.

"I was wondering," he said, descending the stone steps with effortless ease, his hazel eyes catching the morning light in flashes of gold and green, "would you like to come with me? I would like to show you a few places in Tuscany— spots that might inspire your designs."

Isabella's heart skipped a beat. Alone with him, away from the villa and its walls of expectation, it felt both thrilling and terrifying. She hesitated, twisting the hem of her dress between nervous fingers. "I… I do not know… I mean, I do not want to be in your way," she stammered, the warmth rising steadily in her cheeks.

Lorenzo smiled, slow and patient, his expression encouraging and easy in a way that made her chest flutter without warning. "You will not be in my way," he said gently. "I think you will enjoy it. No expectations, no obligations—just a morning among the hills, the vineyards, and a few hidden spots most people never notice. Consider it… a gift for your art."

Her shyness softened at his words, his tone so sincere and light that it seemed to lift some of the weight from her shoulders. She glanced down at her pencil, then back at him, offering a tentative nod. "Okay… I would like that," she admitted, voice quiet but steady.

"Perfect," he said, bowing with a teasing flourish, almost ceremonious. "Then let us go before the sun climbs too high."

They walked along the villa's winding drive until they reached his sleek car. Lorenzo opened the door for her with a polite bow and a playful sparkle in his eyes. She stepped inside, the cool leather seat brushing her hands, while he slid behind the wheel, starting the engine with a soft purr that blended with the morning symphony of birdsong and distant rustling leaves.

The air was crisp and fragrant, carrying the subtle scent of wildflowers, sun-warmed stone, and the earthy richness of the vineyards that rolled endlessly on either side of the road. Sunlight filtered through the olive trees lining the narrow, winding route, casting shifting patterns of gold across the car's interior, dancing across Isabella's hair and making her skin glow in the soft morning light.

After a winding drive through the sun-kissed hills, Lorenzo brought them to a secluded vineyard terrace, hidden from the world as if reserved only for those who truly sought it. The rows of grapevines stretched in neat, endless lines, their leaves still heavy with morning dew, sparkling like scattered diamonds in the sun. Beyond them, the Tuscan hills rose and fell in gentle waves of gold and green, dotted with cypress trees and ancient stone cottages, each a painting come to life. The quiet was profound, broken only by the whisper of the wind and the occasional distant song of a bird.

"This place," Lorenzo said, sweeping a hand over the hills as if presenting a masterpiece, "is one of my favourites. The shapes, the colours, the way the light shifts through the day… perfect for sketching, for inspiration. I thought you might like it."

Isabella stepped carefully out of the car, feeling the sun warm her shoulders and the soft earth beneath her feet. Her eyes widened in awe, the scene spreading before her like something out of a dream. The gentle slope of the hills, dotted with cypress trees and rustic stone cottages, seemed almost magical. Her heart fluttered in her chest, a delicate mix of excitement and a curious, unnamed thrill—the same light, dizzying sensation she had felt the morning she had first arrived at the villa.

"Thank you," she said softly, her voice hushed with reverence. "It is… beautiful. I think… I think I will have so much to draw here."

Lorenzo's smile deepened as he watched her, admiration sparking in his eyes, a quiet warmth that made her cheeks heat and her pulse accelerate. "I have no doubt you will. Tuscany gives its best to those who truly see it… and Isabella, I can tell, you notice everything."

She opened her sketchbook and began to draw, pencil moving as if it had a mind of its own, tracing the gentle curves of the hills, the interplay of light and shadow on the cypress trees, the delicate folds of the vineyard leaves. The landscape inspired her, yes, but it was Lorenzo's presence—steady, watchful, quietly magnetic—that stirred her far more. Each casual glance from him made her chest lift with unspoken anticipation; each easy, teasing smile tugged at something deep inside her. For the first time in weeks, she felt not only the thrill of creative possibility but a tender, dizzying sense of connection—an unspoken current humming between them that neither could ignore.

Lorenzo lingered nearby, leaning casually against the car, arms folded loosely, his gaze intent yet relaxed. He watched her shade the folds of the grape leaves, every stroke deliberate, every line precise. There was a patience in his presence that made her feel safe, yet fully alive in a way she had not expected, a sense that here, in this quiet corner of Tuscany, the world could pause and let them simply exist.

After a while, he straightened, brushing a hand through his dark hair, and a slow, teasing smile curved his lips. "You have earned a little reward, I think," he said, voice low and warm. "Would you like to go for some gelato?"

Isabella blinked, momentarily startled, and then a genuine smile spread across her face, bright and spontaneous. "Gelato? Yes! I would love that."

He extended his hand, and she hesitated only for a heartbeat before placing her fingers in his, feeling the steady warmth of his touch. Together, they walked down the winding path toward the small village at the edge of the vineyard, sunlight sparkling across the cobblestones, the scents of fresh bread and blooming flowers drifting toward them with each step. Each footfall beside him made her heart beat faster, a quiet, exhilarating reminder that this morning, this day, was hers in ways she had never anticipated.

Once they had their cones, Isabella laughed softly as a drop of chocolate ice cream slid down the side. Lorenzo chuckled beside her, deftly catching a stray drip with his napkin.

"Careful," he teased, eyes sparkling. "Tuscany's sun is as generous as its gelato."

Isabella grinned mischievously, flicking a tiny smear of chocolate at him. He dodged with exaggerated indignation. "Hey! That is cheating!" he exclaimed, laughter spilling easily into the warm morning air. The sound was rich, effortless, and it made her chest flutter in a way she had not expected.

They strolled along the narrow, cobbled streets, cones in hand, taking in the village with unhurried delight—the fresh scent of bread from the bakery, the subtle perfume of roses and jasmine climbing the walls, and the gentle murmur of life unfolding around them. Every moment felt alive, unhurried, and entirely theirs.

Isabella felt a lightness she had not known since London. The grief that had clung to her seemed to lift just enough for her to breathe fully, to laugh freely, to feel… hopeful. And as they walked side by side, teasing and sharing small smiles over melting ice cream, she realised with a quiet, thrilling certainty that this morning—this day—might very well mark the beginning of something entirely unexpected, entirely wonderful, and entirely theirs.

Chapter Three

And she was right. Over the next few weeks, Lorenzo sought her out almost daily. Sometimes in the soft, golden light of morning, other times in the warm, honeyed glow of late afternoon, he would find her wandering the gardens, sketchbook in hand, or pausing along the villa's terraces, absorbing the view of rolling vineyards, cypress-lined hills, and the sun catching the pale stone walls. At times they spoke quietly, voices mingling with the whispering breeze; at other times, they simply shared the beauty around them, companionable silence settling like a gentle cloak over the two of them. Gradually, that silence wove a subtle intimacy neither yet dared to name, an understanding built from glances, shared breaths, and the quiet rhythm of presence.

One warm afternoon, they strolled through the gardens, the sunlight striking golden highlights in Isabella's hair, making it shimmer as she moved. They paused behind a tall hedge, hidden from view, where the air was heavy with the scent of jasmine, warm stone, and the faint tang of sun-baked earth. Lorenzo stopped, turning to her with a gaze that made her heart falter—a mixture of reverence, curiosity, and something far more dangerous, something thrilling and electric.

He reached out, brushing a loose strand of hair from her face. His fingers lingered, tracing the curve of her cheek as if memorising the warmth beneath his touch. "Isabella…" he murmured, voice low and husky, almost breathless.

She looked up, chest tightening, pulse racing, breath coming in shallow, uneven draws. Before she could gather her thoughts into words, he leaned closer, pressing his lips softly against hers. The kiss was tentative, delicate, a careful mapping of the contours of her response. Her hands rose instinctively, resting lightly against his chest, feeling the steady warmth beneath her fingers, the reassuring beat of his heart beneath her palm.

Then, as if an unspoken permission had passed between them, the kiss deepened. Lorenzo's arms wrapped around her with a deliberate, protective intensity, while she responded with a quiet courage she had not realised she possessed. The world narrowed around them—the rustle of leaves in the olive grove, the distant gurgle of the fountain, even the birdsong fading into nothingness. There was only him, the taste of the Tuscan sun mingled with the faint saltiness of his lips, and a thrill that was at once tender and electric, leaving her senses alight in a way she had never imagined.

When they finally pulled apart, their foreheads rested together, breaths mingling in the gentle warmth of the hidden garden. Isabella's cheeks glowed, her eyes wide and shimmering, and for a heartbeat, neither spoke, savouring the newness, the sweetness, and the unspoken promise that hung between them.

"It seems," Lorenzo murmured, his lips brushing the side of her temple, "that Tuscany has given us another kind of inspiration."

Isabella laughed softly, a delicate mixture of delight and shyness, and pressed her face against his chest. For the first time in months, she felt fully alive, fully present, and entirely seen.

They lingered behind the hedge, still wrapped in the afterglow of the kiss. Her heartbeat thundered against her ribs, and she pressed her palms lightly against Lorenzo's chest, afraid to let go, uncertain that words could ever capture the swirl of emotions inside her.

"I…" she began, voice trembling, then faltered, swallowed by the sheer impossibility of adequately naming what she felt. Words seemed suddenly too small, too clumsy to contain the intensity of her emotions.

Lorenzo lifted her hands gently, holding them between his. "Shh," he whispered, thumb brushing lightly over her knuckles. "We do not have to say anything. This… it is perfect just like it is."

Her cheeks warmed further, and she lowered her gaze, afraid he might see the rush of feelings she barely understood herself. She had never felt so alive, so fully seen, so safe—and yet, there remained a fragile ache, an awareness of how fleeting happiness could be.

He smiled, quietly, knowingly, and that single expression sent a jolt through her chest. "Isabella, I do not want to rush anything," he said softly, voice steady and low. "But I also do not want to hide what we feel. Not from each other. Not here."

Her breath caught, heart swelling, longing to nod, to confess the whirl of emotions she kept hidden. But shyness and awe held her still. Instead, she rested her head against his shoulder, letting silence speak for them, carrying the words their hearts could not yet form.

They began walking slowly back through the gardens, their hands brushing occasionally, the space between them humming with unspoken promise. Lorenzo kept the conversation light, pointing out clusters of wisteria in bloom, teasing her about a smudge of pencil she had forgotten on her finger. Isabella laughed, the sound ringing bright and clear, like wind chimes in the warm afternoon. To Lorenzo, it was music—unexpected, delicate, and utterly captivating.

By the time they reached the villa, the sun had dipped low, casting long, golden shadows across the stone paths. Isabella felt a bittersweet tug in her chest—the day had been magical, the connection undeniable—but alongside the thrill came a flutter of uncertainty. What did this mean? Could she allow herself to care so deeply again after losing her mother? Could she trust someone with a heart that had already known so much sorrow?

Lorenzo seemed to sense her quiet unease. At the villa entrance, he paused, brushing a loose strand of hair from her face, fingers lingering just long enough to ignite warmth along her cheek. "We don't have to decide anything right now," he said softly, voice low and comforting. "We can just take this… whatever this is… one step at a time."

Isabella swallowed hard, pulse quickening, and a shy, tentative smile broke through her uncertainty. "I… I would like that," she whispered, voice carrying a mixture of hope, caution, and tentative excitement.

They lingered for a heartbeat longer, savouring the moment—the warmth of the touch, the memory of the kiss, the quiet thrill of beginnings that neither fully understood. Slowly, deliberately, they parted, each carrying with them the spark of the afternoon, the gentle certainty that something extraordinary had begun—something neither could yet name, but that would quietly, irresistibly, change their lives.

Over the following weeks, Isabella and Lorenzo fell into a gentle, unspoken rhythm that seemed to grow more natural with each passing day. Some mornings, she would settle in the gardens with her sketchbook, sunlight filtering in dappled patterns through the olive trees, the warm air carrying the mingled scents of jasmine, rosemary, and earth. He would appear quietly, leaning against a terrace railing or standing just beyond the rows of lavender, watching her work with a faint, approving smile that made her chest flutter in ways she could neither name nor anticipate. Other afternoons, he would lead her along winding paths through the villa grounds or beyond the estate, to hidden groves, sunlit vineyards, and hilltop chapels that seemed plucked from a dream, their quiet majesty framed by the golden light of late afternoon.

Each excursion became a delicate, unhurried blend of laughter, quiet observation, and shared wonder. Lorenzo would point out the way sunlight fell on the curve of an olive grove, how it struck the terracotta tiles to reveal subtle shades of ochre and amber, or how the shadow of a cypress created a line that might inspire a new design. Isabella's pencil moved feverishly across the page, almost as if possessed, capturing every shape, shadow, and glint of light he highlighted. Her eyes would occasionally lift, meeting his, and for a heartbeat, the world seemed suspended between them—the gardens, the vineyards, the endless Tuscan hills—all framing a quiet intimacy that had begun to grow like a tender, unspoken promise.

With each passing day, Tuscany—the rolling hills, the golden light, the scent of sun-warmed stone and grapes—became more than a backdrop. It became a living canvas, a place that seemed to shape not only her art but her very heart, guided, subtly, by him. Even the smallest details—the flutter of a bird's wings, the distant hum of a fountain, the curve of a vine—took on new meaning when she captured them with Lorenzo at her side, pointing out the beauty in ways only he seemed to notice.

And Lorenzo, too, seemed to change when she was near. The weight of family expectation, the shadow of his father's cold authority, softened whenever she laughed, whenever she hesitated to show him a sketch only to reveal it with timid pride. The usual hard line of his expression melted into warmth, something lighter, more alive, and Isabella felt it in the quiet stirrings of her own chest. Each glance she caught from him—sharp yet tender, teasing yet respectful—made her heart betray her with a flutter she could not, and did not want to, ignore. In those shared moments, between sketches, laughter, and the golden Tuscan sun, a new rhythm emerged—one neither spoke of, yet both felt deeply, a rhythm that held the promise of something neither had expected yet could not imagine being without.

One radiant afternoon, they wandered a sun-drenched vineyard terrace, the rows of grapevines stretching endlessly toward the horizon, their leaves shimmering like molten green under the golden light. The air was warm, carrying the sweet scent of ripening grapes and the faint perfume of wildflowers growing along the stone walls. Lorenzo paused behind a cluster of tall cypress trees, their long, elegant shadows pooling across the sun-warmed earth. He turned to her, his gaze steady and intense, holding hers with a weight that made her pulse skip, and took her hands in his, fingers entwining with a familiarity that felt both new and inevitable.

"Isabella…" he murmured, voice low and reverent, as though speaking her name aloud carried meaning beyond words. In his eyes was a depth of emotion she had only begun to glimpse—a mixture of longing, admiration, and something unspoken, something that made her chest ache and flutter simultaneously.

She bit her lip, heart hammering so loudly she feared he might hear it, yet she did not pull away, drawn to him by a force she could neither resist nor fully understand. The warmth of his hands, the subtle heat of his body near hers, seemed to ignite a fire that both startled and thrilled her.

When he leaned in, the kiss was deliberate, bolder than before, a kiss that spoke of months of quiet attention, lingering glances, and unspoken desire. His lips pressed against hers at first with gentle, teasing intensity, testing the boundaries of connection, and then, as she responded, allowing herself to let desire bloom, it deepened—urgent, hungry, yet still tender. His hands cupped her face with careful precision, tilting her head as hers threaded into his dark, tousled hair, pulling him closer, anchoring them together, afraid that even the briefest separation might feel unbearable.

Around them, the vineyard seemed to dissolve—the rustle of the leaves, the distant hum of cicadas, the sunlight glinting across the rolling hills—all faded until there was nothing but the warmth of him, the intoxicating ache of his lips on hers, and the electric thrill of discovery that sent shivers through her body.

When they finally parted, breathless, their foreheads resting together, Lorenzo's voice was a husky whisper, intimate and reverent. "I have wanted to kiss you like that—for a long time."

Isabella's cheeks burned with a delicious heat, her lips tingling from the memory of his touch, her heart racing. "Me too," she admitted softly, a quiet confession that left her dizzy with both delight and longing.

In the weeks that followed, their kisses grew bolder, more daring—quick, teasing pecks along sunlit garden paths, lingering embraces hidden behind olive groves, or private moments on terraces that glimmered with the soft afternoon light. Each touch, each stolen kiss, carried a heady mix of heat and tenderness, deepening a connection that was as emotional as it was physical—fragile, exhilarating, and utterly consuming.

Through shared laughter, quiet conversations under the cypress trees, and these stolen moments of intimacy, their bond strengthened. Tuscany itself seemed to conspire with them—its golden light, fragrant breezes, and gently rolling hills weaving a spell over their hearts, as if the entire landscape existed to cradle this burgeoning love, making it feel inevitable, luminous, and entirely theirs.

By the time spring fully settled over the hills, Isabella felt herself transformed. She was no longer the shy, grieving girl who had arrived from London. She was alive—her heart daring to feel, her sketches infused with newfound vibrancy, and her spirit quietly tethered to a young man whose presence had become her most unexpected, irresistible source of inspiration. Every glance from him, every brush of his hand, and every shared smile had ignited a courage she had not known she possessed, leaving her ready to embrace a life that felt, finally, wholly her own.

As the sun began to sink behind the rolling Tuscan hills, painting the sky in deep shades of rose, gold, and amber, Lorenzo led Isabella to a small stone terrace tucked at the edge of the vineyard. The air was warm, tinged with the sweet, earthy scent of ripening grapes and the subtle perfume of wildflowers drifting from the hedgerows. A soft breeze played through her hair, lifting loose strands against her cheeks, and for a long, suspended moment, she simply breathed it in, feeling fully present in a world that had begun to feel like hers.

Lorenzo set down a small blanket he had brought, smoothing it across the cool stone with deliberate care. "I thought we could watch the sunset," he said softly, glancing at her with a teasing, yet gentle smile. "The vineyard looks even more beautiful from here, don't you think?"

Isabella settled beside him, her sketchbook balanced in her lap, though for once she did not feel the urge to draw. She simply wanted to look, to inhale the fading warmth of the day, and to savour the quiet intimacy of the moment— the way the light softened the world, the subtle rustle of vines, the distant chirp of cicadas.

Lorenzo's hand brushed hers, tentative at first, and her heart leapt. She froze, pulse thrumming in her ears. He did not withdraw; instead, he laced his fingers gently through hers, their hands resting together in a warmth that was both steady and reassuring. It was a simple gesture, yet it carried the weight of a silent promise, one that neither of them felt the need to voice.

"Do you ever think about the future?" he asked quietly, voice low, intimate, meant only for her ears.

Isabella gazed out over the vineyard, the long shadows stretching lazily toward the horizon. "I… I used to worry so much about what I would lose," she admitted, her voice soft, almost reverent. "But now… I think I just want to see what is possible. To… to live and not just survive."

Lorenzo turned slightly toward her, the golden light catching the edges of his dark hair, haloing him in warmth. "Isabella… whatever happens, I want you to know that you are not alone. And I…" He hesitated, searching her eyes, the vulnerability in his gaze making her heart tighten. "I do not want to imagine a day without you in it."

Her cheeks flushed, and she squeezed his hand, letting the warmth of his touch flow through her. "I don't think I want to imagine that either," she whispered, her words soft but carrying everything she felt, trembling yet certain.

He leaned closer, the air between them humming with quiet anticipation. Their lips met in a soft, lingering kiss, gentle at first, tasting of sun-warmed air, wild grapes, and the faint sweetness of late summer. She pressed closer to him, heart racing, surrendering to the thrill of desire tempered by the safety and steadiness of his presence.

When they finally parted, their foreheads rested together, breaths mingling in the quiet warmth of the terrace. Lorenzo's hazel eyes were soft, searching, and his voice fell into a low murmur. "I want you to be mine," he confessed, a reverent, almost pleading tone. "Not tonight… not until you are ready. I will wait for you, Isabella. Every moment, every day… if that is what it takes."

He brushed a stray strand of hair from her face, letting his fingers linger as though memorising the sensation. "No pressure. No expectations. Just… us when the time is right."

Isabella's breath caught, her chest tightening with a mixture of longing, relief, and an almost dizzying tenderness. She nodded, words unnecessary, letting the silence between them carry all she already knew—trust, desire, and the quiet certainty that she wanted this, with him, on her own terms.

And there, under the last golden glow of the Tuscan sun, they simply existed together. The vineyard seemed to hold its breath around them, a silent witness to a beginning both fragile and undeniable, a promise suspended in the fading light, delicate yet unbreakable.

The morning sun spilled molten gold across the villa gardens, casting a warm glow over the vineyards alive with birdsong and the soft hum of bees drifting between blossoms. Isabella moved slowly along the winding stone paths; her sketchbook balanced delicately in one hand as she tried to capture the elegant curve of a cypress tree rising against the pale sky. Her pencil moved in quick, deliberate strokes, her brow faintly furrowed with concentration.

A few paces away, beneath the shade of a broad oak, Lorenzo leaned casually against the trunk, arms crossed loosely, his hazel eyes following her movements with quiet intent. The faintest smile tugged at the corners of his mouth—an expression he reserved for her alone, one of fondness and fascination. In that still moment, with the gardens bathed in soft light, everything felt suspended, almost perfect.

Until a voice cut sharply through the morning calm.

"Lorenzo!"

He straightened immediately, the ease in his posture vanishing, a flicker of irritation shadowing his face. From the crest of the hill, a young woman appeared, her silk dress a slash of bright colour against the muted greens of the vines. Valentina—one of the seasonal guests. She descended the slope with the languid confidence of someone accustomed to being noticed, chin tilted, dark eyes scanning the garden until they found him.

"Ah, Valentina," Lorenzo said smoothly, though his jaw tightened ever so slightly. "Good morning. I did not expect to see you here."

Valentina's laugh rang out like the brittle chime of breaking glass. "Oh, I know. I was just thinking how rare it is to catch you alone these days." Her glance flicked toward Isabella—quick, dismissive—before sliding back to Lorenzo. "Or… almost alone."

Isabella's pencil hesitated on the page; the line she was sketching trembling. Her chest tightened with a pang she could not quite name. She told herself it was nothing—Lorenzo had been nothing but kind, attentive, devoted—but Valentina's sudden intrusion felt like a cold draft through a warm room.

Valentina drifted closer, her perfume—rich, expensive, unmistakably deliberate—floating on the breeze like a challenge. "You've been hiding from me, Lorenzo," she said, her tone low, intimate, teasing. "I was hoping we might go riding later—just the two of us, like old times."

"I'm here to enjoy the morning and the view. Nothing more," Lorenzo replied calmly, his voice even but with a quiet edge of steel.

Valentina arched one perfectly sculpted brow, her gaze flicking past Isabella as though she were merely part of the scenery. "Mmm. Well, perhaps you will change your mind," she said smoothly, her hand trailing deliberately along Lorenzo's forearm, a gesture meant to be seen. Then, at last, she turned toward Isabella, her lips curling into a smile that was anything but kind.

"And you must be… Isabella, was it?" Valentina's voice dripped with thinly veiled condescension. "The chauffeur's daughter."

Heat flamed across Isabella's cheeks. Her fingers clenched around the edge of her sketchbook until the paper crinkled. "Yes," she murmured, barely audible.

"Charming," Valentina purred, tossing her head in mock appreciation. "You do keep such… interesting company, Lorenzo." She let her eyes linger on Isabella for a beat longer—dismissive, almost predatory—before turning on her heel and gliding away, the sway of her silk dress trailing a faint echo of her perfume behind her as though she had already claimed a victory.

Lorenzo's jaw tightened. He stepped forward, closing the small distance between himself and Isabella in one decisive movement, his hand brushing lightly but protectively along the small of her back. "Valentina," he called after her, his voice calm but carrying a distinct blade of warning. She paused, glancing over her shoulder, and he added, "Isabella is not someone you insult—or underestimate. She is here by my choice. Only my choice."

For a moment Valentina faltered, surprise flickering across her face before she lifted her chin in a haughty shrug, her mask slipping back into place. Without another word, she moved on, her forwardness checked for now.

When the garden was quiet again, Lorenzo turned fully to Isabella. He tilted her chin gently with his fingers until her gaze met his, his eyes soft but resolute. "Do not let her words touch you," he said, his voice low but firm. "You have done nothing wrong. I am here with you. I choose you. Only you."

Relief and something warmer—something tender, unspoken—bloomed in Isabella's chest. A shy, hopeful smile broke across her face despite herself. "I… I just did not expect her to be so forward," she whispered.

He bent his head and pressed a soft, lingering kiss to her temple, his thumb brushing lightly over her cheek. "She is nothing," he murmured, low and protective. "You are the only one who matters to me. Always."

Chapter Four

A few days later, Isabella lingered in her room, the pale Tuscan light spilling through the shuttered windows in soft, fractured beams. She had drawn the curtains halfway, as though trying to keep the world at bay. Her sketchbook lay open across her lap; pencils scattered beside her like small soldiers fallen out of formation. She tried to focus—tried to lose herself in lines and shading—but her hands wouldn't stay steady. Each stroke of the pencil felt distracted, unfocused.

Her mind kept circling back, again and again, to the gardens, to Valentina's sharp voice, to the way the woman had looked at her like she was an interloper. And always, inevitably, her thoughts drifted to Lorenzo: his hazel eyes, the warmth of his smile, the protective way he had stood between her and Valentina as though shielding something precious.

A soft knock interrupted her restless sketching.

"Isabella? May I come in?"

Lorenzo's voice was gentle, careful, carrying that same warmth that had drawn her to him from the very beginning.

She stared at the page, at the unfinished cypress tree that suddenly seemed like a stranger. "I… I am busy," she murmured, her eyes fixed firmly on the paper. She didn't trust herself to look at him, not yet.

There was a pause—then the door eased open, hinges creaking faintly. He stepped inside anyway, filling the small room with his quiet presence. Concern etched itself into every line of his face, softening the usual easy grace of his posture. "Busy?" he repeated gently. "Rosa told me you have hardly eaten. Hardly sketched. You are avoiding me." His voice dipped lower, steadier. "Tell me what is wrong."

Isabella's fingers tightened around her pencil until the wood bit into her skin. "I… maybe I should spend some time alone," she whispered, her voice so faint it almost disappeared into the room.

He hesitated, a flicker of hurt passing through his eyes, then crouched down before her, kneeling slightly so their faces were level. He reached for her hands, prying them gently from the sketchbook and holding them in his own, warm and steady. "Alone?" he echoed softly. "I thought we wanted this—these mornings, these afternoons, these moments together."

"I do!" she burst out, the suddenness of her voice startling even herself. Her cheeks flushed hot, her eyes darting up to his before falling again. "But Valentina… when she—" She faltered, the words catching, her throat tightening.

"Isabella," he said softly, tilting her chin with two fingers until her gaze met his. His hazel eyes were intense, unwavering, but not hard—steady, like sunlight through glass. "What you felt was only a shadow. A flicker of fear. You are the one I care for. No one else matters—not her, not anyone. Only you."

Something inside her gave way. The tight coil in her chest loosened, tears threatening to spill as relief and lingering frustration wove together, tugging at her heart. She let herself lean forward, pressing her forehead lightly to his shoulder. His arms came up around her at once, drawing her in with quiet certainty. "Okay," she whispered, the word trembling but sincere.

He shifted back just enough to look at her, his thumb brushing a tear from her check. Then he pressed his lips gently to hers—a kiss that was tentative at first, soft and reassuring, a promise more than a demand. When she responded, her fingers lifted to thread through his dark hair, and his hands found her waist with a tenderness that steadied her even as it set her heart racing. The kiss deepened gradually, carrying with it not just desire but patience, a kind of reverence.

When they finally broke apart, their foreheads rested together, breaths mingling, the world outside the small room falling away. Isabella felt something new stir within her—a longing not just for the sweetness of his kisses but for trust, for intimacy, for the slow, deliberate surrender of herself on her own terms, in her own time. And in that quiet, golden moment, she realised how deeply she wanted to let herself fall—not into fear, but into him.

Later that day, the villa gardens glowed in the late-afternoon light, every leaf burnished gold, every breeze carrying the scent of jasmine and sun-warmed stone. Isabella sat on the stone terrace, sketchbook open across her knees, her long, wavy dark-blonde hair catching the sun like a halo. Her doe-brown eyes were bright yet distant, thoughtful, as if her heart was already wandering somewhere far beyond the page.

"Ciao, Isabella," Lorenzo murmured from behind her, leaning casually against the railing. "May I join you?"

She nodded, her pulse quickening at the sound of his voice. Silence stretched between them, broken only by the trickle of the fountain and the rustle of the olive trees.

"You have been quiet," he said gently. "Thinking?"

"Yes... about my designs," she admitted shyly. "And about us." She hesitated, then lifted her gaze to his. "I feel safe with you... and I cannot stop thinking about you."

He reached out, brushing a stray strand of hair from her face. "You do not have to be afraid," he said softly. "I want you to feel, to explore... with me."

Her breath caught. "I... I have never felt this way," she whispered, her voice trembling. "I want to be with you... I want to give myself to you."

Something flickered in his hazel eyes—heat, restraint, and a tenderness that felt like a caress all on its own. Tilting her chin, his thumb brushed along her jaw. "When you are ready, Isabella... I will be here," he murmured. "I will honour every part of you. And soon... I will arrange a place where it can be just us—private, ours—where you will feel safe, and where we can be together like that, without fear or interruption."

A shiver ran through her, part longing, part relief. She closed her sketchbook slowly, fingers trembling. "I want that," she breathed, cheeks flushed.

His hand slid to the back of her neck, warm and steady. "Then we will make it ours," he said softly, his voice low and deliberate. "No rush, no pressure. Just you and me when the moment is right."

The kiss that followed was gentle at first—tender and slow—before deepening into something more consuming, a mingling of promise and restraint, patience, and desire. His hands cradled her face; hers slid into his dark hair, pulling him closer as her heart thundered wildly against her ribs. The warm Tuscan sun kissed their skin, the faint scent of jasmine and sun-baked stone drifting on the breeze, making the moment feel suspended outside time.

His hazel eyes caught the golden light, glowing with an intensity that made her pulse race. "Isabella..." he murmured, his voice low, reverent, almost trembling with something he had held back for far too long. "I have been wanting to tell you this for a long time."

Her heart fluttered, a delicate mix of anticipation and nervous longing. "What is it?" she whispered, her voice so soft it might shatter the spell around them.

His hand lifted to cup her cheek, thumb brushing lightly across her skin. "I love you, Isabella," he said, each word deliberate, heavy with meaning. "From the very first moment I truly saw you—your spirit, your creativity, your heart. I cannot imagine this life without you in it."

Her breath caught, a single tear glimmering at the corner of her eye. The honesty in his words, the warmth in his gaze, the unwavering devotion he radiated seeped into every corner of her soul. "Lorenzo... I... I love you too," she whispered, voice trembling but certain. "I have been afraid... but I cannot deny it. You have... changed everything for me."

For a heartbeat, they simply held each other's gaze, the confession lingering like sunlight through the olive trees—warm, illuminating, unshakable. The cicadas hummed faintly in the distance, the breeze rustled the cypress leaves, and the scent of ripening grapes and lavender floated through the air, weaving a quiet, intoxicating spell around them.

Drawn by an unspoken pull, their lips met again—soft, tender, urgent. The kiss deepened, slow and deliberate, exploring and claiming with a patience that made every second stretch like eternity. Lorenzo pressed her closer, hands cradling her face, while Isabella's fingers threaded through his hair, anchoring herself to him as if to erase every lingering fear. Time seemed to stop; the gardens, the vineyards, the fading golden light—all disappeared until there was nothing left but the heat between them, the rhythm of their hearts, and the intoxicating warmth of Tuscany enveloping them.

When they finally parted, foreheads pressed together, breaths mingling, Isabella laughed softly—a trembling, breathless sound of relief, joy, and desire. "I cannot believe I am saying it out loud," she murmured.

"You never have to doubt it," Lorenzo whispered, brushing his lips gently against hers again, tender, reverent. "I will show you every day that it is true. You are mine, and I am yours. Completely."

Isabella shivered at the weight of his words, leaning into him, feeling cherished, protected, and alive. For the first time since leaving London, she felt fully herself—a young woman in love, an artist inspired by every sight, sound, and scent, and a soul daring to surrender to the full, breathtaking possibilities of life, of passion, and of love.

The morning after their quiet confessions, Isabella busied herself in the kitchen with Rosa, carefully polishing silverware and arranging fresh flowers for the dining room. The familiar rhythm of her hands—folding napkins, lining teacups, smoothing tablecloths—usually grounded her, but today her thoughts kept slipping away. They drifted back to Lorenzo, to the warmth of his touch, the intensity of his confession, and the unspoken promise lingering in his hazel eyes.

Balancing a tray of polished silver, she moved through the villa's cool corridors, the scent of beeswax and sun-warmed stone drifting around her. She paused mid-step, sensing something shift—the air itself felt heavier. Voices, low but tense, floated from an open door down the hall. Familiar voices. She hadn't meant to stop, yet some invisible force rooted her in place.

"Lorenzo, you need to listen to me!"

The sharp, commanding tone sent a twist through her stomach. Her fingers tightened on the tray. That unmistakable voice—Matteo Caravelli. Her heart lurched as she pressed herself against the cool wall, gripping the silver like a shield.

"Yes, Father?" Lorenzo's reply came polite, controlled, but she could hear the taut thread of tension running through it.

"You need to stop spending time with that girl… Isabella Moretti. She is not suitable for someone of your position." Matteo's words snapped like a whip, each syllable cutting through the corridor.

"That is ridiculous, Father," Lorenzo said steadily, but the frustration beneath his calm was impossible to miss.

"You must understand," Matteo continued, cold and unyielding. "Our family, our legacy… it cannot be compromised." Each word pressed down on Isabella like a weight.

Her knuckles turned white around the tray. Even the sunlight streaming through the windows felt harsh, accusatory, as if the villa itself had turned against her. Her heart thudded with a fragile mix of hope and dread—hope that Lorenzo would stand his ground, dread that his father's expectations might crush not only him but the delicate, tender connection they had begun to nurture.

"I forbid you to spend any more time with that girl. It stops now."

Then came the words that splintered her world.

"She is only a bit of fun, Father," Lorenzo said, a soft, nervous laugh following—a laugh that sliced through her like a blade.

Matteo's response was cruel, contemptuous. "Oh, in that case, good. I am glad you realise a girl like that is for the bed, not the altar."

The words landed like blows. A surge of disbelief, fury, and shame crashed over her, but she stayed frozen, listening, her pulse pounding in her ears. Every syllable echoed down the hall and seared itself into her chest. All she felt was betrayal.

Her hands began to shake violently. She clutched the tray as though it could hold her together, but it offered no protection. Her stomach churned, her legs wobbled, and the world tilted beneath her feet. She wanted to cry out, to demand that the words weren't true—but all she could do was stand there, letting them settle, cruel and relentless, like ashes falling after a fire.

Even the sunlight felt mocking now, the gentle Tuscan breeze a silent accomplice to her pain, highlighting her helplessness. Her throat burned as tears welled and spilled freely. She turned away on unsteady legs, the tray rattling faintly in her trembling hands, and stumbled back toward the kitchen.

Rosa's startled, concerned glance blurred in her vision as she set the tray down with a clatter and fled outside to the fountain, desperate for refuge—for air, for space, for a place where her chest could unclench and her heart might find a rhythm again.

Meanwhile, as Lorenzo stepped out of his father's study, a storm of anger and disgust roared through him, relentless and fierce. Matteo's words gnawed at him, scraping against his skin, searing into his blood, but beneath the fury was clarity: defiance carried risks, and those risks could mean Isabella being taken from him. And he would not allow that. Not ever.

He wanted her close. He loved her with a depth he had never known before. He knew, with unshakable certainty, that she was the one he would marry—a wife he could love, a partner to share a life with, children who would grow up knowing warmth, tenderness, and devotion, unlike the cold, merciless legacy that had shadowed his own childhood. Matteo's threats, his rigid demands, his icy authority—they could not, would not, shake him from what he knew in the core of his being: Isabella was his, in every meaningful sense, and he would move heaven and earth to ensure she remained by his side, whatever it took.

By the time Lorenzo reached the fountain, his heart thudded with a mix of fear and longing. He stopped short, and the anger in his chest softened into something fragile when he saw her. Isabella stood a few yards away, shoulders rigid, trembling under the weight of hurt, tears glistening in her doe-brown eyes like sunlight on water. Even in her anguish, even as the world seemed to have shifted beneath her, she radiated a fragile, heartbreaking beauty that made his chest constrict and his pulse spike.

"Isabella…" he began, his voice low and tentative, hope and fear mingling in each word.

She shook her head sharply, cutting him off before he could say more. "I heard. Everything. How… how could you laugh? How could you let him say that about me?" Her words trembled, raw and jagged with pain and disbelief, lacerating him where he stood.

"Isabella, no—it is not what it sounded like," he pleaded, stepping forward, desperation etched into every line of his posture. "My father… he is—"

"Don't!" she snapped, taking a small, unsteady step back. Her chest rose and fell with ragged breaths, tears cascading freely down her cheeks. "I can't… I cannot be with someone whose family… sees me like that. A girl for the bed, not the altar? I… I can't."

Her words hung in the sun-drenched garden like shards of glass, each one slicing through him with an unforgiving edge. She turned abruptly, her retreating figure trembling with heartbreak, and each step she took seemed to etch her absence deeper into his chest. Fury, helplessness, and an aching, desperate longing warred within him. The cruel echo of his father's laughter, the sting of her hurt, the sight of her leaving—it all burned like fire behind his ribs.

Lorenzo's jaw tightened, muscles coiling with a tension that mirrored the storm inside him. Anger, disbelief, and guilt collided, jagged and relentless. He knew, with a clarity that cut through everything else, that winning her back would require more than words. More than apologies, more than explanation. It would demand proof—tangible, undeniable, irrefutable proof—that Isabella Moretti was everything he had ever desired, everything he had ever loved, and that not even his father, nor the oppressive weight of the Caravelli name, could ever come between them.

And in that instant, beneath the warm Tuscan sun, Lorenzo vowed—silently, fiercely—that he would do whatever it took to make her see it too.

Isabella moved through her small room almost mechanically, her hands trembling slightly as she gathered her belongings—her beloved sketchbook, the pencils that had become extensions of her thoughts, and the small, precious keepsakes she could not bear to leave behind. Each item felt like a fragile lifeline, a tether to the world she had known, something she could carry with her into the uncertain expanse of life beyond the villa.

She paused mid-step, chest tight, and let her eyes rest on the neatly made bed, the room bathed in the soft early-morning light filtering through the tall windows. Carefully, she set her sketchbook down and pulled a sheet of paper from her desk, scribbling a note to her father, Marco, with a hand that shook only slightly despite the resolve she was trying to summon:

Papa, it is time I stand on my own. I need to explore, to find my path, and to create a life that is entirely mine. Please do not worry—I will let you know I am safe. Always, Isabella.

Her fingers lingered over the words, tracing the ink as if touching them might anchor her courage. A shuddering breath escaped her lips, a mixture of fear and determination, and with a quiet nod to herself, she left the note neatly on the desk and stepped out into the sunlit corridor. The villa seemed unusually still, the scent of roses and jasmine faintly drifting through the open windows, a reminder of everything she was leaving behind.

The streets of Florence were hushed, bathed in the golden glow of the morning, the warm light catching the cobblestones and turning them almost to honey. She walked without a destination, driven by the urgent, unrelenting need to put distance between herself and the heartbreak that pressed so heavily against her chest. She told no one where she was going—not Lorenzo, not her father— not allowing a single word to escape her lips. In her mind, she mapped possibilities: a train to Milan, a ferry along the Amalfi coast, a winding journey that would carry her far from the villa, far from the man who had captured her heart so completely.

With every step, memories pressed against her like a weight she could not shake: Lorenzo's hazel eyes, the warmth of his hand brushing hers, the soft murmur of his voice promising love and devotion. She loved him—she knew she always would—but the cruel, dismissive words she had overheard from his father cut too deeply, leaving wounds that burned with bitter clarity. She could not remain, not if she was to be seen as nothing more than "a girl for the bed, not the altar." The injustice of it, the sting of rejection, propelled her forward even as her heart fractured with each step.

Each mile she put between herself, and the villa carved another piece from her heart, yet with it grew a quiet, hardening resolve—a steel thread forming inside her, preparing her for the unknown road ahead. She would carve her own path, discover the world on her own terms, and build the life her mother had always dreamed she could. And yet, even as a fragile thread of hope flickered faintly on the horizon, the ache of leaving Lorenzo clung stubbornly to her, a shadow tracing every step she took, whispering that love and loss often walk hand in hand.

By nightfall, she sat on a train heading north, the rhythmic clatter of the tracks a harsh counterpoint to the relentless pounding of her heart. Outside the window, the golden hills of Tuscany dissolved into darkness, carrying with them the villa, Lorenzo, and the life she had cherished and nurtured in secret. She pressed her sketchbook to her chest as though it were a talisman, a small, sacred anchor in a world that suddenly felt vast and unmoored. Silent tears slipped down her cheeks as she whispered a goodbye she could not voice aloud, a farewell tangled with longing, love, and the wrenching uncertainty of a future yet unseen.

The villa was unusually quiet that morning, the kind of silence that pressed against the walls and seemed almost alive, listening, waiting. Lorenzo wandered through the gardens, his steps restless, his gaze sweeping over every familiar corner, searching for her. He half-expected to find Isabella in her usual spot beneath the ancient olive tree, sketchbook balanced carefully on her lap, sunlight catching the gentle waves of her dark-blonde hair, the morning light painting her in a golden glow. Her focus, her calm, her unshakable stillness— had always seemed untouchable to him, serene and timeless, as if she belonged to another world entirely.

But today he needed more than the sight of her tranquil beauty. Today, he needed her to hear him, to believe him, to understand. He needed to explain— urgently—that what she had overheard had never reflected his heart, never reflected the depth of his feelings for her. It had been a mask, a lie forged for self-preservation, a desperate act to prevent his father from sending her away. She was everything to him, and the thought of losing her—losing her touch, her laughter, the subtle warmth of her presence—was unbearable, unbearable beyond words.

So many women had tried to capture his attention over the years, thrusting themselves into his life with calculated smiles, seeking his name, his wealth, his approval. They had been noise, distractions he had brushed aside effortlessly, with nothing more than a polite nod or a disinterested glance. But Isabella… Isabella had never tried. Without plotting, without seduction or guile, she had slipped past every wall he had built around his heart. She had simply been herself—and somehow, impossibly, that had undone him completely.

She was the one. He had always known it, deep in the quiet chambers of his thoughts, in the steady pulse of his blood, in the unshakable truth buried in his heart.

Yet the terrace was empty. At first, he thought she might have wandered along the garden paths, sketching among the olive groves, the sun catching the pages of her book, the gentle scratch of her pencil a familiar comfort. He called her name softly, then louder, but only the wind and the faint rustle of leaves answered him, indifferent and mocking. A tight knot of unease twisted relentlessly in his chest.

He ran through the villa, searching every hall, every corner, calling her again, his voice rising with desperation. Then he reached her door, hand trembling as he knocked. Silence. He pushed it open with careful fingers and froze. On the desk lay a note—her handwriting unmistakable, deliberate, fragile, yet infused with a quiet, defiant resolve:

Papa, it is time I stand on my own. I need to explore, to find my path, and to create a life that is entirely mine. Please do not worry—I will let you know I am safe. Always, Isabella.

Lorenzo read the words over and over, disbelief giving way to a suffocating panic that knotted his stomach and tightened around his heart. She had left—without a word, without warning. His mind spun, racing through images of train stations, ferries, every port and city along the Italian coast, searching for the possibility of finding her, of stopping her before she went too far.

He rifled through the drawers she had left behind. Her belongings—each intimate, carefully chosen, a trace of her presence in the villa—were gone. Her sketchbook, her constant companion, vanished. The pencils she carried as extensions of her thoughts and soul were gone, every tangible piece of her erased. And with it, a part of Lorenzo felt torn away, leaving a hollow ache in its place.

"No… no, this cannot be real," he muttered, pacing the empty room, hands shaking. Every imagined step she took—boarding a ferry, wandering through sunlit streets, leaving Tuscany forever—tightened the grip of despair around his chest. The villa, bathed in the warm morning light, suddenly felt cold, hollow, mocking him with its serene beauty.

He ran back to the gardens, desperate to see her figure among the cypress trees, calling her name until his voice became raw, hoarse, yet met only by the whispering wind and the swaying olive branches, carrying the cruel echo of her absence.

Finally, he sank to the edge of the fountain, pressing his face to his hands, a sharp, almost unbearable ache cutting through him. He had known heartbreak before, but this—this was different. Isabella—his Isabella—had been everything: his calm, his light, the quiet inspiration that had made life feel expansive and full. Now, she was gone. His love, his longing, the life he had imagined with her, all seemed swallowed by the rolling Tuscan hills stretching endlessly beyond Florence.

And yet, beneath the despair, a fierce, smouldering resolve ignited within him. He would find her. He would trace her path through Italy if he had to, across trains and ferries, through bustling cities and quiet coastal towns. He would make her see—beyond any doubt—that she was everything he had ever wanted, and that no family, no pride, no legacy could ever stand between them.

But in this moment, Lorenzo could do nothing but sit at the fountain, heartbroken and helpless, haunted by the memory of her laughter, the brush of her hand against his, and the unspoken goodbye that had lingered between them, stretching like a shadow across every corner of his soul.

Chapter Five

Isabella held the velvet tray with careful reverence, fingertips brushing the delicate sweep of the necklace she had designed. Beneath the warm glow of the studio lights, the piece shimmered—white gold entwined with pale sapphires and pinprick diamonds, arranged to echo the gentle curves of olive branches from the Tuscan gardens she remembered so vividly. Every twist of filigree, every stone, carried a memory, a thought, a fragment of the quiet landscapes and secret moments that had shaped her earliest dreams.

She tilted her head, studying the piece with a critical, almost tender eye. "The stones must catch the light," she murmured softly, as if confiding in the necklace itself, "but never overpower the neckline. She is tall, elegant, with delicate collarbones… it must frame her, enhance her grace, not weigh her down."

Across the wide worktable, Giovanni Bellandi—the distinguished Milanese jeweller whose silver-streaked hair framed a face of sharp, discerning angles— lifted the piece in gloved hands. He angled it toward the light, testing its brilliance the way a maestro tests the pitch of a note. "Your instincts are extraordinary, signorina," he said, voice low but certain. "Many designers chase spectacle, adornment for its own sake. You… you seek harmony. That is rare. That is difficult to achieve without losing the soul of a piece."

A soft flush rose to Isabella's cheeks, a flutter of pride tinged with a familiar thread of anxiety. At twenty-four, she had grown into her elegance—long, wavy hair pinned loosely at the nape of her neck, eyes the deep brown of polished walnut, sharpened by experience and quiet determination. "I want it to feel like it belongs to her," she whispered, as though saying it too loudly might betray how fiercely she felt it.

Giovanni's gaze lingered—not just assessing the necklace, but her: the vision, the hunger, the force yet untamed. "This necklace—it will not simply complement her," he said slowly. "It will define her. And your name… it is already beginning to define a style of its own."

Her chest tightened with longing. This had been her dream: Milan, ateliers humming with quiet energy, the creation of something that shimmered, moved, and spoke without words. And yet, even as she admired the olive branch motif she had drawn from memory, her mind drifted—not to Milan, but to Tuscany: sun-warmed gardens, olive groves climbing toward distant hills, the sketchbook where she had first traced the intricate curves of leaves and branches. She remembered the man with golden-hazel eyes who had told her, with a teasing smile, that she noticed everything. The memory lingered—soft, sharp, impossible to ignore.

She shook her head gently, pushing it back down. This was her life now. Her path. Tuscany lay behind her, but it had shaped her, taught her to see beauty in the smallest gestures, the quiet details that made a piece—and a person—truly luminous.

Giovanni leaned closer, studying her as though weighing the essence of her spirit against the delicate necklace she held. "Remarkable," he murmured. "At your age, I was still apprenticing under my father. And here you are—designing for women who command the Paris and Milan runways. You have a gift, Isabella. Truly."

A modest smile curved her lips. "Grazie, Signor Bellandi. But I have much to learn. Much I have yet to see. To experience."

His dark brows lifted, curiosity sharpening into intent. "Then learn with me. Work only with me, and I will ensure your brilliance is not fleeting. Together, we could make Loren Bella a legacy—something that endures far beyond these ateliers, far beyond the fleeting applause of fashion weeks."

She shook her head, a soft, deliberate laugh escaping as she brushed a loose strand of hair behind her ear. "Giovanni, I am humbled by your offer, truly. But Loren Bella was never meant to be confined to one voice, one master. My craft must drink from many wells—Paris, with its elegance; Vicenza, with its gold; Geneva, with its precision; London, with its heritage; Dubai, with its opulence. Each city has its own lessons, its own brilliance to offer. To choose only one would diminish the collection itself."

Giovanni exhaled, a scoff slipping free despite his best efforts. "Paris? Henri Dubois? That showman—always chasing spectacle, never substance. And Vicenza? Riccardo Santini—flash, no discipline."

"Perhaps," Isabella replied, a mischievous glint warming her brown eyes. "But each has merit in its own way. As do you, Giovanni. As do they all. There is knowledge everywhere—if one has the eyes to see it."

The older man's chest swelled with pride, though he masked it beneath a veneer of restraint, admiration threaded carefully with respect. "You will come back to me, Isabella," Giovanni said, his voice carrying the weight of certainty born from decades of mastery. "In the end, every true artist craves substance. And there is no substance finer than Bellandi."

Isabella gathered her sketches with deliberate care, her movements unhurried yet resolute, as though each page she stacked into order was an affirmation of her independence. Her tone, when she spoke, was steady, unwavering, infused with quiet determination. "Perhaps. But the world is wide, Giovanni. Loren Bella must be wider still. If it is to endure, it must carry more than one man's legacy. It must carry mine."

For a long, weighted moment, Giovanni studied her, his sharp eyes narrowing as if measuring the fire in her spirit against the patience he had cultivated over a lifetime. Then, at last, he inclined his head with the dignity of a master acknowledging the inevitable. "Then go, ragazza. Go, and make the world yours. But when you are ready for substance, you will remember Bellandi."

Memories of her breakout piece—the Aurora necklace—rose unbidden. Worn by Elena Rossi at Milan Fashion Week, its golden lattice entwined with aquamarines had caught the first rays of sunlight like frozen dawn. Cameras had exploded in a frenzy of flashes, social media feeds had ignited with feverish praise, and the press had hailed Loren Bella as daring, achingly elegant—a young visionary redefining luxury itself. Backstage that night, Isabella's heart had raced, not merely with pride, but with the intoxicating knowledge that this was only the beginning. Loren Bella would be more than a collection; it would be her voice, her statement, her defiance against the ordinary.

And now, standing in Giovanni's workshop, she carried that same fire—tempered and refined by the guidance of a man who had spent decades shaping jewels into legacies. She was still learning, still growing, yet the world already knew her name.

Later, stepping into the vibrant streets of Milan, sunlight warm upon her shoulders, sketchbook tucked securely under her arm, Isabella felt the exhilarating rush of possibility. Every corner, every boutique window, every gleam of a gemstone in the display cases reminded her why she had chosen this path: the pursuit of beauty, the command of craft, the hunger to make her mark.

"Paris next week," she told Giovanni, her voice alive with determination, her steps light with purpose. "I will see the ateliers, meet the masters, compare techniques, and gather inspiration for Loren Bella's next collection."

Giovanni raised a brow, the faintest smile tugging at his mouth, half-amused and half-approving. "Paris will challenge you. The ateliers there demand perfection without compromise. But... you already carry the spark, Isabella. Most young designers never find the vision—or the courage—you hold."

A soft laugh escaped her, eyes gleaming with quiet confidence. "I know. That is why I go—to learn, to grow, to push Loren Bella further. My collection must speak to the world, not merely echo one city, one atelier, one perspective."

He shook his head, impressed despite himself, the stern lines of his face softening. "Ambitious, yes—and rightly so. But remember, each master sees the world differently. Take what sharpens your vision. Leave the rest behind."

Isabella lifted her gaze to the Milan skyline, its towers and spires bathed in golden afternoon light, then down to the sketchbook brimming with fresh ideas. "I plan to visit five ateliers in Paris, then London. Each will teach me something unique. Loren Bella will carry it all—my voice, my experience, my evolution. By year's end, it will not merely be a collection. It will be unmistakably mine."

Giovanni chuckled then, the rare sound rumbling warmly, and a flicker of softness glowed in his dark eyes. "You are already making them notice. Keep that fire, Isabella. Keep that heart. Talent alone may open doors—but passion like yours… that will carry you beyond them."

As she moved through the sunlit streets of Milan, the city alive with clamour and colour, Isabella felt the intoxicating pulse of independence. The rhythm of creation throbbed through her veins, promising a future of brilliance—one atelier, one master, one glittering stone at a time. And yet, at the quiet edges of her mind, Tuscany lingered: the amber glow of villa terraces, the whisper of olive leaves swaying in evening breezes, and the memory of a hazel-eyed man whose gaze had once set her heart alight. Longing mingled with determination, threading through her ambition like a hidden melody. Every risk she took, every step forward, was not only for her craft, but for the woman she had become—resilient, fearless, unyielding in her pursuit of beauty—yet still carrying the delicate ache of love remembered, a shadow that gave her fire its depth.

The streets of Paris shimmered like jewels themselves—a labyrinth of light, shadow, and infinite possibility. Isabella moved through the narrow avenues, weaving between the façades of grand, historic ateliers, her sketchbook and portfolio clutched close to her chest. Her heart thrummed with a heady mix of nerves and exhilaration. Every ornate doorway she passed seemed to beckon like a threshold into a new world—one brimming with knowledge, challenge, and inspiration waiting to be claimed.

Her first appointment was with the legendary maître joaillier, Étienne Duval, whose sculptural, avant-garde pieces had captivated Europe's elite for decades. He received her in a lofty atelier where sunlight streamed through soaring windows, glancing off polished marble and gilded display cases. The air itself seemed to hum with artistry and expectation.

Étienne lifted her sketches with long, precise fingers, tracing the bold curves and delicate angles she had laboured over. His eyes, sharp as cut diamonds, flickered with calculation as he studied each page in silence. At last, he looked up, his voice deep, carrying the weight of authority but edged with curiosity. "You have vision. For someone so young… it is remarkable. You understand balance, elegance, and—most importantly—story."

A modest smile softened Isabella's lips, though her spine remained straight with quiet pride. "Grazie. That is what I want Loren Bella to be known for—not excess, not spectacle, but originality. Designs that feel alive. I learned much in Milan, but Paris…" Her gaze drifted briefly to the window, where the city glowed in afternoon light. "…Paris is another world entirely."

Étienne's brow arched, his interest piqued as he returned his gaze to her work. "Paris will test you, signorina. Here, skill alone is never enough. You must be fearless. Your designs must speak louder than your age, louder than your reputation. Otherwise, Paris will forget you before the season ends."

Her chest rose, determination burning steady in her eyes. "I will meet five more ateliers this week, each with its own philosophy and discipline. When I return to Milan, Loren Bella will not carry only one voice but many. Every lesson, every master, every city—it will all be woven into the collection. Into me."

For the briefest of moments she faltered, allowing her thoughts to slip away from the grandeur of Paris and back to Tuscany: rolling hills washed in sunlight, the whisper of olive leaves in the breeze, the warmth of hazel eyes watching her with quiet wonder. A pang of longing curled through her chest—tender, insistent—reminding her that even here, in the heart of Paris, the past walked beside her, shaping the future she was building.

Étienne inclined his head, a faint, approving smile ghosting across his features. "Then show me, Isabella. Show me that courage. Make Paris remember your name."

The next few days unfolded in a blur of glittering gems, polished metals, and minds as sharp and exacting as her own. Isabella moved from atelier to atelier— some steeped in centuries-old traditions, others driven by young prodigies eager to break convention—absorbing every lesson. Each master left her with something new: the delicate trick of refining a clasp so it became invisible, the art of layering stones so they told a story, a philosophy of light and shadow in metalwork that made her pulse quicken with inspiration.

One evening, she paused at a café along the Seine, the city bathed in twilight, its bridges and façades glowing with molten gold. She sat with her espresso, sketchbook open across her knees, and let herself breathe in Paris. The air carried the hum of possibility, the whisper of centuries of artistry. Loren Bella had already taken Milan by storm—her pieces had adorned celebrities, magazines, and runways. Yet this journey through Paris was about more than recognition. It was about mastery. Growth. The staking of her claim as an artist unwilling to be confined by borders, traditions, or expectation.

She turned the pages of her sketchbook slowly, her pencil hovering over unfinished designs. Sunlight spilled across the lines of necklaces, earrings, and rings, and she imagined how each new influence—Parisian daring, Milanese elegance, Venetian precision—would shape her next collection. Loren Bella would not simply be a name; it would be a signature of courage, elegance, and vision. And Isabella Moretti—the girl who had once arrived in Florence with nothing but grief and a sketchbook—was now becoming the designer the world would remember.

When she stepped out of the last atelier that week, the soft Parisian afternoon kissed her cheeks, the hum of the city pressing close. With her portfolio and sketchbook tucked under her arm, her mind raced, alive with ideas for Loren Bella's future, each one a spark waiting to ignite.

Her phone buzzed against the café table, startling her. She glanced down, her brow arching slightly at the name flashing across the screen: Alessandro Venturi. For a heartbeat she hesitated—then answered.

"Ciao, Alessandro," she said, her tone careful but not cold, a quiet warmth threading through.

"Ciao, Bella," he replied at once, his voice rich, familiar, almost teasing. He had taken to calling her Bella—beautiful—insisting it suited her better than her name. Over time, she had stopped correcting him. Against her better judgment, she had even started to like the way it sounded in his voice.

"I just wanted to hear your voice," he continued. "It's been too long."

A small flutter stirred in her chest—a reminder of why she let him close at all. "I'm glad you called," she admitted softly. "I'll be back in Milan next week."

"Perfect," he said, excitement shading his words. "An old friend of mine is hosting a masquerade ball, followed by a week at his private island villa. Come with me."

Isabella stilled, her pulse skipping. The invitation sparked something—curiosity, even anticipation—but beneath it rose the undertow of memory: Lorenzo, betrayal, heartbreak. She had never given herself to a man, had never let intimacy cross that threshold. What she had felt with Lorenzo had been singular—raw, unshakable, and unfinished. Yet with Alessandro, warmth was slowly, unexpectedly, taking root.

"I… I don't know, Alessandro," she murmured, steady but hesitant. "I want to go… but only if we have separate rooms. I'm not ready to share a bed. I need space—to feel safe, to trust."

There was a pause, then his voice, low and amused but entirely sincere: "Separate rooms it is. Bella, I understand. I like you—I care for you—but I will never rush you."

Her shoulders eased, a small smile breaking through despite the ache still lodged deep inside. "Thank you," she whispered. "I really do like you, Alessandro. I just need to take this slowly."

"I know," he said simply, his tone threaded with patience. "And I'll wait. That's all I ask. But next week, I hope we can make memories—unforgettable ones— even with separate rooms."

She nodded to herself, the flutter in her chest both cautious and hopeful. "We'll see," she said lightly. "But yes… I'll go."

"Good." There was satisfaction in his voice, but not the press of demand. "Then I'll arrange everything. Just bring that brilliant mind and heart of yours, Bella. The rest is mine to handle."

When the call ended, Isabella slipped her phone into her bag, her emotions a tangle of relief and anticipation. Alessandro was kind, patient, undeniably charming. With him, she could move at her own pace, carefully, deliberately, on her own terms. For the first time in years, she felt the fragile flicker of hope— not only for her career, but for love that might heal instead of wound.

And yet… she had never crossed that final threshold with anyone. She was still a virgin, not out of fear, but because she had refused to give herself to a man who saw her as unworthy. The echo of Matteo Caravelli's decree—a girl for the bed, not the altar—still shadowed her steps, reminding her of how easily desire could be warped into dismissal. Her heart demanded more. It demanded respect.

Alessandro, for all his golden charm, carried a reputation she could not ignore. Milanese society had long whispered about him—a playboy who moved seamlessly from one beautiful woman to the next. No scandals, but no permanence either. It made her cautious, wary that his patience might one day evaporate, that she would become just another fleeting chapter in his glittering life.

But Lorenzo… Lorenzo was no different. Though he had never married, never been linked to a single woman for long, the rumours had always followed him too. Short affairs, dazzling appearances, nothing lasting. He lived in the pages of glossy magazines, untouchable, gilded, adored. Yet unlike Alessandro, she had known the man behind the mask—the man who once held her hand beneath the Tuscan sun, who whispered love and promises that had shattered under the weight of his father's control.

And that memory—whether she willed it or not—still had the power to ache.

She had told Alessandro she'd been hurt before, confessed to scars left by love, but she had never spoken Lorenzo's name. Lorenzo Caravelli—a name heavy with history, power, and the shattered fragments of her heart—remained locked inside her. To speak it aloud would be to summon a storm she had spent years bracing against.

And still—after five long years—a part of her loved him. Quietly. Relentlessly. Against her will. She had glimpsed him in photographs, seen his name echoed across glossy magazines and news reports, always cloaked in elegance, influence, and the unshakable mantle of expectation. Each sighting was a knife—sharp with memory, dulled only by time, yet never enough to blunt the ache in her chest. His father's death two years ago should have freed him—from duty, from tradition's rigid chains. Yet that truth brought her no peace. It only sharpened the bittersweet sting of longing, the restless pull of a past that refused to let her go.

More than once, her father had asked if he might tell Lorenzo where she was, if he could bridge the silence she herself had carved between them. Each time, she refused. She wasn't ready. Perhaps she would never be ready. To face him again meant reopening wounds she had fought to bind. She still loved him— God help her, she always would—but love had twisted into something jagged. She hated him, too. Hated the man he had been—or perhaps the man she had discovered he was.

Drawing in a deep breath of crisp Parisian air, she anchored herself in the present—the mingled scents of stone streets, warm bread, and blooming flowers grounding her. She let the memories retreat, tucking them behind the careful veil of resolve—acknowledged, but not permitted to rule her. Alessandro was here: steady, patient, attentive. After years of storms, he felt like sunlight breaking through grey skies. With him, love did not resemble a battlefield of betrayal and longing. It was a warm current, steady and sure, a possibility she could nurture—on her terms, and no one else's.

She pictured it then—the slow unfurling of affection, tender and deliberate, like a garden coaxed into bloom without fear of frost or sudden storm. In Alessandro's calm presence, there was safety, a harbour where she might finally set down her burdens. And yet, even as she leaned toward the promise of gentleness, the echo of another name lingered—Lorenzo—a quiet, persistent melody threading the edges of her thoughts. She did not fight it, nor did she yield to it. It was there, like the dull throb of an old scar: a reminder of where she had been, but no longer a chain binding her to the past.

For the first time in years, Isabella allowed herself to envision a future untethered from regret—a life where love could be tender, patient, and wholly her own. Alessandro was patient. Alessandro was present. And as she exhaled into the cool morning air, she felt the faint but unmistakable stirring of belief: that her heart might one day trust again—without fear, without restraint, and entirely on her own terms.

Chapter Six

Lorenzo Caravelli moved with effortless grace across the polished marble floor, his hand resting lightly at the small of his date's back. Valeria De Luca—Rome's darling, fashion editor, a woman whose beauty and poise commanded every gaze—laughed as he spun her beneath his arm, the shimmer of her gown scattering light across the ballroom like falling stars. She was elegance. She was admired. She was everything a man in his position could want.

And yet… nothing.

No spark. No pull in his chest. No quiet thrum of recognition. He had dated many women—actresses, heiresses, women of influence whose names carried weight. Some had warmed his bed for a season, their beauty a pleasant distraction. But none had touched him where it mattered. None were her. None were Isabella.

The memory of her haunted him still: long, wavy dark-blonde hair catching sunlight, eyes like rich earth, steady and unguarded, seeing him in ways no one else ever had. From the first moment he had truly looked at her, his heart had ached for her. And then—she was gone.

He had searched. God, how he had searched. Florence, Milan, Venice—every whisper pursued, every lead followed—yet she remained a ghost always out of reach. Still, sometimes, in glossy magazines or behind the gleam of a boutique window, he would catch sight of jewellery—necklaces, rings, sketches transfigured into gold and light—that stopped him cold. There was something in them, a grace he recognised instantly: the delicate sweep of a line, the quiet harmony between stone and metal.

Each time, his breath caught, his chest tightening with bittersweet pangs. They reminded him of her—of long afternoons when she sketched with fierce concentration, of the way her eyes lit when she spoke of the future she dreamed of. She had confessed once, almost shyly, that she wanted to design jewellery. And every time he saw those pieces, he wondered—achingly, endlessly—if somewhere, somehow, Isabella had made that dream come true.

And always, there was Marco. Loyal Marco—his friend, his conscience, his wall.

"Please," Lorenzo had begged more times than he could count, pride stripped bare. "Tell me where she is. I need to know she's safe."

Marco's answer never wavered. His eyes, steady and regretful, always held the same resolve.

"She is safe. But she asked me to promise I would never tell you—not until she is ready. I gave her my word, Lorenzo. I cannot betray her trust."

The words burned, leaving him hollow. But he could not argue. Isabella had left not only because of his father's scorn, but because of him—because when it mattered most, he had not been strong enough to fight for her, to protect her. That truth haunted him more than Marco's silence ever could.

No other woman lingered in his mind the way Isabella did. No laughter could touch him, no touch could ignite him, no gaze could undo him. Every delicate design he stumbled upon, every echo of her talent in the world, was a reminder of what he had lost—and what no one could ever replace.

Isabella Moretti had been his undoing. And even now, surrounded by beauty and brilliance, she remained the only woman who had ever truly held his heart.

As Valeria's hand brushed his—a playful tease—Lorenzo forced a polite smile, letting her energy wash over him like the faintest breeze. His mind drifted elsewhere: Florence, the sunlit gardens of his family villa, Isabella standing quietly among the roses, pencil in hand, lost in her sketches. Even now, years later, her memory remained vivid, unyielding, impossible to ignore.

Valeria leaned closer as they glided through the waltz, her perfume brushing his skin, her eyes sparkling with mischievous delight. "I'm really looking forward to the house party on the island," she murmured. "A week away, beautiful surroundings… and, of course, with you."

She tilted her head, letting the implication linger. "I'm happy to share your room, if that makes things easier," she added softly, her hand lingering just slightly longer than necessary.

Lorenzo felt the pull of her charm but carefully set it aside, a smooth, polite smile playing at his lips. "Valeria…" he said, tone light yet distant, "I think I'll manage just fine with the accommodations."

Her lips curved in a sly grin. "Oh? No plans to tempt me?"

He chuckled, low and measured, a subtle barrier between them, though his hand still rested lightly on hers during the dance. His gaze swept the ballroom, searching for someone—or something—that wasn't there. He hadn't married, never intended to unless he loved the woman, and he had no desire to sleep with Valeria. She was a plus-one, a social expectation. He would have been content attending alone, but too many eyes, too much gossip, made her presence convenient—necessary even.

"Not tonight," he replied smoothly, the firmness of his words leaving no room for misinterpretation.

Valeria's expression faltered for a heartbeat before she masked it with a playful laugh, unaware of the truth behind his silence: Lorenzo's heart, his desire, his longing were already bound to another. As the music swept them through the final steps, he felt her nearness—her charm, her beauty, her flirtation—all vivid yet curiously empty.

When the dance ended and they returned to their seats, the ballroom shimmered with laughter, clinking glasses, and bright conversation—but Lorenzo barely noticed. Every sound, every flicker of silk and sparkle of jewels faded beneath the steady ache of memory: Isabella's smile, her quiet fire, the life he had lost through his own weakness and his father's cruelty.

Valeria leaned closer, her perfume brushing his senses. "You'll enjoy the gala," she murmured, teasing. "All the guests, the music… and, of course, the company."

He inclined his head politely, his composure intact though emptiness echoed inside him. His thoughts weren't on the gala or its glittering guests—they were on Isabella. Her laughter. Her sketches. The effortless grace with which she moved through the world—self-assured, brilliant, untouchable—and yet, she had claimed his heart with a single glance.

Even as Valeria spoke, light and flirtatious, Lorenzo's mind wandered to Isabella in the garden, pencil in hand, bringing visions to life with quiet intensity. He could almost see her concentration, feel the pulse of her passion—and the ache within him deepened. No other woman, however radiant or charming, could touch what she had awakened.

The contrast was cruel. Valeria's sparkle, her practiced allure, all seemed hollow beneath the chandeliers compared to the enduring weight of memory. She laughed at something he hadn't heard, and he managed a courteous smile, though his gaze had already drifted—to the shadow of a woman who was no longer there.

Surrounded by admirers and murmured intrigue, Lorenzo understood with bitter clarity: no one could ever replace Isabella Moretti. No fleeting attraction or artful charm could erase her imprint—the ache of her absence, the relentless longing, the quiet truth that even amid splendour, his soul remained hers.

He had never married. Never truly given himself again. Valeria was merely a convenient shield against society's questions—but she would never touch the place Isabella had claimed long ago.

After dropping off a visibly disappointed Valeria, Lorenzo returned to his Florence villa. The city lights shimmered faintly in the distance, and the evening air settled cool and quiet around him. He climbed the steps to his bedroom balcony and leaned against the railing, gazing across the gardens below. This was the very spot where, years ago, he had first seen her—the shy, grieving girl with dark-blonde, wavy hair and eyes so deep you could drown in them. Even now, the memory of her tentative smile and the way she clutched her sketchbook like a shield haunted him.

His phone buzzed insistently, pulling him from the memory. Alessandro's name flashed across the screen, and a grin tugged at the corner of his mouth. A whirlwind of charm and mischief, Alessandro had been a friend since childhood, now a constant presence in Lorenzo's social orbit.

"Alessandro," he said, leaning against the balcony railing. "To what do I owe the pleasure?"

"Lorenzo, my old friend," Alessandro's voice was smooth, upbeat, and familiar. "When I come to your island for the gala... might I bring a guest?"

Lorenzo chuckled lightly. "Of course—but why do you ask? I assume she'll be sharing your room, yes? You've never been one for discretion, my friend."

A pause, then Alessandro replied hesitantly. "Actually... I'd like her to have her own room."

Lorenzo blinked, genuinely surprised. "Her own room? That's... unexpected. Not like you to insist on propriety."

"She's important to me, Lorenzo," Alessandro said quietly. "I'm taking this slowly. I want her to feel safe—and I'm not ready to rush anything. Not like... well, never mind."

Lorenzo smiled, shaking his head. "So, let me get this straight—you, the man who dates a different woman every week is actually thinking of taking things seriously?"

"Yes," Alessandro said simply, voice firm with conviction. "You'll understand when you meet her. You'll see why I'm willing to wait."

Alessandro laughed softly. "Just wait, Lorenzo. You'll see—Bella is unlike anyone I've ever known." There was a pause, almost reverent. "I'm hoping that I'll be able to call her my wife one day."

Lorenzo's eyebrows shot up. "Oh… that is unexpected." Alessandro—the notorious playboy, charming and elusive, never tied down—actually considering marriage? It gave him pause, a rare flicker of curiosity about the woman capable of inspiring such devotion.

"She's brilliant, strong, kind, clever… and her heart," Alessandro continued, voice soft, almost reverent, "is unlike anyone I've ever known. You'll understand when you meet her."

The call ended, leaving Lorenzo staring out over the rooftops of Florence. The city sprawled beneath the night sky, quiet, bathed in the pale glow of streetlights. The cool air brushed against his face, but his thoughts were elsewhere—tangled, insistent, relentless.

Isabella. The only woman he had ever truly considered marrying, the girl he had once hoped to wed. The shy, grieving girl with wavy dark-blonde hair and eyes like melted chocolate. She tugged at him still, years later. He saw her in the villa gardens, pencil in hand, absorbed in her sketches. The tenderness in her gaze, the quiet authority of her own world… no other woman had ever stirred him like that, and he was certain none ever would.

Even as Alessandro's words lingered in his mind, a knot of longing twisted in his chest. No charm, no playfulness, no fleeting attraction could ever replace her. She was his measure of everything—desire, regret, and the unshakable echo of a love he had never truly released.

Heartbreak had shadowed him ever since. Her sudden disappearance, his father's cruelty, and his own failure to defend her had left him hollow. Nights were hardest—haunted by her laughter, her touch, the memory of their stolen kisses.

Now, Alessandro's seriousness—the thought of him considering marriage—forced Lorenzo to confront what he had long avoided. He thought of Isabella, and a pang of envy and longing struck sharply. If Alessandro could be so captivated, so completely taken with a woman, what must she be like? What strength, what brilliance, what gentle command could inspire even the most elusive playboy to patience, restraint, and reverence?

Lorenzo exhaled slowly. The night air, scented faintly of the city and the Arno, brushed his face. Everything else faded. His thoughts were occupied entirely by her memory, by the ache that had never left him, by the certainty that Isabella was the one woman who had shaped his very soul.

Alessandro's words echoed again: *'You'll understand when you meet her.'* The idea of seeing Alessandro's Bella, witnessing the effect she had on him, stirred something complex—curiosity, admiration, and an unbidden flicker of hope that perhaps Isabella had not entirely abandoned him in spirit.

He leaned against the balcony railing, fingers tracing the carved marble, allowing himself a rare moment of quiet reflection. Years of searching, longing, and following every whisper of her life had not dimmed the fire of his feelings. They had only sharpened them, honed them into a relentless drive to find her, to know her, to make things right if he could.

His mind wandered further, imagining her in some distant city—Paris, perhaps, or Florence again—sketching with focused intensity, moving through life on her own terms, unaware that every choice she made left a hollow ache in the heart of the man who had loved her without reservation. He pictured her smile, the curve of her lips when lost in thought, the way her eyes seemed to see everything and nothing at once.

And yet, amid the quiet and the ache, a seed of resolve took root. If Alessandro could find his Bella, if fate had allowed him to cross paths with a woman so extraordinary, then perhaps it was not too late for Lorenzo. Perhaps the years, the distance, and the barriers his own family had erected were obstacles that could, with patience and determination, be overcome.

As Lorenzo descended the sweeping staircase, the polished marble echoing softly beneath his shoes, he embodied aristocratic refinement—tailored tuxedo impeccable, crisp white shirt pristine, mask tucked neatly into his pocket, ready for the masquerade. His dark hair caught the light, and the faint scent of his cologne lingered in the air.

At the base of the staircase, Rosa, his longtime housekeeper, and Aldo, the ever-efficient butler, awaited him. Rosa's eyes sparkled with a mixture of pride and affection, while Aldo's posture remained rigid, professional, yet loyal.

"Everything is ready, Signor," Aldo announced, his voice steady, carrying the weight of decades of service.

Rosa nodded, brushing a stray lock of hair from her face. "The staff have attended to every detail, Signor Lorenzo. The guests will descend soon for the ball. You need only walk through the ballroom, and the evening will unfold as it should."

Lorenzo's smile was slight, absentminded, his mind still caught on the memory of the woman who refused to fade from his thoughts. "Excellent," he murmured, folding his hands behind him as his gaze swept the room. "Nothing out of place, I hope?"

"Of course, Signor," Aldo replied. "The villa is flawless—every table and room arranged perfectly. The orchestra is briefed, the lighting set, and the masks await."

Rosa stepped closer, warmth in her expression. "All overnight guests have arrived, Signor, except for Signor Alessandro and his guest. They'll join just before the masquerade begins. He mentioned that Bella has a business meeting she must finish first."

Lorenzo's eyes flickered, curiosity and anticipation crossing his features. Bella… he reminded himself. Whoever inspired Alessandro's patience must be extraordinary.

Rosa and Aldo exchanged a knowing glance, sensing the quiet tension coiling in the room. Lorenzo adjusted his jacket, the tailored fabric settling neatly against his frame, ran a hand through his hair, and prepared himself. The night was poised, the guests ready—but his mind drifted inevitably to the woman who had haunted him for years.

"And, Signor," Rosa added softly, a teasing lilt in her voice, "the guests will not see the true Caravelli until you reveal yourself in the ballroom."

Lorenzo's lips curved into a faint smirk, though shadows lingered in his eyes. "Thank you, Rosa. Thank you, Aldo. Your diligence is appreciated."

He straightened, smoothed his cuff, and settled the mask into place. Tonight, the masquerade would begin—but no shimmer of silk, no graceful laughter, no artful intrigue could chase away the memory of Isabella Moretti, carved indelibly into his heart.

She haunted him still. Had she built the life he once dreamed for her? Was she sketching, creating, shaping beauty from imagination as he had always believed she would? Did she ever think of him—or had time and distance softened her memory of what they'd shared? Had she married, or did she remain the fiercely independent woman he had admired and feared to lose?

He moved through the ballroom like a ghost among the living. The guests, radiant in their masks and jewels, blurred together in a whirl of laughter and flirtation that rang hollow against the ache in his chest. The music, the dancing, the effervescent chatter—all of it felt unbearably trivial beneath the quiet weight of her absence.

As he drifted toward the terrace, his hand brushed the gilded railing, his gaze catching on the turquoise waters below. Every glint of candlelight, every shimmer of crystal reminded him of what he had lost—and the longing that time had only deepened.

No mask, no gown, no whispered compliment could fill the hollow space she had left behind. And as the sun sank into the horizon, gilding the villa in liquid gold, Lorenzo Caravelli felt the truth settle with painful clarity: no matter how many women he courted, how many glittering soirées he endured, no one— not even Alessandro's captivating Bella—could ever replace Isabella Moretti.

Chapter Seven

There was a firm knock at her apartment door. Isabella paused, smoothing the silk of her gown over her hip, and drew a steadying breath. The apartment was large and open, bathed in evening light, but modest compared to the opulence Alessandro was accustomed to. Yet she had grown fiercely proud of it—every polished surface, every carefully chosen piece of furniture reflected the life she had built with talent, perseverance, and sheer determination. It was hers, earned, and she would never apologize for it.

She opened the door. Alessandro stood there, framed by the soft glow of the hallway light, his expression caught somewhere between surprise and something gentler, rarer. He didn't speak at first, simply taking in her presence with quiet intensity.

Her gown shimmered—a long, champagne silk that gathered gracefully at one hip with a delicate jewelled clasp and split high along her leg. Thin straps framed her shoulders, leaving just enough skin to hint at elegance without excess. Her hair fell in soft waves, and her eyes met his with steady composure, masking the faint flutter in her chest.

"You… you look stunning," Alessandro said finally, his voice low and warm, edged with admiration.

Isabella allowed a small, polite smile. "Thank you," she said lightly, aware of his gaze but keeping her composure intact. "Shall I let you in?"

He stepped closer, careful, his eyes still on her, as though afraid to look away. "If you'll have me," he murmured, voice calm and respectful—no push, no pressure, only acknowledgment of the woman before him. Isabella's pulse quickened slightly, not with desire, but with the certainty that he was considerate, patient, and present.

She stepped aside, gesturing toward the interior. "Please, come in."

For a moment, the world outside her apartment fell away—the muted hum of traffic, the distant city lights, the faint laughter—all dissolved. There was only this: the quiet weight of his gaze, the gentle pull between them, and the fragile thread of anticipation neither dared break.

"I'm sorry I kept you waiting," she said softly, tucking a loose strand of hair behind her ear. "I had to finalise a design for Giovanni Bellandi."

Alessandro's lips curved into a slow, deliberate smile, his eyes softening with something warmer than amusement. He reached out, hands settling lightly on her bare shoulders, and bent to press a gentle kiss to one cheek, then the other, lips brushing with unhurried care.

"You're worth waiting for," he murmured, breath warm against her ear.

A faint heat crept into Isabella's cheeks, and she lowered her gaze, lips curving despite herself. She wasn't accustomed to words spoken with such quiet sincerity, and it caught her off guard.

Noticing her blush, Alessandro's smile deepened, patient and knowing. He gestured toward the waiting chauffeur, who stood beside her single, modest suitcase. "Is that all you're taking?"

"Yes," Isabella replied, steady and sure. "That's all I need."

His brows lifted, surprise giving way quickly to admiration. He shook his head slightly. "You're a rare woman, Bella."

The name—Bella—made her breath hitch. In Italian, it meant "beautiful," but in his voice, it carried respect, warmth, and something gently disarming. A quiet part of her long-guarded heart stirred, though she didn't let it show.

They walked down the softly lit hallway, her heels clicking against the polished floor. Isabella turned the key in the lock, the metallic click sharp in the evening hush, then slipped it into her purse with quiet finality. This apartment—her sanctuary, her proof of independence—would wait for her return.

Alessandro was a striking figure in his tuxedo, every line tailored to perfection. The subtle gleam of cufflinks at his wrists, the confident set of his shoulders— he belonged to a world far grander than hers, yet his attention never wavered from her.

Stepping into the night, he glanced down, a half-smile tugging at his lips. "I hope you have your mask?"

She lifted her purse slightly, a faint smile curving her lips. "I do," she replied, the single word carrying a quiet promise.

His gaze softened, holding hers just a beat longer before the waiting car, the glittering night, and the world of masquerades claimed them. For a fleeting moment, the evening seemed to belong only to them.

The chauffeur opened the sleek black car door, and Alessandro guided Isabella inside, his hand resting lightly at the small of her back. The leather interior smelled faintly of cedar and citrus—polished, immaculate, much like the man beside her. As city lights blurred past the windows, Isabella exhaled, letting herself settle into the calm rhythm of the ride. The champagne silk of her gown whispered across her legs, the jewelled clasp catching the glow of passing lamps.

Alessandro leaned back slightly, hand resting casually on the seat between them, his gaze flicking to her with quiet admiration. He spoke easily, sharing anecdotes from past masquerades and teasing hints of the eccentric guests she would meet—tycoons, artists, aristocrats—all concealing more than their faces behind masks. Yet even as he spoke, Isabella remained grounded, attentive but careful, savouring the calm before the night's illusions.

Their journey wound first through the sleeping city, then out toward the coast. Streets narrowed into twisting roads, the hum of traffic fading until only the rhythmic thrum of tyres on stone and the distant crash of waves remained. A little over an hour later, the horizon opened to the silvery expanse of the Tyrrhenian Sea, moonlight spilling across restless waters like quicksilver.

The car eased to a private dock, where a sleek yacht awaited, its lights glowing softly against the dark water. Crew members moved with quiet precision, and Alessandro offered his hand—steady, courteous—to help Isabella aboard.

The deck gleamed beneath lanterns as the engines rumbled to life, the yacht gliding smoothly from shore. Isabella leaned against the railing, the cool night brushing her skin, salt-tinged air filling her lungs. Her gown rippled in the breeze, and her fingers tightened around her purse, where her mask rested—a small talisman, a key into Alessandro's glittering world, yet a reminder that she moved carefully, on her own terms.

Even as the yacht cut through the waves, carrying her further from familiar shores, her thoughts flickered to Florence, to the villa gardens, to a memory she tried not to dwell on. And yet, beneath the anticipation of the night ahead, a quiet part of her remained untethered, aware that some memories—like the pull of certain eyes, certain hands—could not be drowned by distance or luxury.

Hours later, Elba Island emerged like a vision—jagged cliffs softened by moonlight, cypress trees rising tall, and the villa crowning the hill like a jewel. The waters around it glittered with anchored yachts, their lights scattered like stars across the dark sea.

Her breath caught. She had expected opulence, yes, but not this. Lanterns flickered along the harbor, casting golden reflections across turquoise waves, while above, the villa blazed with light. Terraces hummed with music and laughter, drifting down to the quay like a gentle invitation.

She turned to Alessandro, awe mingling with a trace of hesitation. "This is… incredible."

He smiled, his gaze lingering on her as much as the island. "It's a tradition, Bella. A masquerade unlike any other. By the end of the night, you'll understand why."

What she didn't know—and what Alessandro had never mentioned—was that the villa belonged to Lorenzo Caravelli: the man whose memory lingered like a ghost in her heart, the one who had held her gaze among roses and sketches, unaware that fate was drawing them close once more.

At the private dock, the yacht eased alongside the stone quay, bathed in the soft glow of lanterns. Isabella's heels clicked lightly against the planks as Alessandro guided her down the gangway, the distant music from the villa drifting on the night air.

And then, at the foot of the steps, a familiar figure stood—tall, poised, his uniform immaculate, his bearing as polished as the marble floors she had once walked.

"Aldo," Isabella whispered before she could stop herself, heart stuttering, every memory of the villa and its absent master rushing back at once.

The butler's eyes widened, then softened into delight. He stepped forward, ignoring formality, and pressed warm kisses to her cheeks, once on each side. "Signorina Isabella… madonna mia, we were not expecting you. What a joy, an absolute joy to see you again. Your father will be so happy."

The words hit her like lightning. Your father. The villa above—glowing in the night—was his. Lorenzo's. Her breath caught, and for the first time in years, she found herself utterly speechless.

Alessandro blinked, surprise flickering across his features. "You… know each other?"

Aldo, perceptive as ever, caught her silence and Alessandro's glance. Warmth softened his smile. "Signorina Isabella lived with us once, Signor Alessandro. After her mother passed, she came to the Florence villa with her father, who served Mr. Caravelli for many years. She is like family to us—and always will be.”

Alessandro’s brow lifted, intrigue sparking. “Bella… you never mentioned this,” he murmured, voice low and threaded with awe.

Isabella’s lips parted, but no words came. Her heart thundered as her gaze swept to the villa, terraces glowing with lanterns, alive with music. Memories surged—the roses, the sketchbook held like a shield, Lorenzo’s gaze etched into her mind.

Finally, disbelief threaded her voice. “I didn’t know Mr. Caravelli owned an island villa. I only ever lived at the Florence estate. This… this is as much a surprise to me as it is to you.”

Alessandro’s eyes softened as he studied her, taking her hand gently in his. Warmth grounded her amid the shock. “Bella,” he said quietly, voice steady, “it seems this has become a homecoming. I hope… I’ll get to meet your father soon.”

She exhaled, relief mingling with fluttering nerves. Alessandro’s acceptance—calm, patient, without judgment—was a balm, even as curiosity and anticipation stirred inside her.

He stepped slightly closer, eyes never leaving hers, a subtle, playful smile tugging at his lips. “I suppose,” he murmured softly, “we’re about to discover even more surprises tonight.”

Isabella allowed herself a quiet smile, caught between astonishment at the island’s grandeur and the rising thrill of the unknown.

Aldo appeared, guiding them up the sweeping marble steps, both formal and familiar. “The ball has begun, Signorina,” he said, nodding. “You are the last guests to arrive.”

Alessandro reached for her hand briefly as they ascended. “Remember your mask,” he reminded her, a mischievous glint in his eyes as he donned his own. Isabella lifted hers, letting the intricate filigree frame her eyes, heightening the mystery.

She glanced at Aldo with a polite nod. “Please tell my father I will see him tomorrow,” she said softly.

His smile was knowing, gentle. “I will, Signorina.”

They stepped into the grand ballroom together, music and laughter spilling around them. Isabella's chest rose and fell with anticipation. Every footstep carried her deeper into the night's glamour, the villa's secrets, and unspoken possibilities—Alessandro beside her, steady, patient, quietly captivated, entirely unaware of the reunion fate was already arranging.

Lorenzo moved gracefully across the ballroom floor, spinning Valeria effortlessly in the waltz. The masked ball was in full swing—crystal chandeliers glinting overhead, gilded mirrors reflecting the swirl of colour and movement, the delicate rustle of silk and satin blending with laughter and music that mingled in the warm, scented air. He had yet to spot his friend Alessandro, but with so many masked guests and elaborate disguises, it would not be easy. Everyone was a mystery until midnight, when masks would come off and fireworks would ignite the night sky, scattering sparks across the dark heavens.

As Valeria leaned in slightly, her perfume brushing his senses—a soft, floral warmth with hints of spice—Lorenzo's gaze drifted to the necklace at her throat. A delicate piece, it shimmered in the candlelight, catching reflections like liquid gold. Something about it stirred a pang of familiarity he could not yet name.

"The necklace is beautiful, Valeria," he murmured, his voice low and smooth, curiosity threading every syllable.

Valeria smiled, tilting her head with that effortless grace that drew eyes wherever she went. "Oh, it is, isn't it? It's from Loren Bella's range," she said casually, as though the name were nothing more than a passing remark. "They're very sought-after pieces. You have to grab them as soon as they become available—if you can."

Lorenzo's brow lifted, intrigue sparking. Loren Bella… The name tugged at a buried memory, a shadow of recognition that refused to be dismissed. Every glance at the necklace, every sparkle of the jewels, seemed to echo some recollection he could not yet place, but it stirred something deep within him, something that quickened his pulse and drew his thoughts like a lodestone.

He kept his hands steady at Valeria's waist, motions of the waltz precise, elegant, yet his mind raced in a thousand directions at once. Loren Bella. He had seen the name before—admired it in magazines, glimpsed sketches in boutique windows, traced designs that seemed impossibly refined, almost alive.

A shiver slid down his spine. Loren… Bella. The thought flickered through his mind, reckless and impossible: Isabella? Surely not. And yet, a sudden, dangerous pulse of hope refused to be silenced, thrumming insistently beneath his chest.

He would have to investigate once the week was over. Perhaps it was coincidence, just a clever name. But if there was even the slightest chance it could lead him back to Isabella, he could not ignore it.

His pulse quickened with a mixture of anticipation and dread. If she truly was the genius behind Loren Bella—if this name represented her vision, her talent, her artistry—then perhaps, at last, he could find her. Track her down. Hear her voice again. See her eyes, the way they always seemed to hold him captive without trying.

The waltz ended with a flourish, applause scattering across the ballroom like silver dust, and he guided Valeria toward a pair of velvet chairs near the terrace. The orchestra seamlessly transitioned into a slower, more languid melody, but his attention was elsewhere, sweeping the crowd with restless precision, searching, always searching.

He tilted his head slightly, studying Valeria in the soft glow of chandeliers, careful to mask the urgency threading through his voice. "So… this Loren Bella," he asked lightly, as though idle curiosity, though every word carried the weight of unspoken questions, "tell me about them. Italian, I assume?"

Valeria reclined with languid ease, one hand smoothing her gown. Her eyes sparkled with amusement, catching the light like a gem herself. "Oh, everyone assumes so," she said airily. "But no one truly knows who they are. Only a handful of jewellers have ever met her. She's… elusive. Private. And fiercely intentional about it. No interviews, no photographs. Her work speaks for her. Limited runs, bespoke commissions—exquisite, impossible to acquire unless you're already on the list. Every piece vanishes within hours. It's all very mysterious… and very clever."

Lorenzo's pulse leapt, every syllable feeding the fragile certainty flickering in his mind. If this elusive designer is Isabella… then everything I've been searching for—the sketches, the exhibitions, the name—is a breadcrumb she left for me.

A tap on his shoulder pulled him sharply from his thoughts. He turned—and recognition was instant. Alessandro. Of course. He would have known him anywhere, across any crowd, even masked and half-hidden.

"My friend! You made it," Lorenzo exclaimed, clapping him on the back with practiced warmth as they embraced. There was the familiar energy of Alessandro—confident, effortless, with just the right measure of charm.

"Of course we did," Alessandro replied smoothly, his voice calm, unshakable, the kind that drew attention without needing it.

Lorenzo's gaze swept the room instinctively, hungry and precise. "And… where is your Bella?"

A faint, knowing smile curved Alessandro's mouth. "Ah, she has escaped to the powder room," he said, voice casual, yet carrying an unspoken weight. He hesitated for a heartbeat, then added almost offhandedly, "It seems you know my Bella."

Lorenzo's chest tightened, the words like a blade twisting in his ribs. My Bella. The thought struck him with sudden clarity and impossible longing.

"Oh," he managed, the single syllable taut on his tongue, betraying the rapid surge of thoughts he tried desperately to control.

"She used to live at your Florence estate," Alessandro continued easily, oblivious—or indifferent—to the sudden stillness settling over Lorenzo, his posture rigid with unease, yet curiosity glimmering in his eyes.

Disbelief jolted through him, sharp, undeniable, like ice tracing down his spine. Could it truly be her? The girl with the sketchbook in the rose gardens? The woman who had haunted every quiet moment of his life, whose name had been pressed into his heart like a seal he had never dared break. He forced his lips into a polite, controlled smile even as his mind spun, chaotic and unrelenting. Tonight—tonight might finally bring the truth.

"Do you mean Isabella Moretti?" he asked, his tone measured, careful, almost detached.

"Yes," Alessandro confirmed with a casual shrug, as though it were no great revelation. "That's her name. I call her Bella… because she is a beauty."

Lorenzo inclined his head, words smooth, voice steady, though his pulse thundered against his ribs. "Ah… yes. Of course. How wonderful to see her again."

But beneath that composed exterior, his mind roared. Isabella. Here. Now. And with Alessandro.

He felt the echo of Alessandro's earlier words press against him like a curse: *I hope to call her my wife.*

No.

No.

No.

His chest tightened, a mixture of anticipation and caution. He had to remain measured, conceal the fire threatening to betray him, to resist the urge to move across the room, to speak, to touch, to claim in some silent, desperate way. Not yet.

Straightening his shoulders, he forced a practiced ease, letting composure mask the storm of memories that surged with every heartbeat—the Florence villa, the sketchbook clutched protectively to her chest, the light in her eyes that had undone him from the very first glance. "It's been… some time since Florence," he said lightly, tone smooth, almost indifferent. "I trust she's well?"

Alessandro's smile was easy, confident, measured. "Very well. She's thriving. You'll see tonight."

Thriving… and here, under this roof… Lorenzo's chest constricted, a fierce, almost painful longing coursing through him. He had to see her, speak to her, hear her laugh again. Yet outwardly, he remained composed, the perfect host, letting conversation drift with practiced casualness, hiding the tempest inside.

"And you?" Lorenzo asked, voice casual but threaded with curiosity. "How fares our mutual friend, Alessandro?"

Alessandro chuckled, mischief sparkling in his eyes. "I think I am in love."

Lorenzo arched a brow, incredulous. "You? Surely not."

"Oh, I assure you, I am entirely serious," Alessandro replied, his smile widening, self-assured and teasing in equal measure.

Lorenzo's lips tightened, a flicker of unease hidden beneath the veneer of polite amusement. In love… with her? The name echoed in his mind, jagged and undeniable.

Then Alessandro's gaze shifted, a subtle triumph curving his smile. "Ah… there she is."

Lorenzo followed his line of sight—and his breath caught, hard, sudden, irrevocable.

There she stood. Poised. Radiant. Unmistakably Isabella. Every detail struck with clarity—the curve of her jaw, the quiet fire in her eyes, the effortless elegance of her bearing. It hit him so violently the room seemed to recede into shadow, leaving only her in the centre of his world.

The music, the laughter, the swirl of masks and glittering gowns—all dissolved into haze. She was real. She was here. Every pulse in his body quickened, a heady storm of awe, disbelief, and cautious thrill rising that he struggled to suppress.

Her gaze swept the ballroom, searching, eyes flicking with faint anticipation, lips curving with that subtle, familiar restraint. Her movement was fluid, confident, yet tempered with hesitation, and it constricted his chest, drawing him forward despite reason.

Alessandro straightened, a faintly triumphant smile tugging at his lips. "I'll be right back," he said lightly, almost as if nothing monumental had just occurred.

"Of course," Lorenzo answered, voice calm, steady, betraying nothing, though every nerve in his body burned with recognition, alert to every detail.

Alessandro leaned closer to her, murmuring something low, and Lorenzo's jaw tightened at the subtle stiffness in her shoulders, the careful restraint that had always defined her. Then—her head lifted, and her eyes found his across the room. Time fractured.

Recognition flared, quick as lightning, striking every fibre of his being. A heartbeat, a breath—and it was enough.

Her gaze widened, startled yet unflinching.

Isabella.

The name thundered through him, shattering years of control, filling every space he had locked away, awakening every memory, every ache, every longing he had carried in secret.

Chapter Eight

"Ah, there you are, Bella." Alessandro's voice drew her from the swirl of her thoughts. He reached for her hands, warm, steady, grounding her amid the glittering chaos of music and masked faces.

"Come," he added, leaning down slightly, his breath brushing her ear, sending a faint shiver down her spine. "Come meet Lorenzo again. I am sure you remember him."

Her chest tightened. For a heartbeat, she froze, the past pressing close, threatening to surface with the force of memory. Her fingers trembled subtly under Alessandro's hold as she glanced toward the man he was guiding her to—Lorenzo. The man who had once held her heart entirely, who had left an indelible imprint she had thought carefully tucked away. Her breath caught, a rush of old emotions brushing against her carefully maintained composure.

"Of course," she murmured, her voice light though her heart raced like a wild thing in her chest. She slid her hand into Alessandro's arm, allowing him to guide her closer. Each step felt like walking through a memory she had both treasured and tried desperately to forget.

There he was—tall, composed, every inch the man she had loved, impossibly real. Even with the mask concealing half his face, she would have known him anywhere. The breadth of his shoulders, the elegance in his stance, the quiet gravity he carried—it was unmistakable. Her stomach fluttered with tangled threads of nerves, longing, and wary caution, each pulse reminding her of what she had once surrendered.

"Lorenzo," Alessandro said lightly, though a subtle edge of insistence cut beneath his easy tone. "You remember Bella."

Isabella's gaze locked with his, and for a single suspended heartbeat, the ballroom dissolved. Music dulled, laughter blurred, chandeliers shimmered into shadows at the edges of vision. For a fleeting, fragile moment, it was only them. The weight of the past pressed into the present, fierce and undeniable.

She forced a polite smile, even as her body tensed, every muscle bracing against the surge of memory, the ache of what once had been, and the fragile uncertainty of what lay before her now.

"Hello, Lorenzo," she said softly, her voice measured but slightly trembling. "It... it has been a long time."

His hands rested lightly on her bare shoulders, sending sparks through her. He leaned forward, brushing gentle kisses across her cheeks, warm and familiar. "Isabella, it has been far too long. You look as gorgeous as ever."

A shiver ran through her, and she forced herself to inhale slowly, steadying her pulse. Every nerve seemed alive, memories flooding back with vivid intensity—the Florence villa, sunlit gardens, the sketchbook clutched to her chest with the same fierce protection she had once carried.

"Thank you," she murmured, lowering her gaze. Alessandro's presence behind her anchored her, a quiet assurance that she was not alone.

"You… you've changed," Lorenzo said softly, reverently. "But it's still you. I would have recognised you anywhere."

"It… it has been five years," she replied, calm on the surface, concealing the storm beneath.

A woman beside Lorenzo rose with practiced grace, movement fluid, deliberate. Isabella's eyes immediately caught on the necklace resting against her collarbone—a piece she recognised at once, though her expression remained serene, controlled.

"Aren't you going to introduce me to your friends, Lorenzo?" the woman asked, her tone light but carrying a subtle edge of possession as she slipped her arm through his.

Pain flared sharply and unbidden in Isabella's chest. A pang she had no right to feel—but could not deny.

"Oh—yes, of course." Lorenzo's voice was smooth, composed, yet the subtle shift in his posture betrayed him; he disengaged just enough to restore a sliver of space between the women. "Isabella Moretti, Alessandro Vitale… this is Valeria de Luca."

Isabella extended her hand with flawless composure. "A pleasure," she said evenly. Then, inclining her head slightly toward Valeria's throat, she added with careful poise, "Your necklace is exquisite."

Valeria's smile was light, effortless, but Isabella noted its confidence, the slight spark of pride in her eyes. "Thank you. It's a Loren Bella—one of my favourites. Nice to meet you as well."

Alessandro inclined his head politely, then kissed Valeria's cheeks with practiced charm. "Lovely to meet you," he said lightly, voice smooth, leaving Isabella suddenly aware of the fragile, intricate web tightening around her. The world seemed to pulse with possibility and peril at once, the past and present converging in a single, breathless moment.

The orchestra swelled, a rising tide of music that filled the grand ballroom and seemed to vibrate through every polished surface. Before Alessandro could speak again, Lorenzo's hand closed gently yet insistently over hers. "May I have this dance?" His voice was low, urgent, threaded with a need he could no longer disguise, each syllable carrying the weight of years lost and desires unspoken.

Isabella's gaze flicked toward Alessandro. He smiled, warm and unaware, utterly oblivious to the storm roiling inside her. With reluctant grace, she allowed Lorenzo to lead her onto the floor. The world blurred around them—masks, chandeliers, laughter, and the glinting swirl of gowns—all dissolving into a haze until there was only the pulse of the waltz and the man she had not touched in five long, aching years.

"Isabella," he breathed, forehead almost brushing hers, eyes dark, insistent, compelling her attention.

"Don't, Lorenzo," she murmured, fragile yet firm, voice barely more than a whisper against the swell of strings.

"Please… let me explain," he pressed, grip tightening on her hand—not in possession but in desperate pleading.

"There is nothing to explain," she replied, chin lifted though her voice trembled slightly. "I wasn't worthy—and you… you agreed with your father."

"No." He shook his head, a contained, fierce denial. "Not once. I made mistakes—yes—but never that one. I never believed you unworthy, Isabella. Never."

Her eyes glistened, tears threatening, her words slicing through the music like shards of glass. "I cannot forget the pain you caused me," she said, quiet but precise. "You and your father thought I was only worthy if I—if I lay in your bed. You hurt me, Lorenzo. I will never let a man do that again."

His breath shuddered as he bent closer, each word a plea that reverberated through her. "Isabella, please. I did not agree with him. If I had not smiled, if I had not pretended… he would have cast you out at once. I thought that by yielding, I could keep you near. I was powerless—but never willing to wound you myself."

The waltz carried them across the polished floor, each turn drawing them together, tightening the invisible tether between past and present. Lorenzo's hand at the small of her back pressed just slightly, a feather-light contact igniting sparks she hadn't felt in years—a reminder of the girl she once was, and the man who had haunted her heart relentlessly.

"I… I have moved on," she whispered, voice soft, uncertain if the words were meant for him or herself. "I cannot be that woman again—the one who loves too much, trusts too easily."

He held her a beat longer, silence pressing like velvet around them, heavy with unsaid confessions. Then his voice, low and urgent, cut through her resolve. "I searched for you, Isabella. Every city, every whisper… Marco would never betray your trust. But if you cannot believe me now," his gaze darkened, filled with longing so raw it ached, "then I will wait. I will respect your heart, however long it takes. But I will never stop trying to win you back."

Her chin lifted, shielded by composure, each step of the waltz drawing them closer while she remained proud, untouchable, careful. And yet… she felt it— the pull between them, the memory, the ache of what had once been—alive, insistent, impossible to ignore.

"You still feel something for me," he murmured, certain, insistent, a quiet claim threading through his words. "I can feel it."

Her chest tightened, a flutter of panic and resistance. "You are mistaken, Lorenzo," she said, each syllable sharpened by controlled resolve.

"I love you, Isabella. I always have," he countered softly, unrelenting, and the words landed like stones in the quiet spaces of her heart, stirring echoes she had tried to bury.

The music tapered, notes stretching like a long, breathless exhale. Lorenzo released her slowly, reluctantly, hands lingering an instant too long, betraying the storm beneath the surface. He stepped back, composed outwardly, yet every fibre of him ached, eyes following her every movement as she drifted toward Alessandro.

Alessandro's hand extended, steady, warm, a familiar anchor in the swirl of masked dancers. Isabella slid her fingers into his, letting him guide her through the glittering crowd, beneath lantern light and the shimmer of chandeliers. Each step was measured, deliberate—but inside, her chest tightened, caught in a quiet war between the comfort of Alessandro's presence and the restless, unquiet pull of Lorenzo lingering at the edge of her thoughts. He was grounding, kind, patient—but every glance, every memory of Lorenzo tugged at her chest like a weight she had never wanted to acknowledge.

"Come," Alessandro murmured, voice gentle, encouraging, a calm anchor in the whirl of music and movement. "Let us enjoy the ball. Midnight soon… then the fireworks."

Her lips curved into a controlled smile, concealing the flutter of anticipation, the quickened pulse at the thought of Lorenzo across the room. She allowed herself to follow Alessandro, embracing the thrill of the evening without shame—but the shadow of the past, the memory of the man who had once held her heart completely, lingered at the edges of every graceful step.

As the orchestra lifted the next piece, her gaze flicked almost involuntarily toward Lorenzo. There he stood, tall, poised, commanding attention even in stillness, watching, just beyond reach. And though she moved forward with Alessandro, each carefully measured step carried the weight of a longing she had yet to untangle, a pull from a past she could not deny, and a fire she feared might never fully extinguish.

Lorenzo stood rooted in place, his gaze fixed on her every movement. He watched the delicate curve of her fingers as they threaded through Alessandro's, the gentle tilt of her head, the quiet light in her eyes—the same light that had once held only him. A pang of longing twisted through him, sharp, sudden, and impossible to ignore. Every instinct in him screamed to reach for her, to pull her back into his arms, yet he remained perfectly still, forcing his posture into calm, concealing the hunger, the ache, the storm of emotions raging beneath the surface.

Each step she took away from him sent a quiet shock through his chest, a reminder of years spent searching, of longing and lost time, and now, here she was—so achingly near, and yet, somehow, still just beyond his reach. He let the moment linger, savouring it, burning it into memory: the way the lanterns caught the subtle shimmer of her hair, the effortless grace in every motion, the way she carried herself with elegance and quiet authority even while allowing Alessandro's guiding hand. Every detail, every nuance, was etched into him like a portrait he had been painting in his mind for years.

And yet, beneath the ache, beneath the restraint, hope flickered—small, defiant, stubborn. He had found her. He had seen her. And no matter the masquerade, the glittering distractions, the gilded illusions of the ballroom, he would find a way back into her world. Because Isabella Moretti had never truly left his heart, and he would not—could not—let slip away again.

Midnight arrived, and a hush rippled through the grand ballroom as every guest removed their masks. Gasps of astonishment floated through the room as the identities of the attendees became clear, mingling with whispers of admiration and surprise. Alessandro and Isabella exchanged quiet, knowing smiles, their eyes drifting over the glittering crowd, taking in the masked and unmasked alike with a calm, measured attention, unbroken by distraction.

Then Alessandro took her hand—warm, steady, grounding—and guided her through the throng. They moved past swirling dancers and gowns that shimmered like liquid crystal, the chandeliers scattering light across polished floors. Towards the terrace they walked, each step measured yet intimate, until the night air embraced them, cool and fragrant, carrying the heady scent of night-blooming flowers and distant sea spray as they descended the marble steps into the garden.

In a moonlit clearing, he paused, turning her gently into his arms. "You are beautiful, Bella," he murmured, his voice low, reverent, threaded with an intimacy that made her chest tighten. His lips met hers, slow and deliberate, honouring the space she still claimed, as if the world had narrowed to the two of them alone.

Her hands rested lightly on his shoulders. She kissed him back—soft, measured, deliberate—a promise of trust, not surrender. In that suspended, quiet moment, clarity settled over her. She had to move forward. She had to allow herself a love that was steady, honest, and freely given, not stolen or demanded.

Gently, Alessandro pivoted her, pressing her back against his chest. His arms slid around her waist, a protective, grounding embrace that enveloped her entirely. The warmth of him seeped through her, and for the first time in years, Isabella allowed herself to simply breathe—to feel safe, to feel the thrill of being wanted without fear or reservation.

Above them, fireworks ignited, brilliant bursts of colour scattering across the dark sky, mirrored in the restless waves of the sea just beyond the garden. Isabella tilted her head back, letting the kaleidoscope of light dance across her eyes, while Alessandro's chin rested near her shoulder, his breath warm against her neck.

"Beautiful," he murmured again, low and reverent. "Like you."

Her heart fluttered, and a soft, unguarded laugh escaped her lips. "It's incredible," she whispered. Yet even as she leaned fully into him, she could not entirely ignore the shadow of the past. Across the garden, near the terrace, she glimpsed Lorenzo—standing silently, a dark silhouette against the lanterns, his gaze fixed on her, intense, impossibly familiar, threading the present with memories she had thought she had contained.

A pang of old longing struck her chest, but she pressed back slightly into Alessandro's steady embrace. The fireworks mirrored the pounding of her pulse—rapid, bright, inescapable. Alessandro held her closer, unhurried, unwavering, allowing her to feel the constancy of his presence, the quiet certainty of a love that asked nothing but her trust.

Lorenzo remained rigid, every muscle taut, as though even the slightest movement might betray the storm within him. The distance—both physical and unspoken—stretched taut between them, a fragile chasm he could not cross. He had no claim here, no right to intrude upon this moment, and yet the sight of her—alive, radiant, pressed close to another man—pierced him with a pain that was almost unbearable. Beneath the sharp sting, a stubborn, defiant hope lingered. She had once been his heart; she would always remain an indelible part of him, no matter the years or the choices that had separated them.

His gaze never wavered, fixed like a silent sentinel on the woman he had loved. The woman he had lost, and the delicate, tantalizing possibility that their story was far from over. Every subtle tilt of her head, every graceful movement in Alessandro's arms, etched itself into his memory, a living reminder of what had been and what might still be.

The fireworks continued their brilliant display, bursting across the night sky in cascades of light, spilling reflections across the waves below. Yet Lorenzo scarcely noticed them. For him, the world had narrowed to a single point of brilliance: Isabella. Radiant. Unreachable. And the relentless ache of knowing that nothing—neither the shimmer of the night, nor the spectacle surrounding them, nor even the presence of Alessandro—could ever replace the piece of his soul she had carried away.

As the final firework exploded across the night sky, streaking clouds in violet and molten gold, Alessandro turned Isabella gently in his arms. Her hands threaded around his neck, pulling him closer, and he held her with quiet, grounding strength. The world beyond them—the fragrant garden, the scattered guests, the music drifting from the villa—blurred into insignificance, leaving only the warmth of his body, the firm, reassuring press of his hands around her waist, and the rapid thrum of her own heart. His lips met hers, slow and deliberate, carrying desire, tenderness, and the unspoken promise of something new, something steady and enduring.

Isabella responded, but even as her body moved with his, her mind drifted to memory. She felt the ghost of Lorenzo's hands on her shoulders, the heat of his gaze, the echo of his voice earlier in the ballroom—all pulsing beneath the surface, insistent and unyielding. She longed to lose herself in Alessandro, to surrender to the comfort, constancy, and care he offered—but a part of her remained tethered to a past she had never fully released.

Alessandro's lips parted, his forehead resting lightly against hers. "Bella… you're incredible," he murmured, reverent and low. "I've wanted this—wanted you—for so long."

She inhaled the scent of him, felt the reassuring warmth and strength of his presence, yet a shadow of longing twisted in her chest. Lorenzo. She could still see him across the garden, watching, impossibly close in her memory, impossibly far in reality. She wanted freedom from that pull, but the past refused to be silent.

Her lips curved, soft and tentative, responding to Alessandro without fully surrendering. Each heartbeat was a careful negotiation: part thrill, part memory, part caution. She was drawn to Alessandro's warmth, to the safety and stability in his embrace—but she could not summon the wild, consuming intensity that Lorenzo had once ignited in her, the reckless fire that had defined her first love.

Above them, the last embers of fireworks faded into the night, leaving only stars and moonlight to witness their closeness. Alessandro tightened his hold slightly, sensing her hesitation, but he did not push. He whispered against her ear, voice low and intimate: "Tonight… this is ours, Bella."

Isabella exhaled, a shiver running through her—not just from the kiss, not just from the closeness, but from the storm Alessandro could not erase and the echo of Lorenzo she could not silence. She leaned against Alessandro, allowing herself to feel warmth and protection, yet a part of her heart remained suspended elsewhere—between past and present, longing and restraint, love remembered and love still waiting.

Across the garden, Lorenzo's dark gaze remained fixed on her, taut with longing and quiet torment. Every tilt of her head, every subtle movement of Alessandro's arms around her, struck him like a knife. He could see her desire, but he could also see the tether she had never severed. That knowledge both thrilled and ached within him, leaving him powerless yet desperate.

Isabella's hands rested lightly on Alessandro's chest, feeling the steady beat beneath her fingertips, yet she could not let go fully. Tonight had been full of laughter, closeness, and shared joy—but the past, the heartbreak, and the questions that remained were still alive. She was caught between two worlds, and the night, the fireworks, and Alessandro's steady presence only made the tension more vivid.

"I… I am a little tired," she murmured, pulling back just enough to breathe, to regain some control.

"I will walk you to your room," Alessandro said, his voice soft, protective, patient.

"I need to find Aldo or Rosa," she replied, scanning the moonlit garden path. "I'm not sure which rooms we're in."

"Are you sure you don't want to come to my room?" he asked gently, a hopeful edge in his tone, careful not to press.

Isabella met his eyes, tender yet resolute. "Alessandro… tonight has been wonderful. More than I could have imagined," she said, brushing her fingers lightly over his arm. "But… I'm not ready for that yet. I need time… to know my own heart, to be certain I can give it fully."

His hopeful gaze flickered, and he nodded slowly, understanding threading through his disappointment. "I can wait," he said softly, his hand brushing hers. "I just want you to be sure—about everything."

She offered him a small, warm smile, threading her hand lightly through his arm. The closeness remained—comforting, tender, yet measured. "Thank you, Alessandro," she murmured. "I'm not ready. But tonight… it's been perfect."

Alessandro said nothing, walking beside her, allowing her to set the pace. In that careful distance, Isabella realised she could allow herself warmth, trust, and affection—but the pull of the past, the fire Lorenzo had never fully released in her heart, still lingered, unresolved and impossible to ignore.

Chapter Nine

Alessandro walked Isabella to her bedroom door after Aldo had directed them to the wing of the villa where she would be staying. The corridors were quiet, dimly lit, and completely separate from the main bustle of the villa, offering a rare sense of privacy and calm.

She stepped willingly into his arms, letting herself feel the solid warmth and quiet steadiness of him. He leaned down, capturing her lips in a slow, deliberate kiss—passionate enough to stir desire, yet measured, respectful, honouring the fragile boundary she had set.

Pulling back just slightly, his forehead resting lightly against hers, he whispered, low and reverent, "I'll see you at breakfast."

Her pulse still raced, heat lingering in her cheeks, and a small, reluctant smile tugged at her lips. "Yes… see you then."

And with that, she slipped from his embrace, letting the door close softly behind her. The echo of his warmth lingered in the room—a quiet ache of possibility, a reminder of what might be, but a path she wasn't yet ready to fully explore.

Alessandro found Lorenzo in his study, the soft glow of the desk lamp casting long shadows across the room. Lorenzo sat nursing a glass of amaro, the bitter-sweet herbal liquor warming his hands, grounding him against the swirl of thoughts he couldn't yet control.

"There you are, Lorenzo," Alessandro said, stepping into the room, his tone a mix of exasperation and amused reproach.

Lorenzo looked up, relief flickering in his dark eyes. At least Alessandro wasn't hovering near Isabella's room. "You alone?" he asked cautiously, his gesture vague.

Without a word, Lorenzo handed him a glass. Alessandro accepted it, tilting it slowly and letting the warmth of the liquor seep into his palm, a deliberate pause before tasting.

"I cannot believe how far away they've put her," Alessandro said, swirling the amber liquid in his glass. A wry smile tugged at his lips. "The villa is enormous. A man could get lost… or worse."

Lorenzo frowned, feigning casual curiosity while every fibre of him was alert. "Why… where did they put her?" He had to know where her room was, but asking Aldo or Rosa directly would reveal far too much.

Alessandro leaned against the edge of the desk, glass tilted as the light caught it. "West wing. Last room along the corridor."

Lorenzo nodded lightly, striving for nonchalance. "That was probably Rosa. She's always been protective of Isabella."

Alessandro's jaw tightened, and he took another slow sip of the amaro, letting its bitter warmth echo the edge of his frustration. "Protective… yes. I get that feeling."

Lorenzo leaned back slightly, swirling the amber liquid in his own glass, attempting casual ease. "Did you… both enjoy yourselves?" The words sounded light, but the undercurrent was taut with curiosity, a thread he could not fully hide.

"Yes," Alessandro replied smoothly, eyes sharp and appraising. "And what do you think of her now, having seen her again?"

Lorenzo's gaze darkened, tension threading through his voice despite the controlled exterior. "She is… much more beautiful than she was at nineteen, when she lived in Florence. That girl… she has changed—grown into someone impossible to ignore."

Alessandro's lips curved into a subtle, knowing smile. "Changed indeed. And not only in beauty. She creates now—jewellery. The Loren Bella collection. Every piece, her design. All of it… hers."

Lorenzo's glass froze halfway to his lips. His pulse stuttered. Her designs. The name struck him like a lightning bolt—Loren… Bella. Us. His breath caught, chest tightening with a reckless surge of hope. She remembered. She had carried something of them into this new life. That had to mean something.

But the warmth curdled almost as quickly as it had arrived. Or perhaps it wasn't a tribute at all. Perhaps she had named it as a wound, a reminder of what had been broken—of what he had broken. The thought sliced deeper than he had anticipated, leaving him raw, exposed to a longing that had never truly faded.

Across from him, Alessandro sat steady, assured—a man firmly rooted in Isabella's present. Lorenzo, by contrast, felt like nothing more than a ghost from her past, clinging to fragments of a love he wasn't certain he had the right to claim.

He set his glass down slowly, resolve hardening. She might see him as a relic of memory, a shadow of what once was, but he would not remain one. He had waited too long, endured too many empty years. If there was even a sliver of her love left, he would find it—and this time, he would not let go.

Lifting his glass once more, he masked the storm behind his eyes with a deliberate swallow of amaro. The bitterness lingered on his tongue—longing, regret, and something dangerously close to hope.

Alessandro's gaze sharpened, catching the faintest flicker of tension. One brow arched, deceptively casual. "So… did you know her well, back then?"

Lorenzo's lips curved into a practiced smile, smooth but tight at the edges. "Yes. We spent many afternoons in the gardens. She would sketch while I…" His gaze drifted briefly, memory tugging insistently. "…watched. Sometimes we talked. Sometimes she didn't need words at all."

He lifted his glass again, letting the bitter warmth mask the storm that churned behind his eyes. The amaro clung to his tongue, tasting of longing and regret he refused to show.

Alessandro's gaze lingered a beat too long, the faint glint in his eyes weighing Lorenzo's answer. "Hm. Interesting," he said, voice light, casual, but Lorenzo sensed the calculation behind it.

The conversation moved forward with the smooth politeness of men who knew more than they let on, yet the air between them carried an undeniable tension— sharp, electric, unspoken.

"Her father works for you, doesn't he?" Alessandro asked, curiosity threading his tone.

"Yes," Lorenzo said softly. "For many years. That is how she came to Italy. After her mother passed, Marco was all she had."

"And why did she leave?"

Because I was a bloody fool and hurt her badly, he thought, the memory tightening like a knot in his chest.

"She wanted a career," he said aloud, measured, almost detached. "We all knew she was exceptionally talented."

His jaw tightened, a quiet tension pulling at his posture. He wanted to tell Alessandro everything—to confess the truth he had carried for years: that he loved Isabella, that he had never stopped, that he would fight for her if given the chance. The words burned, raw and urgent, on the tip of his tongue.

But he stopped himself.

He swallowed, hiding the storm behind a neutral expression. This was not the time—not here, not with Alessandro so certain and present in her life. For now, he would hold his silence, letting the truth remain locked in his chest, biding its time, a slow-burning fire waiting for the right moment.

Lorenzo left the study with the lingering taste of amaro, but it wasn't bitterness that burned in him now—it was fire. Loren Bella. The words looped endlessly in his mind, each repetition a reminder, a confirmation that she hadn't erased him from her heart, no matter what she claimed.

The villa was quiet, shadows stretching long across the marble corridors as the household settled into sleep. He moved with measured steps, yet every beat of his pulse urged him faster, closer to her. Alessandro's careless revelation had lit a fuse inside him, and there was no chance of snuffing it out. Not tonight.

At the entrance to the west wing, he hesitated. Rosa's doing, he had told Alessandro. Of course. Protective Rosa, ever the sentinel, always guarding Isabella like a hawk. Even now she had placed her as far away as possible—as though walls and distance could shield her from him, keep him at bay.

He walked the corridor slowly, hand brushing the cool stone as if the villa itself were guiding him. At the last door, he stopped. Silence pressed around him. No sound but the rush of his own breathing.

For a long moment, he hovered there, knuckles inches from the polished wood. What am I doing? he asked himself. But the answer was already there, pulsing in his chest. He couldn't stay away. Not after tonight. Not after knowing she had carried their name—their name—into her life's work.

Finally, he raised his knuckles and knocked, soft but insistent.

Inside, movement—a rustle of fabric, the quiet pad of feet. Then her voice, cautious, wary. "Who is it?"

"It's me," he said, low and rough. "Lorenzo."

A pause. He could almost hear her heartbeat, feel her hesitation vibrating through the thick door. Slowly, deliberately, the latch turned.

The door creaked open, spilling a narrow ribbon of soft light into the darkened hall. Isabella stood framed in its glow, clad in a pale silk nightdress, a matching robe draped lightly over her shoulders, clinging just enough to hint at her shape. Her dark-blonde hair tumbled loosely around her face, catching the light like spun gold, her eyes wide—uncertain, startled, caught between caution and something far more vulnerable.

"Lorenzo…" she breathed, his name slipping past her lips like a confession, her voice trembling with equal parts warning and reluctant welcome.

He stepped closer, stopping just at the threshold, unwilling to cross without her permission. "I had to see you," he said, voice low, hoarse with urgency. "After tonight… after everything… I could not let the night end without—without being near you."

Her fingers gripped the edge of the door, torn between shutting it and pulling it wider. "This isn't the time," she murmured, though her eyes betrayed the conflict roiling within her.

He lifted a hand, hovering near her, careful not to touch, as if reaching for her across the fragile distance. "I will not step inside if you do not want me to. But please, Isabella… just look at me. Tell me there is nothing left between us, and I will leave."

For a heartbeat, she stood frozen, caught between reason and memory, between what she knew she should do and what her heart still longed for. Then, with a shaky breath, she stepped back, opening the door wider.

"Just for a little while," she whispered. "To talk. Nothing more."

Lorenzo inclined his head, eyes dark with gratitude and quiet relief. He entered softly, careful not to brush against her, though every fibre of him ached to close the space between them. She closed the door behind them, and the faint click sounded impossibly loud in the stillness, sealing them together in the fragile tension of the moment.

The room was bathed in the muted glow of a single lamp on the writing desk, its amber light softening shadows and gilding her features with warmth. Isabella moved across the room with quiet, measured steps, creating distance between them—as though space alone could shield her from the storm his presence stirred within her.

They remained standing, neither willing to sit, as if settling might anchor them in a place they weren't ready to face. Silence stretched, thick with unspoken words and memories pressing between them like a living weight. Each heartbeat seemed amplified, each breath drawn heavy with restraint, longing, and the memory of a love neither had truly left behind.

At last, she drew a breath and lifted her gaze to him. Her eyes were guarded, her expression carefully schooled, but her voice carried a quiet strength. "Lorenzo," she murmured, steady though hushed, "why are you here?"

His lips curved faintly, bitterly, as though the smile cost him something. "Because I could not bear to end the night without seeing you again. After all these years… and then hearing about Loren Bella—Isabella, you cannot tell me that name means nothing."

Her breath caught, fingers tightening around the sash of her robe as though anchoring herself. "It was… a memory," she said softly, almost defensively. "A piece of my past that shaped me. It is nothing."

"I'd give anything to change that," he countered, stepping closer, his voice low, raw. "I know now you haven't forgotten me."

"I… of course I haven't," she whispered, a tremor in her voice she tried to suppress.

He closed another step, the space between them taut, charged like a drawn bowstring. "I am asking for the chance to show you that I am not the man you think I was. That I never stopped—" His words faltered, jaw tightening as if speaking them cut too deep. "I hurt you, Isabella. I know that. But I love you. I never—"

"Stop," she whispered sharply, eyes glistening with unshed tears. "Don't. You do not get to say that to me. Not after everything that was said."

The silence that followed pressed down on them, trembling with all they could not voice. His chest rose and fell in uneven breaths before he spoke again, softer now, almost breaking. "Let me prove it. Let me be near you. No demands. No promises. Just… let me close again."

Her gaze lingered on him, torn, wavering between heart and mind. For a heartbeat, she almost yielded to the pull of him. Then she exhaled slowly, steadying herself.

Her voice was quiet, firm, unyielding. "No, Lorenzo. I am here with Alessandro."

The words hit him like a blade. His jaw tightened, but he did not step back. Instead, he moved closer still, the charged space between them shrinking until she could feel the warmth of his breath. His dark eyes searched hers, fierce, almost desperate, a storm barely contained beneath the surface.

"Do you feel the same with him as you did with me, Isabella?" His voice was low, trembling with restrained emotion. "Or are you just hiding—because it's easier than facing what you and I still have?"

Her breath caught, fingers clenching at her sides. "Don't," she whispered, though her body betrayed her, rooted in place instead of retreating.

He leaned closer, rough, urgent, his presence like a tide pressing against the walls she had built. "When I look at you, I see it—you still feel it. Do not deny me that. Do not deny yourself. Alessandro may have your attention, but he does not have your heart. Not the way I do. Not the way I always will."

Isabella shook her head, but the motion was trembling, uncertain. Her heart thudded painfully in her chest. "You're wrong," she whispered.

"No." His hand lifted, hovering near her cheek, trembling slightly but not daring to touch. His voice softened, thick with feeling, almost breaking. "You are the only thing I have ever been sure of. And I will spend every breath proving it—whether you want me to or not."

The silence that followed pressed heavily between them, charged with all the words they had never spoken. Isabella's eyes shimmered, lips parting as if to speak—but no words came. The pull between them was magnetic, irresistible, the air itself humming with the weight of what they both still carried.

Then, as if by inevitability, their lips met. Isabella gasped as heat flared through her, a tremor of shock and longing cascading through every nerve. Lorenzo's arms tightened around her waist, drawing her flush against him, and she pressed back without thinking, her hands threading into his hair, fingers curling at the nape of his neck as though she could anchor herself there. Every shared breath felt electric, every touch a pulse of memory and desire.

The kiss deepened—urgent, feral, yet impossibly tender—a collision of passion denied for far too long. Neither had planned it, yet neither could pull away. It was reckless, consuming, and unavoidable. Her silk nightdress and robe offered little barrier; he could feel the heat of her body moulded to his, her heartbeat thundering against his chest. One of his hands slid up into her hair, fisting gently in its softness, while the other rested low on her back, drawing her closer with an almost desperate need.

Isabella moaned softly, startled by the intensity of the sensation, as their mouths met in a heated, desperate rhythm. Every motion, every touch, became a silent confession—years of longing and regret, finally unleashed. Lorenzo pressed closer, his lips claiming hers with a heat that left her knees weak. She clutched at his shoulders, her breath catching, every fibre of her caught between surrender and restraint.

A flicker of reason—of the life she was trying to protect—broke through the storm. She pressed her palms against his chest, just enough to create a sliver of space, though her pulse still thundered in her ears.

"Lorenzo…" she whispered, her voice trembling but firm, "stop."

He froze, forehead resting against hers, dark eyes searching hers, desperate and raw. "I can't," he murmured, voice rough, thick with emotion. "I've waited too long… Isabella, I—"

She shook her head, swallowing hard, the ache of wanting him clashing with the knowledge that she couldn't fully give in. "No, this is wrong," she said softly, though every word carried weight. "I… I am with Alessandro. I—"

"Alessandro," he murmured, each syllable tight with barely restrained emotion. "Do you… kiss him the way you just kissed me?"

Isabella's chest rose and fell unevenly, her pulse a frantic drum in her ears. Every part of her wanted to lean into him, to let the years of longing and ache finally dissolve into something undeniable—but she couldn't. Not yet.

She wanted to say yes, to tell him she no longer felt anything for him—but that would have been a lie.

A shiver ran through her and she instinctively stepped back, smoothing the silk of her robe over her body, reclaiming a fragile composure. Her eyes met his, steady yet shadowed with the conflict she could not fully conceal.

"No," she whispered, quiet but resolute—the single word carrying both truth and the weight of all that remained unspoken.

Hope flared in his chest. "I will fight for you, Isabella. You and I… we belong together. I never meant to hurt you all those years ago. I thought I was protecting you… protecting us."

Isabella's breath caught. Her heart thudded painfully, torn between the ache of old wounds and the undeniable pull of what had never truly faded. Part of her wanted to throw herself into his arms, to surrender to the certainty in his voice—but caution, and the scars of the past, held her back. She remained still, her hands clutching the silk of her robe, eyes locked on his, torn between hope and fear, longing and restraint.

"You should leave," Isabella whispered, her voice steady despite the storm in her chest.

Lorenzo's jaw tightened, eyes dark with longing, but he nodded slowly. "I will leave… but know this, Isabella—I will not stop. Not until I win you back."

He stepped back, his hand lingering a heartbeat longer in the air as if reaching for her, though he did not touch. He gave her one last look—intense, desperate, yet tempered with respect—and turned toward the door. Each step echoed softly against the floorboards, a reluctant retreat carrying the weight of years lost.

Isabella stood rooted in place, her chest heaving, the heat of his words still searing through her. She pressed a hand to her lips, as if to hold back the tremor of emotion that threatened to spill. The room felt impossibly empty once he was gone, the shadows stretching longer, the quiet heavier.

Her mind raced, caught between relief that he had respected her boundaries and the sudden, hollow ache of his absence. She sank onto the edge of the bed, fingers clutching the silk of her robe as if it could anchor her, and whispered to the quiet room, "I can't… this isn't fair to Alessandro."

The soft click of the door closing lingered in the air—more than a sound, it was a promise, a challenge, and a warning all at once. And beneath her ribs, a spark of hope flared, fierce and undeniable, threatening to undo the careful composure she had fought so hard to maintain. Perhaps their story was far from over. Perhaps, no matter how she tried, she could not extinguish it.

Chapter Ten

The corridors lay silent around him, vast and echoing, the hush broken only by the soft whisper of his footsteps across the polished marble. The faint glow of lanterns spilled over the walls, casting long, shifting shadows that stretched like memories he could not outrun. But he barely saw them. His mind was a storm—thick, restless, a tangle of desire, regret, and frustration that refused to quiet.

He had seen her tonight—the way she had looked at him with trembling hands and burning eyes, the almost imperceptible shiver in her breath, the taste of her lips still lingering like forbidden wine—and it was all he could do not to turn back. Not to pull her into his arms again, to let the fire between them blaze until it consumed them both. But he hadn't. She had chosen restraint, and, against every instinct, he had let her.

Yet the memory of her clung to him like a second skin. Her scent, warm and faintly floral, ghosted his senses; the soft press of her fingers against his shoulders had imprinted itself on his flesh. Even now, he could feel the whisper of her warmth and hear the fragile catch in her voice as she almost—almost—spoke his name. It burned in him, a slow ache beneath his ribs.

He walked on, jaw set tight, hands curling into fists at his sides. Could she truly give herself to Alessandro? Could she trust another man with the tenderness she had once given him so completely? The question mocked him. A bitter, humourless laugh escaped his throat, echoing faintly off the stone. He already knew the answer. She could try. She might even succeed for a time. But a part of her—no matter how deeply buried—would always belong to him. Always.

The thought should have brought satisfaction, a kind of savage triumph. Instead, it only sharpened the ache, deepened the hollow in his chest until it felt as though he were walking through the corridors not of a villa, but of his own unquiet heart.

At last, he reached his door and paused, his palm resting flat on the cool brass handle. He inhaled slowly, trying to steady the pulse still racing from her nearness, from the ghost of her lips against his. Isabella's warmth, her scent, the ache in her gaze—they swirled in his head like a fever. He closed his eyes for a moment, forcing a breath in, then turned the handle and stepped inside. The door shut softly behind him, sealing the night—and her—just out of reach.

"Hello, Lorenzo."

His eyes snapped open. She was there—Valeria—lounging across his bed as though she had been poured onto the silk covers, her short nightdress shimmering in the dim light. The low glow traced the slope of her shoulders, the arch of a bare leg as she shifted. She tilted her head, a slow, sultry smile curving her lips like a practiced weapon.

"What are you doing here?" he asked evenly, voice low but edged with steel.

"I thought…" she purred, swinging one leg over the edge of the bed, leaning forward so that the lanternlight kissed the hollow of her throat, "maybe you'd like some company. You looked tense out there. I wondered… could I be the one to help?"

Lorenzo's jaw tightened. He felt nothing—not desire, not intrigue, not even the faintest flicker of temptation. The part of him that once might have been flattered was gone. His heart, his mind, every pulse in his body belonged to someone else. "Valeria," he said carefully, each word deliberate, "I am not interested. Not now. Not ever."

Her smile faltered, just for an instant, before she recovered, lowering her voice to a challenge. "Never? Not even a little? Will you ever choose me?"

He met her gaze, dark and unflinching. "No," he said, the single word ringing through the room like a verdict. "Never."

The finality in his tone made her eyes widen, a flicker of surprise and irritation flashing through them before she masked it with a cool expression. She straightened, the sultry pose slipping, replaced by a reluctant acceptance. "As you wish," she said softly, letting her legs slide from the bed to the floor. "But don't think I didn't try."

Lorenzo offered her nothing more than a cool nod. She lingered only a heartbeat longer, then crossed the room with silent steps. When the door clicked shut behind her, the sound was like a release—a weight lifting, an echo fading. Alone again, he exhaled slowly, tension draining from his shoulders even as his mind immediately returned to the one woman who truly mattered— Isabella. Every other distraction, every other temptation, dissolved into irrelevance.

"She's all I want," he murmured to the silent room, moving to the window and staring out at the moonlit gardens where the shadows rippled like water. "And she always will be."

The morning sun streamed through the grand windows of the villa's breakfast room, spilling long shafts of golden light across the polished oak table, gleaming porcelain, and crystal glasses. A gentle warmth filled the space, yet Isabella felt a flutter of nerves she couldn't quite settle. She smoothed the folds of her gown, took a deep, steadying breath, and tried to centre herself before approaching the table, aware that every step carried a weight she could not entirely shake.

Alessandro was already there, seated near the centre, the picture of effortless elegance. He glanced up as she approached, offering a small, reassuring smile that sent a quiet current of calm through her chest. "Good morning, Bella," he murmured, voice low and steady, carrying that familiar reverence that always made her pulse quicken in a way she could neither ignore nor explain.

"Good morning," she replied softly, sliding into the chair beside him. Her hands rested lightly on the table, fingers brushing the edge as she sought an anchor in the moment, though her thoughts threatened to drift to the night before.

Across the room, Lorenzo entered with his usual quiet grace. Dark eyes immediately found hers, and a shiver ran down her spine. He offered a polite nod and took his seat a few chairs away—not close enough to touch, but near enough for the subtle tension between them to hum, palpable and electric. Her stomach twisted with anticipation and unease, a mixture of longing and caution that left her pulse uneven.

The remaining guests filled the room with polite chatter; a muted current of conversation that underscored the storm of emotion she carried. Valeria de Luca sat across from Lorenzo, her sharp gaze flicking toward Isabella with thinly veiled disdain, while Countess Bianca, a young aristocrat, fidgeted nervously with her napkin and cutlery, casting anxious glances around the room. Two gentlemen, friends of Lorenzo and Alessandro from their business circles, chatted lightly about art collections and recent travels, their voices polite, measured, and utterly oblivious to the silent drama threading its way across the table.

The room itself was elegant yet relaxed, a portrait of refinement and composure—but Isabella's heart betrayed her. It beat with quiet tension, divided between desire and caution, past and present, restraint and temptation. As her gaze flicked between Alessandro and Lorenzo, each exuding a different kind of magnetism, she realised just how precarious this morning would be—and how impossible it might be to keep her heart in check.

A waiter moved silently between chairs, pouring rich coffee and fresh-squeezed juice. The soft hum of polite conversation rose around them, punctuated by light laughter. Alessandro leaned slightly toward her, lowering his voice, warm and steady.

"Did you sleep well?" he asked, his hand brushing hers for the briefest instant, grounding and intimate without overstepping.

"I… yes, thank you," she replied, careful to keep her voice even. But her mind flickered, drifting to last night—the memory of Lorenzo's kiss lingering like a secret flame she could not extinguish.

Lorenzo, meanwhile, remained an unyielding presence in her periphery. He spoke occasionally with Countess Bianca or the other guests, but his gaze never strayed far from her. She felt it, sharp and magnetic, even as she tried to focus on her breakfast—scrambled eggs, fresh fruit—but every glance made her pulse hitch, a subtle ache threading through her chest.

Alessandro, perceptive as ever, seemed to sense her distraction. He didn't speak again immediately, instead allowing her space, his quiet presence a steadying force at her side, patient and unintrusive.

Just then, Aldo appeared, moving with silent efficiency. "Signorina Moretti," he said, voice soft and deferential, "your father is in the study. He asked if you might come see him before departing for the day."

Isabella exhaled, a small tension leaving her shoulders. "Thank you, Aldo. I will go find him."

Alessandro's dark eyes glinted with curiosity. "May I come with you?" he asked, casual but insistent, a subtle warmth threading through his tone. "I haven't yet met your father, and I would like to—if it's all right with you."

She hesitated, caught between propriety and the instinct to include him. Finally, she nodded. "Yes… I think he would like to meet you."

"Excellent," Alessandro said, a faint smile tugging at his lips. "Then let's go together."

Lorenzo's gaze flicked toward her, sharp and calculating, though he said nothing. A quiet tension hummed in the air, unspoken but unmistakable, as Isabella rose from her chair. Her pulse fluttered—not only with the anticipation of seeing her father, but with the awareness that Alessandro's presence at her side made every step feel charged, each movement weighted with meaning, even as the lingering shadows of last night whispered at the edges of her mind.

The other guests continued their breakfast, unaware of the silent storm threading through the villa. Isabella and Alessandro moved through the sunlit corridors, the morning light spilling across polished floors, glinting off tall windows and gilded mouldings. Each step felt deliberate, measured, yet charged with a subtle tension neither spoke aloud.

At last, they reached Lorenzo's study. The familiar scent of leather-bound books and polished wood filled the room, grounding her even as her pulse quickened. Her father looked up from an armchair, his expression softening into a smile as he rose.

"Isabella," he said warmly, stepping forward. "I'm glad to see you." His gaze flicked toward Alessandro, laced with polite curiosity.

"Father, this is Alessandro Vitale—a friend of mine," Isabella said, voice calm but carrying a quiet pride. "Alessandro, this is my father, Marco Fioravanti."

"I am very pleased to meet you, sir," Alessandro said, taking Marco's hand firmly, with respectful ease. "I hope I'm not intruding."

Marco waved a hand, dismissive yet kind. "Not at all. If Isabella calls you a friend, I am happy to meet you." His gaze was sharp, intelligent, but softened by warmth. Alessandro met it without hesitation, a faint glint of charm smoothing the edges of his expression.

Marco's eyes lingered on Isabella for a moment, studying her closely. "Have you seen Lorenzo, Isabella?"

"Yes, last night and again this morning," she replied evenly, steady as ever.

"So, all is well between you two?" Marco asked, his tone measured but probing gently.

"All is well, Father," Isabella said, a subtle warmth threading through her words. Alessandro's presence at her side added an unspoken reassurance, a quiet anchor in the delicate navigation of this conversation.

For several minutes, the three of them spoke, beginning with small pleasantries before easing into more personal topics. Alessandro asked thoughtful questions about Marco's work and interests, attentive without overstepping, his charm understated but effective. Isabella felt the room shift subtly—the balance of respect, curiosity, and quiet magnetism working in Alessandro's favour.

When it came time to leave, Marco extended his hand once more. "I'm glad to meet the man who matters to my daughter," he said, voice firm yet approving.

Alessandro's smile was warm, genuine. "Thank you, sir. I assure you; I only want what is best for her."

Her father nodded slowly, a faint glimmer of satisfaction in his eyes. "Good. That is all I could ask."

As they stepped out of the study, Isabella felt a small, lingering warmth spread through her. Alessandro had made a careful, respectful impression—an unspoken victory threaded through the morning sunlight, quiet and reassuring, leaving her mind surprisingly at ease.

Returning to the breakfast room, the chatter of the other guests swelled softly around them, yet Isabella's attention remained fixed on the encounter. The small triumph carried both comfort and tension, a reminder that the morning's stakes were far from over.

Lorenzo noticed their return immediately. "Did you see your father, Isabella?" he asked, voice neutral yet sharpened with curiosity.

"Yes, thank you," she replied politely, steady and measured.

Valeria's eyes widened in surprise, a flicker of annoyance flashing across her face. "Your father is here?"

"My father works for Lorenzo," Isabella said evenly, quiet pride underlying her calm tone, a subtle assertion of self-possession.

Alessandro, walking beside her, allowed a subtle, knowing glance to meet hers—a small, unspoken acknowledgment of the closeness they were building, even in the shadow of Lorenzo's watchful gaze. The air between them hummed softly with possibilities, careful and restrained, yet undeniably present.

The morning sun bathed the villa gardens in a warm, golden glow, highlighting the neatly trimmed hedges and casting dappled light across the cobblestone paths. Birds chirped merrily from the treetops, and the gentle rustle of leaves mingled with the soft murmur of conversation as the guests gathered for their morning stroll. The air carried the faint scent of roses and freshly cut grass, a delicate perfume that seemed to hang over the entire villa.

Valeria, radiant in a pale silk dress that shimmered with each step, glided toward Alessandro. With an effortless, practiced smile, she slipped her hand around his arm, letting her fingers linger just long enough to announce her presence. Alessandro's gaze flicked down at her, a trace of surprise crossing his composed features, though he quickly masked it with his usual calm.

"Surely you could escort me this morning," Valeria said, her voice light and teasing, yet threaded with intention. "After all, the whole point of this gathering is to meet and converse with new people."

Isabella, standing on Alessandro's other side, caught the subtle movement and stiffened for a fraction of a second. The sharp pang of jealousy she had felt the night before—when Valeria had claimed Lorenzo's arm—did not strike so sharply this morning. Still, a quiet, cautious alertness stirred within her as she studied Valeria, noting the deliberate attempt to draw Alessandro away, and feeling the soft pull of curiosity mingled with guarded wariness.

Alessandro's dark eyes flicked between the two women, steady, measured, alert. A faint, almost imperceptible smile curved his lips—a private acknowledgment of Valeria's subtle challenge—yet he gave nothing away, his control absolute.

"You don't mind, do you, Bella?" he asked carefully, his tone light, testing her mood without pressuring.

Isabella returned a soft, reassuring smile. "Of course not," she said, her voice steady, though a subtle flutter in her chest betrayed the quiet tension threading through her.

Before Alessandro could respond, Lorenzo stepped forward, movements deliberate, precise, confident. "I would be honoured to escort you, Isabella," he said, offering his arm with that familiar mix of charm, authority, and understated intensity.

Isabella blinked, startled, and after a brief pause, accepted his gesture. The touch of his hand against hers, warm and grounding, sent a ripple of recognition through her pulse.

Alessandro's lips curved into a polite, measured smile, unaware that in stepping aside, he had played straight into Lorenzo's hands. The shift was subtle, almost imperceptible to the others, yet the quiet game—the tug between past and present, the invisible stakes of hearts and claims—was unmistakably now in Lorenzo's favour.

Three other couples walked ahead, their laughter and light chatter mingling with the rustle of the gardens. Isabella and Lorenzo fell naturally into step, his arm warm and steady against hers, a subtle anchor that seemed to pull her closer even as propriety dictated restraint. Behind them, Alessandro walked with Valeria, his posture calm, controlled, eyes occasionally flicking forward, noting the understated closeness between Isabella and Lorenzo. A faint, thoughtful smirk played on his lips—he had registered the unspoken claim, filing it carefully away for later.

The group followed the winding stone path, pausing occasionally to admire fountains, sculptures, and flowering hedges. Each couple exchanged polite conversation, soft laughter, and small pleasantries, but Isabella's attention lingered on Lorenzo.

She glanced around, taking in the vibrant colours of the roses, the sculpted greenery, and the sunlight glinting off marble statues. "This place is so beautiful," she murmured, voice touched with wonder. "So inspiring."

Lorenzo's gaze softened as he watched her, a faint, intimate smile tugging at his lips. "It suits you," he murmured, voice low, almost conspiratorial, though they were surrounded by others. "You always find the beauty in everything, Isabella."

She looked up at him, startled for a moment by the closeness in his tone, feeling her pulse quicken. Yet the presence of Alessandro behind her, the careful propriety of the group, kept the moment suspended—balanced precariously between restraint and desire.

As they meandered along the garden path, Lorenzo spoke softly about the flowers, sculptures, and history of the villa, his voice a gentle undercurrent only she could hear. Isabella leaned slightly toward him, drawn to the familiarity in his words, the ease of being with someone who had known her so long, someone who could read the silent rhythm of her thoughts.

Behind them, Alessandro maintained his measured pace with Valeria. She laughed lightly at something he said, her hand brushing his arm ever so deliberately. Alessandro's eyes flicked forward once, noting Isabella's hand resting lightly on Lorenzo's arm, the subtle closeness they shared. A faint, knowing smirk curved his lips. He had seen the unspoken claim, and he would remember it.

Valeria leaned a little closer, voice soft and conspiratorial. "This path is lovely… perhaps we should wander off for a moment, just the two of us?" Her golden hair caught the sunlight as she tilted her head, a deliberate challenge glittering in her eyes.

Alessandro's jaw tightened imperceptibly. He glanced forward at Lorenzo and Isabella, who were laughing quietly at some small remark Lorenzo had made, and then back at Valeria. A faint, indulgent smile curved his lips. "Perhaps," he said smoothly, voice controlled, "we could take a little detour."

Valeria's smile widened, triumphant. She brushed her hand lightly against his, testing him, confident he would take the bait. And he did, eyes flicking toward Isabella one last time before guiding Valeria down a winding side path, leaving

Lorenzo and Isabella slightly ahead. The subtle tension threaded between the two pairs, electric yet unspoken, a delicate web of desire, rivalry, and restrained affection that seemed to hang in the morning air.

Isabella glanced back as Alessandro and Valeria disappeared behind a hedge, letting out a small, almost imperceptible sigh. She leaned into Lorenzo's side, the steady warmth of him grounding her. "It's… nice to have a moment like this," she murmured, her voice soft, almost hesitant, her heart caught between the comforting attentions of Alessandro and the undeniable pull toward Lorenzo.

Lorenzo's gaze softened as he looked down at her, fingers brushing hers lightly, almost unconsciously. "Moments like this," he said quietly, each word deliberate, "are only ours if we let them be." Simple words, yet layered with heat, with promise; she could feel them settle in her chest, pressing gently against her pulse, even as the shadow of Alessandro's dark, watchful eyes lingered at the back of her mind.

The rest of the stroll continued in a careful balance of polite conversation and quiet, private tension. Each gesture, each glance, carried meaning—unspoken but undeniable—and Isabella realised with a start how little control she truly had over where her heart was being drawn.

Alessandro and Valeria did not return to the group. Their absence was immediately noted; subtle murmurs rippled through the remaining guests. Countess Bianca cast Isabella a soft, pitying glance, eyebrows lifting delicately. "They must have… gotten lost," she offered, her tone polite yet inquisitive.

Isabella responded with a tight, controlled smile, conscious of the assumptions forming around her. She kept her gaze forward, mind elsewhere, the echo of last night and the magnetic tension between Lorenzo and Alessandro simmering beneath her calm exterior.

She turned to Lorenzo, seeking a safe, familiar anchor. "I think I will go and see Rosa and Aldo, catch up with them," she said quietly, her voice steady but laced with subtle relief.

"They would like that," Lorenzo replied, a small, warm smile softening the edges of his dark eyes. "I will escort you to the kitchens."

She nodded, comforted by his presence. Together, they excused themselves from the group, slipping into a quieter corridor where the morning sunlight stretched in long golden lines across the polished floors. Behind them, the chatter of the remaining guests continued, punctuated by the quiet absence of

Alessandro and Valeria—a detail that quickened Isabella's pulse, a reminder of the intricate, invisible game playing out around her heart.

The corridor narrowed, the soft light tracing the contours of the walls, gilding the smooth marble floor. Lorenzo matched her pace effortlessly, his hand occasionally brushing hers—not deliberately, yet enough to make her pulse skip. Every subtle contact, the warmth radiating from him, the confident rhythm of his stride, reminded her just how much of herself still belonged to him.

"I haven't seen Rosa in ages," she murmured, glancing up at him. "And Aldo… they've both changed so little, though it feels like decades."

Lorenzo's gaze softened, fixed on hers with quiet intensity. "Some things are meant to stay the same," he said, voice low, almost teasing, yet threaded with something deeper. "Like people who matter to you. They're constants."

Her fingers twitched lightly against his arm, a subtle, almost imperceptible reach. She tried to suppress it, reminding herself she was here for a polite visit, a brief catch-up—not a reunion of hearts and years-long longing. Yet every step beside him, every faint brush of his sleeve, made the ache of their past pulse anew, sharpening both desire and restraint.

They turned a corner, and the warm scent of fresh bread and herbs drifted from the kitchens. Rosa looked up from a tray she carried, her face lighting with a wide, genuine smile.

"Isabella! Lorenzo! You've come just in time," she exclaimed, stepping forward and embracing Isabella in a quick, tight hug. "I thought I might see you this morning!"

Aldo emerged from the pantry, wiping his hands on a cloth, greeting Lorenzo with a firm nod and giving Isabella a quick, conspiratorial wink. "It's been too long," he said heartily. "But now that you're here, we can fix that."

Isabella smiled, tension easing slightly under the warmth of their welcome. Yet even as she laughed and exchanged words with Rosa and Aldo, Lorenzo's gaze never left her. It was attentive, protective, claiming without a word. Every laugh, every gesture she made toward him carried weight; every glance he offered teased a promise she wasn't certain she could resist.

For a brief, suspended moment, standing there between the two people who had shaped so much of her adulthood, Isabella allowed herself to breathe. And yet, at the edges of her awareness, Alessandro lingered—a quiet reminder that the path before her was still uncertain, that choices made and desires felt were far from resolved.

Lorenzo's hand brushed hers again as he passed her a small plate of pastries Rosa insisted she try. The contact was fleeting, almost accidental, yet it sent a shiver through her, part warning, part thrill, impossible to ignore.

"Isabella," he murmured, leaning slightly closer, his voice low and intimate, meant only for her, "I don't think we'll let you go so easily once this visit ends."

Her heart skipped a beat, caught between the warmth of familiarity and the dangerous pull of desire. She smiled softly, unable—or perhaps unwilling—to respond, fully aware that the morning had only just begun and that the undercurrent threading through them would not be so easily ignored.

Chapter Eleven

Lorenzo made his way back to his study, finishing a string of business calls that had stretched longer than intended. The familiar weight of responsibility pressed against his shoulders, yet beneath it all, Isabella's presence lingered in his thoughts like a quiet, insistent drumbeat. He was just about to leave when the door opened without warning and Alessandro slipped inside, carrying with him that usual air of effortless charm, polished and practiced.

"There you are," Alessandro said smoothly, his voice polite yet edged with impatience, as if his search had been too long delayed. His dark eyes swept the room, sharp, probing. "Do you know where Bella is?"

"I left her in the kitchens with Rosa and Aldo," Lorenzo replied evenly. His tone was calm, measured, but every word was deliberate, designed to mask the tension that stirred beneath his surface.

Alessandro gave a curt nod, already half-turned to leave, when Lorenzo's gaze sharpened—and caught something that made him pause. A faint smudge of colour marked the edge of Alessandro's collar. Lipstick. Unmistakably Valeria's.

A muscle ticked in Lorenzo's jaw, irritation flashing across his features before he could smooth it away. He had no patience for games, not when Isabella was involved. No tolerance for men who thought women were toys to be collected and discarded. Not when he had seen first-hand what betrayal did—how his father's infidelities had hollowed out his mother, how that kind of wound left scars that never healed. He would not, could not, allow Isabella to suffer the same fate.

His dark eyes narrowed, glinting with warning as he gestured subtly toward Alessandro's collar. "It seems your… playboy ways are still very much intact." The words were quiet, but beneath them simmered steel.

Alessandro's lips curved into a half-smile, charm layered with mischief, as though the accusation were nothing more than a jest between friends. But Lorenzo didn't flinch. His gaze stayed locked, unyielding, unmoved.

"You may think her affections are yours to toy with," Lorenzo said, his voice dropping lower, carrying the weight of old fury, "but I will not let you play that game. Not with her. Not ever."

Alessandro's brows lifted, mock surprise flickering across his face. "Ah… so there is history between you two. I suspected as much."

"Yes," Lorenzo admitted, the words tearing from him like a confession. "And if I hadn't been so bloody stupid in my youth, she wouldn't be so… available now."

Something sparked in Alessandro's gaze—amusement, intrigue, calculation—all tangled together. "So, you do care for her."

"I love her," Lorenzo said fiercely, his composure cracking just enough to reveal the raw edge of his heart. "I have for a very long time. I've waited for her, searched for her, every day for years. And you, my friend…" His voice hardened, laced with conviction. "You are the one who reunited us."

For a long moment, Alessandro studied him, the calculating gleam in his eyes weighing every syllable. Then, with a faint tilt of his head, he delivered the jab. "Yet she does not seem particularly overjoyed to be reunited with you."

The words cut deeper than Lorenzo expected, a sudden, sharp sting that threatened to unravel him—but he held firm, jaw tight until the ache radiated through his face. The air between them thickened, heavy with unspoken rivalry and the inescapable truth: Isabella was not a prize to be won, but a woman with her own mind and heart.

Yet Lorenzo's determination blazed fiercer than ever—he would never surrender her. Not if even a fragment of hope remained. Not ever. The only way he might relent was if she could prove, beyond all doubt, that her heart no longer belonged to him. But the memory of their kiss from last night scorched his lips like fire, searing away any trace of uncertainty.

"She is the first woman I've met I would consider settling down for, Lorenzo," Alessandro said at last, smooth, confident, and almost taunting. "And I intend to win her."

"And still play around behind her back?" Lorenzo's words cut through the polished veneer Alessandro wore so easily, sharp as a blade.

Alessandro's hand rose to his collar, brushing over the faint lipstick stain as if acknowledging it for the first time. For a fleeting second, the playboy mask slipped, revealing something raw beneath—guilt, maybe shame. "This… was a mistake," he said quietly. "It won't happen again."

"Really, Alessandro," Lorenzo said, his voice low and uncompromising. "If you truly care for Isabella, do not toy with her affections. She is not like the others—like Valeria."

Alessandro met his gaze, weighing Lorenzo's words, considering the weight behind them. But Lorenzo's eyes never wavered—dark, unrelenting. His silence was a decree unto itself. To him, Isabella's heart was sacred, and he would never allow it to be treated as anything less.

After a lively chat with Rosa and Aldo, Isabella felt the familiar stir of inspiration rise within her. The lightness of their conversation still clung to her, but it was the whisper of creativity that tugged at her most insistently. She decided it was the perfect moment to fetch her sketchbook, to slip into the gardens and let the quiet beauty around her take shape on the page. Gathering her belongings, she moved toward the terrace.

The morning sun spilled generously across the polished stone floors, setting the villa's grand façade aglow with a golden warmth. Every gleam of sunlight seemed alive, almost conspiratorial, beckoning her outside as if the very world longed for her to pause, to breathe, to create—even for a fleeting moment.

She was just reaching the terrace doors when a cheerful voice carried from behind her.

"Oh, hello, Isabella! Going for a walk?"

Turning, she found Countess Bianca standing there, her delicate features bright with curiosity and touched by playful amusement. Her eyes shimmered like sunlight dancing over water, their sparkle instantly disarming. There was something about her presence—easy, gracious—that set Isabella at ease before a single step had been taken.

"Hello, Countess. Yes," Isabella replied, warmth softening her smile. "Would you like to join me?"

Bianca's eyes lit with delight. "Yes, please. All the men seem to have vanished into the billiard room, and…" her lips curved knowingly, "well—Valeria appears rather attached to them."

Isabella's own lips curved in a subtle, knowing smile. "Yes, I noticed. You're very observant, Countess."

Bianca tilted her head, mischief glinting in her eyes. "Please… call me Bianca."

"Then Bianca it is," Isabella said, tucking a loose strand of hair behind her ear. "Let's make the most of the quiet before the others realise we've slipped away."

Together, they stepped onto the terrace. The morning air was crisp, tinged with the sweetness of roses and the faint, earthy green of freshly cut grass. Sunlight dappled the cobblestones beneath their feet, glinting off terracotta pots lined neatly along the balustrade. Beyond, the gardens stretched wide and serene, an expanse of carefully tended beauty that seemed to wait patiently for Isabella's pencil to capture its life.

Her chest filled with a familiar, eager flutter. Her fingers itched for the texture of the page, for the scratch of graphite as she translated blooms and shadows into form. The vivid blossoms, the curling ivy, the jewelled dewdrops still clinging to petals—each detail whispered for her attention. And beside her, Bianca's gentle, unassuming presence made the moment feel lighter, a small oasis of calm after the tension of the morning meal.

"You came here with Alessandro, yes?" Bianca asked suddenly, her tone light, almost casual, but edged with quiet curiosity.

"Yes," Isabella answered, her voice steady though brief.

Bianca lifted a delicate brow. "And… Valeria seems to have latched onto him rather quickly."

Isabella's gaze flicked back toward the villa, picturing the laughter and the effortless charm that had unfolded inside. Her lips pressed together in thought. "I've noticed," she said evenly, cloaking her unease in composure.

Bianca's eyes softened, studying her. "I'm sorry if that upsets you."

Isabella shook her head, voice quiet but firm with quiet conviction. "No. It's fine. I have no reason not to trust Alessandro."

Bianca regarded her closely, admiration flickering across her features. "You are very brave. Most women would feel threatened—or at least uneasy—watching someone else stake such a quick claim."

Isabella's smile grew, faint but genuine, a warmth rising in her chest. "Perhaps. Or perhaps I've learned that worry does little good. It's better to see how people truly act—and then decide what to do."

They walked on in companionable silence, footsteps soft on the sun-warmed stone. The gardens unfurled before them, hedges and flowerbeds whispering of inspiration. Isabella's sketchbook, tucked securely beneath her arm, felt almost like a talisman, a promise of clarity and calm. For the first time that morning, she let herself breathe, let the rhythm of the world around her soften the turmoil inside.

"Are you and Alessandro… a couple?" Bianca asked after a pause, her voice airy but edged with curiosity.

"Not really," Isabella admitted, considering her words carefully. "He's been pursuing me for a few weeks, but I haven't decided what I want yet." She brushed a strand of hair from her face, and the sunlight caught in her eyes as she glanced back toward the gardens.

Bianca tilted her head, her gaze thoughtful. "I noticed Lorenzo looking at you quite a lot."

Isabella stilled, a flicker of memory tugging at her. "I used to live at his Florence villa when my mother passed. My father works for him," she said softly. The words carried a weight that had shadowed her for years.

"Oh… I see." Bianca's expression gentled, curiosity tempered with compassion. "I think… Lorenzo likes you."

Isabella blinked, startled by the frankness. "What makes you say that?"

"The way he looks at you," Bianca said simply, her eyes steady. "Every time you are with Alessandro, he does not look happy. Not exactly." Her words lingered, quiet but pointed, like a truth that refused to be ignored.

Isabella's fingers tightened around her sketchbook strap. She forced a calm smile, though her pulse had quickened. The morning light, the serenity of the gardens, even Bianca's gentle companionship—none of it could silence the storm that Alessandro and Lorenzo stirred within her.

"May I ask, Bianca… have you ever been in love?" Isabella's voice was thoughtful, almost tentative, her gaze drifting toward the curve of a nearby fountain.

Bianca's lips curved wistfully, her eyes shining with quiet hope. "No, not yet," she admitted, tucking a strand of hair behind her ear. "But I'm hoping it will happen to me one day. You?"

Isabella's grip on her sketchbook tightened. A shadow crossed her features, memory pressing close. "Yes," she said softly. Her voice was steady, but the weight in it was undeniable. "I have."

Bianca leaned in, curiosity sparkling. "And… did it last?"

Isabella's gaze fell, her thoughts caught between Alessandro's charm and Lorenzo's intensity, between desire and caution. "Some things leave a mark, even if they don't last," she murmured, her words touched with melancholy.

Bianca nodded slowly, understanding glimmering in her expression. "Then perhaps it isn't always about holding on. Sometimes it is about learning what truly matters."

A small smile curved Isabella's lips, tender and knowing. "Yes. And sometimes, it is about knowing what—or who—you can never quite let go of."

The morning breeze drifted across the terrace, carrying the sweetness of roses and the earthy freshness of newly cut grass. For a moment, the world seemed hushed, listening to her unspoken thoughts. Her gaze lifted to the blooms swaying in the sunlight, their petals catching the light like delicate flames.

And with them came the memory of Lorenzo. The way his dark eyes had always pierced through her, seeing not the version of herself the world expected, but the truth of who she was. The remembered warmth of his touch lingered against her skin, unshakable. The dangerous, magnetic pull of him—equal parts comfort and peril—rose from the depths of her heart, a force she had never truly escaped.

Her breath slipped free in a soft whisper, carried off by the wind. She tried to sketch, but her hand faltered, the pencil hovering above the page like a heart unwilling to move forward. Even with the garden stretched before her, vibrant and alive, she felt the invisible tether she could neither sever nor ignore. It bound her to him—unrelenting, irrevocable. In that piercing clarity, Isabella knew: no other love could ever reach her fully while Lorenzo's shadow loomed so insistently.

Bianca tilted her head, studying her with quiet curiosity. "You drifted away for a moment," she said softly, almost conspiratorially. "What were you thinking about?"

Isabella's hand stilled at the edge of her sketchbook, her chest tightening. "If I can forgive," she murmured before she could stop herself. The words rang hollow, even to her own ears.

"Forgive what?" Bianca asked gently, without judgment.

For a heartbeat Isabella considered silence. But Bianca's openness—her delicate patience—disarmed her. Exhaling slowly, she lifted her gaze. "It was Lorenzo's father. He told him I was not enough, that I did not belong in their world. That I was fine for amusement, but never for marriage. And the worst part..." Her voice broke before she steadied it. "Lorenzo laughed with him. He said I was just... a bit of fun."

Bianca's expression softened, shock flickering across her features. "He said that. And laughed at you?"

Isabella nodded, her throat tightening. "I was nineteen. Young, foolish, hopelessly in love. To hear those words—from the man I trusted, the man I thought would fight for me—it shattered me. That is why I left Florence. Why I left him."

"How long ago?" Bianca asked quietly.

"Five years," Isabella admitted, the ache of those years pressing into her voice.

Bianca tilted her head, thoughtful. "Five years is a long time. We do foolish things when we are young—things that leave scars we carry far too long."

"He tells me he's sorry now," Isabella whispered, clutching her sketchbook as if it might steady her. "Terribly sorry. For what he said... for what he did not stop his father from saying. But the words still echo. I do not know if I can forgive—not truly. Not when they cut so deep."

Bianca's eyes warmed with quiet compassion. "The question is not only whether you can forgive him. It is whether you still want to. Sometimes... holding on to the wound feels safer than opening your heart to the risk again."

Isabella's gaze drifted to the roses trembling in the breeze. Their fragile petals mirrored the state of her own heart—soft, bruised, yet stubbornly alive. And in that fragile stillness, she admitted what her pride had long refused: she had never truly let go of Lorenzo.

Bianca hesitated, then leaned a fraction closer, her tone conspiratorial. "May I make one last observation?"

"Yes, of course," Isabella replied quickly, as though bracing herself.

Bianca's gaze held steady. "I have seen the way you look at both men. When your eyes rest on Alessandro, I see warmth—admiration, even affection. But when you look at Lorenzo—" she paused, choosing her words with care, "—I see longing. Longing that cannot be feigned. It's the look of something unfinished. Something still burning, no matter how deeply you try to bury it."

Isabella's breath caught. Her fingers tightened around her sketchbook until the edges pressed sharply into her palms. She wanted to deny it, to protest—but the words tangled in her throat, refusing to form. Bianca was right. The aching pull each time Lorenzo's gaze found hers, the quickening of her pulse at the thought of him—none of it could be smothered by reason, pride, or even Alessandro's gentle affection.

"I…" she began, voice faltering to a whisper. Her gaze lifted to the roses swaying in the wind, their fragile blooms reflecting her own heart—wounded, but still alive. "I thought I had buried those feelings. But perhaps… I only buried myself along with them."

Bianca reached out, resting a gentle hand on her arm. "Sometimes," she said softly, "the heart knows the truth long before the mind dares to admit it. Knowing does not make the choice easier. But it makes it real."

Isabella's chest heaved as the words settled inside her. Every unspoken thought, every stolen glance, every moment of denial rose to the surface. She clenched her sketchbook tighter, the paper cutting into her palms. There was no protest left, no deflection—because there was nothing left to deny.

"I still love him," Isabella whispered. The fragile confession trembled free at last, her eyes shining with raw, unvarnished truth. "Even after everything… even after the hurt… I never stopped."

Bianca's silence carried more weight than words. She offered no answer, only the quiet gift of understanding.

For a long while Isabella watched the roses, the breeze rippling their petals as her thoughts circled back to Lorenzo—the darkness of his gaze, the warmth of his touch, the dangerous gravity he carried wherever he went. She had tried to resist, tried to be fair to Alessandro, but the truth was undeniable: her heart belonged, still and irrevocably, to Lorenzo.

At last Bianca spoke again, her voice soft but knowing. "Be careful, Isabella. Love like this… it is a force. It can lift you higher than anything else, but it can also shatter you if you are not ready. Sometimes, the hardest part is admitting it—even to yourself."

Isabella nodded, her throat tight with unshed tears. "I know," she murmured. "And yet… I cannot help it. No matter what I try, no matter who I care for… he is the one I cannot let go of."

The breeze whispered through the terrace once more, carrying with it the fragrance of roses and the faint, earthy scent of freshly cut grass. Isabella's chest tightened with longing—with the piercing clarity of her own heart, with the realisation that the road ahead would not be simple or safe. Yet for all its peril and its ache, she could no longer deny the truth that had risen within her: she still loved Lorenzo. She always had.

She lingered on the terrace, allowing Bianca's words to settle around her like a soft, protective cloak. The morning sun had climbed higher now, gilding the villa's gardens in molten gold, but the brightness brought her no comfort. The joy she normally found in sketching, in capturing beauty with pencil and page, was absent. Her mind felt too crowded, her heart too heavy, her thoughts circling back to the one admission she had dared to speak aloud at last—she loved him, fiercely and irrevocably, no matter the cost.

Turning toward Bianca, Isabella managed a tentative smile, fragile at the edges. "I… I think I need some time alone. Please—make my apologies for lunch. I am… not feeling myself."

Bianca's eyes softened, understanding shimmering in their depths. She offered no lecture, no questions, only quiet acceptance. "Of course, Isabella. I will tell them."

With a grateful nod, Isabella gathered her sketchbook to her chest, as though its familiar weight might keep her scattered thoughts from unravelling. She slipped away from the terrace, her steps slow, almost reluctant. The villa's sunlit corridors stretched around her, elegant and echoing, yet they felt strangely hollow now—every footfall a reminder of the choices she could no longer postpone.

When she reached her room, she closed the door behind her, the faint click of the latch sounding sharper, more final than it should have. Alone at last, Isabella leaned against the door for a moment, clutching her sketchbook as if it could steady her, the silence pressing in like an unspoken question she was no longer able to avoid.

Chapter Twelve

When Lorenzo entered the dining room for luncheon, the villa's warm, inviting atmosphere felt strangely hollow. The usual murmur of conversation, the soft clink of silver against porcelain, filled the air with its genteel rhythm—but his eyes went first, instinctively, to the chair by the terrace window. Empty. Isabella's place stood vacant, a small absence that swallowed all other sounds.

Countess Bianca, graceful as ever in her seat nearby, caught the flicker of his searching gaze. Leaning toward him, her voice low and touched with regret, she said, "Signor Caravelli… Isabella will not be joining us for lunch today. She asked me to make her apologies."

A knot tightened in Lorenzo's chest, threading unease with concern until the two were indistinguishable. Every instinct urged him to rise at once, to go to her room, to see with his own eyes that she was well. Yet a quieter voice, stubborn in its restraint, warned him it would be improper—perhaps unwelcome. Still, the pull was relentless, tugging at him with every beat of his heart.

He lowered himself into his chair and accepted the plate before him, though his appetite had deserted him entirely. His fork moved in idle motions, food touched but barely tasted, while his thoughts drifted back to the morning—the sound of Isabella's laughter carried on the garden breeze, the warmth in her fleeting glances, the quiet glow of her presence that lingered even in absence.

Across the room, Alessandro reclined with his effortless charm, every movement smooth, unhurried, as if he belonged to the air itself. His dark eyes surveyed the company with lazy confidence, his smile never far from his lips. By his side, Valeria de Luca leaned in with practiced ease, her laughter light and rippling as her hand brushed his arm in a gesture that was casual, yet far too deliberate to be meaningless.

Lorenzo's jaw tightened. His knuckles whitened where his hand gripped the edge of the table. Each tilt of Alessandro's head, each sly smile or murmured word that drew laughter from Valeria, struck like a needle under his skin. The sheer ease of it—the way Alessandro could command a room without effort, charm without consequence—only sharpened the ache gnawing at Lorenzo's chest.

The thought of Isabella seeing him like this—seeing Alessandro's charm directed so carelessly elsewhere, watching Valeria bask in it—burned bitterly through him. He remembered his mother's silences, her dignity masking years of betrayal; remembered the fractures that careless indulgences left behind. He would not—he could not—bear Isabella suffering anything of that kind. She was too luminous, too trusting, too rare to be wounded by another man's whims.

The clink of glasses, the hum of voices, the polite cadence of laughter—none of it anchored him. Each mouthful of food tasted of nothing but unease. His thoughts circled back, again and again, to Isabella: to the shadows he had glimpsed in her eyes, the way her shoulders seemed to carry weight she never spoke aloud.

Leaning back at last, Lorenzo forced a steady breath, forcing himself to listen, to nod, to endure the hollow rhythm of conversation that meant nothing to him. Outwardly, he gave the impression of calm; inwardly, every polite smile, every casual remark from the table, only deepened the ache. He could do nothing—nothing but wait, nothing but hope—that Isabella was safe, that her heart remained untouched by wounds he would never forgive anyone for causing.

The afternoon sun streamed through the tall windows of Isabella's room, casting long, golden shafts across the polished floors and gilded furnishings. She sat near the open shutters, her sketchbook abandoned on the chaise lounge beside her. Her fingertip traced idle patterns across its blank pages, though her thoughts were far from the gardens she had intended to capture.

She turned toward the gilded mirror, her reflection staring back with a calm composure that belied the storm within. Dark blonde waves framed her face, soft and luminous, yet inside, turmoil churned relentlessly. Her heart tugged in two directions at once: the safe, steady comfort Alessandro offered, a quiet haven she could rely on, and the dangerous, magnetic pull of Lorenzo, the man she had never truly stopped loving.

Her fingers grazed the edge of the mirror, as though tracing the contours of the life she wished she could lead—the clarity she longed for but could not yet summon. Pressing a hand to her chest, she felt the lingering ache of unresolved feelings, the sorrow of wounds that had never fully healed. She told herself she had to decide, yet even the thought felt unbearable. She had to be honest with Alessandro, yet Lorenzo lingered in every shadow of her mind, a presence impossible to banish.

A soft chime from the bell downstairs signalled the arrival of the dinner announcement. Isabella exhaled slowly, forcing herself upright. She tucked stray curls behind her ears, smoothed the bodice of her gown, and drew in a measured breath. This evening, she resolved, would be about appearances first, feelings later.

By the time she entered the dining room, the warm glow of the chandeliers bathed the long table in golden light. The rich scent of fresh bread and roasted meats mingled with the crisp aroma of polished silver, filling the room with a comforting, familiar opulence. Lorenzo sat at the head of the table, his gaze immediately seeking her. Relief flickered across his features, tempered by a shadow of lingering concern.

"Isabella," he said softly, voice low yet threaded with warmth that brushed against her awareness. "I trust you are feeling better. We missed you at luncheon."

She inclined her head, offering a small, polite smile. "Yes, thank you. I… I needed some time alone this afternoon."

Her gaze shifted toward Alessandro, lounging with effortless ease across the table, dark eyes sweeping the room with quiet confidence. Valeria hovered nearby, her soft laughter deliberately timed, accentuating every motion of Alessandro's charm. Isabella felt her chest tighten, the familiar tug of indecision stirring once more.

She ate sparingly, picking at her plate with careful, measured motions, all the while observing Alessandro—the tilt of his head, the subtle attentions he offered, the natural charisma that drew others into his orbit. Every glance she cast in his direction was a small, potent tug against her heart, a reminder of how much she had yet to resolve.

Lorenzo's gaze followed her subtly, a quiet sentinel of presence. Each look she gave Alessandro felt like a taut thread stretching between them, and he forced himself to maintain composure, though the tension coiled in his chest, a low, insistent ache he could not shake. He had hoped simply seeing her might calm the storm in his own heart, bring reassurance—but each measured glance toward Alessandro only heightened the quiet fear of losing her, even as she remained at the same table.

He reached slightly across the table, letting his gaze linger a fraction longer, a silent assertion: she was not alone. Each courteous gesture from Alessandro, every smooth word, was noted—but the pull Isabella felt toward Lorenzo ran deep, unspoken, unresolved, a dangerous undercurrent neither could ignore.

The dinner continued around them, conversation light, laughter polite, but for Lorenzo, each word carried weight. Every laugh, every turn of the table, was a potential threat to the fragile balance of Isabella's heart. Desire, restraint, attention, and presence wove together in a quiet, unrelenting battle—and Lorenzo knew the stakes had never been higher, not for him, and certainly not for her.

Dinner drew to a close, the soft clatter of cutlery and polite chatter fading into the warm glow of the villa's lamps. Isabella pushed her plate back gently, the food barely touched. Her heart raced, fingers twisting lightly in her lap, betraying the storm of thoughts she could no longer keep at bay. All afternoon she had avoided the truth—and now it demanded to be spoken.

Alessandro noticed her lingering at the table and leaned slightly forward, his dark eyes calm yet attentive, a faint edge of concern flickering in their depths. "Is everything all right, Bella?" he asked, his voice smooth, carrying the warmth of genuine care.

She drew a measured breath, rising from her chair, her pulse thrumming in her ears. "Alessandro… may I speak with you for a moment? Away from everyone else?"

He nodded, a faint, easy smile softening his features, and followed her to a quieter corner of the veranda. The evening air was cool, carrying the faint scent of roses from the gardens below, and the hum of distant conversation faded, leaving them suspended in a private, almost fragile moment. Isabella's chest tightened as she faced him, her gaze flickering briefly to the darkening sky before settling on his.

"Alessandro," she began, her voice soft yet steady, "I need to be honest with you. I… I cannot be with you."

His half-smile faltered, replaced by a careful, attentive concern. "You… cannot?" he repeated, keeping his tone calm, though his eyes never left hers.

She nodded, summoning all the courage she could muster. "You've been kind, patient, and… generous with your affection. But my heart—" She paused, swallowing hard, her fingers brushing the railing as if it could anchor her. "It belongs elsewhere. I cannot give you what you deserve, because I am not free. I… I cannot love anyone while Lorenzo—" Her voice caught, a tremor betraying the depth of her feelings. "While I am still bound to him in my heart."

Alessandro regarded her quietly, his dark gaze unwavering, the playfulness in his expression giving way to rare solemnity. Then he exhaled slowly, a quiet acknowledgment settling in his eyes. "I see," he said softly, the gentleness of his tone edged with a faint trace of regret. "Then I must accept that. You must follow your heart, Bella. I cannot—and would not—stand in its way."

Relief and a pang of sorrow washed over her in equal measure. She felt the weight of unspoken gratitude for his understanding, for the grace with which he let her go, free of resentment or reproach.

"I am sorry," she murmured, her fingers brushing the edge of the railing as if it could steady her racing heart. "I never wanted to hurt you."

Alessandro's lips curved in a faint, rueful smile, a mixture of warmth and quiet melancholy. "You have not hurt me, Bella. Not truly. You've simply reminded me that some hearts are not ours to claim. Perhaps… that is the truest test of love—knowing when to let go."

She exhaled, a whisper of relief slipping from her lips. "Thank you, Alessandro," she said softly. "Thank you for understanding."

He inclined his head, the light-hearted charm of his usual demeanour replaced by a gravity that spoke to his sincerity. "Always, Bella. Always." After a pause, he added, "I think I will leave in the morning. I came here to try to win you, but now that you have made your choice… I think it is best that I go. So, you may be with Lorenzo without any pressure—or awkwardness—from me."

"I don't want to chase you away, Alessandro," she said quickly, a twinge of guilt in her voice.

He took her hands gently in his, the touch reassuring yet firm. "You are not. But I see that you need the space and time with Lorenzo that you deserve. That is far more important than anything else."

"You are so kind, Alessandro," Isabella murmured, her throat tight. "I hope… I hope I can call you my friend."

"Of course, Bella," he said warmly. Then, bending slightly, he brushed his lips against hers in a soft, tender kiss. She returned it—a gesture of gratitude and farewell, sweet yet tinged with the ache of what could not be.

With a final glance, she stepped away, feeling lighter in some ways, yet heavier in others. Each step back into the villa carried her closer to the heart she had never stopped yearning for—the one whose shadow had lingered over every fleeting moment of happiness, the one she must now face, knowing the truth of her love could no longer remain hidden.

Isabella lingered in the villa's quiet corridors after her confession to Alessandro. Relief still hummed faintly in her chest at how gracefully he had taken it, his understanding words echoing in her mind. Yet that relief was fragile—she had another truth to confront, a confession far more dangerous and terrifying.

Her hands twisted nervously in front of her, fingers knotting and unknotting as she tried to summon courage. She began to pace, slow at first, each step deliberate, then gradually faster, the polished floors reflecting the warm glow of the lamps above. Her pulse hammered in her ears, a relentless drumbeat of anticipation and fear, and she pressed her palms lightly to her thighs, willing her body to steady itself.

"I can't keep hiding this," she whispered to herself, voice low, almost swallowed by the cavernous hall. "I have to tell him… I have to tell him I love him."

She searched first in the billiard room, hoping to catch a glimpse of him among the other men, but it was empty except for the casual laughter of distant guests and the absence of Alessandro. She moved on to his study, imagining he might be there, lost in his papers, but again the room was empty.

Her gaze drifted upward to the grand staircase, instinctively knowing he must be in his bedroom. She closed her eyes for a moment, inhaling deeply, trying to steady the racing of her heart. The memory of his dark, searching eyes, the warmth of his voice, the subtle pull of his presence—everything about him flooded her senses. The thought that she might never speak her heart aloud tightened her chest with a sudden, urgent ache.

Step by careful step, she made her way toward the hall leading to his rooms. Her hands clenched into fists at her sides, and her pulse quickened with a combination of hope and terror.

A sudden doubt made her stop. What if he didn't feel the same? What if she had waited too long and the moment had passed? The very thought twisted her stomach. She shook her head, forcing the fear away. No—she had to tell him. She could not endure another day without him knowing the truth.

Her steps resumed, shorter, more determined now, echoing softly in the hallway. Each turn strengthened her resolve; every breath tethered her to courage. Her heart hammered, reminding her of the vulnerability she was about to embrace, yet whispering of the freedom and relief that might come from speaking honestly at last.

Finally, she neared the doorway of Lorenzo's bedroom, her heart hammering so loudly it seemed to echo off the polished floors. She slowed, steadying herself with a deep breath, repeating the words she had rehearsed countless times: *Lorenzo... I love you. I have loved you all along.* I cannot deny it any longer. Every step, every movement felt measured, sacred—a fragile bridge between fear and the confession she had longed to make.

And then the door opened.

Valeria stepped out, a mess of tousled hair spilling over her shoulders, her gown slightly wrinkled, a faint smear of lipstick on her cheek catching the light. Isabella froze, disbelief rooting her to the spot. For a moment, she thought she might be imagining it, some cruel trick of light and shadow—but no. Valeria's presence, her very air, screamed triumph and malice.

Valeria did not notice her immediately. She fussed with her hair, straightened her bodice with deliberate, languid movements, and even smirked at herself in the hallway mirror. Finally, her sharp gaze fell on Isabella.

The cruel, calculating smile that spread across Valeria's lips sent a chill down Isabella's spine. She stepped forward, every movement slow, deliberate, savouring the effect of her words before she even spoke.

"If you were planning a little... tête-à-tête with Lorenzo," Valeria purred, her voice soft, silky, and venomous, "he may be a little tired. I think I... wore him out."

The words landed with the force of a physical blow. Isabella's stomach dropped, her legs threatening to give way beneath her. Her hands clenched at her sides, nails digging into her palms, a futile attempt to anchor herself against the sudden, sharp surge of panic.

Shock paralysed her for a heartbeat; the carefully rehearsed confession to Lorenzo evaporated into the cold corridor air. Her mind raced, stuttering over every memory, every interaction of the day, now filtered through this single, devastating image.

Valeria leaned forward, eyes glinting with cruel delight. "He seemed... very eager," she added, deliberately slow, drawing out the insinuation with almost sadistic patience. "I think you might have... missed your chance."

Isabella's chest tightened, a low, unbearable ache spreading through her body. Her knees threatened to give way, and she reached for the nearest wall to steady herself. Her vision blurred with the first prickling sting of tears. For a moment, it felt as though the floor beneath her had disappeared.

The hall seemed impossibly long, impossibly silent, except for her ragged breathing and the faint echo of Valeria's soft laughter fading behind her. Each step away from the doorway felt like walking through a storm of shattered hope, every movement heavier than the last. Her mind replayed the cruel implication: Lorenzo… with Valeria… and I was so close to confessing everything.

Her heart ached with the raw, unrelenting pain that made her chest feel hollow. Every beat reminded her of the truth she could not deny, she loved Lorenzo. She had never stopped. And now, she had arrived too late.

Tears blurred her vision, and she swallowed hard, forcing them back, letting the fire of heartbreak fuel her resolve instead. She could not confront him like this—not now, not like this. She needed time. She needed to breathe. And she needed someone who could offer a calm anchor when her world had spun so violently out of control.

Chapter Thirteen

Isabella's legs trembled as she fled the villa's corridors, Valeria's cruel words echoing in her ears like a relentless, sharp refrain piercing every corner of her heart. Each step felt heavier than the last, the polished floors reflecting the dim glow of the lamps above, stretching out before her like a path she had no choice but to follow. Instinct drove her forward, overriding thought, until she reached Alessandro's bedroom. Her hand hovered over the polished door handle, pulse hammering so violently she feared he might hear it through the wood. For a long moment, she froze, drawing in a shuddering breath, trying to gather the fragments of her composure, and then rapped lightly against the door, as if the gentlest touch could convey the storm within her.

The door swung open almost immediately.

"Bella…" Alessandro's voice caught in his throat as he saw the tears streaking her face, the small, trembling sobs she could no longer hide. His dark eyes searched hers, full of quiet, immediate concern—the kind that did not demand answers but offered sanctuary.

"Please… may I come in?" she whispered, fragile and trembling with a vulnerability she had fought so hard to contain all afternoon.

"Of course." He stepped aside, and she entered, her steps unsteady, each one echoing slightly against the polished floors. The door closed softly behind her, a gentle click that felt almost like a promise.

Alessandro's gaze softened as he crossed the room and drew her gently into his arms. Warmth enveloped her, a calm anchor amid the chaos of her emotions, steadying her quaking limbs. "Tell me what's happened," he murmured, voice low and patient, threaded with an understanding that made her chest ache even more.

She shook her head against his chest, tears spilling freely now. "I… I don't know how to explain it," she admitted between sobs, voice cracking under the weight of heartbreak and shock.

Alessandro held her closer, tilting her chin so she could meet his gaze. His eyes, deep and unwavering, carried a tenderness that demanded nothing yet allowed everything. He pressed for no details, offered no judgment—only the quiet reassurance she desperately needed.

"I need… I need to leave here," she whispered, voice barely audible, trembling with both fear and longing.

"All right," he said softly, brushing a stray curl from her temple. "Tomorrow morning. You'll come with me, and we'll go—away from here. No questions until you're ready. You decide when you speak."

Relief surged through her like a tidal wave, mingling with the lingering ache in her chest. She leaned into him slightly, letting his steady presence anchor her frayed heart. "Thank you," she whispered, each word weighted with gratitude she could not fully articulate.

"You're welcome," he replied, voice low and unwavering. "I know tonight has been difficult. Tomorrow… we'll have the sea, the wind, and freedom. You can tell me everything then—if you're ready."

Isabella exhaled slowly, pulling back just enough to clasp her hands in front of her, steadying the tremor that still coursed through her. She did not tell him what had driven her here, did not reveal the sight that had shattered her heart. Alessandro, for his part, assumed—correctly or not—that Lorenzo had rejected her. Even in that assumption, his calm, unwavering kindness filled the void left by her heartbreak, offering a fragile hope she could cling to until morning.

"I… I'll be ready," she murmured, voice tight with emotion. "Tomorrow. Thank you, Alessandro… for… everything."

He inclined his head, a small, understanding smile playing at the corners of his lips. "Always, Bella. Get some rest tonight. Tomorrow, the sea will wait, and when you're ready, you can tell me everything."

Isabella turned toward the door, taking one last shaky breath before retreating to her room. Each step felt heavy, yet somehow lighter than before, as if the burden of uncertainty had been momentarily eased by his steadfast presence. She paused as she closed the door behind her, letting herself breathe, gathering the scattered pieces of her heart. Alone, she pressed her hands to her chest, feeling the lingering ache of loss and longing, steeling herself for the journey ahead—the journey away from the villa, from Lorenzo, and toward the uncertain freedom she desperately needed, even as the shadow of her love stretched long and dark behind her.

The villa lay hushed around her, the soft rustle of leaves outside her window the only sound. Isabella pressed the pillow lightly to her cheek, the faint scent of lavender from her drawers barely reaching her senses. Her mind was a storm, a whirlwind of memory and fear. She replayed the afternoon again and again—the corridors she had paced, the words she had finally spoken to Alessandro, the sight of Valeria emerging from Lorenzo's room. Each cruel, deliberate smirk burned in her mind, leaving her chest tight and her stomach twisting. Her knuckles whitened as she clutched the sheets, trying in vain to hold herself together.

She imagined Lorenzo—near yet unknowable: the warmth of his presence, the depth of his dark eyes, the way each movement anchored her even from afar. And yet, that image was now tainted, marred by Valeria's malicious cruelty, her words cutting through the memory like shards of ice.

Alessandro's calm, understanding presence offered a fragile tether, and she clung to it in the darkness. She pictured the early morning, the soft sway of the yacht, the fresh salt air whipping around them. Perhaps then she could finally unburden herself completely. Perhaps then she could speak the truth without shame or heartbreak.

Sleep came fitfully, fleeting and shallow. Every time she closed her eyes, Lorenzo appeared—alone in the dim villa, unaware she knew the truth, while her heart ached for him. Every breath reminded her of what she had lost and what she had never truly possessed.

Morning arrived too quickly. Sunlight spilled across the polished floors and gardens, glimmering on the waves beyond the villa. Isabella dressed with deliberate care, each motion precise yet distracted, her heart racing beneath the delicate fabric of her gown. She gathered her belongings, checking each item meticulously, her mind replaying Alessandro's soothing words from the night before.

Descending the stairs, she found him waiting, leaning casually against the doorway of the salon, his dark eyes sweeping the horizon. His gentle smile carried the same quiet concern as the night before.

"Bella," he said softly, stepping forward, "are you ready?"

She nodded, her voice barely audible, trembling slightly. "Yes."

He reached for her hand, warm and reassuring. She allowed herself to be guided down the private dock to his yacht. The morning air was crisp, carrying the scent of salt and freedom. The gentle sway beneath her feet grounded her, yet her thoughts remained tangled—between past and present, heart and reason.

Lorenzo woke before dawn, the first pale light of the villa filtering through the tall windows, casting long, ghostly shadows across the polished floors—silent witnesses to his unrest. Sleep had abandoned him entirely, slipping further away with every thought he could not banish. Now, seated in his study in the hushed stillness of early morning, he felt the weight of the night pressing down, relentless and unyielding.

His mind churned with images that refused to fade: Isabella's quiet, hesitant demeanour at dinner; the delicate, almost imperceptible curve of her smile when she spoke to Alessandro; the warmth in her voice during words meant for him alone; the subtle, intimate brush of her hand against his, or the gentle tilt of her head that made his heart twist with longing. Each memory, each fleeting glance, burned itself into his consciousness, leaving him suspended between desire and despair.

The study felt suddenly oppressive, the familiar walls closing in as if mirroring the tightness in his chest. Every flicker of light across the polished wood reminded him of what he had seen, what he had felt, and what he feared he might never reclaim.

Unable to bear the uncertainty any longer, he had followed them after the dining room, moving silently, heart hammering with dread and a desperate curiosity he could not quell. From the shadowed distance of the gardens, he had watched them on the veranda, framed by the soft glow of lanterns: Isabella's smile, beautiful and soft; Alessandro's hands reaching for hers in a gesture so casual yet filled with warmth.

And then—he saw it. A kiss. Gentle, fleeting, almost innocent to an outsider, but to him, searingly intimate, a blade twisting deep into his chest. Time seemed to slow, the air around him thickening impossibly, his pulse thundering in his ears. Every instinct screamed to move, to intervene—yet he remained rooted, powerless, forced to witness what should have been his alone.

The sight left him hollow. Each beat of his heart echoed the impossible truth: Isabella, the woman he had loved and longed for in silence, was giving a piece of herself to another.

And yet, the solitude of his room offered no reprieve. Valeria, predictably audacious, had already claimed the space. She lay sprawled across his bed, limbs draped with careless confidence, hair tousled, lips faintly smudged with lipstick from some earlier encounter.

"What are you doing in here again?" Lorenzo demanded, his voice sharp, edged with exhaustion and frustration. "Do I need to start locking my door?"

Her eyes sparkled with defiance, lips curling in a slow, teasing smile. She rose with deliberate sensuality, the sway of her body impossible to ignore. "Come now, Lorenzo," she purred, voice low and sultry. "Now that Isabella has chosen Alessandro, perhaps you are… more receptive to a little fun?"

Her fingers traced the front of his shirt, sliding down and back again in bold, infuriating precision. Every motion, every glance, was designed to provoke, to remind him of her presence.

Lorenzo's chest tightened, a storm of desire and irritation mingling with the ache already gnawing at his heart. "Why aren't you with Alessandro this evening?" he demanded, voice taut. "You seemed very close today."

Valeria dismissed him with a laugh, tossing her hair over her shoulder. "Oh, he told me after lunch that our little dalliance will not be repeated," she said casually. "It seems Isabella has both of you wrapped around her finger."

Her words hit him like ice, yet it was the memory of Isabella's soft smile with Alessandro that tore him deeper. Every protective instinct, every shred of longing, surged violently through him. He could not—would not—be swayed. The only woman he wanted was beyond his reach, and Valeria's audacity only sharpened that truth.

She stepped closer, arms circling his neck, pressing her body against his. Her lips met his in a kiss that was insistent, teasing, demanding—but he could not give in. His hands pressed lightly on her shoulders, creating space, yet she persisted, tugging at his collar, hair falling in tousled strands across her smudged lips, bodice slipping slightly at the shoulder.

Lorenzo felt every nerve scream. Desire warred with loyalty, temptation with obsession. One touch, one whispered word from her, and his mind might have faltered—but it did not. His heart was already claimed. Only one woman existed in the chambers of his soul, and Valeria's attempts only illuminated the emptiness beside him.

Finally, he removed her fully from his orbit. He stepped back, straightened his shirt, letting out a slow breath, and met her gaze with unflinching clarity.

"I am done," he said, quiet but firm. "The only woman I want—has always been Isabella. No one else will ever be enough."

For a heartbeat, Valeria stared at him as if she hadn't heard correctly. Then her lips curved—not in amusement, but disbelief laced with fury.

"Isabella?" she hissed, her eyes flashing. "What is it about her, Lorenzo? Tell me—what makes her so special? Because I can't see it. She's ordinary. She's a nobody. She's beneath you."

He met her glare, unflinching. "She's everything you'll never understand."

Valeria's breath hitched, and for a moment, something sharp and wounded flickered in her expression before pride took over. She let out a brittle laugh and turned on her heel, the click of her stilettos slicing through the silence as she swept from the room.

But even after the echo of her footsteps faded, the storm inside him raged— relentless and consuming. Desire. Regret. Jealousy. Longing. Every emotion tore through him until only one truth remained, raw and absolute.

Now, in the pale, fragile light of early morning, Lorenzo sank into the familiar embrace of his leather chair at the desk. The cool surface pressed against his back, a faint, fleeting comfort against the firestorm raging within him. His fingers drummed a restless, uneven rhythm against the armrest, a silent echo of the wild, unrelenting hammering of his pulse. The villa beyond the windows— its gleaming halls, manicured gardens, and the first tender rays of sunlight spilling across the polished floors—felt impossibly distant, almost meaningless, as if it existed in another world. None of it mattered.

All he could see, all he could feel, was Isabella. Her delicate smile haunted him—so effortless, so achingly genuine. The soft cadence of her laughter echoed in his mind, entwined with the memory of her gaze—those deep, expressive eyes that had always seemed, in some unspoken way, to belong only to him.

And then there was the warmth he'd glimpsed between her and Alessandro— subtle, unmistakable, a quiet intimacy that should have stirred curiosity but instead ignited a scorching ache in his chest.

The unbearable thought clawed at him: what if she had chosen Alessandro? What if, despite everything he believed, she had given her heart elsewhere, even for a moment? The mere possibility twisted inside him like a knife, each heartbeat a cruel reminder of what he might already have lost.

He couldn't—wouldn't—let her slip away. Every fibre of his being screamed that Isabella was his, that her absence was intolerable. Yet beneath the fury, a reluctant voice whispered: perhaps she had chosen Alessandro. Perhaps he should step aside—allow her freedom, honour her choice.

The thought was almost unbearable, like surrendering a part of himself he had spent years guarding. Love—real love—could not be forced. But the idea of losing her ignited a deeper fire, a fierce determination that refused to be silenced.

He leaned back, eyes drawn to the light spilling through the tall windows. Shadows stretched across the polished floors like silent witnesses to his torment. If she had chosen Alessandro… should I step aside? The question gnawed at him, each repetition twisting the ache in his chest sharper.

Silence wrapped around him, broken only by the relentless pulse of his own heartbeat—the cadence of a man waging war with himself. Every breath carried longing, jealousy, and desperate hope, a tempest that refused to calm.

Beneath it all, one certainty burned: Isabella was his heart, and no force on earth could make him relinquish it—not now, not ever.

A sharp knock jolted him from the spiral of his thoughts.

"Come in," he said, his voice tight.

Aldo entered, urgency shadowing his expression. "Sir… Mr. Vitale asked me to inform you that he and Miss Moretti have departed."

Lorenzo's brow furrowed, disbelief and anger rising like twin flames. "What do you mean—departed?"

"They left on his yacht… about twenty minutes ago," Aldo replied carefully, sensing the tension coiling in the room.

"And I'm only being informed now?" Lorenzo's voice cracked, low and taut with frustration. His hands clenched on the armrests, knuckles whitening as reality struck. Isabella—his Isabella—had left with Alessandro.

Aldo gave a cautious nod and withdrew, the soft click of the door echoing in the cavernous study. Lorenzo remained slumped in his chair, the polished leather pressing against his back but offering no comfort to the ache in his chest.

Images of her flooded his mind: the warmth of her smile, the soft lilt of her voice, the way she had always seemed to belong to him in some quiet, undeniable way. The thought that she might have chosen another was like a blade twisting inside him.

He pressed a hand to his face, struggling to contain the torrent within—desire that burned, jealousy that cut deep, fear that hollowed him, and a reluctant resignation that tasted like defeat. *If she had chosen him… should I step aside?* The question lingered, heavy and cruel. Yet beneath the storm of doubt, deeper than reason, throbbed a fierce, unyielding truth: he could not surrender her. He had to fight—to win her back, whatever the cost.

The room fell silent again, save for the quiet pulse of his own heartbeat—each beat echoing the war within, between honour and desire, love and possession, letting go and holding on.

Chapter Fourteen

As the yacht cut through the waves, Alessandro spoke sparingly, as though instinctively sensing that silence was the only balm Isabella could bear. He offered her space without hesitation, never pressing, never intruding, a quiet presence she could lean on without fear. Sunlight spilled across the water, scattering into shimmering ribbons of gold that danced with the gentle swell beneath her feet. Isabella's gaze followed the horizon, her eyes fixed on the endless line where sea met sky, as if somewhere beyond it lay the answers she had been too afraid to face.

She drew in a deep, shuddering breath, the salt-laden air stinging her throat and filling her lungs with both sharpness and clarity. Soon, she told herself. Soon she would reveal everything—the fear, the heartbreak, the longing she had carried silently for years. But not yet. Not while the ache was still so raw, the wound carved by one woman's cruel words still throbbing with unbearable sharpness. For now, she clung to the quiet companionship beside her. Alessandro's presence was steady, patient, and unassuming—a fragile balm pressed against the bruises of her heart, offering comfort without demand, a sanctuary in motion.

The wind tugged at her hair, loosening strands from the knot at her nape and sending them whipping across her cheeks in playful, chaotic arcs. The waves lulled her with their eternal rhythm, steady and unyielding, whispering of resilience, return, and the persistence of life. And in that fragile moment, Isabella allowed herself something she had not dared in years: hope. A private, trembling hope that the truth she had hidden for so long might finally see the light, and that in telling it, she might reclaim the heart she had lost—but never stopped carrying within her.

Breakfast was served, the gentle clatter of cutlery and the soft murmur of crewmen filling the cabin with a domestic calm that felt almost foreign after the storm of the night before. Alessandro ate with quiet focus, every movement deliberate, measured, as if to remind her—without words—that life could still have order, that not everything was chaos and ruin. Isabella, by contrast, barely touched her plate. She toyed with a piece of bread, moved fruit from one side to another, but appetite eluded her. Her stomach twisted with nerves, her chest heavy with unspoken truths, and the memory of what she had almost confessed to Lorenzo throbbed at the edges of her consciousness.

When the plates were cleared, Alessandro turned his gaze toward her, his dark eyes gentle yet unwavering, patient but attentive. "Bella," he said softly, "can you tell me what happened?"

Her hands tightened in her lap, fingers twisting together in nervous repetition, betraying her unease. She drew in a trembling breath. "After talking to you last night," she began slowly, her voice breaking at the edges, "I went to Lorenzo. I… I wanted, I needed to tell him the truth." Her eyes flickered with remembered pain, the memory raw and sharp. "But just as I reached his door, Valeria came out of his room."

Alessandro's brow furrowed, his expression thoughtful, quietly assessing. "Oh," he murmured. "I see. Perhaps nothing happened—perhaps they only spoke. Did you talk to Lorenzo at all?"

Isabella shook her head, the movement sharp, almost pained. "There was no need. Valeria told me very plainly what they had been doing. I… I couldn't face him. Not after hearing her say it." Her voice cracked, a long sigh escaping her that carried both sorrow and quiet defeat.

Alessandro's eyes softened, sympathy etched into every line of his face. "Perhaps, with time, you might be able to."

She lowered her gaze, shoulders sagging as though the weight of the past half-decade rested there. "No. I think I really need to close that chapter of my life. I can't blame Lorenzo for being with Valeria—it's not as though he and I were together. But it still hurt… it cut deeper than I thought it could. And I just… I can't go through that again. Not with him. Not with anyone."

Alessandro hesitated, his voice careful and measured. "May I ask… why you and Lorenzo parted in the first place?"

Isabella's throat tightened, memories long buried clawing to the surface. She forced herself to speak, each word weighted with old grief. "After my mother passed, I moved to Florence to live with my father. I could have stayed in England, but he wanted me near him—he needed to care for me while I grieved. I agreed." She paused, eyes distant, as though staring back into another life, a life shaped by loss and longing.

"I was only nineteen," she continued softly, "and Lorenzo… he was my world. We grew so close. I loved him, with everything in me. And he told me he loved me too." Her breath faltered. "Then one day, his father demanded he stop seeing me. Lorenzo told him… he told him I was just a bit of fun." Her voice cracked on the words. "That seemed to please his father. He laughed and said, *'A girl like that is only good enough for the bed, not the altar.'* And then he laughed… and Lorenzo laughed with him." Her lips pressed together, trembling. "I left the next morning. I couldn't stay."

Alessandro sat in silence, his expression sombre, the weight of her confession settling heavily between them. He let the quiet linger, let her words breathe before he responded, his tone low and steady, threaded with quiet conviction. "I knew his father. A hard man, cold… never satisfied with anything Lorenzo did. Always treating him like a disappointment. It was wrong. Cruel. Lorenzo… he was always striving to please, always carrying burdens too heavy for one man. But he is not his father, Bella. He is a good man. Perhaps… all of this is a misunderstanding."

Her eyes lifted to his, the faintest flicker of gratitude softening her features. But sorrow still lingered in her voice. "I don't think so," she whispered. "I don't wish him ill—I want him to be happy. Truly. But I need to be happy, too. I need to let him go, Alessandro. It's too painful to keep holding on."

Alessandro reached across the small distance between them, his hand brushing hers—warm, steady, grounding her against the storm inside. The gesture was simple, yet it anchored her, offered a lifeline to hold onto amidst the waves of heartbreak. "Whatever happens, Bella," he said softly, "you are not alone. If you ever need someone to talk to, someone to lean on… I am here."

Her lips trembled into the faintest of smiles, her voice barely audible. "Thank you, Alessandro. Truly."

The yacht swayed gently beneath them, the morning sun climbing higher over the horizon, painting the sea in brilliant shades of gold and sapphire. Isabella drew a slow, deliberate breath, letting the rhythm of the waves and the steady presence of Alessandro soothe some of the ache inside her. For the first time in what felt like forever, the grip of the past began to loosen, if only slightly.

And as sunlight spilled across the water, glinting and sparkling like liquid gold, Isabella allowed herself a fragile, tentative hope—that her heart, battered and scarred though it was, might one day be whole again, and that the future might still hold a joy she had thought forever lost.

It had been a week since Isabella had stepped off Lorenzo's island with Alessandro, and still the echoes of that night clung to her like the faint scent of smoke after a fire. She refused to linger on them. Instead, she poured herself into the one constant in her life, the companion that had never betrayed her— her work.

Every morning, she rose with the sun, sketchbook open before her, the sharp scent of graphite filling the air as her pencil moved in restless, purposeful strokes. The lines that spilled onto the page were more than designs—they were confessions, unspoken truths she dared not voice aloud. Curves of metal softened into tenderness, clusters of gems cradled sorrow like captured stars. And today, more than any other, those truths demanded to be seen.

A nervous energy accompanied her across the cobbled streets of Milan, the city alive with the low hum of anticipation that always preceded Fashion Week. She had an appointment with Giovanni Bellandi, the most respected jeweller in Milan, to see the finished pieces she had designed just before the disastrous house party. These creations were meant to crown the runway, destined for the throat and ears of one of the season's most prominent models. Now, bruised though her heart remained, Isabella approached the unveiling with quiet resolve.

Bellandi's atelier was bathed in late-afternoon light, the air faintly scented with polish and velvet. Jewels glittered beneath glass domes, trays lined with silk gleaming like treasure, and the hush of reverence filled the space as though it were a chapel.

On a central table, laid against deep navy velvet, rested her creation. The necklace was unlike anything she had shaped before—a collar of brushed white gold, formed in fluid, interwoven arcs that mimicked rippling water. At its heart cascaded moonstones and pale sapphires, each gem set so that light transformed it into something alive: pearl one moment, silver-blue the next, then a whisper of violet, like twilight captured in stone.

The earrings, slender counterparts, carried the same motif with daring grace: threads of white gold hung like droplets of rain, each tipped with a moonstone that shimmered when touched by light. When worn, they would sway with every movement, scattering reflections as if carrying water itself onto the runway.

Isabella leaned over the tray, her brown eyes sharp, studying every detail with the precision of both artist and critic. "The necklace must frame her collarbones without swallowing her," she murmured, half to herself, half to Giovanni. "The stones are soft, ethereal—they should glow, not compete. The earrings draw the eye upward… together, it should feel like light caught in motion, not restrained, but free."

Giovanni, silver-haired and sharp-eyed, lifted the necklace with gloved hands, holding it toward the sunlit window. The gems ignited, moonstones flickering like fireflies across water. He let out a low breath, his voice edged with reverence. "You have not designed jewellery, ragazza. You have captured water itself. This—" he tilted the piece, sapphires flaring like drops of twilight— "is extraordinary."

A faint smile ghosted across Isabella's lips, though her pulse raced. For a moment she stood taller, reminded why she had chosen this path, why she had fought to define herself—not as someone's daughter, not as someone's lost love, but as Loren Bella. Her brand. Her voice. Her truth.

And yet Giovanni's gaze did not linger on the jewels alone. His eyes, dark and perceptive, shifted back to her, as though weighing more than artistry. "Brilliance such as this," he said quietly, "does not come from steady hands alone. It comes from something deeper. A fire, a wound, a hunger. I see it in you. In the way you look at your work." He leaned closer, his tone edged with warning. "Be careful, Isabella. Passion can shape genius, but distraction? Distraction destroys it."

Her throat tightened. She pressed her palms against the table, steadying herself. "I design what I feel," she said softly. "That is all I know."

"Mm." Giovanni tilted his head. "And what you feel is powerful… but dangerous. The olive branches, the moonstones, the twilight stones—you have poured memory into this design. Memory and longing. Do not let the wound consume you. If it remains open, it will devour the hand that shapes it."

His words landed too close to truth. For a fleeting second, Lorenzo's face surged in her mind—the hazel of his eyes when they had softened for her, the heat of his kiss on a terrace scented with night jasmine, the sound of his laugh when she had believed herself loved. She blinked hard, forcing the images back into shadow, her gaze fixing on the stones before her.

"I am not distracted," she whispered. But even to her own ears, the words sounded fragile, as if they might shatter at any moment.

Giovanni's lips curved faintly, not in triumph, but in recognition. "Perhaps. Or perhaps you are stronger than you think—turning heartbreak into beauty. But beware, ragazza. Loren Bella may make you immortal. It will also betray you. Jewellery does not lie. It speaks the truths its maker cannot."

The words struck her like a chord pulled too tight. In the mirror across the atelier, Isabella caught her reflection. Loren Bella glittered there—flawless, untouchable, radiant as moonlight. And yet she knew—Giovanni had seen what lay beneath: the confession buried in her work, the story of love and loss carved too deep into stone to be hidden.

After a pause, Giovanni asked, his tone deceptively casual, "Tell me, Isabella—will you be present when this creation is unveiled next week?"

Her fingers curled around the edge of her sketchbook, leather warm beneath her touch. She drew in a quiet breath, willing her voice to stay even. "Yes. I will be there."

She hesitated, then added, "Tomorrow, I travel to Vicenza. Riccardo Santini has agreed to meet with me—his mastery of goldsmithing is legendary, and I want to study his techniques. But I will return in time for Milan."

Giovanni's brow arched, his mouth curving in faint disapproval at the mention of Santini's name. Still, he inclined his head. "Vicenza," he murmured. "Ambition carries you far. So be it. The world will know Loren Bella not only for brilliance, but for breadth."

Isabella allowed herself a small smile, though it did not reach her eyes. "That is the hope," she said softly.

But as Giovanni turned back to his papers and Margherita stepped into the light, wearing her necklace like flowing silver rain, Isabella's chest tightened. She had promised herself she would not falter—but in the hollow of her heart, she felt the truth Giovanni had named. Jewellery did not lie.

And if Loren Bella revealed the secrets she still carried, then when Milan looked upon her collection next week, they would not only see beauty. They would see the shadow of a man she had never truly stopped loving.

Lorenzo's hands were clenched tightly around the crystal glass, the amber liquid inside long forgotten as he stared out over the city from his penthouse balcony. Two weeks. Two endless, excruciating weeks since he had last seen Isabella, and each day had carved itself into him like a slow, unyielding blade.

The first week had been swallowed by obligations—the high-profile house party he could not simply walk away from. Guests had filled the villa with laughter, clinking glasses, and the hollow chatter of luxury—but Lorenzo had barely registered a single word.

His mind had been entirely elsewhere, obsessively replaying every detail of Isabella's face: the tilt of her head when she smiled, the way sunlight had caught her hair, the memory of that devastating, impossible kiss she had given Alessandro. Each recollection felt like fire through his chest, a cruel reminder that she had chosen another man.

And yet, that knowledge did nothing to extinguish the inferno within him. He could not, would not, accept that she was lost. He had told her, insisted to her trembling heart, that he loved her more than anything. That she was safe with him. That she belonged to him. And he had meant it—every word burning like a truth that could not be denied.

The second week had been worse, if that were possible. The villa emptied of guests, the echo of laughter fading into memory, and Lorenzo had thrown himself into a frantic, desperate search. He did not know which city she now inhabited, only that Alessandro had taken her away. He had tried to reach Alessandro himself—calls unanswered, messages ignored, the image of the yacht glinting on distant horizons haunting him—but the man was elusive, as always, moving through the world with the casual command of wealth and influence.

He paced the length of the balcony, the night air doing little to cool the coiled fire in his chest. Every hour without news of her was a betrayal of time, every second a reminder that she might be laughing, speaking, or smiling—not with him, but with another. The thought clawed at him. It was unbearable.

And yet, beneath the fear, beneath the raw ache, there was resolve. A singular, unshakable certainty. He would find her. He would reach her. And when he did, he would remind her—again, if necessary—that no man could love her as fiercely, completely, or relentlessly as he did. She had felt it before. He needed only to make her feel it again.

His jaw tightened, and he pressed a hand to his forehead, fighting the rising tide of desperation. He did not know the city streets, the alleys, the docks Alessandro might use—but he knew her. He knew the rhythm of her steps, the tilt of her head, the way her eyes searched for truth in the smallest gestures. He would follow that instinct, across oceans, through cities, past every distraction, until he stood before her once more.

Because the world could try to pull her away, fate could intervene, Alessandro could flaunt his wealth and charm—but none of that could alter one immutable truth: Isabella was his heart. And he could never, ever forget her.

Tomorrow night, the grand ball that would mark the opening of Milan Fashion Week would take place. Lorenzo had caught wind that the debut of the latest Loren Bella collection was scheduled around this event. His pulse quickened at the thought—perhaps Isabella would be there, radiant, untouchable, commanding attention, her creations coming alive beneath the lights.

He wasn't certain how the unveiling would occur. The launch could take place at the ball itself, amidst glittering chandeliers and opulent guests, or on the runway the following day, bright lights cutting through the shadows, cameras flashing. Either way, he could not afford to miss it. He had to see her, even if only from a distance. Even if he had to push through a sea of fashion editors, designers, and socialites just to catch a single glimpse.

He ran through possibilities in his mind, each more urgent, more desperate than the last. His name carried weight in Italy—doors would open when whispered in the right circles. He could slip into the ballroom unnoticed, pass as another wealthy guest, or infiltrate the backstage chaos of the runway, moving silently, unseen, until he found her. Every scenario, every risk, seemed worth it if it brought him one step closer to Isabella. One moment. One chance.

Lorenzo clenched his jaw, raking a hand through his dark hair, imagining every way he could reach her. Tomorrow night, he decided with absolute certainty, he would do whatever it took—not for the grandeur of the collection, not for the spectacle of Milan's elite, but for Isabella herself. To see her radiant in her element, to speak to her, to remind her—again—that no other man could love her with the depth, the devotion, and the fire that he did.

Even if she had chosen Alessandro, even if her heart had leaned toward another, Lorenzo would not stand idly by. He would track her through the crowds, slip past the glittering elite, and find a single, perfect moment—just one—to reach her. And when he did, he would make her remember what she had always known: her heart had never truly belonged to anyone else but him.

The city lights stretched beneath him like a glittering river, and he let his gaze linger, memorising every stone and street, every flicker of movement that might lead him to her. Each breath he drew tasted of anticipation and obsession. And with the first sharp thrill of dawn approaching, Lorenzo felt a singular, burning certainty: tomorrow night, he would see her. And nothing—neither time, distance, nor deceit—would stop him from reclaiming the heart that had always been his.

Chapter Fifteen

The ball shimmered with anticipation, a glittering prelude to Milan Fashion Week. Crystal chandeliers hung from the vaulted ceiling, scattering prisms of light across the polished marble floors. Guests drifted through the grand hall in lavish gowns and perfectly tailored suits, champagne flutes tinkling in their hands, laughter and conversation weaving a tapestry of elegance and intrigue. Every detail—the soft strains of a string quartet, the low murmur of voices, the glint of jewels and satin—was designed to dazzle. Yet Lorenzo felt none of it. None of the frivolity, none of the spectacle. His gaze swept across the glittering crowd with a single, burning focus: Isabella.

He moved deliberately, his steps measured but urgent, weaving through throngs of photographers, fashion editors, and socialites. Each laugh, each chatter, each sparkle of a jewel made him feel further from her, as if the world were conspiring to keep them apart. Perhaps she was here, he thought, moving quietly behind the scenes, overseeing the debut of Loren Bella's latest collection. Perhaps she had chosen this moment to appear—radiant, untouchable, commanding attention without even trying.

His pulse throbbed in his ears. Every nerve in his body screamed for her, the image of her face—her soft brown eyes, the way her hair tumbled across her shoulders, the curve of her smile—burning itself into his mind. He could blend in, he told himself. He could pass unnoticed among the glittering guests, slip behind the velvet ropes of the runway prep area, and move silently until he found her. Every risk seemed trivial compared to the thought of seeing her, of knowing she was near.

And then, from a quiet alcove near the terrace, movement caught his eye.

Alessandro.

His posture relaxed, his arm slung casually around a woman who was not Isabella. Their heads leaned together, lips meeting in a slow, deliberate kiss. Lorenzo's chest constricted, a surge of fury and disbelief flooding through him like ice. How could he? How dare he flaunt such intimacy—especially now, when Isabella was not there to witness it herself?

Lorenzo's fists clenched, knuckles white, and he fought to contain the storm within. Every instinct screamed at him to charge forward, to tear Alessandro away from the woman who did not deserve him. But he paused, muscles coiled like springs, mind racing, heart hammering. He waited, every fibre of his being tense, until the woman finally pulled away, leaving Alessandro alone for just a moment.

Seizing it, Lorenzo stepped forward. Dark eyes blazing, every movement taut with barely restrained rage and desperation, he stopped just short of Alessandro. His voice, low and dangerous, cut through the quiet of the terrace. "What are you doing?"

Alessandro looked up, surprise flickering across his features before a practiced, easy smile replaced it. "Lorenzo... I didn't expect—"

"Don't," Lorenzo snapped, cutting him off sharply. "Don't try to explain. I saw exactly what you were doing."

Alessandro's brows furrowed, confusion warring with caution. "Saw what?"

"You think you can play games? You think anyone would—" Lorenzo's chest heaved, words catching in his throat. Then he noticed Alessandro's pause, the careful way he measured his next words, and a sharp, jarring realisation hit him like a physical blow. "Where is she?" His voice was raw, desperate, fraying at the edges.

"Where is who?"

"Isabella," Lorenzo ground out, jaw tight, heart hammering. "You and she... you left the island together. Is she here?"

Alessandro's eyes softened, and he chose his words with careful precision, as though each one carried the weight of a delicate truth. "Lorenzo... Bella is not here. Isabella... she is not with me."

Lorenzo's heart lurched. "What do you mean? Not with you?"

"You think Isabella left your island because she chose me?" Alessandro asked gently, almost pitying, reading the storm in Lorenzo's expression.

"Yes," Lorenzo admitted, jaw clenching, a coil of anger and fear tightening in his chest.

"She didn't," Alessandro said firmly. "She left because of you... and Valeria. Not because she wanted to be with me."

Lorenzo froze. "Because of me... and Valeria?" His voice caught, disbelief and fragile hope colliding in a single, unsteady breath.

Alessandro nodded slowly. "She saw Valeria—coming out of your room. Valeria told her you were together. She made her believe you had moved on, that you had been unfaithful. That is what drove her away, Lorenzo. Not me."

Lorenzo's chest constricted, the air leaving his lungs in a single, shuddering exhale. For a heartbeat, the words did not register—then they did, hitting him like a wave. Isabella had not chosen Alessandro. She had fled, wounded and deceived. The realisation surged through him—fierce, consuming, and blinding.

"She… she was going to your room to tell you she'd chosen you," Alessandro continued quietly. "She told me on the veranda the night before we left. That was why she ran—not for me, but because of what she thought she saw."

Lorenzo's throat tightened. "But… you kissed." The words came out broken, raw. Then the truth began to dawn. "Were you… kissing each other goodbye?"

Alessandro met his gaze without flinching. "Yes. She only came to me to be honest. She told me she couldn't be with me—that she loved you. Then she went to find you."

The weight of the revelation struck Lorenzo like gravity itself. His fists curled, knuckles white, breath shallow. "She… she chose me," he whispered, awe and heartbreak threading every word.

"Yes," Alessandro said softly, the certainty in his tone steady and sure. "Every glance, every word—she has always belonged to you, Lorenzo. Not to me. Not to anyone else."

Silence settled, thick with emotion. Lorenzo's pulse pounded in his ears as relief, fury, and yearning collided within him—a storm of everything he'd feared and everything he'd hoped. And beneath it all lay one undeniable truth: Isabella had never left his heart. And now he knew—she had never truly been gone.

Alessandro's tone gentled. "I take it Valeria was lying?" He hesitated. "Why was she in your room that night?"

Lorenzo's gaze hardened, the memory flashing like a blade behind his eyes. "Because you told her you were no longer interested that afternoon," he said bitterly. "She assumed I would be. She was in my room when I arrived—I never invited her. And when I told her to leave… she must have ran straight into Isabella. If she told her that I had touched her…" His voice cracked, then dropped to a low, dangerous growl. "Then Isabella believed I betrayed her. Every word—every insinuation—was a lie."

Alessandro exhaled slowly, understanding settling in his features. "So, she drove Isabella away—with deceit."

"Yes." Lorenzo's voice deepened, fierce and raw. "For a moment, I thought I had lost her forever. But now… now I know the truth. She did not leave me. Valeria took her from me." He drew a sharp breath, conviction burning in his eyes. "And I have to win her back. My Isabella… she is mine."

A spark of determination ignited within him, fierce and consuming. He would see her. He would find her. And nothing—not Valeria, not Alessandro, not anyone—would ever come between them again.

"You need to convince her," Alessandro urged, voice low and urgent. "Tell her Valeria was lying. Nothing she heard is true."

Lorenzo hesitated, then straightened, dark eyes blazing, mind racing with possibility and urgency. "Do you… do you know where Isabella is?"

Alessandro nodded slowly. "She'll be at the fashion show tomorrow. Tonight… I assume she's at home, resting, preparing herself."

Lorenzo's chest tightened, hope and anxiety coiling like fire. His voice was low, steady, but threaded with determination. "Where exactly? I need to find her tonight."

Alessandro met his gaze, respect—and a quiet pity—lingering there. He sent her address to Lorenzo's phone. "Be patient. She needs truth, not force."

Lorenzo's fists unclenched slightly, replaced with a sharp, burning resolve. "Thank you, my friend. Truly."

Alessandro inclined his head, eyes softening. "Go, Lorenzo. Win Isabella back. She has always been yours. You are a lucky man—never forget that."

And with that, Lorenzo turned, each step measured but charged with purpose, propelled by the weight of the past, the fire of his heart, and the certainty that the woman who had never truly left him would soon know that her heart had always belonged to him.

The streets of Milan shimmered beneath the soft glow of streetlights, the city alive yet hushed in the late evening. Lorenzo sat in the back of his black limousine, fingers drumming a restless rhythm against the leather seat, the amber liquid in his glass long forgotten. His mind raced with anticipation, fear, and hope, each heartbeat pounding like a drum of urgent intent. The address

Alessandro had given him now felt impossibly close, yet every passing block stretched the seconds into an eternity.

He exhaled slowly, forcing his pulse into submission, and gave the driver a quiet instruction. The tyres whispered against the cobblestones as the car turned into a narrow street, finally stopping before an elegant apartment building. Warm light spilled onto the quiet sidewalk, illuminating wrought-iron balconies and casting long shadows across the stone. The city seemed to hold its breath with him; the world suspended in a fragile moment of possibility.

Lorenzo's chest tightened. He imagined her there, inside that apartment, oblivious to the storm of emotion waiting just beyond the door. Isabella—safe, perhaps brushing a loose strand of hair back, or reading quietly—appeared in his mind in intimate, fleeting snapshots that made his chest ache with longing. A flicker of doubt threatened to rise, but he shook it away. He had to see her. He had to tell her the truth.

The evening air bit gently at his skin as he stepped from the limousine. Each stride toward the entrance was measured, deliberate, purposeful. The faint scent of night-blooming flowers drifted from a nearby courtyard, mingling with the soft hum of distant traffic, grounding him in the moment. He reached the apartment door, hand hovering over the bell for a heartbeat longer than necessary, as if willing her to appear before he pressed it. Then, with a steady push, he rang. The chime echoed softly through the quiet hall; a sound charged with expectation.

Moments later, the door opened. There she was—Isabella, framed in the soft glow of her foyer, eyes wide, lips parted in shock. Her hair tumbled in gentle waves around her face, catching the light like threads of silk, and her expression was a delicate mix of surprise, relief, and apprehension, as though her heart recognised him before her mind could catch up.

"Lorenzo…" Her voice trembled, barely audible, a fragile whisper that breathed life into the hope she had nearly buried.

"I had to see you," he said, his voice low and unwavering, each syllable carrying the weight of weeks spent in torment, sleepless nights, and unanswered questions.

"You shouldn't be here, Lorenzo," she murmured, her voice shaky but determined, as if the words were an armour she was trying—failing—to hold between them. Beneath the steel of her tone flickered a raw vulnerability she could no longer deny.

"Isabella… you need to hear what I have to say. Alessandro just told me what Valeria said to you."

Her brows drew together, a shadow of pain passing through her eyes like a wound reopening. "Lorenzo…" she began, voice strained and hesitant, as though afraid to let hope take root.

He stepped closer, each movement deliberate, closing the distance with a quiet intensity that sent a tremor through the air between them. "What you were told—it was lies. None of it was true."

"I… what do you mean?" Her voice was barely above a whisper, trembling as she tried to anchor herself against the possibility of disappointment.

Lorenzo reached for her hands, his fingers sliding around hers with a gentle insistence that spoke of longing, regret, and urgency. "Valeria lied. She told you I was with her that night, that I touched her. None of it happened. Every word was a fabrication. Isabella—please—believe me."

Her gaze dropped for a heartbeat, the memory of Valeria's deceit flashing across her mind, sharp and bitter. "But… she was coming out of your room. Her hair, her clothes…"

"She tried to," he interrupted softly, voice taut with restrained anger and shame. "…But I pushed her away. Isabella, the woman I want—the only woman I have ever wanted—is you. Always you."

Tears glimmered in her eyes as his words sank in, the tension in her shoulders beginning to ease, trembling like glass about to crack. "I… I thought…" she whispered, voice breaking, fragments of fear and heartbreak spilling into the quiet.

He drew in a long breath, his eyes never leaving hers. "I will be honest with you, Isabella. These last five years… I have not lived like a monk. There were women—but none of them ever meant anything. Not one. And for months now, I have not touched another soul."

"Lorenzo…" His name escaped her lips like a confession—soft, trembling, almost a prayer.

"You never left my heart," he said quietly. "Not for a single day. I know I hurt you when my father said those things about you, but I swear—I never believed them. I was afraid he would send you away. I should have fought harder, and I did not." His voice was low, unwavering, the sound grounding her as his fingers closed around hers—warm, steady, unrelenting. "Isabella, I am sorry for the pain I caused you. I would undo it all if I could. But I am yours—I always have been. And I will never again let lies or deception steal you from me."

Her lips trembled into a fragile, tearful smile as emotion broke through the fragile composure she'd fought to keep. "You... you came for me."

"I had no choice," he murmured, brushing a strand of hair from her face. His fingertips lingered at her temple, tracing the soft curve of her skin. "I thought you left because of Alessandro—but now I know it was because of Valeria's lies. I will not let anyone come between us again. If you tell me to walk away, I will. But if there is even the smallest part of you that still loves me—let me prove that you are the only woman I have ever wanted. The only one I will ever love. I will spend the rest of my life making you happy."

She drew a shaky breath, her heart pounding as the weight of his words settled deep within her. Every syllable rang with truth, steady and certain, melting through years of pain and distance. His gaze never wavered—dark, intense, filled with the kind of devotion that didn't fade with time.

"I... I don't know what to say," she whispered, her voice breaking, as fragile as glass. "I was so afraid... so lost..."

"You only have to say one word," he said softly, his thumb tracing slow circles against her skin. "Just say yes. Trust me. Let me show you that nothing—not lies, not time, not doubt—could ever destroy what has always been ours."

The city beyond the window dissolved into a blur of muted lights and shadows, as though Milan itself had faded away, leaving only the two of them suspended in that fragile, electric moment. The hush of the room wrapped around them, and for an instant, time seemed to bow, the world narrowing to the sound of their hearts—two frantic rhythms beating in unison. Their breaths mingled, their clasped hands becoming a silent, unspoken promise that spoke louder than any words could.

For the first time in what felt like an eternity, Isabella allowed herself to believe—not in fate or circumstance, but in the man standing before her. The man who had never truly left her heart, who had been the quiet ache in every moment of absence.

"I love you, Lorenzo," she whispered, the words fragile and trembling, breaking beneath the weight of her honesty. Her voice was spun glass, glinting and delicate, trembling on the edge of shattering.

"I love you too, Isabella. So much," he answered, his tone low and resonant, each word vibrating with months of longing—nights he had ached for her, mornings when her absence burned like a wound he could not close.

Her body stiffened, her pulse spiking as the reality of his nearness crashed through her. "Lorenzo... I—" Her voice faltered, breath catching, the magnetic pull of him stirring every guarded corner of her soul, every fragment of longing she had tried so desperately to deny.

"You're trembling," he murmured, fingers brushing a stray lock of hair from her face, his touch achingly tender. "Not from fear, I hope?"

She shook her head quickly, but her chest rose and fell with frantic urgency, betraying the secret she had kept locked away even from herself. "It's... it's just... I've never been with anyone," she admitted softly, her palms pressing lightly to his shoulders. Sparks leapt at the contact, a thrilling, terrifying charge. She thrilled at being held—cherished, claimed—but another part of her, the fiercely protected part, flared with instinctive resistance.

Surprise and something like wonder flickered in his dark eyes. "No one?" he asked, his voice a low murmur of disbelief.

She shook her head again, silent confirmation, her pulse fluttering under the weight of his gaze.

"Isabella..." His voice dropped, rich and intimate, each syllable a tether to the unspoken longing of years past. He drew her into his arms with exquisite care yet with an insistence that anchored her to him, every heartbeat pulling them closer to inevitability.

Lorenzo's gaze deepened, fierce yet tender—a storm contained by devotion. "We belong together, Isabella," he murmured hoarsely, raw emotion scraping through every word. "Always have, always will."

Then his lips claimed hers—tender and demanding all at once—igniting a fire she had only dared to imagine. She opened to him instinctively, their mouths sliding, seeking, devouring, until the world collapsed into nothing but the fevered rhythm of breath and heartbeat.

"I want you, Isabella," he groaned against her jaw, his lips searing a path along her skin. "I've always wanted you."

"I... I want you too," she breathed, the confession trembling from her lips— terrifying in its vulnerability but liberating in its truth.

He held her close, inhaling the scent of her hair, feeling the warmth of her body pressed to his. Every touch, every brush of skin, became a vow—a silent promise that this was not fleeting, but the reclamation of something that had always been theirs.

He lifted her effortlessly, carrying her to the bedroom with reverent care, setting her down on the bed as if she were sacred. For a long heartbeat, he lingered above her, drinking her in, his chest rising and falling with the weight of all he felt yet could barely put into words.

Their clothes fell away slowly, each piece discarded like a barrier shed. He undressed her as though every button, every zipper, was a ritual, and when she reached for him, her hands trembled with both desire and wonder.

And then he worshipped her. With his hands, tracing the lines of her body as though memorising a masterpiece. With his mouth, tasting her like a man starved, devouring yet reverent. With a hunger honed sharp by years of restraint and longing. His touch was unhurried yet consuming, a patient claiming that left her trembling, a slow, inexorable unravelling of her defences, stripping away every last veil of fear until she lay before him unguarded, utterly his.

When his tongue rasped over her nipple, Isabella cried out, her back arching helplessly. He caught the sound with his mouth, greedy for every note of her surrender.

His hand slid between her thighs, parting her gently, reverently, exploring with aching precision. He touched her like she was sacred, every caress a prayer, every movement an act of devotion.

When he lowered his head and tasted her, she nearly sobbed.

"You taste," he murmured, his voice rough silk against her, "incredible."

"Lorenzo…" She gasped his name, broken and breathless. "Please."

He smiled against her heat, wicked and tender all at once—then gave her everything. His tongue teased and stroked until her legs quaked, until her fists twisted the sheets, until her head fell back in exquisite abandon.

She shattered with his name spilling from her lips, a broken, beautiful cry that etched itself into his soul, unforgettable.

Lorenzo kissed his way slowly back up her body, lingering over every curve as though memorising a sacred map. Her skin was dewy with release, her breath shallow, her body pliant, but her eyes—her eyes burned wide and dark, brimming with want and wonder.

Hovering above her, he cupped her face, his thumb tracing her cheek with reverence. His voice trembled with restraint. "Isabella... I want you. We've waited so long."

She reached up, framing his face with both hands, her touch steady despite the tremor in her fingers. "Yes, Lorenzo," she whispered, her voice fierce despite its softness. "I want this. I want you."

Lorenzo's breath caught at her words, at the trembling certainty in her voice. His control, always a thin thread around her, frayed and snapped. He lowered his mouth to hers, kissing her deeply, hungrily, pouring years of longing and regret into the meeting of their lips.

"I'll be gentle," he whispered against her mouth, though the rough edge in his voice betrayed the hunger he could barely contain. "You're everything to me, Isabella. Always have been."

"I trust you," she breathed, her hands sliding into his hair, pulling him closer, offering herself with a vulnerability that made his chest ache.

His lips trailed down her throat, lingering at the pulse that fluttered wildly beneath her skin. His hands moved with deliberate reverence, stroking down her sides, learning every curve, every secret place that made her shiver. He wanted to mark this moment into her memory, to ensure she felt worshipped, never rushed, never afraid.

When he parted her thighs with the weight of his body, she gasped, her breath quickening, her fingers gripping his shoulders like she might fall without him. He steadied her with a kiss, soft and coaxing, his forehead pressed to hers.

"Look at me," he murmured, dark eyes holding hers with unshakable intensity. "Don't look away."

She nodded, her lips trembling as she whispered, "I'm ready."

He eased into her slowly, carefully, every muscle taut with restraint. She tensed, a small sound escaping her, and he froze, pressing soothing kisses along her temple, her cheek, her mouth.

"Breathe, amore," he whispered, his thumb stroking her jaw. "I've got you. Just feel me... let me love you."

She exhaled shakily, her body gradually yielding around him. The sting softened, replaced by a fullness that made her clutch at him with wonder, her eyes dark with awe.

"That's it," he murmured, his own breath ragged as he sank deeper, holding himself still as she adjusted. "My beautiful Isabella…"

When her body relaxed, when her soft gasp shifted into a moan, he began to move. Slow, reverent thrusts that rocked through them both, a rhythm of discovery and surrender. Her nails dug into his shoulders, her mouth finding his in desperate, clumsy kisses as pleasure built between them like a rising tide.

Every sound she made undid him, every shiver and arch of her body unravelling his control. But he held back, desperate to give her everything, to make her first time a memory carved in gold.

"Lorenzo," she cried, her voice breaking as sensation consumed her. "Oh God—"

He swallowed her cry with his kiss, his pace quickening only when she begged for more, when her body clung to his with unashamed need. And then she shattered again, her release pulling him under with her, dragging a hoarse groan from his chest as he followed her into the fire.

Chapter Sixteen

When the storm finally eased, he drew her into his arms, holding her as though he could fuse them into one. Their bodies remained entwined, their breaths mingling in the tender hush of afterglow. He kissed her damp hair, her temple, the corner of her mouth—unable, unwilling, to stop touching her.

Lorenzo cupped her face, his thumb grazing her swollen lips with a reverence that made her heart ache. His voice was low and raw, but steady, carrying the weight of a vow. "I love you, Isabella. I'm yours—forever."

She nestled closer, her lips brushing the strong line of his throat, her body soft, languid, wholly sated against him. "And I'm yours," she whispered, the words trembling with both truth and relief. "I always have been."

Wrapped in each other, they finally surrendered to sleep, drifting into a peace neither had known in years.

But it did not last.

In the very early hours, before even the faintest light touched the horizon, Isabella stirred. Her body shifted against his, her leg sliding languidly across his, her hand gliding down the hard plane of his chest. The moment her palm brushed the taut muscle, his breath hitched, his body responding instantly, as though he had been waiting for her touch even in his dreams.

A low groan rumbled from deep within him as he pulled her tightly into his arms. "Isabella…"

The sound of her name—hoarse, rough with need—shattered the fragile calm between them. Their mouths met in an instant, the kiss hungry and consuming, nothing of the slow tenderness of the night before. This was different. Reckless. Desperate. A fierce collision of two souls who had been denied too long and could no longer endure the ache of restraint.

Her hands clutched at his shoulders, nails biting into his skin as though to anchor herself, while he rolled her beneath him, his weight pressing down with unrelenting force. The world beyond the walls ceased to exist; there was only heat, the frantic thunder of their hearts, the inexorable need to drown in each other again and again.

"Lorenzo—please," she gasped, her voice breaking, trembling with raw longing.

pants and draped his shirt across her bare shoulders. Then, without warning, he swept her into his arms once more.

She gasped, then laughed, the sound light and shimmering in the stillness. "You do know I can walk?" she teased, lips brushing his shoulder.

"Yes," he murmured, grinning, "but I'm not ready to let you go yet."

He set her gently on the counter, sunlight spilling through the windows, gilding her skin in soft gold as he moved about the kitchen. Her fingers reached for him, trailing absently over the lines of his chest, the faint touch sparking reminders of their night—of fire that refused to fade.

They ate slowly, sharing warm croissants and fresh fruit, the air rich with coffee and contentment. Knees brushed beneath the table, fingers intertwined between bites, and laughter came easily, quiet and unguarded.

And when the last plate was cleared, silence settled once more—not of distance, but of inevitability. Their eyes met, and in that lingering glance, they both knew hunger—of the body, of the heart—was far from sated.

By late afternoon, steam curled around them as they stood beneath the shower's warm cascade. Lorenzo's hands moved over her body with exquisite care, his touch reverent at first—until tenderness gave way to something deeper, something that pulsed with need.

"Lorenzo…" Isabella breathed, her voice trembling with longing.

He caught her mouth in a fierce, lingering kiss. "I know, amore mio," he murmured against her lips, his breath ragged. "I want you again."

In one fluid motion, he lifted her, pressing her back gently against the cool tiled wall. Water streamed between them, tracing the lines of their joined bodies as their eyes locked—steady, unblinking, consumed.

When he entered her, it was slow, deliberate, a claiming and a homecoming all at once. She gasped softly, her hands clutching his shoulders as he began to move—each thrust a wordless confession, each breath a vow.

"You're perfect, Isabella," he whispered, kissing her again, deeper this time. Her body met his with desperate urgency, and together they found a rhythm that built, tightened, and broke—until the world dissolved into heat, water, and the shattering pulse of love rediscovered.

Lorenzo had arranged for a tuxedo to be delivered earlier, and after their shared shower—full of teasing, laughter, and lingering kisses—they finally dressed for the Milan fashion show.

He looked devastatingly handsome in a dark, perfectly tailored tuxedo, the deep midnight-blue fabric sculpting his broad shoulders and narrowing to a lean, powerful waist. When Isabella turned, his breath caught.

She was radiant—draped in a floor-length gown of white silk that clung and flowed like liquid moonlight. The soft fabric skimmed her curves with effortless grace, the plunging neckline offering a whisper of temptation, while the delicate draping at her hips framed her slender waist. Her hair fell in loose, luminous waves, and her eyes—bright, calm, and impossibly beautiful—met his with quiet confidence.

Lorenzo moved behind her as she checked her reflection, his hands sliding around her waist, drawing her back against him. "Perfection," he murmured, his lips grazing the shell of her ear.

A soft laugh escaped her, low and musical. "You're biased," she teased, meeting his gaze in the mirror.

"Yes," he said simply, his dark eyes gleaming with warmth and hunger. "Always."

He pressed a kiss to the nape of her neck, and her soft, involuntary sigh made his pulse quicken.

"Stop that," she warned playfully, though her smile betrayed her pleasure. "Or we'll never leave."

He chuckled, low and rough, a promise threading through the sound. "Then perhaps Milan will have to wait."

She laughed, a musical, teasing sound, and shook her head. "No, my love— you will have to wait."

"As long as it's not too long," he murmured, his voice dark with longing, "I will follow you anywhere."

She gathered her small clutch, letting her fingers slip into his as they descended toward the limousine waiting below. Once inside, Lorenzo's curiosity could no longer be contained. He glanced at her, eyes alight with admiration and something more. "No one knows you're the designer of Loren Bella?"

She shook her head, a secretive, playful smile tugging at her lips. "That is right. Only a very few know. I am not interested in fame. I want the jewellery to speak for itself—to tell its own story."

Lorenzo's gaze softened, his eyes tracing her face with reverence and desire. "It always does," he said quietly, brushing his thumb over her hand, "just like you."

The limousine glided through the streets of Milan, the city alive with anticipation as the sun dipped lower, casting long golden streaks across the façades of elegant buildings. Lorenzo's hand rested lightly on hers, their fingers entwined, but his gaze never left her. She looked radiant, almost otherworldly, in the soft silk of her gown, the white fabric catching the light with every subtle curve of her body.

As they arrived at the venue, the buzz of the crowd and the shimmer of flashbulbs greeted them. Designers, models, and journalists milled about, yet Isabella moved through it all with quiet grace, a ghost among the glittering throng. She never announced herself; she let the jewellery and the models speak, preferring the anonymity that allowed her creations to shine without distraction.

Lorenzo followed closely, protective and enthralled. His eyes lingered on her every movement—the sway of her gown, the gentle curve of her shoulders, the serene confidence in her posture. "It astounds me that no one has any idea," he murmured softly, leaning close so only she could hear.

She smiled, brushing a loose strand of hair behind her ear. "I prefer it this way," she replied. "The designs are the focus, not me."

He chuckled, brushing his thumb across the back of her hand. "Even so, it is extremely hard not to notice you. But I will let you keep your secret."

They settled into a quiet spot near the front, a perfect vantage point to watch the models glide down the runway. Lorenzo's arm rested lightly around her shoulders, protective, possessive yet gentle—a silent declaration of the claim he had already made on her heart. Isabella leaned into him, feeling the warmth of his body, the steady beat of his heart against her own, and allowed herself to savour the moment—the calm before the spectacle, the intimacy before the world took notice of her genius.

Every model carried a piece of her vision, a fragment of her soul, and Lorenzo's pride in her was palpable. "You've done it again," he whispered, pressing a soft kiss to her temple. "Every piece… flawless. Just like you."

Isabella leaned back against him, letting the applause and flashing cameras fade into the background, her heart full. In that moment, she didn't need recognition or acclaim—she had him. And for Isabella, that was more than enough.

After the show, the after-party was in full swing—chandeliers scattering sparkling light over elegantly dressed guests, laughter and music weaving through the grand hall. Glasses clinked, conversations overlapped, and everywhere Isabella looked, people buzzed about the gowns that had just graced the runway.

Amid the chatter, she caught snippets of praise for her jewellery—the delicate pieces that had adorned the models, each one glinting under the lights. A designer's name was seldom spoken aloud, yet admiration for her work rippled through the crowd.

Lorenzo, standing beside her, noticed the way her eyes lit up at each compliment. When a guest remarked on the brilliance of her designs, he leaned closer, brushing his hand lightly over hers, and gave her a slow, proud smile— a look filled with quiet reverence and unspoken awe.

It was a smile only she truly understood. A smile that said: I see you. I know what you've created. And I'm in awe of you—always.

She returned his gaze, heart swelling, and for a fleeting moment, the noise of the party melted away. Among the glittering crowd, among the clinking glasses and swirling gowns, it was just the two of them—connected by love, by pride, and by the shared knowledge of what they meant to each other.

A voice cut through the hum of the after-party. "Lorenzo… Isabella."

They turned to see Alessandro, calm and composed, a soft smile on his face. "I see you two finally found one another," he said warmly, without a trace of envy or edge.

He leaned in and kissed Isabella gently on the cheek. "We did… thank you, Alessandro," she replied, her voice sincere.

He pressed a kiss to her other cheek. "I can't pretend it doesn't sting a little… but you and Lorenzo belong together. That's what matters."

Lorenzo met his gaze, and for the first time, a genuine, unguarded smile softened his features. They shook hands, a quiet acknowledgment passing between them. "Alessandro… thank you," he said, his voice steady yet layered with gratitude. "For everything."

Alessandro inclined his head modestly, almost deferential. "You deserved this. I'm just glad it worked out—and that I could help, even in a small way."

Isabella's hand slid into Lorenzo's, their fingers intertwining naturally. He glanced at her, then back at Alessandro. "I'll never forget it," he said, the depth of his gratitude clear in his dark eyes.

Alessandro's smile deepened. "Good." Then, lowering his voice slightly as he turned to Isabella, he added with a knowing nod, "Your designs are a hit, I see."

She smiled, grateful yet modest, warmth radiating as she shared a look with Lorenzo, who squeezed her hand gently. Their eyes met—a silent conversation passing between them: relief, love, and the private joy of finally being together—while Alessandro watched on, quietly approving, his presence the perfect punctuation to their hard-won happiness.

They chatted a little while longer, Alessandro's presence warm and easy, and agreed to meet again soon, but before long he melted back into the crowd, his tall frame swallowed by glittering gowns and the hum of conversation.

Lorenzo threaded his fingers through Isabella's, tugging gently, his thumb brushing the inside of her wrist in a way that sent a shiver spiralling up her arm. "Shall we step outside for a breath?" he murmured, his dark eyes glinting with mischief—and something far deeper: longing, hunger, possession.

Isabella's laugh was soft, low, like a secret meant only for him. It rose above the clinking glasses and muted music, a melody he'd ached to hear for years. "I think we deserve it," she whispered back, the words carrying a flicker of playful defiance and something softer beneath.

Hand in hand, they slipped through the crowd, a pair apart from the whirl of the after-party, until the door closed behind them and the cool night air wrapped around them like a balm. The noise faded to the hum of the city— distant horns, muted footsteps, the faint hiss of a passing car—leaving only the two of them suspended in a quieter world. A breeze slid over their skin, sharpening every spark of sensation between them.

Lorenzo pulled her close, pressing his forehead to hers, his breath warm on her lips. "Finally," he whispered, his voice rough with desire and relief, like a man exhaling after years of holding it in. "Alone with you again."

Her lips curved into a soft, knowing smile, eyes glinting beneath the streetlight. "Finally," she echoed, her body melting against his, her hands sliding up his chest as if she couldn't stop herself.

Their kisses began slow—a gentle tasting, an exploration—but the moment the first sigh escaped her, the tension of months of longing and fear erupted between them. Hands roamed, fingers tangled in hair and fabric, breaths came quick and shallow. The city lights blurred into a distant glow; there was only the heat of his mouth, the strength of his arms, the wild drum of their hearts.

When they finally paused, chests heaving, Lorenzo held her against him, his thumb tracing slow circles at the base of her spine, his eyes dark with devotion. "I'll never let you go again," he murmured, his voice thick with the weight of a vow.

"And I don't want you to," she whispered back, nuzzling into his neck, her fingers tracing the hard line of his jaw. "Not ever."

The private moment stretched, intimate and unhurried, a pocket of stillness carved from chaos—a sanctuary where nothing else existed. No crowd, no city, no past. Just them.

Then he lowered his head, lips brushing the shell of her ear, his voice rough and raw. "Marry me."

She gasped, her heart stuttering in her chest. Slowly, she lifted her gaze to his and saw only sincerity there—no games, no pretence, just the man she had always loved.

"Please, Isabella," he said quietly, his hands cradling her face as though it were something precious. "I love you. I want to spend the rest of my life with you— wake up to you every morning, build a family with you. I want to fill the Florence villa with laughter and love, with children running through the halls. I want it all—with you."

Isabella's breath caught, her hands trembling as they rested on his chest. Her eyes shimmered in the soft glow of the streetlights, wide with disbelief, joy, and the fragile hope she had dared to feel again.

"Lorenzo…" she whispered, her voice barely audible yet carrying the weight of everything she had held inside for months. "All this time… all these years… I—" She shook her head, laughing softly through her tears, a mixture of relief and awe. "I've waited for you. I've always waited for you."

He cupped her face, thumbs brushing away a stray tear, his gaze locking with hers. "And now you don't have to wait anymore," he murmured, his voice thick with emotion. "I'm here, Isabella. Always. And I'm never leaving."

She pressed her forehead to his, inhaling the familiar scent that had haunted her dreams—the strength and warmth that had called to her heart even in his absence. "Yes," she whispered, her voice trembling but resolute. "Yes, Lorenzo. A thousand times yes. I will marry you. I've always been yours."

A slow smile spread across his face, dark eyes glinting with a mixture of triumph and reverence. "Yours," he echoed, his lips finding hers in a kiss that was gentle, claiming, and full of promises, sealing their reunion, their future, their forever.

Her hands tangled in his hair, holding him close as if she could never let him go, and he lifted her slightly, spinning her once before setting her down gently. "You have no idea how long I've dreamed of this," he murmured against her lips.

"Then don't stop," she breathed, her body pressing against his, her heart overflowing. "Don't ever stop reminding me."

Lorenzo smiled—dark, tender—and kissed her again, slower this time, savouring every moment, every second of the woman who had always been the centre of his world. Around them, the city continued its hum, but for Lorenzo and Isabella, the universe had finally narrowed to just the two of them—and the promise of a life they would build together.

Epilogue

Five years later…

The soft morning sunlight spilled through the wide windows of the Florence villa, bathing the marble floors in a warm, golden glow. Dust motes danced lazily in the light, drifting like tiny stars caught in a serene, sunlit universe. The walls, adorned with carefully curated art and family photographs, seemed to hum with the quiet energy of a household alive with love. Outside, birds sang in the gardens, their songs threading through the open windows, mingling with the subtle scent of jasmine drifting in from the courtyard.

In the kitchen, the aroma of freshly baked pastries mingled with the rich, earthy scent of coffee brewing, filling the air with a warm, inviting comfort. Isabella stepped in, her silk robe brushing the polished floors, toes curling slightly as she moved quietly to avoid disturbing the cheerful commotion. Her heart swelled at the scene before her.

At the large wooden table, Lorenzo knelt on the floor beside Gabriel, their four-year-old son, and Elena, their three-year-old daughter. Aldo, ever-dignified, was carefully handing out warm croissants and golden pastries, while Rosa hovered nearby with a tray of jam tarts and chocolate-dusted delights. Even Marco, Isabella's father, had joined in the morning chaos, laughing warmly as he helped Gabriel smear chocolate across his small fingers.

Gabriel's curls bounced as he leaned toward Lorenzo, who lifted him gently so he could reach a particularly chocolatey treat. The boy's giggle erupted and echoed off the kitchen walls, mixing with Elena's squeals of delight as Rosa placed a mini tart in front of her. Crumbs were scattered across the table and floor alike, a sweet mess of morning joy.

Isabella shook her head, a warm smile tugging at her lips. "You are all spoiling my children!" she called softly, though her voice held both amusement and affection.

Rosa chuckled, smoothing Elena's sticky hair from her forehead. "They deserve it, señorita," she said fondly. "And you've already done so much for them."

Lorenzo looked up, eyes dark with affection, a slow grin spreading across his face. "Isabella," he murmured softly, voice low and playful, "I think we both know who really gets spoiled around here."

"Dio, Isabella," he rasped against her throat, his mouth hot and demanding as it traced her skin. "I can't get enough of you. I'll never get enough."

His mouth crashed down on hers as he surged into her, deep and unyielding, her legs wrapping around his waist in pure instinct.

She moaned into his kiss, the sound swallowed by him as though he needed even that part of her. He gripped her hips in both hands, fingers biting into her skin as if he would never let her go again.

"Dio, Isabella…" His voice broke, reverent and raw. "So perfect."

She clung to him, arms looped around his neck, her body arching in helpless surrender to every fierce, driving thrust.

Their bodies moved together in a rhythm that was wild, unrestrained—every thrust a vow, every gasp a confession, every moan a prayer of desperate love. They clung as if the world might tear them apart again, as though only this unrelenting closeness could heal the years of longing and loss.

When release finally claimed them, it was violent, devastating—an obliterating surrender that left them trembling, gasping, utterly undone.

They stayed tangled for a long, breathless moment, bodies slick, hearts hammering, minds still reeling from the storm they had unleashed. Lorenzo's hands roamed lazily over her curves now, tracing lines, memorising the soft heat of her skin, fingers brushing where he had left marks of his need. Isabella shivered under his touch, leaning into him, letting herself be both claimed and cherished.

"I could stay like this forever," she murmured, her voice husky with sleep and the echo of desire, nuzzling into the curve of his neck.

"Me too," he replied, low and rough, pressing a tender kiss to her temple. "But I think we've earned a little sustenance."

She smiled, drowsy and breathless, tugging him back down beside her. Their limbs tangled easily, bodies moving in a slow, languid rhythm—soft touches replacing the desperate urgency of before. Fingers traced idle paths across warm skin, lips brushed in unhurried kisses, and laughter rippled between them like a quiet song. In those tender, stolen moments, it wasn't just passion binding them—it was trust, belonging, and the kind of intimacy that lived between heartbeats.

When hunger—or perhaps the simple need to catch their breath—finally coaxed them back to the world beyond the sheets, Lorenzo slipped into his

Isabella laughed, stepping fully into the kitchen, brushing past him to plant a quick kiss on his cheek. He caught her wrist lightly, tugging her closer for a brief embrace before letting her go. Their family life was messy, chaotic, full of laughter and crumbs, but it was perfect.

Of course, Lorenzo was right. They had married just a week after his proposal, a small, intimate ceremony in the villa's sunlit gardens. Over the five years since, he had made sure every day that Isabella knew exactly how much she meant to him—and she had returned the devotion tenfold. Their love had deepened and grown richer with the joys and challenges of raising a family.

Gabriel squealed again, reaching up to hug Lorenzo's neck, while Elena tugged at her mother's hand, demanding attention in her own insistent, joyful way. Marco chuckled, settling into a chair with a satisfied sigh. "You two have created quite the little army," he said, eyes twinkling. "They're already running the house."

"They keep me running too," Isabella admitted, scooping Elena onto her hip. She glanced around at the lively kitchen—family laughter ringing through the room, the aroma of pastries and coffee mingling with the warm sunlight—and felt a wave of contentment settle over her. This, she thought, this is everything we ever wanted.

Lorenzo reached out, tugging her close and pressing a kiss to her temple. "Five years," he murmured, voice husky with emotion, "and I still fall for you every single day."

Isabella pressed her head to his chest, listening to the steady beat of his heart— a rhythm that had always been hers. "And I for you," she whispered, a smile curving her lips. "Always."

The children continued their joyful chaos, knocking over a cup or two, grabbing extra pastries, and squealing as Gabriel attempted to teach Elena a new hand-clapping game. Aldo and Rosa quietly cleared plates and refilled milk cups, while Marco launched into another exaggerated story, sending the little ones into fits of laughter. Isabella watched, feeling life's messy, beautiful perfection settle warmly around her. Love, family, and a home full of laughter— they had it all.

A mischievous glint lit Lorenzo's eyes. "I have to show you something," he said, taking Isabella's hand and guiding her through the sunlit halls toward the study. The children squealed at a game Gabriel had just invented, chasing each other through the open spaces, but Isabella barely noticed, her curiosity growing with each step.

Once inside the study, Lorenzo closed the door behind them and gestured toward his desk. Spread across it were glowing reviews from top magazines and fashion blogs, celebrating her Loren Bella jewellery collection. Each headline and photograph spoke of her artistry, her vision, and her extraordinary talent.

"I'm so proud of you," Lorenzo whispered, voice thick with admiration, taking her hands in his and letting his thumbs trace the delicate curves of her fingers. "Look at this. All your hard work, all your passion—it's being recognised. You've done something incredible, Isabella."

Her chest warmed, and a radiant smile spread across her face. She tightened her grip on his hands, drawing strength from the shared intimacy of the moment. But she had news of her own, news that made her heart leap and breath catch. Drawing in a steadying breath, she lifted her gaze to his, eyes sparkling with both excitement and awe.

"Lorenzo…" she whispered, voice trembling with anticipation. "I did a test this morning." She paused, squeezing his hands, lips curving into a radiant smile. "It was positive. We're having another baby."

For a heartbeat, time seemed to hold them in suspended wonder. Then Lorenzo's dark eyes widened, breath shuddering from him before a roar of unrestrained joy broke free.

"Another little one?" His voice was rough with disbelief and happiness. He swept her into his arms, spinning her around as laughter burst from his lips. He kissed her relentlessly—her mouth, her cheeks, her hair—his joy spilling into every touch. "Oh, Isabella… this is perfect. Absolutely perfect!"

She melted against him, laughter caught between his kisses, heart soaring. His arms held her as though he would never let go, as if this happiness were too precious to risk.

Hand in hand, he practically dragged her back through the villa, laughter echoing down the polished halls. The familiar scents of pastries, coffee, and sunlit wood wrapped around them as they returned to the kitchen. Aldo, Rosa, and Marco were gathered around the table with Gabriel and Elena, the children giggling and crumbs dusting their chins.

The room was alive with warmth, love, and laughter, every corner echoing the joy only family could bring.

Lorenzo's grin was unstoppable as he lifted Isabella's hand high, voice booming with excitement. "We have news! Isabella and I—we're having another baby!"

Gabriel's eyes widened, and he jumped up, clapping his hands. "I hope it's a boy! I want a brother!" he declared, chest puffed out in mock determination.

Elena squealed, spinning in a happy circle. "Another baby! Another baby!"

Rosa gasped, hand flying to her mouth before enveloping Isabella in a tight hug. Marco's eyes glistened as he pulled both of them into a bear hug, laughing and shaking his head. "Another one? This family just keeps getting better and better!"

Lorenzo lifted Isabella again, spinning her slightly as the children cheered, and pressed a long, joyous kiss to her lips. "This family... it's perfect," he murmured, dark eyes sparkling.

In that chaotic, blissful moment, Isabella watched Lorenzo laugh with their children, the love and happiness radiating from him. Five years had passed, filled with longing, storms, and heartache, but the love that had begun as a tempest between two hearts had grown into something enduring, something unshakable.

It was steady, unwavering, and all-encompassing. Surrounded by laughter, warmth, and family, Isabella knew a single, unshakable truth: this love, this family, would last forever.

The End

Second Glance

Alison Reid

A complete standalone romance

Previously published individually

Chapter One

The Roberts family home, a sprawling estate perched in Bellevue Hill on the edge of Sydney, buzzed with the sounds of a warm afternoon gathering. Jackson Roberts and Nathan McRae, both twenty-five and fresh from their day at a prestigious law firm, sat at the kitchen island, sipping scotch and catching up. Jackson's relaxed posture and easy smile contrasted sharply with Nathan's more composed demeanour. They had been friends for years, ever since high school. Jackson's sister, Phyllis, was excited about her upcoming trip to Perth with her best friend, Jessica Watson, who was visiting Phyllis before returning to university.

Phyllis, always the life of the party, breezed in from the garden, a radiant smile on her face. She was chatting animatedly, her energy filling the room. "I can't wait to go with Jessica to Perth," she said, setting down her glass of water on the counter. "We're going to have the best time when I'm there. She's had such a great time here."

Jackson's gaze flickered briefly to his sister. He knew all about Jessica Watson, Phyllis's best friend from high school. Jessica had been visiting Phyllis but was leaving tomorrow to return to Perth. Phyllis was going with her for a week, just before Jessica starts university. Phyllis had moved to Perth to live with her aunt after both of her parents were killed in a car accident six months ago.

"Oh, right," Jackson said, his tone light. "Is Jessica ready to go back home?" He didn't really care, but the casual question seemed polite enough.

Phyllis's eyes lit up. "Yes, we're both packed. I think she's really looking forward to starting university."

Nathan smiled, though his expression was more curious than enthusiastic. "That's good to hear. She's studying civil engineering, isn't she?"

"That's right," Phyllis smiled at Nathan.

Jackson swirled the ice in his glass, his attention drifting elsewhere. He had always found Jessica Watson to be... well, forgettable. She was Phyllis's quirky, shy best friend. Not someone he'd ever given much thought to, even when they'd all hung out together during the school years. Jessica was never the type to stand out in a crowd—awkward, wearing those big glasses, never quite fitting in with Phyllis's popular group.

"She's so smart," Phyllis continued, her tone soft with affection. "I'm so proud of her."

Jackson raised an eyebrow, his lips curling into a slight, amused smile. "I don't know why you are friends with her," he said, leaning back in his chair and looking at his sister with a teasing glint in his eyes. "She's so… unattractive."

The words hung in the air like a bad aftertaste. Nathan's eyes widened in disbelief, and Phyllis's smile faltered for a moment before hardening into a thin line. Her gaze snapped to Jackson, and for a split second, there was a dangerous flicker of anger in her eyes.

"What?" Phyllis said, her voice sharp and incredulous. "Are you serious? You think Jessica is unattractive?"

Jackson, taken aback by Phyllis's reaction, shrugged. "I mean, she's just not my type, Phyll. You know, she's always been so… plain." His words came out without much thought, his tone casual, as though discussing someone he had no real connection to.

Phyllis's eyes narrowed, her fingers gripping the edge of the counter. "You're unbelievable, Jackson," she snapped, her voice rising. "There's more to a person than looks, you know. You can't just judge someone by their appearance."

Jackson's smirk faded, but his confidence remained. "I'm not judging her," he said dismissively. "I'm just being honest. She's always been so… forgettable. You know that."

Nathan shifted uncomfortably in his seat, glancing between the siblings. "Hey, Jackson, maybe you should—"

"No," Phyllis cut him off, her voice low but seething. "You don't get to talk about her like that. She's my best friend. And for the record, Jessica's way more than her looks. She's kind, smart, and funny—way more than you'll ever see because you can't look beyond the surface."

Jackson opened his mouth to respond, but Phyllis didn't let him get a word in. She was on a roll now, her anger and frustration boiling over. "You always do this, Jackson. You dismiss people because they don't fit some stupid mould you've created. And that's why you'll never find someone who actually matters to you. You don't get it. You never have."

Phyllis turned on her heel and stormed toward the door. "You're my brother, but sometimes you're just an ass," she spat over her shoulder, her voice trembling with emotion.

Jackson blinked, surprised by the intensity of her reaction. He had never seen her so upset—and all because of a comment he had made without thinking. The tension in the room hung thick, and Nathan stared at Jackson, silent disapproval in his eyes.

The words Phyllis had said echoed in his mind. Had he really been that harsh? Was it possible he'd overlooked something about Jessica? As he sat there in stunned silence, he realised for the first time that he might have gotten her completely wrong. And now, it was too late to take back the damage he had done.

Jessica Watson, eighteen years old, stood in the middle of the guest room at her best friend's home, finishing the last of her packing. Her suitcase was nearly zipped up, and she glanced around one final time to make sure she hadn't missed anything. She was in Sydney visiting Phyllis Roberts, and tomorrow they would both leave for Perth, where Phyllis would stay with Jessica for a week before they started university.

Six months ago, Jessica had moved to Perth after her parents tragically died in a car accident. The pain of losing them never seemed to lessen, and the ache of missing them was a constant presence in her heart. But her aunt, though a stranger in many ways, had been kind to her and tried to make her feel at home.

With a deep breath, Jessica zipped up her suitcase, marking the end of her time in Sydney. She wasn't looking forward to leaving, but at least she had one more week with Phyllis. Their friendship had been a bright spot in the wake of so much sorrow. They had shared countless memories over the years, and though Phyllis would soon return to Perth with her, saying goodbye was still hard.

But for now, Jessica wanted to soak up these final moments with Phyllis in Sydney before they left for the airport in the morning.

She made her way downstairs, her steps light but laden with the bittersweetness of the moment. She could hear the hum of voices from the kitchen as she neared. Phyllis was probably chatting with her brother Jackson and his best friend, Nathan. Phyllis always brought an energy to any room, while Jackson, well, he remained a mystery.

He was Phyllis's older brother, a person she didn't know very well, but one who had always intrigued her. Though he wasn't unkind, he never seemed to pay much attention to her. And in the quiet corners of her heart, Jessica couldn't help but admire him—more than she probably should. Jackson was smart, confident, and undeniably attractive. The kind of guy who left a lasting impression without even trying.

Jessica paused outside the kitchen, steeling herself before stepping inside to say goodbye to both Jackson and Nathan. But before she could open the door, she froze. Jackson's voice drifted across the room, cutting through the air.

"She's so… unattractive."

The words sliced through Jessica, leaving her breathless. Her heart skipped a beat. Was he talking about her? No, it couldn't be. He must have been talking about someone else. Her mind tried to reason with her, but the words lingered, biting at her like an open wound.

And then she heard Phyllis's voice rise in protest, filled with sharp emotion. It was unmistakable.

"What! Are you serious, Jackson? You think Jessica is unattractive?"

The realisation hit Jessica like a tidal wave. They were talking about her. Jackson, the one she secretly admired, the one who never seemed to notice her, had just called her unattractive. Her chest tightened, and her breath caught in her throat.

Then he continued, "I mean, she's just not my type, Phyll. You know, she's always been so… plain."

The sting of rejection was almost suffocating. Her pulse raced as she stood frozen outside the kitchen, unable to move or speak. The words echoed in her mind, each one sharper than the last. She had always known, in some corner of her heart, that Jackson didn't see her the way she wished he would. But hearing him say it aloud—hearing him dismiss her so casually—felt like a cruel punch to her gut.

Phyllis's voice broke through her spiralling thoughts, filled with fury. "You're unbelievable, Jackson," she snapped. "There's more to a person than looks, you know. You can't just judge someone by their appearance!"

Jessica's heart pounded in her chest as Phyllis's words rang in her ears. She wanted so badly to step into the kitchen, to say something, to defend herself, but she couldn't. The weight of the moment was too much. The hurt was suffocating, and she could hardly bear it.

Jessica felt her eyes fill with tears, but she didn't want them to see her. She couldn't bear to witness the conversation any longer, but her feet refused to move. She couldn't escape it, even though every part of her wanted to.

As Phyllis's voice continued to rise, Jessica's knees weakened. She turned on her heel and fled upstairs, her heart pounding in her chest. The walls of the house seemed to close in around her. She barely made it to her room before the floodgates opened. The tears that had been quietly building up over the months—grief over her parents, loneliness, and now the sting of rejection—finally broke free.

She collapsed onto her bed, burying her face in the pillow, the sound of her sobs muffled by the soft fabric. She had hoped, just maybe, that Jackson would one day see her differently. That he would look past the awkwardness, the self-doubt, and the insecurity. But now, the painful truth was out in the open. To him, she was nothing more than *'unattractive'*.

Phyllis had defended her, yes, but that didn't change how Jackson saw her. The man she had admired from afar would never view her the way she longed for. And now, she didn't know how to face him. She didn't know how to walk into that kitchen again without feeling utterly exposed.

As her sobs gradually quieted and her tears dried, Jessica lay there in the dim light of her room, her mind racing with all the thoughts she had tried to keep buried. She had never imagined that something so simple, so casual, could hurt this much.

Chapter Two

Five years later...

Jessica Watson, now twenty-three, stood in the arrival area at Sydney Airport, her heart racing with a mix of excitement and nerves. It had been five long years since she had left Sydney, moving to Perth to live with her aunt after her parents' tragic death. Now, after her aunt's remarriage and the sense that it was time for a change, Jessica was coming back to the city she once called home.

But this return wasn't just about moving back—it was also for her best friend Phyllis's wedding. Phyllis had asked her to be the maid of honour, a role Jessica was honoured to take on. The wedding was in two weeks, and right after that, she would start her new job at the Sydney office of her engineering firm. It felt surreal to be here again, and there was an unfamiliar heaviness in her chest. But she was also excited to reunite with Phyllis and Nathan McRae, who had become such an integral part of her life in their own way.

Jessica had kept in touch with Phyllis all these years, and despite the distance, their friendship had remained strong. Phyllis had visited her in Perth several times, but this was the first time Jessica had returned to Sydney since the move. She had grown a lot in those five years—both personally and professionally. She had finished her degree, secured a good position as a civil engineer, and now she was ready to start the next chapter of her life.

She heard a familiar squeal just behind her, and before she could turn around, she was swept up into a bear hug.

"Jessica! You're finally here!" Phyllis's voice was filled with excitement and warmth. Her infectious energy was exactly as Jessica remembered it.

Jessica laughed, feeling the familiar sense of home in her best friend's embrace. "Phyllis, it's so good to see you!" She pulled away slightly to look at her. "I can't believe I'm actually here for your wedding."

Phyllis grinned, her eyes sparkling with joy. "Of course you are! I wouldn't have it any other way. You're my maid of honour, remember?" She squeezed Jessica's shoulders. "It's going to be perfect."

As Jessica glanced around, her eyes landed on Nathan making his way toward them. His broad smile was instantly recognisable, and though it had been years since she'd last seen him in person, the warmth in his expression felt as familiar as ever. They'd kept in touch over the phone often but seeing him now brought a wave of nostalgia she hadn't expected.

"Oh my god, Jess, you're gorgeous!" Nathan exclaimed, his voice filled with genuine surprise and admiration.

Jessica blinked in surprise before laughing softly. Nathan had always been kind and thoughtful, the sort of person who could make anyone feel at ease. It was one of the reasons she had always liked him. But seeing him now, standing next to Phyllis, his obvious happiness only amplified his charm.

Phyllis burst into laughter, playfully swatting Nathan's arm. "Watch it, Nathan. I'll get jealous," she teased, though the affection in her tone was unmistakable.

Nathan's cheeks turned a faint shade of pink as he turned to his fiancée, a sheepish grin tugging at his lips. "You're the only one I love, sweetheart," he said earnestly, slipping an arm around Phyllis's waist.

Jessica couldn't help but chuckle at the exchange. "Thanks, Nathan," she said, her green eyes sparkling with amusement. "It has been a while since you've seen me, so I'll let the surprise slide."

Nathan grinned, still a little flustered but clearly happy to see her. "It really has, Jess. I think the last time I saw you; you were—what, just starting university?"

"That sounds about right," Jessica replied, nodding. "A lot can change in five years."

Phyllis beamed, stepping between them and linking arms with both. "And change it has! I've been telling Nathan how amazing you're doing, Jess. Civil engineer, transferred to Sydney, back here for my wedding—what can't you do?"

Jessica shook her head with a small laugh, her auburn hair catching the light as she spoke. "Let's not exaggerate, Phyll. I'm just trying to figure things out like everyone else. But I'm glad to be back, especially for you two."

"Well, we're glad you're back," Phyllis said, squeezing Jessica's arm. "This wedding wouldn't be the same without my best friend." Her voice softened. "You've always been such a big part of my life, Jess. Having you here means everything."

Jessica felt a lump rise in her throat but managed a smile. "I wouldn't miss it for the world, Phyllis."

Nathan chimed in with a playful grin. "And don't forget, you're not just here for the wedding. You're officially back in Sydney now. I hope you're ready for us to drag you to every brunch, barbecue, and game night we can think of."

Jessica laughed. "I think I can handle it. Though you might regret saying that when you see how competitive I've gotten at board games."

Nathan raised his hands in mock surrender. "Noted. I'll make sure to pick the games carefully."

As the trio walked toward the exit, the lively chatter between Phyllis and Nathan filled the air. Jessica trailed slightly behind them, her suitcase in tow, a faint smile lingering on her lips. It felt good to be surrounded by their energy, their love, and their unwavering acceptance.

But as they stepped out into the bustling Sydney evening, a flicker of unease stirred in Jessica's chest. She was back in the city she'd left behind, the place filled with both fond memories and painful ones. She wasn't the same girl who had walked away five years ago, and she wasn't sure if the people she had left behind—especially one in particular—would see that.

For now, though, she pushed those thoughts aside. This was Phyllis's moment, and Jessica was determined to make it perfect. There would be time later to face the ghosts of her past.

As they approached Nathan's sleek black sedan, he opened the boot and carefully placed Jessica's suitcase inside. "There we go," he said, brushing his hands together. "All set. Let's get you back home."

Jessica slid into the backseat while Phyllis took her usual place in the passenger seat. As Nathan started the car, Phyllis twisted around to face Jessica, her eyes sparkling with excitement. "It's going to be so much fun having you stay with us again. Mum and Dad can't wait to see you, and you'll have plenty of time to settle back into Sydney life before the wedding."

Jessica smiled warmly. "I've missed your parents. They were always so good to me. And thank you for letting me stay. Two weeks is more than enough time to sort out a permanent place."

Nathan glanced at her in the rearview mirror. "Looking to rent or buy?"

"Buy," Jessica replied confidently. "Thanks to my parents' estate, I have the funds to invest in something nice. I'm hoping to find something close to my new office so the commute won't be a nightmare."

Phyllis's expression softened, and she reached out to squeeze Jessica's hand. "I know how hard it must have been after everything, but it's amazing that you've managed to build such a great life for yourself. Mum and Dad were always so proud of you, even when you moved away. Now you're coming back to stay."

Jessica swallowed the lump in her throat, a mix of gratitude and bittersweet memories swirling in her mind. "Your parents were always like a second family to me, Phyll. I'll never forget that."

Nathan cleared his throat, a light-hearted smile playing on his lips as he tried to shift the mood. "Well, with the property market the way it is, you've definitely got a challenge ahead. But if anyone can tackle it, it's you. And hey, if you need any help, just let me know. My friend Terry's pretty well-connected in real estate—he could be a great resource."

"Thanks, Nathan. I might just take you up on that," Jessica said, her smile genuine.

The drive through Sydney's bustling streets felt nostalgic. The familiar landmarks brought back memories of her childhood, of carefree days before everything had changed. The city felt both familiar and foreign, like a past life she was stepping back into.

When they pulled into the long driveway of the Roberts' sprawling family home, in Bellevue Hill, Jessica felt a rush of warmth. The house looked as grand as ever, its manicured gardens and ivy-covered walls welcoming her like an old friend. It was a place that had always been filled with laughter, love, and the comforting sense of belonging.

As Nathan parked the car and stepped out to grab her suitcase, Phyllis turned to Jessica with an excited grin. "Mum's probably already baking something ridiculous. She's been buzzing about you coming back for weeks."

Jessica laughed, stepping out of the car and stretching her legs. "That sounds like her. I can't wait to see them."

Nathan retrieved her the suitcase, and the three of them made their way up to the front door. Before they could even knock, the door swung open, and Mrs. Roberts appeared, her arms wide open and her face lit up with joy.

"Jessica, darling! You're here!" she exclaimed, enveloping Jessica in a warm, motherly hug.

Jessica felt a wave of comfort wash over her. "It's so good to see you, Mrs. Roberts. I've missed you."

"And we've missed you too, sweetheart, and it's Mary," Mary said, pulling back to look at her. "Now, come in, come in! Dinner's almost ready, and you must be starving after your flight."

Jessica stepped inside, the familiar scent of home-cooked meals and freshly polished wood greeting her. She glanced around, taking in the warmth of the house that hadn't changed much in five years.

Phyllis grabbed Jessica's suitcase from Nathan with a smile and turned to Jessica. "I'll put this in your room. Go on into the dining room—Dad's in there waiting for you. He's been excited to see you again."

Jessica nodded, feeling a small wave of nostalgia wash over her. She had always loved the Roberts' home. It wasn't just the grandeur of the place but the warmth of the family that made it special. Walking through the familiar hallway, memories of her teenage years spent laughing with Phyllis here surfaced, mingling with the nervous excitement of being back.

As she stepped into the dining room, Mr. Roberts was already rising from his seat. His face lit up with a broad smile as he opened his arms. "Jessica! Look at you! Welcome home, dear."

Jessica returned his embrace, the familiarity and kindness of the gesture comforting. "It's so good to see you, Mr. Roberts. Thank you for having me here again."

He pulled back and studied her with mock seriousness. "Mr. Roberts? Have you forgotten? It's John to you. Always has been."

Jessica laughed. "Right—sorry, John. Force of habit."

"Well, I'm glad you're here," he said warmly, gesturing for her to sit. "Phyllis tells me you're staying for two weeks. That's not nearly long enough, you know. You'll have to let us twist your arm into visiting more often now that you're back in Sydney."

Jessica smiled as she sat down. "I'll definitely be around more now. It's good to be back, though it feels a little surreal after all these years."

John nodded, his expression softening. "I can imagine. Moving back must be a big step, but I hope you know you've always got family here. If you need anything at all, just say the word."

Touched by his sincerity, Jessica felt a lump rise in her throat. "Thank you. That means a lot."

Phyllis entered the room just then, beaming. "Dad don't go getting all sentimental already. Jess has barely been here five minutes." She turned to Jessica, her tone teasing. "Careful, or he'll start digging out embarrassing stories from our childhood."

John chuckled. "Ah, but there are so many good ones to choose from. Remember that time you two tried to bake cookies and nearly burned down the kitchen?"

Jessica groaned, hiding her face. "Don't remind me! I'm still mortified about that."

Phyllis laughed, plopping down into a chair. "Hey, it was your idea to double the sugar."

"Because you said it would make them better!" Jessica shot back, grinning despite herself.

John shook his head, his eyes twinkling. "You two were a handful back then. It's nice to see that some things never change."

The three of them continued chatting, the room alive with laughter and warmth. Jessica couldn't help but feel a sense of comfort she hadn't experienced in years. She was pulled from her thoughts when Mary and Nathan entered, carrying dishes of steaming food, their long-time housekeeper, Helen, trailing behind with an extra platter.

Jessica stood and made her way toward Helen, a genuine smile spreading across her face. "Helen, it's so good to see you," she said, embracing the woman who had been such a constant presence in the Roberts household.

Helen returned the hug warmly. "Jessica! Look at you—you're all grown up and absolutely stunning. It's been far too long."

Jessica laughed. "It has. I've missed seeing you."

"You've been missed too," Helen replied fondly. "And I've heard about all the amazing things you've been doing in Perth. You should be proud of yourself."

Touched by the kind words, Jessica felt a blush rise to her cheeks. Before she could respond, Helen gently patted her arm. "Now, let me get dessert sorted. Enjoy dinner, love." With that, Helen left the room, her familiar presence adding to the evening's nostalgia.

As everyone settled around the table, Nathan poured wine while Mary dished out portions of roast chicken and vegetables. The aroma was heavenly, and the conversation flowed easily as they enjoyed the meal together.

It wasn't until halfway through the dinner that Mary, with a smile, casually mentioned, "Jackson will be joining us for dinner tomorrow night."

The words hit Jessica like a jolt. She stiffened involuntarily, her fork pausing mid-air.

Nathan chuckled and said, "He's going to get a shock when he sees you, Jess. I can already picture his face."

Jessica forced a small smile, trying to mask the tension creeping through her. "Oh, I'm sure he'll be just as charming as ever," she said lightly, though her tone was tinged with sarcasm.

Phyllis smirked, clearly catching the undercurrent of tension. "Don't worry, Jess. I'll make sure he behaves himself. He's not as bad as he used to be."

Jessica let out a dry laugh. "I'll believe that when I see it."

Mary interjected with a curious look. "What's the story between you two, anyway? I always got the feeling there was… something."

Jessica's cheeks heated, and she quickly shook her head. "There's no story, really. He ignored me most of the time, which was fine with me."

Nathan raised an eyebrow. "I don't think he will ignore you now, Jess. Jackson's sharper than most, but he's not as heartless as he might seem. You'll see."

Jessica bit her lip, unsure how to respond. The truth was, the idea of facing Jackson again after all these years stirred a mix of emotions—nerves, irritation, and a hint of something she didn't want to admit. She could only hope that tomorrow's dinner wouldn't dredge up old wounds she thought she had left behind.

Chapter Three

Saturday morning dawned sunny and warm, the perfect kind of day to relax and unwind. Jessica felt well-rested after an early night. She had unpacked most of her belongings after dinner and now felt more settled in her temporary home.

Slipping into an emerald-green bikini, she admired how the colour complemented her fair complexion, auburn hair, and green eyes. She threw on a pair of denim shorts and a white T-shirt over the top, opting for casual comfort. Phyllis had mentioned the night before that they'd spend the day lounging by the pool, and Jessica was looking forward to a peaceful morning.

As she made her way downstairs to the dining room, the scent of freshly brewed coffee and sizzling bacon wafted through the air. Jessica's stomach growled in response. She entered to find John and Mary already seated, enjoying breakfast.

John Roberts looked up from his newspaper, his warm smile immediately making Jessica feel at ease. "Good morning, Jessica. Sleep well?"

"Morning, Mr. Roberts," Jessica replied with a polite nod, moving toward the table. "I slept great, thank you. It's so peaceful here."

"Please, call me John," he said, waving her formality away. "And help yourself to breakfast. Helen has made us feast, as usual."

Mary gestured to the spread of eggs, toast, fresh fruit, and pancakes. "Good morning, Jess. Sit down, you need to eat something before Phyllis drags you out to the pool. She's already outside setting up towels and sunscreen."

Jessica laughed softly, taking a seat. "Thanks, Mary. This looks amazing. I forgot how much I missed Helen's cooking."

As she reached for a piece of toast, John folded his paper and leaned back in his chair. "So, any plans besides soaking up the sun today? Or are you two keeping things low-key?"

"Just relaxing, I think," Jessica said with a small shrug. "Phyllis and I thought it'd be nice to catch up properly before things get busy with the wedding."

John nodded approvingly. "Good idea. Once the guests start arriving in a week, it'll be nonstop chaos. Enjoy the calm while you can."

As they continued chatting, the terrace door slid open, and Phyllis's cheerful voice called out. "Jess! Hurry up! The pool's calling our name!"

Jessica grinned and quickly finished her coffee. "Guess that's my cue. Thanks for breakfast!"

Mary chuckled. "Go on, have fun. And don't let Phyllis rope you into one of her elaborate schemes. You know how she gets."

Jessica laughed as she made her way toward the terrace. "I'll try, but no promises."

She stepped outside to find Phyllis already lounging by the pool, sunglasses perched on her nose and a wide-brimmed hat shielding her face. A stack of magazines sat next to her, along with a pitcher of iced lemonade.

"There you are!" Phyllis exclaimed, waving Jessica over. "I was starting to think you'd gotten lost."

"Just fuelling up for the day," Jessica replied, settling into a lounge chair beside Phyllis and sliding her sunglasses on.

The warm sun kissed her skin, the sound of water gently lapping against the pool's edge provided a soothing background, and the promise of a carefree day made Jessica feel completely at ease. For the first time in what felt like forever, she could let her guard down and simply enjoy the moment.

A few minutes later, Nathan appeared, strolling out to the pool area with a casual confidence that matched his easy-going personality. He grinned as he approached. "Don't worry, I'm not staying," he said, bending down to kiss Phyllis on the forehead. "I'm just off to meet my friend Terry."

Phyllis tilted her head up to smile at him. "Tell him I said hi."

Nathan straightened and turned his attention to Jessica. "Jess, I just wanted to ask—do you want me to mention your house hunting to Terry? He's got a pretty solid network in real estate, and he might be able to help you out."

Jessica sat up slightly, her sunglasses sliding down her nose as she looked at him with appreciation. "Oh yes, please. I'm starting my search on Monday, so any leads would be great."

"Consider it done," Nathan said with a wink. "I'll text you later if he has any good suggestions."

"Thanks, Nathan," Jessica replied with a warm smile. "I really appreciate it."

"Anything for you, Jess," Nathan said lightly before turning back to Phyllis. "See you later, sweetheart. Love you."

"Love you too," Phyllis said, watching him as he headed back toward the house.

As Nathan disappeared inside, Jessica turned to Phyllis, a small smile on her lips. "You really hit the jackpot with him."

Phyllis leaned back in her chair, her face lighting up. "I know, right? He's the best. And he adores you too, you know. He's always talking about how proud he is of you."

Jessica felt a warm blush creep up her cheeks. "He's a good guy. You two are perfect together."

Phyllis reached over and squeezed Jessica's hand. "And don't you worry. We're going to find you a gorgeous place, and maybe even someone who adores you just as much as Nathan adores me."

Jessica chuckled, shaking her head. "One thing at a time, Phyll. Let's focus on the home first."

Phyllis laughed, raising her glass of lemonade in a toast. "To new beginnings!"

Jessica clinked her own glass against hers, a sense of optimism filling her chest.

"So, tell me, Phyllis," Jessica asked with a teasing smile as she adjusted her sunglasses, "what colour dress am I wearing for the big day?"

Phyllis didn't miss a beat, grinning as she leaned back in her lounge chair. "Green, of course. Emerald-green, to be exact. You look absolutely gorgeous in that colour, Jess. It makes your eyes pop."

Jessica laughed softly, brushing a strand of hair away from her face. "Are you sure? This is your day. I'll wear anything you want. Honestly, I'm just happy to be there for you."

Phyllis reached over and gently squeezed Jessica's hand. "You're my best friend, Jess. Having you by my side means the world to me, no matter what you wear. But trust me on the green—it's perfect on you. And it ties in beautifully with the theme. The groomsmen will have green accents, and you'll match perfectly without overshadowing me."

Jessica tilted her head, mock serious. "Well, we can't have me stealing the spotlight from the bride. That would be a disaster."

Phyllis laughed. "Not a chance. Nathan would drag you back down the aisle if you tried!"

Jessica joined in the laughter, shaking her head. "Fine, emerald-green it is. But I'll draw the line at wearing a ridiculous hat."

Phyllis giggled. "No hats, I promise. Just you looking stunning and standing next to me on the most important day of my life."

Jessica's expression softened, her voice warm. "It really is the most important day, Phyll. I can't wait to see you walk down the aisle. You and Nathan are perfect for each other."

Phyllis smiled, her eyes glistening slightly. "And I can't wait for you to see the man you're destined for. Who knows? Maybe he's already out there, waiting for you to notice him."

Jessica chuckled, shaking her head. "Let's not get ahead of ourselves. I'm still focusing on getting my life back on track in Sydney. One step at a time, remember?"

Phyllis grinned mischievously. "Fair enough. But don't be surprised if someone unexpected catches your eye at the wedding. Love has a funny way of sneaking up on you."

Jessica raised an eyebrow, smirking. "Is this your way of warning me that you've set me up with someone?"

Phyllis laughed. "I'd never! But if it happens, it happens."

Jessica smiled, her heart light as they continued to chat. This was the Phyllis she loved—optimistic, supportive, and always dreaming big for the both of them.

"So, tell me, Jess," Phyllis began, leaning back in her chair with a curious grin. "Did you leave anyone special behind in Perth?"

Jessica shook her head, laughing softly. "No, not really. The four years at university kept me pretty busy. I wasn't interested in dating much then—civil engineering is full-on, and I wanted to focus on my studies. No distractions."

Phyllis raised an eyebrow, intrigued. "And after uni? Come on, you're gorgeous and smart. Surely you didn't stay single forever."

Jessica chuckled, taking a sip of her lemonade. "Well, after I started working for the engineering firm, there was definitely plenty of interest. Let's just say being in a male-dominated occupation comes with its fair share of attention." She laughed again. "I went on dates, sure, but there wasn't anyone special. No one I'd write home about or even miss now that I'm back in Sydney."

Phyllis tilted her head, a sly smile forming. "So, basically, you've got the perfect fresh start here. No baggage, no strings."

"Exactly," Jessica replied with a grin. "And I'm more than fine with that. Right now, I just want to focus on my career and settling into Sydney again. If something happens, it happens, but I'm not in a rush."

Phyllis studied her for a moment, her playful smile fading into something more thoughtful. "You know, Jess, it's okay to let your guard down. Not every guy is like… well, you know."

Jessica glanced at her, catching the subtle reference. "Like Jackson, you mean?"

Phyllis winced slightly, guilt flickering across her face. Jessica had confided in her years ago about overhearing Jackson's comments about her being 'unattractive'. Phyllis had been deeply apologetic at the time, but Jessica had assured her there was no need for blame. All she'd asked was that Phyllis never tell Jackson, because the humiliation of him knowing she'd heard was unbearable.

Phyllis nodded hesitantly. "Yeah… like Jackson. I just don't want you to carry that hurt with you. You've grown so much since then, Jess. You're confident, successful, and absolutely stunning. If he doesn't see it now, that's entirely his loss."

Jessica smiled faintly, appreciating her friend's loyalty, but unwilling to dwell on old wounds. "Thanks, Phyll. But honestly, I don't care if he sees it or not. I know he's your brother, and I love you, but I'm not interested in shallow people who only care about appearances and can't see what actually matters. That's just… not the kind of energy I need in my life."

Phyllis reached over and squeezed Jessica's hand, her expression soft with affection. "Right. I get it, and I'll always have your back. No matter what. If anyone tries to mess with you, they'll have to answer to me—and Nathan."

Jessica laughed, the warmth of their friendship soothing any lingering tension. "Thanks, Phyll. But don't worry about me. I've got thick skin now, and life's too short to waste on people who don't matter."

Phyllis smiled, her pride for Jessica shining through. "Damn right. You're amazing, Jess, and don't you forget it."

Jessica laughed, the warmth of their friendship easing any lingering tension. "I'll keep that in mind. Now, enough about my love life—or lack thereof. What about you? Are you ready for this wedding? Cold feet yet?"

Phyllis rolled her eyes dramatically. "Not even close. Nathan's my person, Jess. I can't wait to marry him."

Jessica smiled; her heart full as she watched her best friend glow with happiness. This was what love should look like—steady, supportive, and true.

Helen brought down bowls of fresh salads, topped with colourful vegetables, and drizzled with dressing, along with more chilled lemonade. The delicious aroma filled the air, and Helen set everything down on the table with a smile.

"Thanks so much, Helen, you're a godsend," Jessica said, her smile wide as she accepted a plate.

Phyllis smiled, watching Jessica. "I swear, Helen could run a five-star restaurant, and we'd never even need a menu."

They dug into their salads, enjoying the light and refreshing meal as they chatted about the upcoming wedding and Jessica's settling into Sydney. After a while, Jessica leaned back, stretching her arms above her head as she finished her lemonade.

"Well, that's lunch done," she said, grinning at Phyllis. "Now, it's time to get wet."

She stood up, pulling off her shorts and t-shirt to reveal the emerald-green bikini she had on underneath. Her toned, sun-kissed skin caught the light as she moved toward the pool.

Phyllis laughed, shaking her head in awe. "God, Jess, I'm glad Nathan didn't stay. You're looking toned as."

Jessica laughed, brushing her hair from her face with a carefree flick. "I like running. It works for me," she said, flashing a playful grin.

Phyllis couldn't help but chuckle as she followed her friend toward the pool. "I can tell. I need to start hitting the track more often. Maybe I'll catch up to you eventually."

"You're doing just fine," Jessica teased, her confidence radiating as she dipped her toes into the cool water. "But if you want to race, I'm game."

Phyllis laughed, shaking her head. "You're on, but don't say I didn't warn you!"

The two of them laughed together, their carefree energy blending seamlessly with the warm afternoon sun, knowing that nothing could interrupt the peaceful, perfect moment.

Phyllis raised an eyebrow. "You sure you want to get that luscious hair wet?"

Jessica grinned, flicking her hair over her shoulder. "It's time for a wash anyway, all good." With that, she launched herself into the pool with a graceful dive, her body cutting through the water effortlessly as she began swimming laps.

Phyllis watched her for a moment, a mix of admiration and envy in her gaze. Jessica moved through the water with such ease and fluidity, a clear reflection of the dedication and discipline she'd cultivated over the years.

"Show off," Phyllis muttered playfully under her breath, but there was a sparkle in her eyes as she settled back into a lounge chair, content to enjoy the view of her best friend effortlessly owning the pool.

Chapter Four

Thirty-year-old Jackson Roberts woke up on a lazy Saturday late morning in his sleek penthouse apartment, the city skyline stretching out beyond his windows. The week had been gruelling—long hours spent in court, defending his clients in the often cutthroat world of criminal law. As a criminal lawyer, it was never easy, but Jackson thrived in the intensity.

He rubbed his eyes, sitting up in bed before stretching his tall, athletic frame. Standing at six-foot-two, Jackson's body was the product of years of dedication to his physical fitness. Dark blonde hair, always neatly styled, framed his chiselled face, complementing his piercing blue eyes. His jawline was sharp, giving him a striking, almost timeless look. He was well-groomed and had a confidence in his appearance that only came from years of self-discipline and hard work.

He moved into the bathroom, running a hand through his hair as he gazed into the mirror, momentarily lost in thought. The weight of the week lingered, but he knew a hot shower would wash away the exhaustion. Stepping under the warm stream, he let the water soak into his muscles, the tension slowly melting away.

After a quick shower, Jackson stepped out, the steam curling around him as he dressed in a pair of dark, well-fitted pants and a simple black T-shirt that hugged his athletic build, highlighting the muscles in his chest and arms. His physique was a result of both genetics and his near-daily morning runs—part of a lifestyle focused on maintaining strength and fitness.

As he finished dressing, he glanced at the clock—plenty of time before he needed to be anywhere. The dinner with his family later still hung in the back of his mind, but something felt off. A strange, unsettled feeling lingered, one he couldn't quite place. Maybe it was the weight of everything happening recently, or the tension of the evening ahead. Regardless, he couldn't shake the feeling that today was going to be different.

Sliding into the driver's seat of his sleek, dark blue BMW, the cool leather beneath his fingertips brought him a small sense of comfort. As the engine purred to life, Jackson couldn't help but feel like something had shifted in the air around him. Whatever it was, he wasn't sure, but it felt like the calm before a storm.

As he drove out of the underground carpark, his mobile rang, breaking his train of thought. Seeing Nathan's name on the screen, he smiled, hitting the green button.

"Hey, mate. What's up?"

"Hey, Jackson. Nothing, man, all good. Just checking if you're gonna be at dinner tonight," Nathan's voice was as relaxed as always, but there was a hint of something else in his tone.

"Yep, I'll be there," Jackson replied, his mind already on the evening ahead. He had agreed to attend, but he didn't quite understand why his parents were so insistent.

In the background, he heard voices—faint but unmistakable.

"Who you with?" Jackson asked, his curiosity piqued.

"Just having lunch with Terry," Nathan replied, his voice a bit distracted as if talking to someone else at the same time.

Jackson chuckled, shaking his head. "Terry, huh? What's he up to?"

"Same old. We just met up for lunch. Anyway, just wanted to confirm. You're gonna be at dinner, right? Should be a good time."

"Of course, mate, but what's so important about tonight?" Jackson asked, his thoughts lingering on the dinner, but his mind still restless. Something felt off, but he wasn't sure what. He hoped a good meal with the family would settle things for him.

"You'll see. See you tonight," Nathan said quickly, and Jackson could hear him turning his attention back to his lunch plans.

After ending the call, Jackson took a moment to think about the conversation. Something felt like it was coming to a head—he could sense it, but the details eluded him.

With that nagging thought still in his mind, Jackson decided to shake it off for a moment. He needed a bit of space to think things through. After all, it had been a long week. He drove to his favourite café, enjoying the quiet solitude that came with sipping a coffee in his favourite corner. It was a brief respite from the whirlwind of his thoughts.

After a leisurely lunch, Jackson decided it was time to head to his parents' home in Bellevue Hill. He drove through the familiar streets of Sydney, the city's pulse quiet in the mid-afternoon lull. As he made his way up the long, winding driveway of his family's estate, he couldn't help but feel a sense of anticipation, though he wasn't entirely sure why. It was still hours before dinner, but he knew his father would keep him occupied.

As he entered the grand house, the soft murmur of his mother's voice greeted him. "Your father is on the terrace," she said with a smile, clearly delighted to see him.

Jackson nodded, heading toward the terrace at the back of the house. He found his father standing just inside the terrace doors, gazing out over the pool, his hands clasped behind his back as if contemplating something.

"What's so interesting?" Jackson asked, raising an eyebrow.

His father turned slightly and smiled. "Hi, son."

Jackson followed his father's gaze, curious. What could possibly capture his father's attention like this?

It didn't take long for Jackson to see what his father was looking at. And when he did, his stomach dropped.

There, at the edge of the pool's shimmering water, stood a vision. She was tall—close to six feet—and her body was toned and strong, every inch defined with effortless power. Her auburn hair, soft and wavy, cascaded down her back, catching the sunlight with every movement. She wore a striking emerald-green bikini, the vibrant colour contrasting beautifully with her sun-kissed skin. Every movement she made exuded confidence, grace, and undeniable allure. Jackson's gaze lingered on her, captivated by how perfectly she fit into the scene.

Then, without a moment's hesitation, she flicked back her gorgeous hair and made a graceful dive into the clear water. She began swimming laps, her movements fluid and rhythmic, the water parting effortlessly around her.

Jackson stood frozen, his thoughts racing. It took him a moment to catch his breath as his father's amused chuckle broke the spell.

"Who the hell is that?" he asked, his voice strained as he tried to hide the surprise that flooded through him.

His father chuckled, a low, knowing sound. "Jackson, that's Jessica."

Jackson's eyes widened in disbelief. "Phyllis's Jessica?" He repeated, still trying to process the image before him. He never expected to see her like this. The shy, unassuming girl he remembered from years ago had transformed into someone completely different, someone who seemed to radiate confidence and allure.

His father's amused smile remained, but there was a hint of something more in his eyes. "I think you might be in for a surprise, son."

Jackson stood frozen, still stunned by the sight before him. The transformation was immense, and the impact it had on him was immediate. His mind struggled to process the change, the girl he once thought of as 'Phyllis's plain friend' now standing before him as something entirely different—someone utterly captivating. The way she moved, the effortless grace with which she swam, it was as though she had become a completely new person in the years since he'd last seen her.

He had no idea what to expect from the evening, but one thing was already crystal clear: Jessica was no longer the shy, awkward girl he remembered. She had grown into someone he couldn't ignore, someone who made an immediate and undeniable impact.

Mary entered the room with a smile, but the moment she saw the tension in Jackson's posture, she hesitated. "John, we have another guest for dinner tonight."

John, who had been focused on the evening's preparations, turned away from his son's shocked face. "Who, darling?"

"Terry," Mary replied, her tone casual, though she clearly didn't notice the way Jackson's expression hardened. "Nathan called and asked if he could come. He wants Terry to meet Jessica and apparently help her find her new home." Her eyes rested on Jackson and explained. "She's moving to Sydney and needs all the assistance she can get."

Jackson's jaw tightened at the mention of Terry. The thought of Nathan's friend—the suave, handsome, and exceedingly wealthy real estate agent—being involved in Jessica's life, sent a surge of irritation through him. "Damn Nathan," he muttered under his breath, his stomach knotting. It felt like yet another way his best friend was getting too close to something he wasn't sure he even had the right to claim.

Mary, oblivious to the tension in the room, continued chatting, but John, ever perceptive, raised an eyebrow as he glanced between Jackson and his wife. "Jackson, you seem… less than thrilled about the guest list. I thought you liked Terry?"

Jackson's hands clenched into fists at his sides, his knuckles turning white for a brief moment. He quickly forced the tension out of his body, smoothing over the unease that was building inside him. "I do," he said, voice flat, trying to mask the unsettling feeling tightening in his chest. "Just tired, that's all."

John gave him a sceptical look but didn't push further, though he could tell something was off. Jackson's attempt to shrug it off barely fooled him. Still, he let it slide, turning back to Mary. "Well, it'll be good to have Terry over. He's a solid guy, and you'll enjoy the company, son."

Jackson's eyes darted to the door as the sound of laughter grew louder. Phyllis and Jessica entered, the energy between them infectious, as they breezed through the terrace doors. Jessica, still in her emerald-green bikini, was holding her discarded clothes and a towel, her long auburn hair still damp from the pool. Her sun-kissed skin glowed, but Jackson's attention was drawn to the way she moved—confident and effortless, a far cry from the shy girl he had once known.

Phyllis, grinning ear to ear, noticed him first. "Hello, big brother!" she called out, planting a quick kiss on his cheek. "You're here early."

Jackson's gaze flickered to Jessica, who seemed to freeze for a split second before she quickly looked away, her shoulders tensing. Her eyes didn't meet his, but the faintest hint of something—embarrassment, or maybe just discomfort—passed over her features.

He opened his mouth to say something, but the words caught in his throat. Instead, he gave a stiff nod, trying to ignore the strange pull in his chest. "Yeah, I got here early," he managed, his voice flat, as he took in Jessica's presence.

Jessica, feeling the weight of Jackson's stare, gave a tight smile and quickly dropped her eyes to the ground, as if trying to avoid further attention. "Hello, Jackson," she said softly, her voice carrying a note of politeness, but there was something in her tone that made him feel like she was keeping her distance.

Phyllis, ever the cheerful one, didn't seem to notice the tension. "We had such a great time by the pool! The water was perfect." She beamed at Jessica, who gave a small smile in return, though her discomfort was evident.

Jackson took a deep breath, trying to ignore the knot in his stomach. He had never imagined seeing Jessica like this—radiant, confident, and somehow... distant.

"You look good, Jess," Jackson said, his voice thick with uncertainty as he tried to push through the tension in the room. The words felt awkward, like they didn't belong to him.

"Thanks," Jessica replied distantly, not even glancing his way as she adjusted her towel and clothes. Jackson's chest tightened, the familiar comfort he once felt around her now replaced with a strange, prickling discomfort.

Mary, oblivious to the silent tension, spoke up. "Jessica, Nathan is bringing Terry to dinner tonight."

Phyllis, bouncing with excitement, turned to Jessica. "Oh Jess, you'll love him! He's such a nice guy," she gushed, nudging her friend playfully. "He's single, you know and gorgeous."

Jessica let out a light laugh, the sound light and clear—like a melody, Jackson thought, the most wonderful sound he had ever heard. "For goodness sake, Phyll, I only just got back," Jessica responded with a chuckle, she glanced quickly at Jackson before turning her attention back to Phyllis.

"If he's helping you find a home, you'll be spending plenty of time with him," Phyllis teased, grinning mischievously as she grabbed Jessica's arm and began to tug her towards the stairs. "Come on, we need to wash your hair and make it look beautiful for Terry. You look like a drowned rat."

Jackson couldn't help the small smile that tugged at his lips. He thought Jessica looked nothing like a drowned rat—she was effortlessly beautiful, even with damp hair and a towel wrapped around her.

John chuckled, shaking his head as he watched his wife turn toward the kitchen. "Poor Jessica, Phyllis will have her married off before we know it," he said with a fond smile, clearly amused by his daughter's enthusiasm.

Mary laughed softly, her voice warm with affection. "Well, whoever he is, he will be a lucky guy," she replied, turning to leave the room. "I'll leave you two men to talk about whatever it is you talk about."

John looked at his son, his expression thoughtful. "Come on, Jackson, let's head to my study. I need a drink."

"Good idea," Jackson replied, sensing the need for a change of pace.

The two of them moved toward the study, the quiet of the house enveloping them as they left the bustle of the living area behind.

John poured two drinks from the decanter on his desk, handing one to Jackson before settling into his chair behind the large mahogany desk. He took a sip, savouring the taste as he looked at his son.

"So how long is Jessica staying here?" Jackson asked, his tone casual but his mind still drifting back to the pool.

John leaned back in his chair, swirling his drink. "As long as she likes. She's been transferred to the Sydney office of her engineering firm. She's looking for a place of her own, but your mother and I have been hoping she'll stay with us for a while longer. We've missed her. She's such a lovely girl."

Jackson nodded, a bit of curiosity creeping in. "So, she's doing well?"

John chuckled softly. "Well? That's an understatement. She finished her civil engineering degree with honours, landed a job at one of the top engineering firms in the city, and now she's looking to buy a place. She's been nothing short of outstanding. I couldn't be prouder of her. To do all that, and without her parents… God rest their souls. When I promised my best friend, I'd take care of his daughter if anything happened to him, I never thought I'd actually have to. But Jess? She's made your mother and me incredibly proud. More than I could ever put into words."

Jackson nodded, his own thoughts momentarily distant. He hadn't realised how much Jessica had accomplished since leaving for Perth, and hearing his father's praise for her made something stir inside him. He remembered the shy girl who had often seemed lost in Phyllis's shadow. And now… now she was someone entirely different. Strong. Independent. Beautiful.

"That's impressive," Jackson replied, trying to keep his tone neutral. "Sounds like she's really got her life together."

John looked at him, a slight smile playing on his lips. "She does. She's a fighter, that one. Your mother and I have always believed in her. And she's proved us right every step of the way."

Chapter Five

Jessica stepped into the shower, the warm water washing away the lingering tension from the afternoon. As the steam filled the small bathroom, her thoughts drifted back to Jackson. His surprise when he saw her, the way he looked at her as though he was seeing her for the first time, and that tight jaw of his that didn't escape her notice. She let the water cascade over her, trying to focus on the rhythm of the droplets hitting her skin rather than the whirlwind of thoughts in her mind.

You need to get it together, she told herself, mentally shaking off the butterflies that seemed to flutter every time she thought about him. You've come so far, Jessica. You're stronger than that.

The words were a reminder to herself more than anything. She had spent so many years building herself into someone who could stand tall, not just in a room full of strangers, but in front of her own reflection. She'd worked for everything she had, and she wasn't about to let anyone—least of all Jackson—undermine that.

He means nothing to you, she silently reminded herself. Just focus on the bigger picture. You have a life to build here. You don't need to let someone like him—who barely knew you—make you feel like this.

As she finished her shower, the warm water running down her back, she took a deep breath, trying to centre herself. She'd made it through so much more difficult things. She could handle this, too. You've got this, Jessica.

When she stepped out of the shower, the steam swirled around her like a cocoon, and she dried off quickly, wrapping a towel around her body. She could already hear Phyllis talking animatedly in the hallway. Soon, they'd be back to the carefree moments of their teenage years, drying each other's hair and chatting about everything and nothing. That felt like the right distraction— one she could handle without letting her mind wander back to Jackson.

Phyllis walked into Jessica's room, talking on her mobile phone. "Okay, I'll see you soon, love you," she said before hanging up.

Looking over at Jessica, she grinned as she held up the hairdryer. "Alright, let's get your hair looking spectacular," she said, her voice upbeat and enthusiastic.

Jessica, still in her towel, sat down in front of the mirror. She gave Phyllis a big smile, shaking off the tension that had been hanging over her since the awkward encounter with Jackson earlier. "Thanks, Phyllis. You're the best hairdresser I know."

Phyllis got to work with a smile.

Jessica looked at her reflection in the mirror, her eyes widening slightly as she took in the results. Phyllis had worked her usual magic—her hair was smooth, shiny, and styled in soft waves that framed her face perfectly. She looked…different. Not just physically, but confident too. The reflection staring back at her was a reminder of everything she'd accomplished in her life, and for a moment, she felt like she could take on anything.

"You weren't kidding," Jessica said with a soft laugh, her tone light. "It's perfect. Thanks again, Phyll."

Phyllis beamed, pleased with her handiwork. "Of course! You're always going to look amazing, Jess. Now, let's get you into something that'll make you feel just as great as your hair looks."

Jessica stood up and walked to the closet, her hand brushing lightly over the fabric of the dress she had chosen for dinner. It was elegant yet simple—nothing too flashy, just a black dress that hugged her figure in all the right places. It felt right for the occasion. She hadn't planned on making an impression tonight, but somehow, everything was aligning to make her feel like she could stand out if she wanted to. She pulled the dress from its hanger and began to slip it on.

"Are you excited to meet Terry?" Phyllis asked from where she was perched on the bed, waiting for Jessica to finish getting ready.

Jessica paused for a moment, her thoughts drifting to Terry, if Nathan thinks he is a nice guy, then he was a nice guy, she had no doubt about that. He was going to help her find a home, after all.

"I'm just… focused on getting settled in Sydney," Jessica replied, her voice steady but guarded. "I'll meet Terry, see what he has to offer, and then go from there. It's just another step in all of this."

Phyllis nodded, standing up and walking over to the mirror, her eyes glinting with understanding. "You know, Jess, you're amazing. You've got this. You're doing so well."

Jessica smiled, feeling her confidence grow. "Thanks, Phyllis. I needed to hear that."

Once she finished getting dressed, she turned to face her friend, taking in the full effect of her appearance in the mirror. She looked good. No, she looked great. Now all she needed was to show everyone, especially herself, that she could handle whatever came her way.

With a final glance at her reflection, Jessica walked out of the room, ready to face the evening ahead. As she turned the corner, she nearly collided with Nathan, who stepped forward just in time to steady her.

"Whoa," Nathan said, his hands landing gently on her shoulders before quickly dropping back to his sides. "Wow, Jess, you look bloody beautiful."

Jessica blinked, caught off guard by the compliment, but the words warmed her. "Thanks, Nathan. And thank your amazing fiancée," she said, gesturing to Phyllis, who had just joined them in the hallway. "It's all her doing."

Phyllis grinned, clearly pleased with herself. "It's all about making sure my best friend looks her best," she teased, winking at Jessica.

Nathan chuckled, taking a moment to look Jessica over once more. His gaze lingered for just a second too long before he cleared his throat. "Well, you definitely knocked it out of the park. I mean, you always look great, but tonight… wow."

Jessica couldn't help but feel a little self-conscious under the intensity of his gaze, though she quickly masked it with a smile. "You're not so bad yourself," she replied, her voice light and playful.

Phyllis raised an eyebrow, a teasing glint in her eye. "I think we're going to have trouble keeping Terry away from her tonight, Nathan," she said, elbowing him lightly.

Nathan laughed, "I think so, he's a great guy, Jess."

Jessica nodded, feeling a mix of emotions. "I'm sure he is, hopefully it won't take long to find something."

"Well, we're here for you," Nathan said with a warm smile. "And Terry's going to be great. He's got tons of ideas for your house hunting, trust me."

Phyllis, ever the optimist, clapped her hands together. "Alright, let's get this party started! Come on, Jess, let's make sure you enjoy yourself tonight."

Jessica nodded, ready to face whatever the evening had in store. Taking a deep breath, she walked past Nathan and Phyllis, her steps steady and confident as she descended the stairs.

Jessica felt her heart skip a beat as she entered the living room. Terry and John stood by the fireplace; his posture relaxed yet exuding a quiet confidence. He was tall, with dark hair that had just the right amount of tousled charm, and his smile was warm, genuine. His eyes met hers, and for a brief moment, she forgot to breathe.

"Ah, there you are, Jessica," John said with a grin, placing a hand on her shoulder and guiding her towards Terry. "Come meet Terry."

Terry's smile widened as he turned to face her. "It's a pleasure to finally meet you, Jessica," he said, his voice smooth with a hint of curiosity, like he was trying to read her in a way that felt almost personal.

Jessica extended her hand, smiling politely despite the flutter of nerves in her stomach. "Nice to meet you, Terry. I've heard a lot about you."

Terry's handshake was firm yet gentle, his touch lingering just a moment longer than necessary. "All good things, I hope," he said, a playful glint in his eyes.

"Of course," Jessica replied, feeling the faint warmth of a blush creeping to her cheeks. She couldn't deny there was a certain magnetism about him, something that made her momentarily forget the tension of the evening.

Meanwhile, across the room, Jackson was engaged in a light conversation with his mother, Mary, but his attention was far from their discussion. His eyes were fixed on Jessica. She looked stunning—elegant, poised, and confident. While he'd been caught off guard by her earlier in her bikini, now, in that dress with her hair styled to perfection, she was breathtaking. A knot of something unnameable tightened in his chest, but he shook it off.

Phyllis, ever the social butterfly, jumped in to steer the conversation. "So, Terry, are you going to find Jess the perfect home?"

Terry grinned, his gaze lingering on Jessica. "I'll certainly try my best. I've already started looking into some properties that I think will really suit your needs. I'm confident we'll find something great."

Jessica raised a sceptical eyebrow, though she couldn't hide her amusement. "I appreciate that. It's a bit overwhelming, honestly. I'm not exactly experienced when it comes to house-hunting."

"Don't worry," Terry said warmly. "That's what I'm here for. We'll take it one step at a time. By the end of this, you'll feel like a seasoned pro."

Jessica chuckled softly, the sound light and genuine. "I'll hold you to that."

Terry leaned forward slightly, his tone curious but professional. "What's your budget?"

Jessica told him the figure, her voice calm yet firm.

Terry whistled, visibly impressed. "That's a healthy budget."

"It sure is," John interjected, his tone faintly curious as he studied Jessica.

Sensing the question behind his words, Jessica offered a small, confident smile. "I invested the money from my parents' estate. Made a few strategic moves and turned a good profit."

Phyllis blinked in astonishment, her admiration clear. "Jess, you never cease to amaze me."

John's chest puffed with pride as he beamed at her. "I couldn't agree more," he said warmly.

Jessica glanced around; her confidence bolstered by the warm support from everyone—everyone except one. Jackson. His expression was hard to read, but there was an undeniable edge to it, almost as if he were angry. She frowned inwardly, the thought prickling at her. What right does he have to be angry at me?

Before she could dwell on it further, Helen appeared in the doorway, her cheerful voice breaking the tension. "Dinner is served, everyone."

Terry turned to Jessica with a charming smile, holding out his arm. "Shall we?"

Jessica hesitated only for a moment before returning his smile. "We shall," she said, slipping her arm through his.

As they made their way to the dining room, Jessica resisted the urge to glance back at Jackson, refusing to let his mood affect her. Instead, she focused on the easy warmth of Terry's company, determined to enjoy the evening ahead.

The scent of roasted lamb, garlic, and herbs filled the air, mingling with the faint aroma of wine being poured into glasses. Jessica took her seat beside Terry, her fingers grazing the edge of her napkin as she glanced at the elegant table arrangement. The soft glow of the chandelier above added a warm intimacy to the room, though she couldn't quite shake the weight of Jackson's gaze from across the table. His dark eyes were fixed on her, intent and assessing, as though he were waiting to catch her off guard. Quickly, she looked away, forcing a polite smile as Terry pulled out her chair before settling into his own seat beside her.

"So, Jessica," Terry began, leaning toward her slightly with an easy, open smile, his tone light and conversational, "what made you decide to move back to Sydney?"

Jessica returned his smile, grateful for the friendly tone. "When Phyllis asked me to be her maid of honour, I realised how much I missed her—and John and Mary, too. They've always been like family to me. So, I asked my firm if I could transfer to Sydney, and they agreed. And here I am."

"That's wonderful," Terry said, his voice warm with approval. "What sort of work do you do?"

Jessica chuckled lightly. "I'm a civil engineer."

Phyllis, who had been sipping her wine, chimed in with a teasing grin. "Yeah, Terry, she told me she works with more men than she can poke a stick at."

Jessica laughed, shaking her head. "That's not exactly how I put it, Phyll." She turned to Terry, her tone good-natured but explanatory. "It's a very male-dominated field, so yes, I do work with a lot of men."

Nathan, seated further down the table, leaned forward with a mischievous smirk. "Yeah, I bet they can't keep their eyes off you." His teasing tone filled the room with a ripple of laughter.

Jessica blushed, her cheeks warming as she looked down at her plate. "It's not like that," she said, trying to suppress her own amused smile.

Terry gave her an encouraging grin. "I'm sure you more than hold your own. Civil engineering isn't easy—you must be incredible at what you do."

Jessica's blush deepened, though she appreciated the compliment. "Thank you, Terry. It's challenging, but I love it. I enjoy seeing a project come to life, knowing I had a hand in making it happen."

From across the table, Jackson's fork paused mid-cut, his dark eyes narrowing as he watched the exchange. His jaw tightened almost imperceptibly, and though his expression remained outwardly calm, Jessica couldn't miss the way his gaze lingered on her—sharp and unreadable.

She forced herself not to look his way, focusing instead on Terry, whose kind and engaging demeanour helped to ease her nerves. But the sensation of Jackson's unyielding attention remained, a silent weight she couldn't quite ignore.

Across the table, Jackson's fork clinked against his plate a little too sharply, drawing Jessica's attention despite herself. His expression was neutral, but his eyes held something unreadable.

"So, Jessica," Jackson interjected, his voice calm but carrying an edge that cut through the light-hearted atmosphere, "what exactly are you looking for in a home? Big, small, modern? Or is it just about location?"

Jessica's polite smile faltered ever so slightly. She reached for her water glass, taking a measured sip to collect her thoughts before answering. "Location is definitely a major consideration," she said evenly. "I believe I can afford something nice, but I'm not looking for anything too extravagant." Her tone was polite, but there was a noticeable restraint—a stark contrast to the warmth she'd shown Terry moments earlier.

Jackson nodded slowly, his gaze fixed on her, probing. "Makes sense. But it's a big decision. Don't you think it might help to have someone who knows the market—someone with experience—guide you through it?"

Jessica's fingers tightened around her glass, the tension in her posture subtle but undeniable. "That's why I have Terry," she replied, her tone cool, though her tight smile didn't quite reach her eyes. She turned deliberately back to her plate, signalling the end of that particular discussion.

Terry, ever the diplomat, laughed lightly, breaking the awkward pause. "Don't worry, Jackson. I've got it covered," he said, giving Jessica a reassuring pat on her arm. "I'll find her the perfect home soon enough."

Mary, sensing the shift in energy, chimed in with her usual warmth. "Not too soon, Terry. I don't want to lose Jessica too fast."

John nodded in agreement, his voice steady and affectionate. "Exactly. We only just got her back. Let's not rush her out the door."

Jessica smiled at Mary and John, their support like a balm against the simmering tension. "Don't worry," she said softly. "I'm not going anywhere just yet."

Jackson's jaw tightened imperceptibly, his fork pausing mid-motion. But he said nothing, his gaze dropping to his plate as the conversation moved on without him.

By the time dessert was served, Jessica felt as though she'd run a marathon. Her interactions with Terry had been light and enjoyable, but Jackson's presence across the table had been an unrelenting weight. Each guarded answer she gave him felt like a victory, a way to hold onto the walls she'd built around herself.

As the evening wound down, Terry turned to her with a smile. "I'll send you some property listings tomorrow. Maybe we can visit a few later this week?"

"That sounds great," Jessica replied, genuinely grateful for his kindness.

From across the table, Jackson's jaw tightened, his gaze lingering on her for a moment longer than necessary.

Jessica met his eyes briefly, her expression unreadable, before turning her attention back to Terry. She wasn't going to let Jackson rattle her—not tonight. Tonight, she would focus on the people who made her feel welcome, not the one who seemed determined to unsettle her.

Chapter Six

Jackson wasn't sure why he had decided to stay the night at his parents' house. He'd told his mother he'd had a bit too much wine at dinner, but that wasn't the truth. The real reason was Jessica. There was something about her that tugged at him, something he couldn't quite explain. It wasn't just her transformation or the way she looked—though he'd be lying if he said her beauty didn't captivate him. No, it was more than that. It was the way she carried herself, radiating strength, confidence, and a quiet happiness that seemed unshakable. He wanted to be near her, even if she clearly didn't feel the same.

After changing into his usual gym shorts and a T-shirt, Jackson decided to go for a run. Running had always been his way to clear his mind, and after the awkwardness of last night, he needed it. Heading out to the porch to stretch before starting, he froze mid-step.

There she was. Jessica.

Dressed in sleek gym gear that hugged her athletic frame, she was bent forward, stretching her hamstrings, completely absorbed in her warm-up. Earbuds were firmly in place, her head lightly bobbing to whatever music she was listening to. She hadn't noticed him yet, which gave him a moment to take her in without interruption.

The sight of her, so focused and self-assured, sent an odd pang through his chest. How had he not seen her before—*truly* seen *her?*

Shaking the thought away, he approached her and tapped her lightly on the shoulder.

Jessica jumped, startled, and spun around, pulling out one of her earbuds. "Oh!" she exclaimed, her green eyes wide. When she saw who it was, her expression cooled almost instantly. "Morning, Jackson."

Her tone was polite but distant, her indifference cutting deeper than he expected.

"Morning, Jessica," Jackson said with a smile, determined to ignore her chilly demeanour. "What are you doing up so early?"

She shrugged as she tucked a loose strand of auburn hair behind her ear. "What does it look like? I'm getting ready for a run."

"Mind if I join you?" he asked, keeping his tone casual, even though he braced himself for rejection.

Jessica hesitated, her gaze flicking to him before glancing away. "If you must," she replied coolly, turning back to her stretches without another word.

Jackson frowned, perplexed. She wasn't outright rude, but she was far from friendly. Last night, when she spoke to his family and their guests, she'd been warm and polite, her smile lighting up the room. But with him? She barely looked at him, let alone smiled.

What had he done to deserve such frost?

As they set off down the driveway and onto the quiet, tree-lined street, Jackson matched her stride, stealing a glance at her profile. Her jaw was set, her gaze fixed ahead, and she didn't say a word.

He wasn't used to being ignored, especially not by women. And yet, there was something about Jessica's aloofness that only made him more determined to figure her out.

He was impressed. Jessica could run, and she could run well. Her pace was steady, strong, and unwavering. She didn't let up or slow down, even as the early morning sun began to warm the air. Jackson, who prided himself on being fit, found himself working a little harder than usual just to keep up with her. She didn't seem to notice, though. She was entirely focused, her breathing controlled, her strides purposeful.

He admired her determination. It wasn't just the running—everything about her seemed to embody strength. She had a quiet resilience that made him want to know more, even if she insisted on keeping him at arm's length.

But his admiration turned sour as they rounded a corner and passed a construction site. A group of tradies, already hard at work, noticed Jessica and immediately started calling out.

"Hey, beautiful!" one shouted, his voice carrying across the street.

Another whistled, loud, and sharp, followed by a chorus of laughter and a few crude comments Jackson couldn't make out.

Jessica didn't falter, her eyes fixed straight ahead as if she hadn't heard them. Her expression was unreadable, but Jackson saw the faint tightening of her jaw.

It bothered him more than it should have. His hands clenched into fists as they ran past the group, his protective instincts flaring. He hated the way their leering eyes followed her, as if they had any right to her attention.

"Don't they have anything better to do?" he muttered, glancing over at her.

Jessica didn't respond immediately. She just kept running, her pace as steady as ever. Finally, she spoke, her voice cool and even. "You get used to it."

Her words made him bristle. "You shouldn't have to get used to it," he said firmly.

Jessica glanced at him briefly, her green eyes sharp. "And what do you suggest I do? Stop running? Stay indoors? Let them control what I do with their behaviour?"

"No, of course not," he said quickly, realising how his words might have sounded. "I just mean—it's not right. They shouldn't—"

"They shouldn't," she agreed, cutting him off. "But they do. And they will. So, I ignore it and keep moving."

Her calm acceptance of the situation unsettled him. She didn't sound bitter or angry, just resigned, and that only made him angrier. She shouldn't have to accept it.

They ran in silence for a while after that, the rhythm of their footsteps the only sound between them. Jackson stole another glance at her, but her face was unreadable again, her focus firmly ahead.

He wasn't sure what frustrated him more—the fact that she had to deal with that kind of harassment or the fact that she wouldn't let him see how it affected her.

They eventually made it back to the house, both slightly winded but steady. The early morning sun was brighter now, casting a warm glow over the yard as they moved into a cooldown routine. Jessica stretched effortlessly, her movements fluid and precise, while Jackson stole glances at her, still mulling over what had happened earlier.

"Do you get that kind of attention a lot?" he asked, unable to let it go.

Jessica glanced at him, her green eyes calm but distant. A half-smile curved her lips, but it didn't reach her eyes. "Yes."

That was it? Jackson waited for her to elaborate, but she didn't. She simply moved into another stretch, her expression unbothered.

"And it doesn't bother you?" he pressed.

"Why should it?" she said, her tone almost casual. "If I see a good-looking guy, I look and appreciate the… beauty. They're doing the same, just being a little more vocal about it than I would be." She straightened and moved into a forward bend, holding the stretch with ease. "And besides, if it did bother me, I wouldn't be working in the field I'm in. I get a lot… and I mean a lot of male attention at work."

Jackson's jaw tightened. He didn't like the idea of other men leering at her, but he wasn't sure he had the right to feel that way. She wasn't his—not even close. Still, the thought of men making inappropriate comments or ogling her at work made his chest tighten with something uncomfortably close to jealousy.

"Is that why you did civil engineering?" Jackson asked, eager to steer the conversation toward safer ground—or so he thought.

Jessica paused mid-stretch and turned to him, arching a perfectly shaped brow. "Really?" she said, her tone laced with dry amusement. "What do you think, Jackson? Do you honestly believe I was so starved for male attention that I deliberately chose to work in a field dominated by men?"

Jackson opened his mouth to respond but closed it just as quickly, caught off guard by the sharpness in her tone. "That's not what I meant," he said, raising his hands in defence.

"Oh?" She straightened, crossing her arms over her chest as she fixed him with a steady, almost challenging look. "Then enlighten me. What did you mean?"

He sighed, running a hand through his hair. "I didn't mean anything by it, Jessica. I was just curious."

She tilted her head, her green eyes narrowing slightly. "Curious about what, exactly? Why would a woman choose a profession where she'd have to constantly prove herself? Why I'd want to work alongside men who sometimes don't take me seriously until I make them? Or are you just trying to figure out if there's some deep psychological reason behind my career choice?"

Jackson shifted uncomfortably under her scrutiny. "I didn't mean it like that," he repeated, his voice quieter this time. "I guess I just… admire it. Civil engineering isn't exactly an easy path."

Jessica's stance softened slightly, though her expression remained guarded. "It's not," she admitted, her tone more even now. "But I didn't choose it because I needed validation or because I wanted to make a statement. I chose it because

I love it. I love solving problems, building things that last, creating something tangible. And yeah, maybe I also enjoy proving people wrong when they underestimate me. But mostly? I just wanted to do something that made me feel proud at the end of the day."

Jackson nodded slowly, her words sinking in. "That's… impressive," he said honestly.

"Is it?" she asked, a wry smile tugging at her lips. "Because I'm pretty sure five minutes ago, you were picturing me surrounded by male coworkers and thinking how tough that must be for me."

He winced, realising how poorly his earlier question had come across. "Okay, I deserved that," he admitted. "But for the record, I wasn't judging you. I was just… trying to understand."

Jessica studied him for a moment, her expression unreadable. Then she let out a small sigh and uncrossed her arms. "Fair enough," she said, her tone softening further. "I guess I'm used to people making assumptions. Especially you."

Jackson was taken aback, her words hitting him harder than he expected. "What do you mean by that?" he asked, frowning.

Jessica tilted her head, her eyes sharp but calm, as if she had been waiting for this moment. "Come on, Jackson," she said, her voice steady but edged with a hint of bitterness. "You made it perfectly clear how insignificant I was before I left for Perth. What's changed? I'm still the same person—I just don't look so… unattractive anymore. Or plain. Wasn't that how you described me?"

Her words felt like a punch to the gut, and for a moment, Jackson was at a loss. He remembered those words, all right—words he hadn't even realised she'd overheard. They'd been said offhandedly, in a private conversation with his sister and best friend, but now they hung in the air between them like a wall he wasn't sure how to break through.

"Jessica," he began, his voice quieter now, "I—"

She held up a hand, cutting him off. "It's fine, Jackson. I'm not bringing it up to make you feel guilty. I've moved past it. I had to. But let's not pretend you're suddenly interested in me because I'm the same girl I was back then. I'm not. You wouldn't have given me the time of day five years ago."

"That's not fair," he said, stepping closer. "I—"

"Isn't it?" she countered, her eyes narrowing slightly. "Be honest with yourself, Jackson. If I showed up today looking exactly how I used to, would you even notice me? Would you even bother to talk to me?"

He opened his mouth to respond but faltered, her words cutting deeper than he wanted to admit. Had he been so shallow back then? Had he dismissed her simply because she didn't fit the image of what he thought he wanted?

Jessica sighed, her expression softening but her guard still firmly in place. "Look, I've dealt with worse. But don't stand here and act like you're interested in understanding me now when you didn't care to back then."

"I was an idiot," he said suddenly, his voice firm.

Jessica blinked, startled by his bluntness.

"I was shallow and stupid," he continued, his gaze locking onto hers. "I judged you without really seeing you, and that's on me. But I'm not that guy anymore, Jessica. And if you'll give me the chance, I'd like to prove that to you."

She stared at him for a long moment, her expression unreadable. Then she shook her head, a faint, almost wistful smile tugging at her lips. "You don't have to prove anything, Jackson," she said softly. "I'm not looking for anything from you. I just want to get through this wedding and start my new life here."

Her words stung, but he nodded, knowing he couldn't push her. "Fair enough," he said, stepping back. His voice softened as he continued, "But for what it's worth, I do see you now, Jessica. And I'm sorry it took me this long to realise how incredible you are—not just because of how you look. It's the way you built a life for yourself after losing your parents, the way you graduated with honours, the way you handle the challenges of your work with strength and grace. It's how you treat the people who matter to you, how you've planned for your future, and how you carry yourself with confidence. That's what I see, and it's all you."

Jessica's eyes flickered with something—surprise, perhaps, or a glimmer of vulnerability—but she quickly masked it, her expression slipping back into neutrality. "Thanks," she said quietly, her tone hard to read.

Without another word, she turned and headed into the house, leaving Jackson standing there in the quiet morning light, watching her retreating figure. Determined and resolute, he vowed to find a way to break through the walls she had every right to keep firmly in place.

Chapter Seven

Jessica entered the house, her emotions churning. She felt like kicking herself. *Why did I let him know I overheard him? Why did I let him see that his opinion actually bothered me?* She sighed, shaking her head at her reflection in the hallway mirror. *You're an idiot, Jessica. You were supposed to be indifferent, remember?*

Determined to brush it off, she headed upstairs for a shower. As the warm water cascaded over her, she took a deep breath, trying to wash away the lingering frustration. She wouldn't let Jackson get under her skin again.

Afterward, she slipped into a cheerful yellow sundress, her mood lifting slightly as the fabric hugged her in all the right places. She swept her auburn hair into a high ponytail, accentuating the graceful curve of her neck. *There,* she thought, giving herself a nod in the mirror. *You're untouchable.*

Downstairs, she found Mary and John already enjoying their morning coffee in the bright, sunlit dining room.

"Morning, Mary. Morning, John. How are you two this morning?" she greeted with a warm smile.

"Morning, Jess," they replied in unison, their voices cheerful.

"No Phyllis yet?" Jessica asked, glancing around.

Mary chuckled. "You know Sundays are her lazy days. She'll roll out of bed eventually, and then she and Nathan will head over to his parents' place for lunch."

Jessica smiled knowingly, imagining her best friend's relaxed routine.

John looked up from his coffee. "What are your plans for today, Jess?"

Before she could answer, Jackson entered the dining room, freshly showered and dressed in a crisp white shirt and jeans. Jessica noticed him but kept her expression neutral.

"I'm going to visit Mum and Dad today," she replied softly. It had been too long—she hadn't visited their graves since the funeral. Now that she'd decided to stay in Sydney, that would change.

Mary's brow furrowed in concern. "Oh, how are you getting there?"

Jessica shrugged lightly. "Probably an Uber," she said brightly, not wanting to make a fuss.

John shook his head. "No, that won't do. If you wait until after lunch, I'll take you."

Jessica waved him off, her tone cheerful. "It's fine, John, really. I'm happy to take an Uber."

"I'll take you," Jackson said quickly, his voice cutting through the conversation.

Jessica turned to him, her brows arching in mild surprise. "That's not necessary, Jackson. I can manage."

"I insist," he said firmly, meeting her gaze. "It's no trouble, and it's better than you going alone."

Mary glanced between them, sensing the tension but choosing to stay out of it.

Jessica hesitated, her walls firmly in place. "I appreciate the offer, but—"

"Jess," John interrupted gently, "let Jackson take you. It'll give you some company, and we'll feel better knowing you're not on your own."

Jessica glanced at Jackson again, his expression unreadable but determined. She didn't want to accept, but she also didn't want to turn it into a bigger deal than it needed to be. Finally, she nodded.

"Fine," she said, her tone measured. "But don't expect me to entertain you on the drive."

Jackson smirked faintly, sensing her guardedness. "Wouldn't dream of it," he replied, already planning how to make the most of the time with her.

After finishing her light breakfast, Jessica turned back to Mary and John, plastering on a polite smile.

"Thank you, both," Jessica said, her tone polite but distant. Then, turning to Jackson, she added, "I'll just get my things and wait for you when you're ready to leave."

As she left the room, her yellow sundress swaying lightly with each step, Jackson's eyes lingered on her retreating figure. His resolve hardened. He had offered to drive her out of a genuine desire to help—but he couldn't deny that it was also another chance to chip away at the walls she had so firmly built around her heart.

"Jackson," his father's voice broke through his thoughts.

"Yes, Dad?" Jackson turned, his brow furrowing slightly at the concerned look on John's face.

"You keep an eye on her," John said gravely, setting his coffee cup down. "I don't think she's going to be as strong as she thinks she is when she gets to the graves. That kind of thing has a way of sneaking up on you."

Jackson nodded, understanding the weight of the moment. "I will, Dad. Don't worry."

Mary, who had been quietly listening, chimed in, her tone soft and reflective. "She was extremely close to her parents," she began, glancing toward the doorway where Jessica had disappeared. "I'll never forget the day we had to tell her."

John sighed deeply; his expression clouded with memory. "Terrible day," he agreed, his voice heavy with regret.

Mary nodded wistfully. "She didn't cry much, you know. Not at first. Just stood there, looking lost. It wasn't until later, when she thought no one was watching, that the tears came. Broke my heart to see it."

Jackson felt a pang of guilt he couldn't quite place. He wasn't there for her back then, and the weight of his past indifference pressed harder against him now.

"I'll stay close," he said, his voice firm. "Don't worry. She won't have to face it alone."

John gave his son a nod of approval. "Good. She'll need someone. Even if she doesn't think she does."

Mary smiled softly, though her concern was still evident. "You'll do the right thing, Jackson. I know you will."

Jackson didn't respond immediately, instead glancing toward the doorway Jessica had left through. He had a feeling today would be a turning point—for her and, perhaps, for him too.

Jessica went upstairs, her steps slow and deliberate. Once in her room, she grabbed her phone and bag, checking its contents carefully. She made sure she had tissues—lots of them. She knew she would need them. The thought of standing at her parents' graves after all this time made her chest tighten. She loved them dearly, and not a day passed that she didn't miss them.

Still, she wasn't thrilled about Jackson coming along. It was kind of him to offer, sure, but she didn't want him to see her like this—vulnerable, emotional, raw. That wasn't the version of herself she wanted him to know. With a resigned sigh, she slung her bag over her shoulder and made her way back downstairs.

Jackson was already waiting for her by the front door, his posture relaxed but his expression unreadable. "Ready?" he asked softly when he saw her.

"Yes," she replied, her voice steady as she walked past him toward the car.

He followed her out, stepping ahead to open the door of his sleek blue BMW. She paused for a moment, briefly taken aback by the gesture.

"Thank you," she said quietly, slipping into the passenger seat.

He closed the door gently, walking around to the driver's side. As he slid in and started the engine, a comfortable hum filled the air, but neither of them spoke.

Jessica glanced out the window as they pulled out of the driveway, trying to focus on the passing scenery instead of the knot tightening in her stomach. She could feel Jackson's presence beside her—calm, steady, yet impossible to ignore.

After a few minutes, he broke the silence. "Have you been back to visit them since…?"

She shook her head, her gaze still fixed on the window. "No. This will be my first time."

Jackson nodded, not pressing her further. He could sense that this wasn't easy for her, and the last thing he wanted was to make it harder.

The drive continued in silence, broken only by the occasional sound of the turn signal or the faint hum of the tires on the road. Jessica's fingers tightened around the strap of her bag, her mind racing with memories of her parents—good and bad, joyful, and heartbreaking.

When they finally arrived at the cemetery, Jackson pulled into the lot but made an unexpected stop at the small in-house florist.

"Give me a minute," he said, glancing at Jessica before stepping out of the car.

Jessica watched him walk into the shop, not fully registering what he was doing. She stayed in her seat, absently looking at the nearby headstones, her mind already beginning to churn with memories.

When Jackson came back, he was holding a large bouquet of fresh flowers—roses, lilies, and sprigs of baby's breath artfully arranged. He opened the door, handed them to her, and said, "For your parents."

Jessica blinked, startled by the thoughtful gesture. "Thank you, Jackson. You didn't have to—"

He cut her off, his tone firm but kind. "I wanted to."

She looked down at the bouquet, her fingers brushing over the soft petals. The gesture touched her deeply, though she wasn't quite sure how to express it. "They're beautiful," she said softly.

Jackson gave a small nod, started the car again, and drove a little farther, carefully parking as close to her parents' graves as possible. Turning off the engine, he turned to her.

"Take your time," he said, his voice calm and steady, as if willing her to feel the same.

Jessica nodded, though her throat tightened as she reached for the door handle. Her hand trembled, the weight of the moment pressing down on her, but she quickly steadied herself, exhaling slowly.

Jackson got out first, walking around to her side to open the door. She stepped out, clutching her bag in one hand and the bouquet in the other. Her eyes scanned the rows of headstones, already zeroing in on the ones she knew so well yet hadn't seen in five long years.

"Thank you," she murmured, her voice barely above a whisper, as if afraid speaking louder would shatter the fragile strength she was holding onto.

"I'll be right here," Jackson said, his gaze meeting hers. His voice was soft but resolute, offering quiet reassurance.

Jessica nodded again, inhaling deeply and squaring her shoulders before beginning the slow walk toward her parents' graves. Each step felt heavier than the last, her heart pounding in her chest. She wasn't sure if she was ready, but she knew she had to do this—for them, and for herself.

As she reached the graves, Jackson stayed by the car, his eyes never leaving her. He watched her approach the two simple headstones, noting how she stopped a few feet away and seemed to gather her strength before kneeling down.

He tried to imagine what it would be like if he were in her position—if it were his parents lying beneath those cold stones. The thought made his chest tighten.

The loss she had endured, at such a young age, was incomprehensible to him. He knew his parents meant the world to him; losing them would shatter him. And yet Jessica had faced that reality and managed to not only survive but thrive.

That kind of strength, he realised, wasn't something you were born with—it was something forged through pain, loss, and sheer willpower. Watching her now, he felt an overwhelming sense of admiration for her. But he also felt a pang of guilt for how he had underestimated her in the past.

She knelt by the graves, placing the bouquet gently in front of them. Jackson couldn't hear what she was saying, but he could see her lips moving, her expression shifting between sorrow and something softer, almost serene. She was saying goodbye again, perhaps, or maybe just letting them know she hadn't forgotten.

Whatever it was, he could see how much it cost her. And as much as he wanted to go to her, to offer some kind of comfort, he stayed where he was. This was her moment, and he wouldn't intrude.

Instead, he waited, ready to be there when she needed him—whether she realised it or not.

Jessica knelt beside her parents' graves, her fingers trembling slightly as she placed the bouquet Jackson had bought in the small vase beside their names. The flowers were beautiful, and she could feel the weight of their significance as she arranged them carefully, as if every movement was an offering of love and gratitude.

Once she was finished, she sat back on her heels and began speaking, her voice soft but steady. She told them how much she missed them, how much their absence had left a hole in her life that no one else could fill. She talked about everything she had accomplished since their passing—her career, her degree, her independence—and how she still felt them with her, guiding her every step of the way.

"I've made it, Mum, Dad," she said, her voice thick with emotion. "I'm doing okay. I know you'd be proud." She smiled through her tears, feeling their presence in the quiet air around her.

"I'll come visit more often," she promised, her voice almost a whisper, as if she were afraid, they might not hear her if she didn't speak just loud enough.

She continued, sharing everything—her struggles, her triumphs, the moments when she wished they were there to see her grow, to cheer her on. For at least twenty minutes, she spoke as if they were still there, as if nothing had changed.

She let her heart pour out in words she had never said to anyone else, hoping they could hear, hoping they were proud.

But as the last words left her lips, a suffocating wave of grief crashed over her. The ache of missing them, of knowing she would never hear their voices again, was overwhelming. It was as if the last five years had been a blur of coping, but now, in this moment, the reality of her loss hit her all over again.

Her hands instinctively covered her face, as though that could somehow shield her from the pain. She sank lower on her knees, her shoulders shaking as her breath caught in her throat. Her body trembled as she tried to control the sobs that wracked her chest, but it was impossible. The grief was too much.

She let go, finally giving in to the sorrow that had always lingered just below the surface. Her sobs were loud and uncontrollable, raw, and heartbreaking. She wept for the parents she had lost, for the moments they would never share with her, for the empty space they had left in her heart.

As she sat there, unable to stop the tears, she didn't notice Jackson moving closer. He had been standing by the car, but now he approached quietly, not wanting to disturb her but knowing she needed someone.

Without a word, he crouched down beside her, his presence a quiet support. He didn't say anything, didn't try to comfort her with empty words. He just stayed close, giving her the space to grieve, offering the silent reassurance that she wasn't alone.

For several minutes, Jessica's sobs were the only sound in the air. Jackson remained by her side, his hand hovering near her but not touching her, as if he knew this was something she needed to do on her own.

Finally, her tears began to slow, and her sobs softened into quiet, shaky breaths. She sniffled and wiped her eyes, but it was clear she wasn't done yet. The pain was still there, buried deep beneath the surface, but for now, it was enough to simply let it out.

Jackson, ever patient, stayed with her. He offered her tissues from his pocket, wordlessly handing them to her as she wiped her face. There was no rush, no pressure—just the quiet comfort of knowing someone cared, that someone was there when she needed them most.

"Whenever you're ready, Jessica," Jackson said quietly after a moment, his voice calm and low, "I'll be here."

Chapter Eight

Once Jessica had gathered herself enough to stand, she let Jackson guide her gently, helping her back into the car. She felt exhausted—physically, emotionally, every part of her worn thin from the grief she had just released. Her head was spinning, and all she wanted was some space, but at the same time, she didn't want to be alone.

"Is it okay if we go to my apartment for a minute?" Jackson asked quietly as they started driving. "I just need to get some clothes for tonight."

Jessica nodded, not trusting her voice to say anything more. She wasn't sure what to say, but Jackson's offer to take her somewhere else felt like a small break from the emotional weight she had been carrying.

The drive was short, and soon they arrived at Jackson's building. He pulled into the parking garage, parking in his designated spot. He turned to her, his gaze soft. "Do you want to wait here, or would you like to come up?"

Jessica, still numb from everything, didn't want to be left alone, even if it meant being in Jackson's space. "I'll come up," she replied quietly.

Jackson didn't say anything else but got out and helped her out of the car, his touch warm but gentle. He guided her through the entrance and into the elevator, making sure she was steady before pressing the button for his penthouse.

When the doors opened, Jessica followed him inside but didn't seem to notice much around her. The apartment was stunning, with floor-to-ceiling windows overlooking the Sydney Harbour, but all she could do was walk toward the glass and stare. The sight of the water should have been calming, but her mind was still racing with everything that had just happened.

Jackson disappeared briefly into the bedroom, and she could hear the sounds of him moving around. She stayed by the windows, feeling small in the vastness of the room. The weight of the moment pressed down on her, but she didn't have the energy to do anything about it.

After a few minutes, Jackson returned, throwing his bag on the sofa. He moved quietly towards her, touching her lightly on the elbow. "Ready to leave?" he asked softly.

Jessica turned and looked at him, really looked at him for the first time since they had arrived. His expression was gentle, but there was something in his eyes she hadn't seen before—something vulnerable, something real. In that moment, everything seemed to slow down. The walls Jessica had spent so long building around herself, the walls she thought were impenetrable, began to crack in that instant. Everything she had kept buried, all the hurt, the loneliness, the pain from the past few years, seemed to fade into the background as Jackson's presence filled the space between them. There was something undeniable between them, a pull that neither could explain.

Before either of them could process what was happening, they found themselves in each other's arms, the intensity of the moment overriding everything else. The kiss was urgent, driven by something raw, something neither of them could control. It was a kiss of need, of longing, of emotions that had been buried too long.

Jackson's hands moved to her back, pulling her closer, as if afraid she might slip away. Jessica's fingers found their way to his shirt, gripping it, pulling him in deeper. The kiss was desperate, neither of them holding back, as if the world outside no longer mattered.

Jessica felt her heart race in her chest, her breath coming in shallow bursts. The heat of the kiss enveloped her, every nerve igniting as she felt Jackson's pulse beneath her fingertips, the urgency of it all consuming her. In that moment, there was no past, no grief, no fear of what might come next—only the intensity of the kiss, the undeniable connection between them. Their tongues clashed, a battle for dominance, but neither one wanted to pull away.

Then, almost as if on instinct, they both broke apart at the same time, gasping for air, the reality of what had just happened crashing over them.

Jessica stumbled backward, her hands shaking as she pressed them to her lips. "That was a mistake," she said, her voice trembling, as though she needed to convince herself just as much as him.

Jackson took a step toward her, his face a mixture of confusion and regret. "Jessica…"

"No!" she cut him off, her voice more forceful this time, though still laced with uncertainty. She held up her hand, as though to keep him at a distance, both physically and emotionally. "This—this can't happen."

Her heart was still pounding, and part of her wanted to believe the heat they'd shared was something worth exploring, but another part of her, the part that had been so carefully protecting herself for so long, screamed at her to stop. She couldn't let this in. She couldn't let him in.

Jackson's gaze softened, the tension between them palpable as he fought the urge to press further. He wanted to push, to make her understand that he didn't regret the kiss, that maybe this—whatever this was—could be something more. But he knew better than to take advantage of her vulnerability, especially now.

Instead, he let out a quiet breath, his voice gentle. "Let's get you home."

Jessica didn't respond right away, her eyes flickering to his before she looked away, almost as if she couldn't bear the intensity of the moment. She nodded, though, the simple movement enough for him to understand that she was ready to leave.

Jackson didn't try to touch her again, didn't push for an explanation. Instead, he turned and walked toward the elevator, his movements slow and measured. Jessica followed, her steps hesitant, her mind clearly elsewhere. He couldn't help but watch her, the way her shoulders were slumped, the tightness in her posture that had returned after the kiss.

As they stepped into the elevator and made their way to the car park, Jackson led the way, his steps deliberate, giving Jessica the space she seemed to need. The silence between them was thick, charged with unspoken tension, both unsure how to bridge the gap that had grown since the moment they'd shared in his apartment.

Once they reached the car, Jackson held the door open for her, and Jessica slid into the passenger seat without a word. As he settled behind the wheel and started the engine, the hum of the car filled the quiet. The road stretched ahead, the sun high in the sky, casting its warmth over the city as they drove in an uneasy silence.

Jackson couldn't shake the feeling that Jessica was pulling further away with each passing mile. He could almost feel the walls she'd so carefully constructed going back up. She had allowed him in, just a little, but now it seemed as though she was retreating, and he couldn't help but wonder how, or even if, he could break through those walls. He had been foolish to think that small crack meant more.

Just before they reached his parents' house, Jessica's phone buzzed in her bag. She reached for it quickly, and Jackson's eyes flickered toward her, a brief moment of curiosity gnawing at him. But he didn't ask who it was. Instead, he focused on the road, a knot tightening in his stomach as she spoke.

"Hello?" she answered, her voice light and polite.

Jackson stole another glance at her, noticing how her tone shifted as the conversation continued.

"Oh, hello, Terry, yes, I'm fine. You?"

He couldn't stop himself from feeling that sting in his chest. The way her voice softened, how she became more engaged—it made him feel like an outsider in that small exchange.

"That would be lovely," she said after listening for a moment. "Okay, I will see you tomorrow. Thank you."

Her voice had a warmth to it now, and Jackson couldn't help but notice how the distance between them seemed to close, even if only for a moment. It was fleeting, though, and the tension that had been hanging between them remained, thick and unyielding.

"Goodbye," she said quietly before slipping the phone back into her bag.

The silence settled between them once more, but this time it felt different— less tense, but more uncertain. Jackson couldn't quite pinpoint why, but he had a nagging feeling about the phone call. He knew Terry, but something about their conversation didn't sit right with him. What bothered him even more was how at ease Jessica had been with Terry, how natural their exchange had flowed, in stark contrast to the distance she kept with him. The sting of her emotional walls was sharp, and he couldn't help but feel the growing frustration and confusion beneath the surface.

When they arrived at his parents' house, Jackson parked the car with a heavy sigh, gripping the steering wheel as if it could somehow steady his racing thoughts. He didn't know how to break the silence or what to say, and it felt as though there was no way to bridge the gap between them. He could feel the shift, the distance growing, and the helplessness of not knowing how to reach her.

Jessica turned to him; her gaze soft but guarded. "Thank you for taking me," she said, her words polite but distant, as though she were already miles away emotionally.

"You're welcome," Jackson answered, his voice almost a whisper. Before he could say anything else, she was already out of the car, moving quickly toward the front door, leaving him there, unable to find the right words.

He watched her walk away, her figure retreating into the distance, each step feeling like a blow he couldn't stop. The weight of her departure pressed heavily on him, and the words he longed to say stayed lodged in his chest, unspoken. His mind kept replaying the moment they had shared—the way she felt in his arms, the way her lips had moved against his, the electric charge that had sparked between them. It wasn't just physical; it was something deeper, something that felt undeniably right.

She belonged there, with him—he felt it in every fibre of his being. But now, as she disappeared into the house, that connection felt further away than ever. And for the first time, Jackson realised just how much he wanted to fight for her. The question was, would she let him?

Jackson stepped out of the car, his steps heavy with the weight of the day, and made his way inside. The warmth of his parents' home enveloped him, but it did little to ease the knot in his chest. He found his parents sitting on the terrace, the soft hum of conversation halting as he approached.

John was the first to break the silence. "How was she?"

Jackson leaned against the doorframe; his face clouded with emotion. "She was broken," he admitted, his voice thick. He rubbed the back of his neck, clearly struggling with the memory of her vulnerability.

Mary's expression turned sombre, her brows knitting together in concern. "Oh, dear," she said softly, her hands resting on her lap. "Do you think I should go talk to her?"

John shook his head gently, his voice calm but firm. "No. She knows we're here if she needs us," he said. "Pushing her right now might make her retreat even further."

Jackson nodded, though his jaw tightened. "She's been through so much," he said quietly. "And she's strong—I can see that—but today, it was like the weight of everything hit her all over again."

Mary sighed, looking out at the view as if searching for answers. "Sometimes grief does that," she murmured. "You think you've learned to carry it, and then something reminds you just how heavy it is."

John placed a steadying hand on Jackson's shoulder. "You were there for her, son. That's what matters."

Jackson nodded again, though the knot in his chest remained. "I just wish she'd let me in," he confessed. "Even a little."

Mary gave him a sad but knowing smile. "Give her time, Jackson. Some walls take longer to break down, especially when they've been built to protect a heart that's already been shattered."

Jackson didn't respond immediately. He just stared out at the horizon, the weight of his parents' words sinking in as he resolved to be patient, no matter how hard it was. Jessica was worth it.

Chapter Nine

Jessica didn't come down for lunch, choosing instead to spend the day in her room. She rested, read a few chapters of her book, and let music fill the quiet spaces in her thoughts. It wasn't until just before dinner that a knock came at her door.

"Come in," she called softly.

Phyllis stepped inside, her face warm with concern. "Hi, Jess. Mum told me you went to see your mum and dad today. Are you okay?"

Jessica managed a small smile. "Yes, I'm fine. It was emotional, but I'm glad I went. I needed to." Her smile grew brighter as she changed the subject. "How are Nathan's parents?"

Phyllis beamed. "Oh, they're wonderful. I love them almost as much as I love Nathan." She sat down on the bed beside Jessica and gave her a playful nudge. "You coming down to dinner?"

Jessica stood, stretching her arms. "Sure am. I'm starving—I could eat a horse!"

Phyllis laughed and linked her arm with Jessica's. Together, they made their way to the dining room.

Everyone was already seated when they arrived, the table buzzing with light conversation. Jessica slipped into the seat next to Jackson, feeling his gaze on her briefly as she settled in.

Mary leaned forward, her voice soft with maternal concern. "You okay, Jessica?"

Jessica nodded, offering her a reassuring smile. "I'm good, thank you." She glanced at Jackson and added, "And thank you again for taking me."

Jackson met her gaze, his smile gentle. "No problem. It was my pleasure."

For a moment, their eyes held, an unspoken connection passing between them. But Jessica quickly looked away, focusing on the plate in front of her.

Dinner continued with its usual light-hearted energy, but Jackson couldn't help stealing glances at Jessica. She was smiling, laughing even, but he could see the subtle traces of the day's weight still lingering in her eyes.

Phyllis, ever the cheerful presence, leaned over to Jessica. "Don't forget, the fitting for your bridesmaid dress on Tuesday afternoon. You're going to look stunning in what I've picked out!"

Jessica laughed, grateful for the shift in focus. "Oh, I'm not allowed to be stunning. You're the bride-to-be—I couldn't possibly outshine you."

Phyllis grinned mischievously. "We'll see about that."

Nathan chimed in, his tone light but teasing. "Terry mentioned you're checking out some properties with him tomorrow."

Jessica nodded. "Yes, I'm looking forward to it."

Nathan's grin turned wicked. "So is he, Jess."

Jackson's head snapped toward Nathan, his voice sharper than he intended. "What's that supposed to mean?"

Nathan raised his hands in mock innocence. "Come on, Jackson. Terry's smitten." He turned to Jessica, his expression softening. "He can't stop talking about how lovely you are."

Jessica's cheeks flushed, the unexpected attention making her shift uncomfortably.

John, ever the composed patriarch, added with a kind smile, "You couldn't do better, Jessica. Terry's a stand-up guy."

Jackson's scowl deepened, his jaw tightening as he tried to keep his emotions in check. He didn't trust himself to respond, so he picked up his glass of water and took a long sip, willing the conversation to move on.

Jessica, sensing the tension, smiled politely. "That's kind of him. Terry's been really nice."

Mary, noticing the shift in the air, smoothly changed the subject. "So, Phyllis, your last day at the salon is Friday, right?"

"Yep!" Phyllis replied brightly. "Then it's four weeks off for the wedding then honeymoon. I just hope you won't be too bored while I'm not here this week, Jess."

Jessica shook her head with a soft laugh. "No, I'll be busy looking for a property, and I might start car shopping too. I need to be mobile."

Nathan perked up. "New or used?"

"I think new," Jessica said thoughtfully. "I only need a small car, but I have the funds to get something reliable."

Nathan asked, "So, Jess, are you all set for Phyll's bachelorette party?"

"Yep, sorted it all out last week—guest list, venue, and, of course, the stripper," Jessica replied with a laugh.

Nathan groaned dramatically. "You make sure my fiancée doesn't get too loose, alright?"

Jessica smirked. "Don't worry, Nathan, the stripper is for us single girls, not the engaged one."

"Hey, that's not fair!" Phyllis teased playfully. "I should get to have a little fun too!"

Jessica raised an eyebrow, grinning. "We'll see, bride-to-be."

Laughter rippled through the table, lightening the mood, and even Jackson managed a faint smile. But as Jessica laughed along with everyone else, he couldn't help but steal a glance at her, wondering how many more little pieces of her he'd have to watch slip away into someone else's orbit.

As the meal wound down and the others laughed over dessert, Jackson leaned back in his chair, arms crossed, his mind far from the conversation. One thing was becoming painfully clear: he couldn't keep ignoring how he felt about Jessica. She wasn't just anyone to him—she never had been. It had taken him far too long to recognise it, but now the truth was undeniable.

After dinner, Phyllis and Nathan excused themselves, heading upstairs for an early night. Mary soon followed, leaving Jackson and his father, John, to retreat to the study for a drink. Jessica, meanwhile, decided she needed to clear her head. The night was warm, and the thought of a swim seemed perfect.

Upstairs, she slipped into a modest one-piece swimsuit. She tied her hair back and padded quietly down the stairs and out to the pool. The cool night air wrapped around her as she approached the water, the faint sound of crickets in the background.

She dived in smoothly, the water enveloping her in a calming embrace. She swam lap after lap, her strokes steady and rhythmic. With each movement, the tension in her body began to ease. She wasn't sure how long she'd been swimming—minutes or hours—but the physical exertion was a welcome distraction from the swirling thoughts in her mind.

Abruptly, she froze mid-lap when she heard the distinct splash of someone diving into the pool. Her head shot up, droplets of water trailing down her face. The pool lights were on, but in her exhaustion, it was hard to make out who it was.

Then, a figure broke the surface right in front of her, water cascading down his face as he ran a hand through his hair.

"Hello," Jackson said, his voice low and amused, his dark eyes locking onto hers.

Jessica blinked, startled. "What are you doing here?"

"Same as you, apparently. Wanted a swim before I go home." He treaded water effortlessly, his gaze never leaving hers.

She frowned, suddenly self-conscious under his steady stare. "Well, I'll leave you in peace."

Jackson moved slightly closer, his tone soft but insistent. "No, don't go."

Her brows knitted together. "Why?"

"Because I want to spend time with you."

Jessica's heart skipped a beat, but she quickly masked it with a sceptical look. "Why?"

"Jessica," he said, his voice dipping with a mixture of regret and determination, "can't we put the past behind us?"

"I don't know." She shook her head, water droplets clinging to her lashes as she avoided his gaze.

"I know I was a bloody idiot five years ago, but surely we can be friends now."

"Friends, huh?" Jessica's voice held a hint of mockery, though her heart wasn't as guarded as she wanted it to be.

Jackson sighed, his expression softening. "Yes. Friends. Or at least, we could try."

She studied him for a moment, searching his face for any hint of insincerity. There was none. "Okay, we could try."

He smiled, the light from the pool casting a soft glow on his face. "How about a race? You nearly did me in this morning with the running, I need to redeem myself."

Jessica raised an eyebrow, intrigued. "Okay. Four laps. You're on."

They moved to their starting positions, both stretching out their muscles in preparation. The air between them was lighter now, as if the tension had been momentarily lifted. With a nod from Jackson, they both dove into the water, the coolness of the pool rushing over them.

Jackson's strokes were powerful, cutting through the water with practiced ease, but Jessica was no slouch. She pushed herself harder, her arms slicing through the water with all the energy she could muster. The first lap was neck and neck, but Jackson's long reach gave him a slight advantage as they rounded the turn.

As they reached the third lap, Jessica's determination kicked in, closing the distance between them. She surged forward, her muscles aching but pushing past the fatigue. Jackson's pace had slightly slowed, but he wasn't giving up. With one last burst of energy, Jessica reached the wall just a split second before Jackson did.

"Just by a smidge," she said, breathless, a smile tugging at her lips as she leaned against the edge of the pool, trying to catch her breath.

Jackson grinned, shaking his head in mock disbelief. "I can't believe I lost to you again."

Jessica laughed, her voice light and teasing. "Don't worry, Jackson. I'll let you redeem yourself next time."

He swam up beside her, leaning against the pool edge as they both caught their breath. "Next time. I'm going to beat you."

Jessica raised an eyebrow. "We'll see about that."

For a moment, they were silent, the only sound the gentle lapping of the water against the pool's edge. Their gazes locked, an unspoken understanding passing between them. Then, as if they both shared the same thought, they reached for each other.

The urgency was instant—neither of them able to wait any longer, as if everything they had been holding back had finally come to a head. Their bodies collided, and in the next breath, they pulled each other closer. There was no hesitation—just an overwhelming need to connect, to feel the heat of each other's touch.

Jackson's breath caught as he cupped the back of Jessica's head, his fingers tangling in her damp hair. She responded immediately, her hands threading through his hair, pulling him in with equal force. Without thinking, without words, their lips met—fierce, desperate.

It wasn't frantic, but it was desperate, as though every moment apart had led to this. The kiss was deep, consuming, a mixture of longing and relief. Neither of them cared about holding back anymore. Jessica's legs wrapped around Jackson's waist, her body pressing against his as their tongues tangled, battling for control.

The world around them seemed to fade away, leaving only the two of them—lost in the shared current of their desire.

A deep groan rumbled in Jackson's chest as he pulled her even closer, her hands threading through his hair, fingers gripping the back of his neck. The warmth of the water, the steady pulse of their heartbeats, and the heat of their kiss consumed everything.

Jackson's hand slid urgently to her breast, his touch tender despite the intensity of the moment. The shift in his touch was enough to make Jessica's breath catch, and a soft moan escaped her lips against his, the sound only deepening their connection. Every nerve in her body seemed to hum, and she responded with a quiet urgency, pulling him closer, as though she couldn't get close enough.

Jackson murmured against Jessica's lips, his voice low and filled with longing. "Jessica, I want you."

Jessica's response was a breathless, simple, "Yes."

The kiss deepened, more urgent now, their bodies moving in perfect harmony, as if they were two halves of the same whole. Their tangled limbs seemed to blur together, until it was impossible to tell where Jessica ended, and Jackson began. The world outside the pool ceased to exist, leaving only the sensation of skin against skin, the rush of shared desire.

The feeling of his arousal pressing against her sent an intoxicating rush of desire through her veins.

"You're not close enough," Jackson whispered, his breath warm against her lips, his voice thick with desire.

"Jackson," she whimpered, her body yearning for more.

"I want you so badly, Jess," he murmured in her ear, trailing soft kisses along her cheek. "You don't know how much I want you."

Jessica's heart raced as his words washed over her, a mixture of heat and need building inside her. "Jackson," she whispered, her voice breathless, barely able to form the words.

"I want to hear you scream my name when I make love to you," he confessed, his voice husky with want.

The pool area was suddenly flooded with light. Jessica pulled away from Jackson's arms instinctively, the loss of contact immediate and jarring.

"Hello?" John called from the edge of the yard.

Jessica quickly started climbing out of the pool, her heart still racing. "Hello," she replied, trying to sound casual.

John came into view, his silhouette outlined by the poolside lights. "I thought I heard someone down here."

Jessica quickly wrapped her towel around herself and replied, "Jackson and I had the same idea to get in a swim before bed."

As she passed John, she leaned in and kissed him on the cheek. "Goodnight, John."

"Goodnight, sweetheart. Sweet dreams," John replied warmly.

Jackson watched as Jessica made her way toward the house, feeling the desire and need still lingering in his body. Her departure was a jarring reminder of the moment that had just passed, and the rush of passion still surged through him.

John gave him a look, one that Jackson couldn't quite place. "Everything okay?" he asked.

"Yeah," Jackson replied, his voice steady but his thoughts far from calm. He finally pulled himself out of the pool, careful to avoid making eye contact with his father as he wrapped his towel around his waist.

"Good night, Jackson," John called as he started to head back toward the house.

"Night," Jackson muttered in return, his mind a whirlwind. He knew he needed space, but what he truly wanted was to follow Jessica—chase what they had, whatever it was. But tonight, had been too much, too fast. He had to figure out where they stood, and what was real, before he made any more moves.

Chapter Ten

"Are you ready to find your new home?" Terry asked as he navigated the bustling streets of Sydney, the sun reflecting off the sleek glass buildings around them.

"Sure am," Jessica replied with a smile, her excitement palpable. It had been a long time since she'd felt so in control of her life and today felt like a new beginning.

They pulled up to the first property. Terry led Jessica towards the entrance of the building, a striking modern glass-and-steel structure that soared high above the bustling streets of Barangaroo. The sleek, minimalist design stood out against the skyline, with reflective glass panels that gleamed in the morning sun, offering panoramic views of the surrounding city and harbour. The building's lobby was elegant and spacious, with polished marble floors, contemporary art pieces lining the walls, and lush greenery scattered in decorative planters, creating a serene, upscale atmosphere.

They walked to the elevator, and as the doors closed, Terry glanced at Jessica. "You'll love this one, it has a fantastic view."

When they arrived at the apartment floor, the door to the unit opened, revealing a spacious open-plan living area. The apartment had floor-to-ceiling windows that bathed the entire space in natural light. The harbour views were breathtaking, stretching out across the water and the iconic Sydney Opera House in the distance. The room itself was sleek and modern, with polished timber floors, soft neutral tones, and high-end finishes.

The kitchen was a dream—state-of-the-art appliances, quartz countertops, and an island that could comfortably seat four. The living area featured a cozy sectional sofa and a dining table, both set against the backdrop of the expansive view. The apartment's layout was open, allowing for a seamless flow between spaces.

Jessica walked toward the balcony, her fingers brushing along the sleek glass railing as she took in the view. "Wow, this is incredible," she whispered, feeling the rush of excitement. The apartment felt both luxurious and inviting, with every detail thoughtfully curated for comfort and style.

Terry stood in the doorway, watching her with a knowing smile. "I thought you'd like it. It's got everything—modern, stylish, and in the heart of everything you need. The building has great amenities too—gym, pool, concierge."

Jessica nodded, feeling a spark of excitement at the prospect of calling this place home. "It's perfect," she said softly, already imagining herself living here, her new chapter in Barangaroo just beginning.

Terry led Jessica back toward the elevator, his steps light with excitement as they headed to the next viewing. "I'm glad you like this place," he said, grinning. "I have a feeling you'll be making a decision soon."

Jessica smiled, feeling a mix of excitement and caution. "I'm definitely leaning toward something in Barangaroo, but I still want to see what else is out there. You know, keep my options open."

"Of course," Terry nodded, understanding. "It's a big decision. But this one is prime real estate, and being so close to work is a huge plus."

As they walked out of the building and into the car park, Terry motioned to the car. "Next stop let's see what else Sydney has to offer. The next few are more on the outskirts of the city, but they have their own charm."

Jessica settled into the passenger seat, her mind buzzing with thoughts of the apartment they just toured. "I'm excited to see them," she said, her eyes glancing at Terry. "Thanks again for setting all this up. You've made it so much easier for me."

"Anytime," Terry replied, starting the engine. "That's what I'm here for. Let's find you the perfect place.

As the car pulled out of the parking lot, the city's skyline glimmered in the distance, offering endless possibilities. Jessica couldn't help but feel like she was on the brink of a new chapter in her life, one that was waiting just beyond the horizon.

They toured the other two properties, each with its own set of pros and cons. Jessica felt the weight of the decision beginning to settle on her, knowing this was going to be a big choice. As they pulled up to her temporary home and walked to the front door, Terry stopped, his expression shifting to something a little more serious.

"Jessica, before we head inside, there's something I've been meaning to ask you," he said, his tone catching her off guard. She raised an eyebrow, sensing the shift. "What's up?" she replied, her curiosity piqued.

"Well," Terry began, his gaze locking onto hers with an intensity that made her heart skip a beat, "I was wondering if you'd be my date for the REB Awards at The Star in Sydney, on Thursday."

Jessica blinked, the suddenness of the invitation catching her off guard. The REB Awards were one of the most prestigious events in the real estate world. "That's… a pretty big event, Terry," she said, her voice betraying her surprise.

Terry's face softened, and he shrugged with a sheepish smile. "I know it's not exactly a casual night out, but I thought it might be fun. Besides, I think we'd have a great time together."

Jessica hesitated, glancing over at the front door of John and Mary's house. Her mind briefly wandered to the tension between her and Jackson—the lingering pull she still felt, the way their last interaction had left her conflicted. But maybe she was overthinking things. She needed to move forward, not backward.

After a brief pause, she turned back to Terry and smiled, deciding to leave her doubts behind. "Alright, I'll go with you. It sounds like fun."

Terry's face lit up, his relief palpable. "Great! I promise I'll make sure you have a good time."

Jessica couldn't help but laugh, her nerves easing as she gave a playful smile. "I'll hold you to that."

They went inside and found John and Mary on the terrace, enjoying the evening breeze.

John turned and smiled as they approached. "Hello, you two! How did it go?"

"Terry showed me some lovely places," Jessica replied, a thoughtful expression on her face. "Now I just have to decide if I need to see any more."

Mary raised an eyebrow. "That sounds like a big decision."

"It is," Jessica agreed, pouring herself an iced tea. She handed a glass to Terry with a smile. "Here you go."

"Thank you," Terry said, accepting the drink with a grateful grin.

Jessica paused for a moment, her mind still on the logistics of her new home. "Terry was telling me that it'll take about six weeks for everything to settle after I pay the deposit. Do you think you could put up with me for that long?"

"Of course, of course!" John insisted, his voice warm and welcoming.

Mary nodded in agreement. "It would be lovely for you to stay. We're really enjoying having you here."

Jessica smiled, feeling a wave of gratitude for their kindness. "Thanks, both of you. I appreciate it more than you know."

"You're a delight to have around, Jessica," Mary insisted, her smile warm and genuine.

"Thanks," Jessica replied, her voice soft with appreciation. "Terry is taking me to the REB Awards on Thursday. That should be fun."

John's eyes lit up. "Good on you, Terry. You make sure you look after our girl here."

Terry smiled, giving a slight nod. "Oh, I will. Promise." His tone was light, but there was sincerity in his words, and Jessica couldn't help but feel a sense of relief at his reassurance.

Nathan and Phyllis walked in, both looking a little worn from their day.

Mary asked, "How was work, dear?"

Phyllis sighed, brushing a strand of hair from her face. "Tiring. You know how it is. On my feet all day with clients in the chair, but it's rewarding."

Nathan nodded, looking equally tired but with a hint of pride. "Busy day. Got a new client—seems guilty, but you have to do your job, I suppose." He was a criminal lawyer, just like Jackson, and they worked at the same firm. "Jackson had a rough day in court today. He looked shot when I saw him. He said he didn't sleep last night. That case must be weighing on him."

Mary frowned slightly. "Poor Jackson. He's been under a lot of stress lately."

Jessica's thoughts immediately drifted to Jackson, wondering if he hadn't slept for the same reason she hadn't. After the kiss in the pool, it was a wonder neither of them had managed to get any rest. The tension between them was still fresh in her mind, and she couldn't help but wonder if Jackson was lying awake thinking about it, just as she had been.

But then, Nathan's words echoed in her mind. Maybe he was right—Jackson was probably just consumed by thoughts of his client, the case, the pressure of it all. That made more sense. Jackson wouldn't be dwelling on their kiss, would he? After all, she doesn't mean anything to him.

Terry turned to Nathan with a grin. "By the way, Nathan, she said yes."

Nathan looked at Jessica with a raised eyebrow, a teasing smile tugging at his lips. "Good on you, Jess. Terry was worried you'd say no."

Jessica chuckled, feeling a bit self-conscious under the attention. "Well, it did sound like fun. Plus, it's been a while since I've attended anything like that."

Terry gave a playful sigh of relief. "I told you she'd say yes." He shot her a warm smile.

Jessica smiled back, feeling a mix of excitement and uncertainty about the event.

Phyllis laughed, shaking her head. "You guys are such big gossips. They say women gossip, but clearly, you two are just as bad."

Terry and Nathan exchanged amused glances before Terry shrugged with a grin. "What can I say? We have to keep up with the important details."

Nathan chuckled, leaning back in his chair. "It's all in good fun, Phyllis. We're just looking out for Jess."

Jessica laughed, feeling a warmth spread through her at the easy camaraderie between everyone. "I guess I'm just the subject of today's gossip then."

Phyllis winked. "Only because you're too interesting not to talk about!"

Chapter Eleven

"She what!" Jackson's voice was sharp, a mix of surprise and frustration. "What the hell, Nathan?"

Nathan chuckled, clearly amused by Jackson's reaction. "Come on, Jackson. What's with the attitude? Why do you care so much about Jessica going out with Terry? You've always been so dismissive of her. I, on the other hand, always liked her. She was a great girl, and now, she's a great woman. I'm proud to call her my friend. And Terry? He thinks she's hot—and honestly, I can't blame him."

"What do you mean, I was always so dismissive of her?" Jackson asked, his brow furrowing.

Nathan rolled his eyes, exasperated. "You used to ask Phyllis why she even bothered being friends with Jessica. I never understood it. Jessica's always been a nice girl. You were just too blind to see it."

Jackson hesitated, his voice softening as he reflected. "I didn't know her. Not really."

Nathan shook his head, his frustration evident. "Yeah, but you didn't even try. I used to have great conversations with Jess before she moved to Perth."

"When?" Jackson asked, his confusion deepening.

Nathan shot him a pointed look. "She was at your place more than her own. After her parents died, she lived there for a month. So, when do you think I had the chance to talk to her? Come on, mate, you were so blind."

"Is Terry taking her out tonight?" Jackson's voice tightened, a hint of unspoken tension slipping through.

"Yep, to the REB Awards," Nathan replied, casually. "Phyllis told me they've been spending a lot of time together this week."

Jackson ran a hand across his face, his frustration bubbling to the surface. "Bloody hell!"

Nathan's eyes widened as the truth hit him. "Oh my god… you like Jess?" His voice held both disbelief and amusement.

Jackson looked up at him, his gaze steady but conflicted. "Yes," he admitted, the single word weighted with both frustration and a newfound vulnerability.

Nathan's brow furrowed as his protective instincts kicked in. "Do you like her for who she is, or just because she's hot now? Because if it's just about her looks, forget it. You're my best friend, but I'm not letting you mess with Jess."

Jackson's expression softened, his sincerity evident. "She's not just attractive," he said firmly, his voice resolute. "She's incredible—strong, smart, sexy… and honestly, way out of my league." He sighed, the weight of his realisation settling over him. "I wish I'd seen it sooner. I wish I hadn't been such an idiot."

Nathan smirked, unable to suppress his amusement. "You're not the only one who missed the mark, mate. But hey, at least you see it now." His tone shifted, teasing but thoughtful. "The real question is, what are you going to do about it?"

Jackson let out a frustrated sigh, running his hands through his hair. "I have no idea."

Nathan shrugged, his grin widening. "Well, you'd better figure it out fast. Terry already mentioned that Jessica is marriage material."

Jackson's jaw tightened, his frustration clear. "Why did you even introduce them, Nath?"

Nathan raised an eyebrow, unbothered. "How was I supposed to know you'd finally take an interest?" He smirked, enjoying the discomfort he was causing.

Jackson glared at him. "You're loving this, aren't you?"

"To be honest?" Nathan leaned back with a grin. "Yeah, a little. Jess deserved better from you, and now you're finally realising it."

"Don't tell Phyllis about this, Nath," Jackson said firmly.

Nathan raised his hands in mock surrender, a mischievous glint in his eye. "I won't bring it up. But if she asks, I'm not lying."

"Oh, Jess, you look gorgeous! Terry's going to lose his mind," Phyllis said, her eyes sparkling with excitement.

Jessica turned to the mirror, taking in her reflection. She wore a dark blue cocktail dress with a slim A-line silhouette that hugged her figure perfectly. The fabric shimmered subtly under the light, adding an air of understated elegance. Her auburn hair was swept into a sleek chignon, with a few soft tendrils framing her face. Paired with matching deep blue stilettos, the ensemble gave her a graceful, poised appearance. Her makeup was light but refined—a hint of blush, soft eyeliner, and a natural lip colour that enhanced her features without overwhelming them.

"Thanks, Phyllis," Jessica said with a small smile, smoothing down the dress. "But don't get carried away."

Phyllis grinned, undeterred. "Oh, I'm not. I'm just stating the obvious!"

From downstairs, Mary called out, "Jessica, Terry's here!"

Phyllis clapped her hands in excitement. "Moment of truth!" she teased before darting out of the room, leaving Jessica to finish getting ready.

Jessica grabbed her clutch, tucking her phone and credit card inside, and took a steadying breath. As she descended the staircase, the soft click of her heels against the polished wood echoed through the house.

At the bottom, Terry stood waiting, looking sharp in a tailored suit. Nearby, Phyllis, Nathan, John, and Mary watched with smiles of admiration. Terry's gaze locked on Jessica as she approached, his expression one of open awe.

"Wow," he said under his breath, his admiration unmistakable.

Jessica managed a small smile, but before she could respond, the front door burst open with a thud. The abrupt noise startled everyone.

Jackson stormed in, his eyes immediately finding Jessica. His chest rose and fell as though he'd been rushing, his expression unreadable yet brimming with urgency.

Mary broke the heavy silence. "Oh, Jackson, I didn't realise you were joining us for dinner tonight."

Jackson barely spared his family a glance, his focus locked on Jessica. He cleared his throat, attempting to sound casual, though tension radiated off him. "Where are you off to?"

Terry, standing confidently beside Jessica, answered smoothly. "She's coming to the REB Awards with me." He held out his hand, his smile widening as Jessica placed hers in his.

"You look stunning," Terry said warmly, his voice filled with genuine admiration. "Ready to go?"

Jessica nodded, her expression calm despite the intensity of Jackson's gaze. "Yes," she replied steadily. Without looking back, she turned toward the door with Terry.

Jackson stood frozen, his jaw tightening as he watched them leave. His eyes lingered on Jessica, an unspoken storm of emotions flickering in their depths.

Nathan, observing from the sidelines, couldn't suppress the wide grin spreading across his face. "Well," he murmured, his tone dripping with amusement, "that was fun to watch."

Terry escorted Jessica into The Star's grand ballroom, the venue buzzing with the hum of conversation and the clinking of glasses. The space was lavishly decorated with elegant chandeliers casting warm light over round tables adorned with crisp white linens and glittering centrepieces.

Jessica felt the weight of many eyes on her as they entered, her dark blue cocktail dress catching the light with every step. Terry stayed close by her side, his hand resting lightly on the small of her back.

"You're turning heads," Terry whispered with a playful smile as they found their table near the stage.

Jessica chuckled softly. "I think it's more the dress than me."

"Not a chance," he replied, his voice warm. "It's all you."

Throughout the evening, they mingled with other attendees, exchanging pleasantries with some of the biggest names in the real estate industry. Terry introduced Jessica to several colleagues, proudly calling her his date, which earned them a few approving nods and smiles.

Dinner was an indulgent affair—a three-course meal featuring dishes like seared salmon with a delicate beurre blanc and a decadent chocolate fondant for dessert. Jessica sipped her champagne, her laughter easy as Terry recounted a particularly funny story from a past deal gone awry.

As the awards ceremony commenced, the room grew quiet, the spotlight shifting to the stage where the host began announcing winners. Terry leaned over and murmured, "I told you this would be fun."

Jessica smiled, relaxing into the evening. "You were right."

But every so often, her thoughts drifted to Jackson—the intensity in his eyes when he saw her before she left, the way he seemed to struggle with something unspoken. Shaking it off, she refocused on Terry, who was attentive and charming, making her feel like the centre of the room.

The night ended with a celebratory toast as one of Terry's acquaintances won an award. On the drive back, Jessica glanced at Terry, feeling grateful for the light-heartedness of the evening.

"Thank you for inviting me," Jessica said softly as Terry's car came to a stop in front of John and Mary's house.

"It was my pleasure," Terry replied, his smile warm and genuine. "I couldn't have asked for a better date."

He stepped out, quickly coming around to her side to help her out of the car. As they approached the front door, Terry paused, gently taking her hand and turning her toward him. His gaze met hers, a mix of affection and admiration in his eyes. Slowly, he pulled her closer, his hand resting lightly on her waist.

Before Jessica could process what was happening, Terry lowered his head and kissed her. It was sweet, tender at first, but it deepened into a kiss full of passion. She felt herself momentarily caught in the moment, her heart racing.

Then, suddenly, the sound of the front door swinging open broke the spell.

Jessica and Terry turned simultaneously, startled, to see Jackson standing in the doorway. His expression was unreadable, his piercing blue eyes shifting between the two of them.

"Am I interrupting something?" Jackson's tone was calm, almost too calm, but his clenched jaw betrayed the tension simmering beneath the surface.

Jessica instinctively stepped back from Terry, her face heating with embarrassment. Terry, however, maintained his composure, slipping his hands casually into his pockets.

"Just making sure Jess got home safe," Terry said evenly, his gaze steady on Jackson's.

Jackson didn't respond immediately, his focus settling on Jessica, his expression a storm of emotions she couldn't decipher. The tension in the air was palpable, the silence heavy.

Jessica cleared her throat awkwardly. "Thanks again, Terry. I'll see you later."

Terry hesitated for a beat, his eyes briefly flicking to Jackson before nodding. "Goodnight, Jess." He turned and walked back to his car, leaving her alone with Jackson.

As the door clicked shut behind her, Jessica barely had time to react before Jackson grabbed her hand, his grip firm but not painful. Without a word, he led her into the empty study, shutting the door behind them with a decisive thud. The sound of the key turning in the lock made her heart jump.

"What the hell was that?" Jackson's voice was low but seething, his stormy eyes boring into hers.

Jessica crossed her arms, refusing to be intimidated. "A goodnight kiss, I think."

"Don't be smart," Jackson snapped, his jaw tightening as he struggled to contain his frustration.

Jessica tilted her head, her voice calm but laced with defiance. "What business is it of yours, Jackson?"

He took a step closer, the space between them charged with tension. "You don't think it's my business when I open the front door to find him kissing you on the doorstep?"

Her eyebrows shot up, a mix of disbelief and annoyance flashing across her face. "No, Jackson. It's not your business. Terry is a gentleman, and I enjoyed my evening with him. So what if he kissed me goodnight?"

Jackson let out a bitter laugh, running a hand through his hair. "A gentleman? You barely know him, Jessica."

"And you barely know me," she shot back, her voice rising slightly. "You've made that perfectly clear over the years."

Her words hit him like a slap, and for a moment, Jackson said nothing. The silence that followed was deafening, the weight of her statement hanging heavy in the air. Finally, he looked away, his expression torn between regret and something else she couldn't quite place.

Jessica took a deep breath, her tone softening. "You don't get to storm in here and act like you have any say in my life, Jackson. Not after the way you've treated me."

His eyes snapped back to hers, filled with something raw and unguarded. But before he could respond, she shook her head.

"I don't owe you an explanation," she said firmly, turning toward the door. "Now unlock it, or I'll scream."

For a long moment, he didn't move. Then, with a sigh that sounded almost like defeat, Jackson reached into his pocket, pulled out the key, and unlocked the door.

As Jessica walked out without looking back, Jackson stood alone in the study, the weight of his own emotions pressing down on him like a storm he couldn't outrun.

Jessica stormed upstairs, her mind racing. How dare he? The audacity of Jackson to act as if he had any claim over her infuriated her. She marched into her room, slammed the door shut, and leaned against it, taking a deep breath to calm herself.

She walked to the vanity, wiping the makeup off her face with swift, deliberate strokes, the anger still simmering under her skin. Slipping into a soft silk nightgown, she sat on the edge of her bed, her phone in hand. After a moment of hesitation, she opened her messages and typed a text to Terry.

Thank you for tonight. I had a lovely time.

The reply came almost instantly, and her lips curved into a small smile as she read it.

So did I. I'm hoping we can do it again.

Her fingers hovered over the keyboard, a warmth spreading through her chest as she considered her response. Maybe I deserve a fresh start. Someone who actually sees me.

But before she could reply, her thoughts drifted back to the intensity in Jackson's eyes, the way he had looked at her in the study. Frustrated with herself for allowing him to still have such an effect, she set the phone down with a sharp exhale. She climbed under the covers, trying to push the chaos surrounding Jackson out of her mind. She reminded herself that tonight had been about Terry, about enjoying her time with someone who respected her.

After a few moments, she grabbed her phone again, determined to focus on what had felt like a genuine connection. She typed out a quick response to Terry.

Would love to *(lips emoji)*

She hesitated for a second before hitting send, her heart racing as she realised how much she was looking forward to seeing him again. The simple message felt like a small step toward something new, something promising. She lay back, allowing the warmth of the night to settle over her, pushing away thoughts of Jackson for just a little while longer.

Chapter Twelve

Friday marked the official start of the wedding celebrations. Nathan's parents, Jackson, Mary's brother and his wife, along with John's sister and her husband, were all coming to stay at John and Mary's home for the week, right through until after the wedding. It was going to be a full house, with everyone bustling about, preparing for the big day. The atmosphere was already charged with excitement, and Jessica couldn't help but feel a mix of anticipation and nerves as she prepared for the whirlwind of activity ahead.

The visitors would be arriving throughout the day, and Jessica was busy helping Helen get everything ready. From making beds to ensuring all the ensuites were fully stocked with fresh towels and toiletries, Jessica was on her feet, making sure everything was in order. She also helped chop vegetables for the first-night dinner party, working alongside Helen in the kitchen. Helen thanked her numerous times, her gratitude evident as they worked together to prepare for the full house that would soon be bustling with activity.

The first to arrive were Nathan's parents, Judy and Eric. Since everyone else was still at work, Mary, John, and Jessica greeted them warmly. Jessica showed them to their room, making sure they had everything they needed. Soon after, Mary's brother, Joseph, and his wife, Anita, arrived, followed by John's sister, Jane, and her husband, Samuel. Finally, Jackson, Nathan, and Phyllis arrived, all finishing up their work for the next week. The house quickly began to fill with familiar faces, and the energy shifted as the celebration preparations continued.

Dinner was served at seven, and Jessica helped Helen set the table and get the food ready. Feeding twelve people was no small task, but everything went off without a hitch. After the meal, Phyllis insisted that Nathan, Jessica, and Jackson go for a swim since it was such a warm night. Most of the older visitors had either gone to bed early or were settled in the living room, chatting. Phyllis and Jessica quickly changed into their bikinis and made their way to the pool, with Nathan and Jackson joining soon after. The cool water was a welcome relief from the heat, and the group enjoyed the peaceful evening under the stars.

"Phyllis, are you ready for your bachelorette party tomorrow?" Jessica asked, giving her a playful grin.

"Sure am, looking forward to wearing those sparkly hot pants," Phyllis replied, excited.

Nathan raised an eyebrow. "What? Who's wearing hot pants?" He didn't seem impressed.

Phyllis laughed. "Jessica organised for all of us to wear skin-tight sparkly hot pants tomorrow night." She then turned to Jessica with a teasing look. "It's alright for you, though—look at those legs. They're to die for."

Nathan and Jackson both looked at Jessica's legs. "Stop, Phyllis. Your legs are gorgeous," Nathan said, but his voice had a hint of admiration.

Jackson's thoughts drifted to when Jessica's legs were wrapped around him in the pool. He quickly shook the thought off, trying to focus on the conversation.

Jessica looked at Jackson, a mischievous smile on her face. "What about Nathan's bachelor party? All organised, Jackson?"

Jackson smirked. "Yep." He then turned to Nathan with a teasing grin. "Sorry, Nathan, no strippers."

Nathan laughed. "I'm happy with that. Less likely I'll get in trouble," he said, clearly relieved.

Jackson glanced at Jessica with a raised eyebrow. "So, what colour are these hot pants?" he asked, his tone curious yet teasing.

Jessica smiled, her eyes twinkling with mischief. "Hot pink, of course," she replied, enjoying the playful moment.

Jackson raised an eyebrow at her. "Hot pink, huh?" he said, a smirk tugging at his lips. "I can only imagine how that'll look on you."

Jessica's smile widened, a playful glint in her eyes. "You'll just have to wait and see," she teased, enjoying the way his gaze lingered.

"I can't wait," Jackson said, his tone a mix of amusement and anticipation.

Jessica dived into the pool gracefully, cutting through the water with ease. When she surfaced, Jackson's voice rang out, teasing.

"When am I going to get my rematch?" he asked, a playful challenge in his eyes.

Nathan, confused, glanced at him. "What rematch?"

Jessica grinned, her eyes sparkling with mischief. "Oh, the poor baby is upset because I beat him in both running and swimming the other day."

Phyllis laughed, shaking her head. "Really, Jackson? You let a girl beat you?"

"Rematch?" Nathan asked, raising an eyebrow.

Jessica grinned, her confidence unshaken. "Anytime, bring it on."

Without missing a beat, Jackson stood up, a competitive glint in his eye. He dove into the pool with a splash, surfacing a moment later. "Rematch now."

Nathan and Phyllis both stood up, their amusement evident. "Okay, you two," Nathan said. "How many laps?"

Jessica and Jackson exchanged a look, each sizing the other up. Jessica quirked an eyebrow, a challenge in her smile. "Six?" she suggested, her voice playful.

"Sounds good," Jackson agreed, his competitive spirit fully engaged.

Phyllis stood at the edge of the pool, her hands on her hips. "Okay, out you get, proper start," she said, looking between the two swimmers.

Jessica and Jackson positioned themselves at opposite sides of the pool, both getting into their starting stance. Nathan stood at the edge, ready to start the race. "Go!" he called.

In an instant, Jackson shot forward, his powerful strokes pulling him ahead. His form was flawless, cutting through the water with precision and speed. Jessica struggled to keep up at first, but her determination was clear in her eyes. She pushed herself harder, each stroke becoming more efficient as she closed the gap between them.

By the time they hit the halfway point, Jackson had built a strong lead. His confidence was evident as he glanced over his shoulder, only to see Jessica gaining on him. Her breaths were steady, her rhythm smooth as she surged forward, her legs kicking with extra force.

The final two laps were a blur of motion as Jessica's speed increased, her focus unshakable. With every lap, she closed the distance between them, her hands slicing through the water like blades. Jackson, sensing her gaining momentum, pushed harder, but the exhaustion from his earlier lead was starting to show.

In the last stretch, just as Jackson's stroke faltered for a split second, Jessica surged ahead, her fingertips grazing the poolside just a fraction of a second before his. She had done it.

Jessica, breathless and triumphant, turned to see Jackson pull himself out of the water, his face a mix of admiration and frustration.

Phyllis was jumping up and down with excitement. "Yes, Jess! You beat him!" she cheered, her voice filled with pride.

Nathan clapped Jackson on the back, his tone light but teasing. "You went too hard, too fast," he said with a grin. "Guess you underestimated her."

Jackson, panting from the race, shot Nathan a playful glare but couldn't hide the smile tugging at his lips. "Alright, alright. She's faster than she looks."

Jessica climbed out of the pool, water dripping down her body as she rushed over to Phyllis for a tight hug. "I won!" she exclaimed, her voice filled with excitement and a wide grin of pride.

As Jackson pushed himself up, still catching his breath, Jessica turned toward him with a mischievous glint in her eye. She jumped into his arms, wrapping him in a playful, tight hug. "Poor baby," she teased, her voice dripping with mock sympathy.

Before Jackson could muster a response, Jessica leaned in and pressed a quick kiss to his cheek. Her lips lingered just long enough to send an unexpected rush of warmth through him. He froze, eyes widening, completely caught off guard by the gesture.

Phyllis raised an eyebrow, clearly enjoying the playful dynamic between them, while Nathan simply shook his head, a knowing smile tugging at his lips.

"I think it's time for bed," Jessica said, her tone light as she picked up a towel and wrapped it around herself. The warmth of the moment lingered in the air between them.

"I agree," Nathan chimed in, still smiling at the exchange.

With that, they all made their way upstairs to their respective rooms, the laughter and light-heartedness of the evening gradually giving way to the quiet of the night.

Chapter Thirteen

The day of the bachelor and bachelorette parties had arrived, and the excitement in the air was palpable. Jessica had organised everything down to the last detail. The girls were gathered at Phyllis's house, each one getting ready for the night ahead. They had all changed into their hot pink, skin-tight sparkly hot pants, and shimmering silver halter tops, looking absolutely stunning.

Jessica couldn't help but smile as she took in the sight of her friends. Each of them looked incredible, and she was beyond excited for what was to come. The party bus would be picking them up shortly, and the night promised to be full of music, laughter, and plenty of fun.

As the girls continued to chat and make last-minute adjustments, Jessica pulled something from her bag.

"One last thing," she said, her voice playful but full of excitement.

The girls turned to her, curious. With a grin, Jessica revealed two tiaras—one that read "Bride" and the other "Bridesmaid."

She carefully placed the tiara with "Bride" on Phyllis's head, her fingers lingering for just a moment. Then she set the "Bridesmaid" tiara atop her own head, giving it a little twirl as if to signal that the night was officially underway.

"Perfect," Jessica said with a satisfied nod. "Now, the bus will be here any minute, so let's get this party started!"

The girls cheered in unison, clapping and laughing as they made their way to the stairs. The energy was electric, and Jessica could tell this was going to be a night they'd all remember for years to come.

As they made their way downstairs, the guys—Nathan, Terry, and Jackson— were waiting for a few more of their friends to show up. The sight of the girls in their hot pink hot pants and shimmering silver halter tops made the room fall silent for a moment.

"Oh my god. Jessica, what have you done?" Nathan said, his eyes wide in surprise as he took in the view of the girls.

Jessica raised an eyebrow, not quite understanding. "What do you mean, Nathan?"

Nathan looked over at Jackson, who was still staring at the girls, his jaw practically on the floor. "You girls need a bloody bodyguard. Look at them, Jackson. Are you seeing this?"

Jackson, still standing there in shock, nodded but said nothing for a moment. His eyes landed on Jessica, who was standing proudly with the rest of the girls. His thoughts trailed off as his gaze moved over Jessica. His breath hitched as he noticed how the hot pants clung to her figure, hugging her perfect curves, accentuating her legs—legs he could still feel wrapped around him in the pool. He shook his head slightly, trying to get rid of the memory, but it lingered.

Phyllis, ever the show-off, did a twirl in front of Nathan. "Do you like?"

Nathan laughed, pulling her into a hug. "Do you get to keep those pants?"

Jessica grinned mischievously. "Yes, Nathan, she can keep them," she teased, earning a burst of laughter from the rest of the girls.

Terry, always the charmer, walked up to Jessica with a big grin. "You look awesome," he said, his eyes appreciative.

"Well, thank you, kind sir," Jessica replied with a wink before planting a quick kiss on his cheek.

Jackson's face went stone cold, his jaw tightening as a wave of jealousy surged through him. His eyes narrowed as he tried to mask it, but the tightness in his chest was impossible to ignore. He didn't like the way Terry was looking at Jessica, or the way she kissed him so casually. He wanted to say something, to confront him, but he kept it inside, the frustration simmering beneath the surface.

Jessica, oblivious to the tension, walked up to Jackson with a playful glint in her eye. "You look after the groom, okay, Jackson?" she teased, her voice light.

"I will," he replied stiffly, his words clipped as he tried to maintain control.

Jessica tilted her head, studying him. "What's wrong, Jackson? Don't you approve?" she asked, her voice barely above a whisper, but sharp enough for him to hear.

Before he could stop himself, Jackson reached for her, pulling her into his arms with a force that surprised them both. Without thinking, he pressed his lips to hers, a kiss that was firm and demanding—an unspoken challenge, an attempt to claim her as his own in some way, though he wasn't entirely sure why.

The sound of Phyllis's voice snapped him back to reality. "Stop manhandling my bridesmaid!" she shouted, clearly not amused.

Jackson immediately released Jessica, stepping back in shock as he realised what he had just done. Jessica stared at him, wide-eyed, her expression a mix of surprise and something else—something he couldn't quite place. Terry didn't look pleased, his brow furrowed with a hint of annoyance. Nathan, on the other hand, wore a smug smile, clearly enjoying the tension, while Phyllis stood fuming, hands on her hips, her fury palpable. The other girls stood frozen in shock, exchanging glances and whispering amongst themselves.

Before anyone could react further, the loud beep of the party bus horn broke the silence. The door swung open with a blast of upbeat music, instantly shifting the mood. The girls cheered, their energy skyrocketing as they piled inside, eager to kick off the night. They took their seats, adjusting their outfits and preparing for the ride. The bus would take them to different venues around the city, each stop promising laughter, dancing, and plenty of surprises. The tension between Jackson and Jessica was momentarily forgotten as the girls settled into the rhythm of the evening, the sound of music and laughter drowning out any lingering awkwardness.

After the girls left, the sound of the party bus fading into the distance, Terry turned to Jackson, his face tight with anger. "What the hell was that?" he demanded.

Jackson, leaning casually against the railing, didn't flinch. "What are you talking about?" he replied coolly, though the tension in his jaw betrayed him.

"You know what," Terry shot back, his voice rising. "Kissing Jessica like that. What the hell were you thinking?"

Jackson's eyes met Terry's, unwavering, his tone calm but challenging. "She's not yours yet," he said evenly, letting the weight of his words settle between them. "And if I have anything to say about it, she won't be."

Terry's fists clenched at his sides; his anger barely contained. "You think this is some kind of game, Jackson? She's not a prize you can win."

Jackson pushed off the railing, stepping closer to Terry, his gaze sharp. "You're right. She's not a prize. She's Jessica. And I'll fight for her if I have to, because I'm not about to let her slip away."

Nathan, sensing the tension boiling over, stepped between them, his tone firm and commanding. "Alright, enough. This is Phyllis's and my wedding week, not a boxing ring. Cool it, both of you."

Terry took a reluctant step back, though his glare stayed locked on Jackson. "This isn't over," he muttered, his voice low and brimming with frustration, before turning and stalking off.

Jackson stood his ground, a faint smirk tugging at his lips, though the adrenaline in his veins betrayed his outward calm. "Didn't think it would be," he murmured under his breath, his thoughts already drifting to Jessica—her kiss, her laugh, her everything.

Nathan leaned closer to Jackson, his voice dropping to a whisper. "You've got a fight on your hands, mate. Terry's not going to back down."

Jackson's gaze hardened, his jaw tightening with resolve. "Neither am I," he said with quiet determination. "Jessica's mine."

Nathan chuckled softly to himself, shaking his head as he stepped away. He knew this was far from over, but he also knew better than to get in the middle of it. With a smile tugging at his lips, he turned to greet the rest of his friends, who had just arrived, ready to kick off his bachelor party.

The next morning, Jessica laced up her running shoes and set off for her usual solo run. The crisp morning air filled her lungs, refreshing her as her feet pounded rhythmically against the pavement. By the time she returned, a light sheen of sweat glistened on her skin, and her mind felt clear and focused.

After a quick shower, she dressed casually in denim shorts and a button-up shirt, her damp hair falling loosely around her shoulders. She headed downstairs for breakfast, her stomach grumbling in anticipation.

The dining room buzzed with the sounds of clinking utensils and light conversation. Most of the group was already seated, except for Jackson, Nathan, and Phyllis.

"Morning, all," Jessica greeted with a cheerful smile as she entered.

"You're the first one up," John noted, looking mildly impressed.

Jessica grinned as she poured herself a cup of coffee. "I think I might be the only one up for most of the day," she quipped, her laugh light and infectious.

Her comment earned a round of chuckles from the table, the camaraderie easing everyone into the morning.

"Did you have a good time, dear?" Mary asked warmly, her motherly tone filled with genuine curiosity.

"Yes, thank you," Jessica replied as she took a seat. "I know Phyllis had a blast, but something tells me her head might be a little sore this morning," she added with a knowing smirk.

The group laughed, picturing the aftermath of the previous night's festivities.

After breakfast, Jessica's phone buzzed in her pocket. She pulled it out and answered in a bright tone, "Hello, Terry. How are you feeling today?"

"I'm good, Jessica. How are you? Did you have a good time last night?" Terry asked.

"Sure did," Jessica replied with a laugh. "What about you?"

"Yeah, but I think Nathan might be feeling a bit dusty today," Terry said with amusement.

Jessica chuckled. "Same with Phyllis. Last night was definitely one for the books."

Terry's voice grew lighter. "Would you like to go for a picnic today?"

Jessica smiled at the suggestion. "That sounds lovely. Yes, I would."

"Great," Terry replied enthusiastically before his tone shifted slightly. "By the way, have you seen Jackson today?"

Jessica frowned faintly. "No. Why?"

"No reason," Terry said casually, though there was a slight hesitation in his voice. "I just thought he might be sporting a hangover after last night."

Jessica tilted her head, sensing there was more he wasn't saying, but before she could ask, Terry changed the subject. "I'll swing by around eleven to pick you up for the picnic?"

"Sounds perfect. See you then," Jessica replied, still smiling.

"See you soon, Jessica," Terry said before hanging up.

"What do you mean she's not here?" Jackson asked his mother, his tone sharper than he intended.

Mary looked up from her book, raising an eyebrow at his abruptness. "She's out with Terry. He picked her up around eleven."

Jackson's jaw tightened. Bloody Terry. "Where did they go?" he asked, his voice clipped.

Mary tilted her head, studying him with mild curiosity. "Jessica mentioned something about a picnic, but she didn't say where exactly. Why do you ask, dear?"

Jackson hesitated for a moment, running a hand through his hair in frustration. "No reason," he muttered, turning toward the door. But his clenched fists and stiff posture told a different story.

Terry had chosen Hyde Park in the city for their picnic, a serene spot surrounded by lush greenery and the gentle hum of city life in the background. He laid out a checkered blanket under the shade of a large tree, setting a picnic basket in the centre.

"I've got cold chicken, salads, and sparkling wine," he said with a smile, pulling out the items and arranging them neatly. "But I also brought apple cider if you'd prefer that."

Jessica settled onto the blanket, smoothing her denim shorts as she sat. "No, a glass of wine will be nice," she replied, her tone light and appreciative.

Terry poured her a glass and handed it to her before pouring one for himself. "So, you didn't drink much last night?" he asked, studying her curiously.

Jessica shook her head, her auburn hair catching the sunlight. "No, drinking to excess isn't really my thing."

"Same here," Terry said, nodding in agreement. "I prefer to actually remember the fun I had."

Jessica laughed softly. "Exactly. Plus, I didn't want to wake up with a pounding headache. Phyllis probably won't be so lucky."

Terry chuckled. "Nathan won't either. I think he will be regretting a few of his choices."

They both laughed, the easy camaraderie between them making the moment feel relaxed and natural. The conversation flowed effortlessly as they started on their food, the sparkling wine adding just the right touch to the sunny afternoon.

After they had eaten, Terry leaned back on his elbows, watching Jessica with a thoughtful expression. "Can I ask you something, Jess?"

She glanced at him, curiosity sparking in her green eyes. "Of course."

Terry hesitated for a moment, then asked cautiously, "What's going on between you and Jackson?"

Jessica's brow furrowed, and she shook her head. "Nothing. Why?"

"That kiss last night," Terry reminded her, his tone gentle but probing.

Jessica sighed, a faint blush creeping into her cheeks. "I don't know where that came from, Terry. I was as shocked as all of you were."

Terry sat up straighter, his gaze steady as he looked at her. "You know what he said to me last night? 'She's not yours yet, and if I have anything to say about it, she won't be.'"

Jessica's head snapped toward him, her eyes wide with disbelief. "What?"

Terry nodded, his voice calm but serious. "He said it plain as day—like he's staking some kind of claim on you."

Jessica frowned deeply, her fingers tightening around her glass. "I don't belong to anyone, least of all him," she said firmly, her voice sharp with irritation.

"I know that," Terry replied, his voice softening. "But I thought you should know. He wasn't exactly subtle when it comes to you, Jess. And I… I just want to make sure you're okay with everything."

Jessica took a deep breath, her emotions swirling. "Thanks for telling me, Terry. I need to have a serious talk with Jackson."

Terry nodded, his expression understanding. "Just know I'm here, Jess. Whatever you decide."

Jessica offered him a small, grateful smile, though her mind was already racing ahead, trying to make sense of everything.

When Terry took her back home, he walked her to the door, the atmosphere between them charged with unspoken tension. As they reached the doorstep, he turned to face her, his hand brushing lightly against her arm.

"Thank you for today," Terry said, his voice low and sincere.

Jessica smiled softly, meeting his gaze. "It was really nice, Terry. I needed a break from everything."

Terry nodded, stepping a little closer. "I'm glad I could give you that," he said, his hand gently cupping her cheek.

Before she could respond, he leaned in slowly, his lips brushing against hers. At first, Jessica froze, her mind still tangled in the events of the day. But as the kiss deepened, she instinctively wrapped her arms around his neck, pulling him closer. The kiss was warm and urgent, a kind of sweetness that made her momentarily forget everything else.

But as the kiss lingered, something became clear. It was nice, yes, but there was no spark—no magnetic pull, no electric charge that made her feel alive the way Jackson's kisses did. With Jackson, it was always intense, as if his lips were calling to her very soul. This… it was just a kiss. Pleasant, but nothing more.

When they finally pulled away, breathless and slightly dazed, Jessica's heart was pounding, but not in the way she wanted. There was a brief moment of silence before she stepped back, her emotions swirling. She glanced at Terry, a polite smile on her lips, but there was no denying the truth inside her.

"I… I should go inside," she murmured, her voice unsteady, betraying the conflicting emotions within her.

Terry nodded, his expression soft but unreadable. "Of course."

Jessica turned and opened the door, her heart heavy with the realisation that something wasn't quite right. Terry watched her enter, and though he didn't say anything more, she felt the weight of the moment settle between them. As the door clicked shut, Jessica was left standing in the quiet of her own thoughts, the image of Jackson's kiss lingering in her mind.

Chapter Fourteen

As Jessica stepped inside, she was met by Jackson, who was walking toward her in the entryway.

"Jessica," he said, his voice low and steady.

"Jackson," she replied, her gaze steady but cautious.

"Out with Terry again?" he asked, his tone tight, carrying an edge of something unspoken.

"Yes, and he told me something interesting," Jessica replied, her voice calm, though there was a guarded edge to it. Her eyes met his, wary yet searching.

"Oh? What was that?" Jackson asked, his brow furrowing, a mix of confusion and curiosity crossing his features.

"That you staked a claim on me," she said, her words deliberate, their weight hanging between them.

Jackson's expression tightened, a flicker of frustration in his eyes. "Didn't say that," he muttered. "I said you're not his yet, and I don't want you to be. And no, I didn't mean it like you're some property. I meant he can't call you his girlfriend yet."

"Maybe I want to be his girlfriend?" Jessica challenged, her voice quiet but firm.

Jackson's eyes darkened with an unreadable intensity as he took a step closer, his posture suddenly tense. "Tell me you don't feel it, Jessica," he said, his voice low but with an undeniable force. "If you tell me, you feel nothing for me, I will walk away."

Jessica's breath hitched, her eyes going wide. "What do you mean?" she asked, her heart racing at the challenge in his voice.

He took another step closer, their bodies almost touching now. The air between them felt charged with electricity. "Tell me you don't want me," he whispered, his voice rough with desire. "Tell me you don't feel it, and I will walk away."

The challenge was clear in his eyes, but there was a vulnerability there too, a part of him hoping she wouldn't say the words he feared.

"Just tell me," Jackson murmured, his voice strained with a raw urgency. "Put me out of my misery. If you don't want me, I'll leave you alone."

He stared at her lips, his own mouth dry, before his gaze flickered up to meet her eyes, searching for any sign of her true feelings.

The silence between them stretched longer, heavy with unspoken words, as Jessica's heart raced in her chest. Her thoughts tumbled in a disarray of uncertainty, but Jackson's intense gaze held her in place, urging her to say what she had kept hidden for so long.

Finally, her voice broke through, barely a whisper. "I do want you."

The words lingered, fragile and raw, and for a long moment, neither of them moved. The air between them crackled with anticipation, a magnetic pull that neither could deny.

Without a word, Jackson reached out and took her hand, guiding her upstairs. His grip was firm but gentle, as if he were afraid to break the fragile connection between them. When they reached his bedroom, he closed the door behind them, the soft click of the lock echoing in the room.

He turned toward her, his gaze searing. "Tell me again," he murmured, his voice low, thick with desire.

Jessica froze, the weight of his words pressing on her chest. She stayed silent, unsure of what to say, unsure of how much of herself she was willing to give away.

Jackson stepped closer, his presence overwhelming. He was so near now that all she had to do was lean in slightly, and their lips would meet. Her breath hitched in her throat, and she felt the heat of his body against hers.

"Tell me," he demanded softly, his voice laced with intensity, sending a shiver down her spine.

"Jackson don't…" Jessica whispered, her voice trembling, a mix of hesitation and longing in her words.

His eyes darkened with something raw, something he couldn't hold back any longer. "Tell me," he repeated, his tone firm yet coaxing, as if he needed to hear it just to make sure he wasn't imagining it.

Jessica closed her eyes, frustration bubbling up inside her as the weight of the moment pressed down on her. She took a deep breath, trying to steady herself, but the truth surged through her like wildfire. "Damn it, I want you, alright?" she said, her voice sharp with emotion, the words spilling out before she could stop them.

The room seemed to hold its breath. And in that instant, all the space between them disappeared. They were in each other's arms instantly, as if the tension that had been building for so long finally erupted. Their lips locked together, urgent, and fierce, as their tongues engaged in a heated battle for supremacy. Every movement was a mix of desire and desperation, their bodies pressing closer as if trying to merge into one. The world outside ceased to exist as they lost themselves in each other, the weight of their feelings finally coming to the surface.

Jackson backed Jessica against the wall, his hands framing her face as their lips remained fused, the kiss deepening with every passing second. Her fingers gripped his shoulders, anchoring herself as his body pressed firmly against hers, leaving no space between them. The cool surface of the wall contrasted with the heat radiating from them both, heightening the intensity of the moment.

Jackson's hand slid down her side, stopping at her waist, his grip possessive yet gentle, as if he couldn't bear to let her go. Jessica's breath hitched, her hands sliding into his hair, pulling him even closer. Neither of them spoke; the kiss said everything their words couldn't.

In one smooth motion, his hands slid lower, cupping her buttocks, and he lifted her effortlessly into his arms as though she weighed nothing.

"Wrap your legs around me," he demanded against her lips, his voice a low growl that sent a shiver through her.

Her heart raced, and without hesitation, she obeyed, her legs locking securely around his hips as he pressed her back against the wall. The intensity between them crackled like fire, their connection undeniable, consuming them both as they gave in to the magnetic pull that had been simmering between them. He ground his arousal into her soft centre, trying to get some relief.

Jackson's lips left hers, trailing soft, heated kisses across her cheek and to her ear. His warm breath sent shivers down her spine as he lingered there for a moment.

"God, I want you, Jess. You don't know how much," Jackson murmured desperately against her ear, his voice raw with longing.

Jessica shivered at his words, the heat of his breath brushing against her skin. Her heart raced; her body pressed against his as if they were drawn together by some invisible force she couldn't fight.

She closed her eyes, trying to steady herself, but his words and the way he held her so tightly made it impossible to think straight.

"Jackson," she whispered, her voice low and husky.

She was completely lost in him, her own desires echoing the intensity of his. She could feel his arousal, hot and hard against her as he ground it against her soft flesh. His lips moved lower, his mouth finding the curve of her neck, his kisses slow and deliberate.

Jessica's hands tightened in his hair as her head fell back against the wall, giving him full access. Her breathing quickened, her heart pounding as his lips explored the sensitive skin of her neck, leaving a trail of fire in their wake. Each kiss seemed to draw them deeper into the moment, the world outside completely forgotten.

"I need you, please, now," Jessica said with passion, her voice trembling with urgency as she gazed into Jackson's eyes.

Her words hit him like a lightning bolt, his restraint crumbling under the weight of her desire. "Jessica…" he breathed, his hands tightening on her buttocks as he pressed her firmly against him.

Their lips collided again, fiercer this time, the heat between them palpable. Her legs still wrapped around his hips, effortlessly he carried her to the side of the bed, their connection unbroken.

"Stand up," he commanded softly, she did as he asked, her legs feeling weak.

They both urgently removed their clothes until they stood there naked in front of each other, fully aroused. The world outside didn't exist, leaving only the intensity of the moment, raw and undeniable.

He gently picked Jessica up and laid her on the bed, her hair fanning out across the pillows like a halo. For a moment, he didn't move, just stood there looking down at her, his breathing heavy and his heart pounding.

Her cheeks were flushed, her lips slightly swollen from their kisses, and her green eyes locked onto his, shimmering with anticipation and something deeper—longing.

"You're so beautiful," Jackson murmured, his voice low and reverent, as though the words were meant only for her.

Jessica reached up, her fingers brushing against his jaw. "Jackson," she whispered, her voice soft but full of emotion.

That one word, spoken in that way, undid him. Jackson eased down beside her, leaning on one elbow, his gaze fixed on her as though she was the only thing that mattered in the world. His other hand found her waist, his grip firm but tender, as he gently pulled her closer.

Jessica's breath hitched as their bodies aligned, his arousal hard up against her thigh, her hand instinctively resting on his shoulder. She could feel the steady rhythm of his heartbeat in his chest next to hers. His hand glided from her waist to her firm, milky white breast, moulding it to his hand, softly pinching her rosy pert nipple. His touch was electric, igniting something deep within her, yet the moment was laced with an unexpected tenderness that took her by surprise.

"Oh, yes," she breathed, her voice trembling as her eyes fluttered closed. She surrendered to the sensation, letting herself focus entirely on the warmth of his touch, the way his hand moved against her skin, igniting a fire within her.

Jackson watched her for a moment, captivated by the way she responded to him. Then, unable to resist, he leaned in and claimed her lips again, while his fingers teased her tight nipple. The kiss was deeper this time, more intense, his passion pouring into every movement.

Jessica melted against him, her hands gripping his shoulders as if anchoring herself in the moment. The world outside the room disappeared, leaving only the heat between them and the unspoken promises lingering in the air.

His hand released her breast, the sudden absence left Jessica feeling an unexpected ache, an instant sense of abandonment. His hand gliding down her taut stomach to cup her feminine mound at the apex of her thighs. The warmth of his touch was all-consuming. He lifted his head and looked at her intently.

"Jackson," she whispered, her voice soft yet filled with yearning. Her hand reached up, brushing against his jaw, trying to pull him back to her. "Please don't stop."

"Jessica, you don't know what you're doing to me," he murmured, his voice rough with emotion.

His eyes never leaving hers as his fingers slid into her hot moist folds. Her eyes fluttered closed as she releasing a soft moan of pleasure from her swollen lips.

He lowered his lips to her neck and kissed and nibbled his way to her breast taking the taut peak into his hot moist mouth and sucked. She whimpered and squirmed under him, while his fingers gently parted her fleshy folds to seek out her secret nub. His fingers gently circled the aroused flesh then rubbed gently at first, building the pressure gradually, while taking turns sucking and licking her rosy nipples.

The pressure was building within her, she was seeking release, his fingers, mouth, and tongue evoking exquisite torture. Then there was a flash of bright white light under her eyelids as the flood gates opened and her whole body exploded intense pleasure.

Her fingernails dug into the flesh on his shoulders, and she softly screamed, "Jackson!"

He slid a finger into her, as her internal muscles convulsed, gripping him, he took her lips in a passionate kiss as her body trembled with the intensity of her climax.

He lifted his head and looked down at her as her eyes opened, searching his face, and she saw the conflict flickering in his expression.

"Jessica…" he murmured, his voice a low rasp that sent a shiver down her spine, "I don't have protection."

She looked up at him, her green eyes wide and vulnerable, "I'm on the pill," she whispered, her voice barely audible.

He let out a groan and lowered his head, their lips locking together, urgent, and fierce, as their tongues tangled. Knowing that she was ready for him, he lifted himself and settled between her parted, soft thighs, positioning himself at her entrance.

Jessica tensed slightly, anticipating the discomfort of her first time. She bit her lower lip as he pressed kisses along her neck, lingering over her pulse, which throbbed beneath his lips.

He eased into her body slowly, giving her body time to relax and adjust. Then, with one deep, powerful thrust, he buried himself fully into her hot tight centre, drawing a gasp from her lips.

He quickly looked down at her, concern etched in his eyes. "Are you okay?" he asked softly, his brain not wanting to engage in what his body was telling him.

Unable to speak from the sharp ache, she nodded, burying her face in his neck to hide the pain. He placed his elbows on either side of her head.

Resting on his elbows he whispered against her skin, he murmured, "God, you feel incredible…, you're so hot and wet, just perfect."

He began to move, withdrawing slowly from her honeyed warmth before easing back in, each motion igniting a new wave of sensation. Her eyes flew open, her breath catching as exquisite pleasure replaced the pain, filling her with an intensity she had never known.

"Yes," she cried, "Jackson, yes!"

Jackson groaned, capturing her mouth with his, as his tongue plundered her mouth, his body plundered her sweet centre. Grinding into her with each thrust, he increased his pace, driving them both to the edge. Jessica's body instinctively matched his rhythm, succumbing to the rising tide of pleasure that enveloped them.

As the pleasure built, his body pounded into hers over and over again. Finally, they both tethered on the brink, almost, then they both fell over the edge, crying out each other's names in ecstasy. A deep primal groan escaped Jackson's lips as he released himself inside her, feeling the warmth of Jessica's body pulse around him with her powerful climax, milking him dry. He held still, savouring the moment as they were both caught in the ebb and flow of their mutual ecstasy.

Chapter Fifteen

After catching his breath, Jackson rolled off Jessica and gently pulled her into his arms, guiding her half on top of him. His voice was hoarse, a mix of urgency and uncertainty, as he looked up at her. "Please tell me that wasn't your first time."

"Okay, I won't tell you," she murmured, resting her head against his chest.

"Jessica?" His voice softened, concern edging his words.

"You asked me not to," she teased, a smile tugging at her lips, warm against his skin.

A sigh escaped him as he tightened his arms around her. "I could have hurt you. You should have said something."

She lifted her head, meeting his gaze with quiet intensity. "Well, you didn't," she reassured him, offering a smile that barely touched her lips. "No harm done."

Jackson kissed the tip of her nose, his voice filled with awe. "That was incredible."

"Yes, it was, wasn't it?" she replied, a playful glint in her eyes as she stood and walked toward the ensuite. The door clicked shut behind her, and she leaned against it, breath shaky. *What have I done?*

As the door closed, Jackson stood, picked up his discarded underwear, and slid them on, noticing the blood on him. He sat at the edge of the bed, a smile tugging at his lips. He didn't want to let her go—not yet—but he needed a moment to think. He couldn't believe she hadn't told him she was a virgin, and the thought lingered in his mind, making him feel both privileged and possessive. The way she'd responded to him—so completely—only deepened the urge to protect what they shared. But now, with her in the other room, he wrestled with his emotions, torn between desire and the overwhelming need to claim her in every sense.

Jessica cleaned herself up, then returned to the bedroom. Jackson was waiting, sitting on the edge of the bed. He held his arms out, and without hesitation, she walked over, settling on his lap. His arms wrapped around her waist as he leaned in to kiss her softly, savouring the connection.

"Does this mean no more Terry?" he asked, his tone light but with an edge of expectation.

Jessica pulled back slightly, raising an incredulous brow. "I didn't say that."

"What?" He looked confused. "Surely, you're not still going to see him after what just happened."

"I don't know," Jessica said, her voice quiet but steady.

"What do you mean you don't know?" Jackson's brow furrowed; disbelief written all over his face. "After everything…?"

She pulled away from him, slipping out of his hold. As she began dressing quickly, her movements sharp, purposeful, he watched in growing frustration.

"Just because we had sex doesn't mean I'm yours," she said firmly, refusing to meet his gaze as she buttoned her shirt.

Jackson stared at her, his face hardening with anger and confusion. "It wasn't just sex, Jessica," he said, his voice tight. "You lost your virginity to me. You said you wanted me. It meant something to me."

"I did want you," she said coldly, pulling on her jacket. "Now that it's happened, I thought you'd be over it."

"Over it?" Jackson snapped, his anger rising. "What the hell, Jessica?"

"Jackson, you know you don't want me," Jessica said, her voice firm but bitter. "You wanted me physically. You've had me. Now you can go back to your perfect life and forget about me."

"What are you saying?" He stepped closer, his voice low, hurt and frustration flickering in his eyes.

"I don't want to be hurt by you again," Jessica's voice trembled as she struggled to keep her emotions in check. "You didn't even look at me sideways five years ago. You didn't talk to me after my parents died. I wasn't 'attractive' enough for you then."

Jackson moved toward her, his voice urgent. "I know I was an idiot back then. But I'm not like that anymore. I want you in my life."

Her tears spilled over as she took a shaky step back. "What happens if a dog mauls me? If my face is scarred or my arm gets ripped off on a construction site?" Her voice cracked with anguish. "Do you just discard me because I'm not 'attractive' anymore?"

Anguish filled Jackson's eyes as he took a step closer, his voice raw. "I'm not shallow, Jessica. I see how amazing you are—all of you. I don't care what you look like. I like you—every part of you, not just the outside."

"Five years ago, I thought the sun shone out of you," Jessica said, her voice trembling. "Even though you barely gave me the time of day. Then I heard what you thought of me, and it hurt. It hurt so badly."

"Jessica—" Jackson started, his voice soft, but she cut him off, raising her hand.

"No," she said firmly. "Now you want me to risk my heart on someone I believe will discard me the moment I don't fit the image he wants me to be." Her voice broke as she took a shaky breath. "You're a higher risk than most."

Her words hit Jackson like a slap, leaving him silent. He stepped closer, his voice low, pleading. "Please, let me prove I'm worth the risk."

Jessica looked at him, sadness in her eyes. "I need to think."

A flicker of hope ignited inside Jackson. He walked to her, pulling her gently into his arms, holding her close. He looked down at her, his voice soft, almost fragile. "What did what happened here mean to you?" he asked, hoping to glimpse her heart.

"Everything," she whispered, leaning into his embrace. Her hands trembled against his chest, the weight of her emotions too much to bear.

Jackson tightened his arms around her, relieved yet uncertain. "I don't want to lose you," he murmured, his voice thick with emotion.

"I don't know if I can trust you," she said sadly, her voice breaking.

Jackson's heart sank, but he didn't pull away. He cupped her face in his hands, his eyes earnest. "I've never felt like this with anyone. What we have... it's real. I need you to believe that."

Before she could respond, a loud knock at the door startled them. Jackson instinctively wrapped her tightly in his arms, his body protective, as he called out, "Yes?"

"Jackson, it's Phyllis. Have you seen Jessica? I can't find her," came the voice from the other side of the door.

Jackson glanced down at Jessica. Her face was pale, and she shook her head slightly, signalling that she didn't want Phyllis to know she was in here with him.

"Mum said she went out with Terry," Jackson called back, his voice steady but unsure.

"Oh, did she?" Phyllis replied casually, though suspicion lingered in her voice. Jackson glanced at Jessica, his arms still holding her close. The tension in the air thickened.

Then, suddenly, the doorknob rattled.

"Why is your door locked?" Phyllis's voice was sharp with growing concern.

"Go away, Phyllis," Jackson said, his tone firm but strained. His heart raced as Jessica stiffened in his arms. This moment was spiralling.

Jessica whispered urgently, "Get dressed."

Jackson reluctantly let go of her, quickly throwing on his clothes while Jessica straightened the bed, her movements quick but distracted. She then sat at the end of the bed, trying to compose herself.

"She's in there, isn't she?" Phyllis demanded, her voice rising, unmistakably laced with accusation. "Open this door, Jackson."

Jackson glanced at Jessica, and she nodded, a quiet signal that it was okay to let Phyllis in. With a deep breath, Jackson walked to the door, opening it just enough to grab Phyllis's arm, dragging her inside before quickly closing it behind them.

Phyllis glared at Jessica, then Jackson, her eyes flashing with anger. "You better not be hurting my best friend again," she said, her voice tight with both concern and accusation. The words hung heavy in the room, and Jackson could feel the weight of their meaning pressing down on him.

Jessica gently reassured Phyllis, her voice steady but soft. "He's not, Phyllis. We needed to talk."

Phyllis looked at her, her expression still full of concern, but she sat down next to Jessica and wrapped her arms around her. "Are you sure?" she asked, her voice laced with worry.

Jackson stood there, watching the exchange, frustration creeping in. He glanced at his sister, his jaw clenched. "Why do you think I would hurt her?"

Phyllis shot him a withering look, her eyes narrowing. "Because you have in the past. You were bloody horrible to her."

Jackson's heart twisted. "I care about Jessica," he said, his voice firm and sincere.

Phyllis raised an eyebrow, incredulous. "Since when?" she demanded. "Since Terry's been interested?"

"No!" Jackson snapped, the defensiveness clear in his voice. "It has nothing to do with Terry." He stepped closer, his voice firm and vulnerable, his words heavy with truth. "I've always cared about her, I just… was too stupid and self-absorbed to see it."

Phyllis let out a sharp laugh, the sound laced with disbelief. "Ha," she said, shaking her head. "You really expect me to believe that? After all this time?" She stood up, her arms crossed, eyes glaring at him. "You broke her heart once, Jackson. You don't just get to waltz in now and pretend everything's different. Did you know Jessica didn't come to visit me for five years because of you?"

"Phyllis," Jessica tried to stop her, her voice panicked. She hadn't told Jackson that, and she wasn't sure if she wanted him to know, especially not in this moment.

Jackson looked at Jessica, his eyes searching hers. "Is that true?" he asked softly, his voice barely above a whisper, as if the weight of her words had struck him harder than he'd expected.

Jessica nodded, her gaze dropping to the floor, the weight of Phyllis's words pressing on her chest.

Phyllis, not missing a beat, crossed her arms and glared at Jackson. "Of course it's true," she said, her voice laced with frustration. She paused, her expression softening as she looked at Jessica before turning back to Jackson. "And I don't want to lose my best friend again because my brother is an ass."

Jackson stood silent for a moment, the sting of Phyllis's words sinking in. His chest tightened, guilt gnawing at him, but there was also a sense of resolve. He had to prove to both of them that he was different now, that he wasn't going to repeat his past mistakes.

Phyllis looked at Jackson, her expression softening, but her tone still firm. "Jackson, you are the smartest person I know, and you're a damn good lawyer, and I love you," she said, her voice filled with sincerity. "But I love Jessica too, like a sister. You can't play with people's feelings."

Jackson took a deep breath, the weight of her words settling in. He met Phyllis's gaze with determination in his eyes. "Phyllis, I know I screwed up. But I am going to prove to both of you that I'm not that idiot anymore. I'm not going to hurt her again. I swear."

His voice, low and steady, left no room for doubt, as if he was finally ready to make things right.

Jessica stood up and looked at Phyllis, her heart swelling with gratitude. She walked over to her, wrapping her arms around her in a tight embrace. "I love you too," she whispered, her voice thick with emotion.

Phyllis hugged her back, holding her tightly as if trying to reassure both of them. When they pulled apart, Jessica turned to Jackson, her gaze steady, but there was a flicker of something uncertain behind her eyes.

"Okay," she said, her voice quiet but resolute. "I will give you a chance."

Jackson's face lit up instantly, the relief flooding through him like a wave. Without a second thought, he rushed to her, his arms pulling her close. He kissed her hard, a kiss full of passion and urgency, as though trying to convey everything he couldn't say in words. His hands cradled her face gently, but his lips were firm, desperate to show her how much this moment meant to him.

For a moment, nothing else mattered but the two of them, the uncertainty of the past replaced by a spark of hope for the future.

Finally, Phyllis looked at them both, her arms crossed with a playful yet knowing smile. "Well, I know Mum and Dad will be happy," she said, her voice light. Then she let out a small laugh, the tension in the room easing.

She walked up to them and pulled both Jackson and Jessica into a tight group hug, her arms wrapping around them both. "Don't blow this, Jackson," she added, her voice turning serious, but her tone still filled with affection. "Jessica is special."

Jackson squeezed both of them tightly, nodding. "I won't, Phyllis," he promised, his voice full of determination. "I won't."

Jessica caught in the middle of their embrace, couldn't help but smile, a mixture of relief and excitement filling her chest. For the first time in a long while, she felt like maybe, just maybe, they were heading in the right direction. She was scared, for sure, but love is worth the risk, *isn't it?*

Chapter Sixteen

Jessica and Jackson walked into the dining room together, their hands intertwined, a subtle but undeniable connection between them. It wasn't just the way they held hands—it was the way their eyes lingered on each other, the quiet warmth they shared. Nathan glanced up from his seat, and a wide grin spread across his face.

"About time, Jackson," Nathan teased, leaning back in his chair. "Make sure you treat her right." His tone was playful, but the sincerity behind his words was clear.

John followed closely behind the pair, immediately catching on to the shift in their dynamic. He clapped his son on the back, a knowing smile tugging at his lips. "Looks like you finally woke up, Jackson," he said, his voice filled with good-natured amusement, before moving to take his usual seat at the head of the table.

Jessica felt her cheeks flush as she slid into her seat, Jackson settling beside her and casually resting a hand on her thigh beneath the table. The small, protective gesture sent a warm flutter through her chest, though she tried to keep her expression neutral.

Dinner was served by Helen and Sarah, the two women moving seamlessly through the room as they catered to the now twelve people staying in the house. The clink of plates and the low hum of conversation filled the air, creating a lively but comfortable atmosphere.

Mary, seated at the far end of the table, caught Phyllis's eye with a knowing smile. "So, Phyllis," she began in a teasing tone, "did you girls have a good time last night?"

Phyllis grinned, leaning back in her chair with a contented sigh. "Oh, we had the best time, Mum. Jessica absolutely nailed the planning—she even booked us a stripper."

Nathan, who had been mid-sip of his drink, choked slightly. "A stripper?" he repeated, his brows furrowing as he glanced at his fiancée. "What does that mean?"

Phyllis's grin widened as she reached over to pat his arm. "Relax, Nathan. He danced, I blushed, and then Jessica got a freebie." She winked at Jessica, who immediately flushed a deep shade of red.

"I did not!" Jessica protested, her voice rising just enough to catch the attention of a few nearby. "She means dance. A free dance." Her tone was slightly too quick, and the table erupted into laughter at her flustered response.

Phyllis wasn't ready to let it go. "It's true, though. I was a bit… distracted, but Jessica stayed sensible. Didn't even drink much."

John chuckled from his end of the table. "We noticed. She was out jogging at the crack of dawn this morning."

Jessica offered a sheepish smile, brushing a strand of hair behind her ear. "Excessive drinking isn't really my thing. I'm not a fan of headaches."

Phyllis leaned forward, a mischievous glint in her eye. "But her idea for us all to wear pink hot pants was genius. We were the life of the party."

Jessica rolled her eyes, though a small smile tugged at her lips. "That's an exaggeration."

"It's not." Phyllis's grin widened. "Amanda and Kylie got a few numbers, and I'm pretty sure Jessica could've left with half the bar if she wanted."

Jessica's blush deepened as she ducked her head. "That's not true," she muttered, her voice barely audible.

"Oh, come on," Phyllis pressed. "How many coasters with phone numbers did you get?"

"Just a few," Jessica admitted reluctantly, her eyes fixed firmly on her plate.

Jackson, who had been quietly enjoying the exchange, leaned closer with a raised brow. "Just a few?" he echoed, his tone teasing. "I'm going to have to keep an eye on you."

Jessica shot him a sideways glance, her lips twitching into a small smile despite her embarrassment. "You don't have to worry."

Nathan's father, Eric, leaned forward, raising an eyebrow as he fixed his son with a curious look. "What about you, Nathan? How was your night? Your mother and I noticed you didn't show your face until late this afternoon. I take it you had a bit too much to drink?"

Nathan shifted uncomfortably in his seat, shooting a sideways glance at Jackson. "You could say that."

Jackson, never one to miss an opportunity, leaned back with a broad grin. "Don't look at me—I wasn't as bad as you. And you're lucky I wasn't, mate. The other boys were all for stripping you down and tying you to a lamp post."

Nathan's face went pale, his eyes widening in disbelief. "They didn't!" he exclaimed, his voice rising slightly.

Jackson's grin only grew wider, a mischievous twinkle in his eye. "Let's just say you owe me. I talked them out of it. But trust me—you were close. Not sure your dignity would've survived the night."

Nathan groaned, muttering something under his breath as he stared down at his plate, clearly trying to salvage a shred of pride.

His mother, who had been listening quietly until now, gasped, her eyes widening as she fixed Nathan with a scandalised look. "Oh, my lord!" she exclaimed. "What kind of trouble have you boys been getting into?"

The table erupted into laughter, the playful teasing only adding to Nathan's embarrassment. He sank lower into his seat, a sheepish smile tugging at the corners of his lips. "Next time, I'll be the sensible one," he muttered, though the faint humour in his tone betrayed him.

Phyllis, ever the quick-witted one, leaned toward Nathan with a teasing glint in her eye. "There won't be a next time," she quipped, her tone both playful and pointed. "You're only getting married once, remember?"

Nathan groaned again, slumping further in his chair as a chorus of laughter filled the room. But this time, he joined in, shaking his head in resignation as he chuckled along with the rest.

Mary, who had been enjoying the banter, leaned forward with a warm smile. "Don't forget," she said, addressing the group, "the big barbecue is Tuesday afternoon. It'll start at three."

Phyllis perked up at the mention of the event, her eyes lighting up with excitement. "How many people are coming?" she asked, her tone bright and eager.

Mary grinned, clearly just as thrilled. "We're expecting about a hundred guests, including all of us."

Phyllis clapped her hands, a wide smile spreading across her face. "I can't wait!" she exclaimed, her enthusiasm so infectious that everyone around the table exchanged amused, knowing looks.

After dinner, the warm February evening beckoned the group outside. Phyllis, Nathan, Jackson, and Jessica decided to take a late-night swim; the clear night sky dotted with stars adding a touch of magic to the moment.

The water was cool and refreshing, and laughter echoed softly as they splashed and teased each other. Nathan and Phyllis sat at the edge of the pool, their feet dangling in the water, while Jackson held Jessica gently, her body floating effortlessly in his arms.

Nathan leaned back, a mischievous glint in his eyes as he looked at Jackson. "So," he began, his tone casual but laced with teasing, "are you going to let Terry know that Jessica's off the market?"

Jackson chuckled, his grip on Jessica tightening ever so slightly. "I think he'll figure it out at the barbecue Tuesday," he replied smoothly. "But if not, I'll make sure to set him straight."

Jessica, her head resting against Jackson's chest, felt a blush creep up her neck at the mention of Terry. "Terry's just a friend," she said softly, her voice warm but firm. "He hasn't done anything wrong."

Nathan raised a brow, clearly enjoying the moment. "A friend? Is that what they're calling it these days?" He grinned as Jessica shot him a look, and Jackson let out a low laugh.

"Don't worry," Jackson said, his tone turning slightly more serious. "I'll be respectful. But he'll get the message loud and clear."

Phyllis leaned forward from her spot at the edge of the pool, a playful smirk on her face. "Oh, Terry's going to figure it out. When he sees how Jackson looks at you, Jess, he'll know he doesn't stand a chance."

Jessica's blush deepened, but she couldn't help the smile that tugged at her lips. "Just don't make it a scene," she murmured, her green eyes meeting Jackson's. "I don't want to hurt him."

Jackson's expression softened as he met her gaze, his voice gentle but firm. "I won't," he promised. "But I'm not letting anyone think they can take you away from me."

Nathan let out a low whistle, shaking his head with a grin. "Looks like you're serious, mate. You're a lucky man."

Jackson smiled, his eyes never leaving Jessica's. "I know."

Nathan and Phyllis went to bed soon after, leaving Jackson and Jessica alone under the soft glow of the outdoor lights.

The stillness of the night wrapped around them, accompanied by the faint chirping of crickets and the gentle lapping of the water. Still in the pool, Jackson adjusted Jessica in his arms, so she was facing him. His hands rested on her waist, holding her close, while her arms instinctively looped around his neck.

"You're beautiful, inside and out," he said, his voice low but filled with sincerity. The words carried a depth that made her heart skip a beat.

Jessica tilted her head, a playful smile tugging at her lips. "You're not so bad yourself," she teased, her tone light, though her cheeks flushed under his intense gaze.

Jackson chuckled softly, brushing a stray strand of wet hair from her face. "Cheeky," he murmured, his thumb gently tracing her cheek.

Jessica's teasing expression softened, her eyes locking with his. "You wouldn't have me any other way."

Jackson's gaze deepened, his heart tightening at her honesty. "I'll take you any way I can," he said firmly, his voice brimming with emotion.

The distance between them disappeared as Jackson tilted his head, his lips brushing hers in a kiss that was slow and filled with unspoken promise. The world around them faded away, leaving only the warmth of the moment and the undeniable connection between them.

When they finally pulled apart, Jessica let out a soft laugh, her cheeks flushed. "That was unexpected," she said, though her radiant smile betrayed her delight.

"Unexpected?" Jackson repeated, a smirk tugging at his lips. "I've been wanting to do that all night."

Jessica shook her head, laughter spilling from her lips. "You're impossible."

"And yet, here you are," he teased, his tone light, though his gaze held a quiet intensity.

"Here I am," she echoed softly, her voice tinged with a warmth that mirrored his.

The moment stretched between them; the air charged with emotion. The gentle sounds of the night seemed to hold their breath, framing their newfound connection in perfect stillness.

After a beat, Jackson cleared his throat, breaking the quiet spell. "It's getting late," he said, his voice a little huskier than usual. "We should go up."

Jessica nodded, her heart fluttering at his thoughtfulness. Together, they stepped out of the pool, the cool night air brushing against their damp skin. Jackson draped a towel around her shoulders before grabbing one for himself, his protective gesture drawing a shy smile from her.

They made their way back inside, the house silent except for the soft creak of the staircase under their feet. The warm glow of the hallway lights illuminated their path as they walked side by side, the comfortable silence between them speaking volumes.

At the door to her room, Jessica turned to face Jackson, her hand resting lightly on the doorknob. "Have a good sleep," she said softly, her gaze flickering to his.

"You too," Jackson replied, his voice low. He hesitated for a moment before stepping closer, his hand brushing hers where it rested on the door.

"Good night, Jess," he murmured, his eyes searching hers.

"Good night, Jackson," she whispered, her voice barely audible.

Before she could turn away, Jackson leaned in, pressing a tender kiss to her lips. It was soft and unhurried, filled with a quiet promise that made her toes curl. When he pulled back, his thumb grazed her cheek for the briefest moment.

Jessica's breath hitched, and she offered him a smile that was equal parts shy and luminous. Without another word, she slipped into her room, closing the door gently behind her.

Jackson stood there for a moment, his hand still resting on the frame, a satisfied smile playing on his lips. Then, with a quiet exhale, he turned and headed down the hall, his steps lighter than they'd been in years.

Chapter Seventeen

The barbecue was in full swing. Laughter and chatter filled the warm afternoon air, blending with the sizzling sound of meat cooking on the grill. Waiters moved seamlessly among the guests, serving cold drinks and replenishing the tables laden with colourful salads, grilled vegetables, fresh fruits, and an array of condiments.

Phyllis and Nathan were clearly the centre of attention, surrounded by friends and family offering heartfelt congratulations and good-natured teasing about their upcoming wedding. Nearby, Jackson stood beside his father, John, flipping burgers and turning skewers on the massive barbecue grill. His easy banter with John and the other guests passing by added to the lively atmosphere.

Across the yard, a few people were cooling off in the pool, their laughter punctuating the hum of conversations. Jessica stood to the side, sipping a cool lemonade. She'd just finished a pleasant conversation with Nathan's parents, who had spoken warmly about their joy in welcoming Phyllis into their family.

She glanced up to see Terry walking toward her, his easy smile lighting up his face. Jessica returned the smile as he approached.

"Hello, Jessica," he greeted warmly.

"Hi, Terry. Nice day for a barbecue," she replied, her tone cheerful.

Terry nodded, glancing around. "It certainly is."

A brief silence settled between them, both seeming to search for the right words. Then, they spoke at the same time.

"Jessica—"

"Terry—"

Jessica let out a small laugh. "Sorry, you go first."

"No, please, go ahead," Terry said, his smile encouraging.

Jessica hesitated for a moment, then looked up at him, her expression soft but resolute. "I need to let you know that Jackson and I have started dating," she said, her tone apologetic.

Terry's smile faltered slightly, but he recovered quickly, nodding. "I had a feeling that was going to happen."

Jessica's brows drew together, and she shifted on her feet. "I'm really sorry, Terry. I never meant to—"

Before she could finish, Jackson's familiar voice cut in.

"Hello, sweetheart," he said as he slid his arms around her waist from behind, pressing a light kiss to the side of her temple.

Terry's expression remained polite but tinged with something unreadable. "Hey, Jackson," he said, his tone even as he extended a hand for a firm handshake.

"Terry," Jackson replied with a nod, his hand resting protectively on Jessica's hip.

Jessica glanced between the two men, sensing the slight tension beneath their friendly exteriors. Before she could say anything, Phyllis called her over from across the yard.

"Excuse me," Jessica said, offering both men an apologetic smile. "I'll be back in a bit." She gave Jackson a quick squeeze on the arm before walking off toward Phyllis.

The moment she was out of earshot, Terry crossed his arms and leaned slightly toward Jackson, a wry smile playing on his lips. "Well, mate, congratulations," he said, his tone cordial but with a subtle edge.

Jackson raised an eyebrow. "Thanks," he replied, his tone steady, meeting Terry's gaze evenly.

Terry's smile widened, though it didn't quite reach his eyes. "I mean it. Jess is an amazing woman. But just so we're clear..." He stepped a little closer, his voice lowering slightly. "If you screw this up, if you hurt her in any way, I'll be right there to pick up the pieces. And trust me, I won't waste any time showing her what she really deserves."

Jackson's jaw tightened, but he didn't rise to the bait. Instead, he smirked, his confidence unshaken. "Good to know, Terry. But you won't get the chance. I know exactly what I've got, and I don't plan on letting her down."

Terry tilted his head, studying Jackson for a moment before nodding slowly. "For her sake I hope you don't, but we will see," he said with a faint shrug, his tone still friendly but unmistakably pointed.

Jackson watched as Terry walked away, his grip tightening slightly on the bottle of beer in his hand. After a beat, he took a steadying breath, his gaze following Jessica across the yard as she laughed with Phyllis.

His determination only grew. He wasn't going to let anyone—least of all Terry—doubt his intentions or his ability to cherish the woman who had quickly become the centre of his world.

Jessica watched from the corner of her eye as Terry and Jackson exchanged words. She couldn't hear what was being said, but the subtle tension in their stances told her it wasn't just small talk.

Beside her, Phyllis followed her gaze, arching an eyebrow. "I assume Terry knows about you and Jackson now?" she asked casually, taking a sip from her glass.

Jessica turned back to Phyllis, letting out a soft sigh. "Yes, I told him before you called me over just now," she admitted, her tone tinged with guilt. "I hope I didn't hurt him."

Phyllis smiled reassuringly and gave Jessica a gentle pat on the arm. "Don't worry about it. It's not like you've known him for long. And besides, it's better to be honest upfront than to lead him on."

"I know," Jessica agreed, her brows furrowing slightly. "But he did make his intentions clear, and you know I don't like hurting people."

"Jess, you're one of the kindest people I know," Phyllis said warmly. "But sometimes, you have to prioritise your own happiness. And clearly, for you that happiness involves Jackson, like Nathan is for mine."

Jessica smiled faintly, the tension in her shoulders easing just a little. Before she could respond, the two men in question approached them. Jackson walked with his usual confident stride, while Nathan followed with a more relaxed demeanour, holding a plate of food.

"Ladies," Nathan greeted cheerfully, setting the plate down on the nearby table. "You're both too far away from the food. Care for some barbecue?"

Phyllis grinned, immediately grabbing a piece of grilled corn. "Don't mind if I do. Thanks, babe."

Jackson's gaze immediately found Jessica's, his expression softening as he reached her side. "Everything okay?" he asked, slipping an arm around her waist.

Jessica nodded, her smile growing. "Yeah, just catching up with Phyllis."

Nathan glanced between them, an amused smirk tugging at his lips. "Well, isn't this cozy?" he teased, earning a playful nudge from Phyllis.

"Don't start," Phyllis warned with a grin, though her eyes sparkled with mischief. "I'm just happy to see Jessica smiling."

Jackson chuckled, his thumb brushing absentmindedly against Jessica's side. "I'll do my best to keep it that way."

Jessica rolled her eyes but couldn't suppress her smile. "I'm always smiling."

Nathan leaned back against the table, eyeing the group with a playful grin. "So, I assume Terry knows now? How'd that go?"

Jackson's jaw tightened slightly, but his tone remained light as he replied, "He knows."

Phyllis gave Jessica a knowing look but said nothing, choosing instead to take another bite of her corn.

Jessica glanced at Jackson, sensing his tension despite his calm exterior. She reached up, lightly resting her hand on his chest. "Are you okay," she asked softly, meeting his eyes. "What did Terry say to you?"

Jackson's expression softened further, and he gave her a small nod. "Everything is fine," he murmured.

Nathan, sensing the shift in the mood, clapped his hands together. "Alright, enough of the heavy stuff. How about we all grab some dessert? I saw someone bring out a chocolate fountain earlier, and I don't plan to miss out."

Phyllis laughed, grabbing his hand. "You and your sweet tooth. Let's go."

As the pair walked off toward the dessert table, Jessica turned back to Jackson.

"They're right, you know," she said, her tone gentle. "Let's just enjoy the day."

Jackson smiled, brushing a strand of hair from her face. "As long as I'm with you, I already am."

She laughed softly, shaking her head. "Come on, Mr. Smooth Talker. Let's catch up with them."

But as they began walking, Jackson leaned down to whisper in her ear, his voice low and teasing. "I'm not letting you get away; you know."

Jessica glanced up at him, her smile turning playful. "I'm not going anywhere."

The barbecue had been a complete success. The food was devoured, the laughter had flowed effortlessly, and the party had stretched on into the night. As the final guests departed, there was a sense of contentment in the air, as though the joy of the gathering still lingered like the warmth from the grill. After a quick round of cleaning up, Phyllis, Nathan, Jessica, and Jackson found themselves in the cozy living room, the soft hum of the house creating an atmosphere of contentment as the night began to wind down. They had spent the evening chatting and laughing with friends and family, but now the chatter had died down, and only the sound of glasses clinking and the occasional soft laugh broke the quiet.

Nathan, lounging back in his chair with a magazine in his hand, broke the silence with a teasing question. "So, Jess," he said, looking up from the pages with a grin, "have you decided to buy a home yet?"

Jessica, her fingers absently tapping the glass of lemonade she had refilled earlier, shook her head. "No, not yet," she said thoughtfully. "I had a really good conversation with John last night. He convinced me to hold off for a little while longer. He thinks I should settle into my new job first before I make any big decisions about where I want to live."

Phyllis, sitting beside Nathan with a mischievous twinkle in her eye, let out a small laugh. "You know, Dad's got an ulterior motive," she said, her grin widening.

Jessica raised an eyebrow in confusion. "What could that possibly be?" she asked, genuinely puzzled.

Phyllis leaned back, crossing her legs casually, and gave her a playful look. "Mum and Dad want you to stay here," she explained with a wink. "He wasn't happy when you went to Perth. You know how he promised your father that he'd look after you, then you went off and decided to live with your aunt, who you hardly knew. He wasn't too thrilled about that. In fact, he sulked for months after you left."

Jessica looked at Jackson, her expression thoughtful. "She's right. I remember Dad mentioning how you should have stayed here with your friends. He said it would have been easier on you."

Nathan, who had been listening quietly, gave a small nod in agreement. "He did say that a few times," he said, his voice soft.

Jessica took a deep breath, her fingers still playing with the edge of her glass. "The thing is, I left Sydney because I felt like I needed to get away. I needed space. To be honest, I was only planning to stay in Perth for a year, and then I thought I'd transfer. But then my aunt's marriage fell apart, and she needed me. It felt like the right thing to do, to stay and help her out. When you asked me to be your maid of honour, though, that really made me think about how much I missed you, Nathan, John, and Mary." Her gaze shifted to Jackson, and she gave him a soft smile. "I even missed you."

Jackson's face softened as he met her eyes. "Aww, thanks," he said with a grin, but there was a tenderness in his voice that made her heart skip a beat.

Jessica continued, her voice growing more reflective. "My aunt had just remarried, so I thought, why not move back? I knew I'd have support here. I knew my company had a branch over here, so I asked if I could transfer. If they'd said no, I was ready to quit and figure something out when I got back to Sydney. But then the Sydney office needed another civil engineer, and I got lucky. It all fell into place. Honestly, I don't regret coming back at all."

Nathan, who had been watching her with an appreciative smile, nodded. "Sounds like it was meant to be," he said softly. "You're back home, and everything seems to be falling into place."

Jessica smiled, her eyes glancing around the room, at the faces of her friends and family. She felt a sense of peace, something she hadn't felt in a long time. "Yeah," she said quietly, her voice filled with emotion. "It really does feel like it was meant to be."

Jackson, who had been watching her intently, reached over and gently squeezed her hand. "I'm glad you came back," he said, his tone sincere. "I'm glad you're here."

Jessica's heart warmed at his words. She had no doubt that her decision to return had been the right one, not just for her career but for the people in her life who mattered most. And, with Jackson's hand in hers, she couldn't help but feel that everything was falling into place just as it was supposed to.

As the conversation turned toward lighter topics, the laughter and chatter filling the room, Jessica felt a quiet contentment settle over her.

Later that evening, the house settled into a peaceful quiet, Jackson walked Jessica to her bedroom door. They stood in the hall, their eyes meeting in a soft, lingering gaze. Jackson brushed a stray lock of hair from Jessica's face, his touch gentle yet full of intent. Without a word, he leaned in, and their lips met in a passionate kiss, the kind that spoke of everything they hadn't yet said.

When they finally pulled apart, breathless and flushed, Jessica placed a hand on his chest, her voice soft and eager. "When can I be with you again?"

Jackson knew exactly what she meant. The desire in her eyes mirrored his own, but he wanted to be careful, to savour the moments between them without rushing. "We don't have anything planned tomorrow," he said, his voice low and inviting. "I was actually going to ask if you wanted to spend the day with me at my penthouse. Just the two of us."

Jessica's face lit up, her smile widening. "Yes, that sounds wonderful."

Jackson's lips curled into a satisfied smile. "Great. We will leave after breakfast."

"Okay," Jessica replied, her voice filled with anticipation.

"Are you going for a run in the morning."

"Yes."

"Well, I will see you then."

With one last lingering kiss on her cheek, Jackson turned and walked down the hall to his room, her heart racing with excitement for the day ahead.

Chapter Eighteen

The sun had barely risen, casting a soft golden light across the streets as Jessica and Jackson slipped quietly out of the house. It was just after 6:30 a.m., the early hour giving them the kind of quiet and calm that only a morning run could provide. The air was crisp and fresh, a perfect contrast to the warmth of the beds they'd just left behind. Jackson was already outside, stretching his legs in preparation for their usual run.

Jessica grinned as she stepped onto the porch, finding him waiting, looking every bit as eager for the morning run as she was.

"You sleep well?" she asked, tying her sneakers with a practiced hand.

"Yep," Jackson replied with a wink. "Ready to beat me again?"

Jessica smiled, eyes twinkling. "I'll try my best."

They took off together, immediately falling into a familiar rhythm. Jessica let Jackson set the pace, but they matched each other stride for stride, pushing themselves hard. They ran through the neighbourhood in comfortable silence, enjoying the morning stillness, the occasional sound of birds in the distance, and their steady breathing.

"I'm looking forward to spending some time with you alone," Jessica said, as they slowed to a jog, nearing the end of their route.

Jackson shot her a playful side-eye. "So am I," he replied, but she could see the glint of anticipation in his eyes.

They jogged the last stretch back to the house, the sweat on their skin catching the morning light. As they reached the porch, they both slowed to a walk, their chests rising and falling with exertion. Jackson smiled, reaching over to give Jessica a light, playful nudge.

"Not bad, Jess. Not bad at all."

"I'll take that as a compliment," she grinned back.

After cooling down a bit, they went inside, keeping quiet so as not to disturb anyone still asleep. Each of them headed straight to their respective rooms for a quick shower, their bodies still warm from the run. Jessica turned on the water, letting it warm up while she stood in front of the mirror, admiring the glow of sweat on her skin. She ran her fingers through her hair, appreciating the chance to rinse off and start the day fresh.

When she stepped out of the shower, wrapped in a towel, she noticed how calm the house felt. The stillness seemed to seep into her, giving her a moment of peace before the busy day ahead. She dressed quickly, pulling on a comfortable blouse and a short skirt, then met Jackson downstairs. Together, they walked into the dining room where John and Mary were sipping coffee, the only ones awake at this hour.

"Good morning, you two," John said, offering her a cup of coffee. "How's the run this morning?"

"Great," Jessica replied, taking a seat. "Keeps me fit."

"Good to hear," Mary chimed in, a cheerful smile on her face. "You both look like you've already conquered the day."

"I think we have," Jackson said, glancing at Jessica with a playful grin.

The conversation flowed easily between them as they ate. John and Mary weren't in any hurry, chatting about plans for the day and sipping their coffee. The rest of the house remained quiet, everyone else still asleep.

As they finished breakfast, Jackson leaned over toward Jessica, his voice low enough that only she could hear. "Ready to go?" he asked, a glint of excitement in his eyes.

Jessica nodded, feeling a flutter of anticipation. She glanced around, noticing that no one else had stirred. The perfect opportunity.

"Let's go," she said with a smile, standing up and leaving her plate behind.

Jackson gave a small nod of approval, then casually stood up as well, offering his hand. They both said their goodbyes to John and Mary, who were none the wiser to their plans, and slipped out of the dining room quietly, careful not to disturb anyone else in the house.

He led her to the car, and before long, they were on their way. As they drove through the busy streets of the city, Jessica found herself glancing over at Jackson, her heart beating a little faster. She couldn't help but feel a growing sense of excitement about the day ahead, where they were headed only adding to the anticipation.

They arrived at his apartment, and Jessica smiled as she recognised the familiar building in front of them. She had been here before, but this time, the atmosphere felt different, this time was special.

"Here we are," Jackson said, turning off the engine. "Are you happy to spend the day here, just the two of us?"

Jessica nodded, her heart skipping a beat. "Sounds perfect."

They walked into the building together, their hands brushing as they headed for the elevator. Jackson pressed the button, and they rode up to the penthouse floor in comfortable silence. Jessica couldn't help but smile at the thought of spending the day with him in this private space. It felt like an escape from the world—just the two of them.

The elevator doors slid open, and they stepped out onto the sleek marble floor of the penthouse. The soft lighting and stylish decor immediately made Jessica feel at home, but it was the view that took her breath away. She walked over to the large windows, her gaze drawn to the magnificent expanse of Sydney Harbour stretching out below them. The early morning light danced off the water, casting a warm, golden glow across the skyline.

Jackson joined her, standing quietly by her side, his hands in his pockets as he admired the view. But soon, his attention shifted. His gaze softened as it settled on Jessica, her face illuminated by the sunlight and her expression filled with quiet wonder.

Jessica turned to face him, her heart pounding as the moment stretched between them. The air felt charged, thick with the weight of everything unspoken. She couldn't keep the longing from her voice as she met his eyes, her breath hitching slightly.

"Jackson… make love to me," she said softly, her words filled with want and the depth of something far more profound.

Jackson didn't reply. He simply stepped closer, his hands gently settling on her waist as his eyes searched hers, as if asking for certainty. When he saw her resolve, her desire mirrored in her gaze, he closed the distance between them. His lips brushed hers, soft at first, tentative. But as their connection deepened, the kiss became more, speaking volumes in ways words never could.

The world outside faded away. Jessica's arms slid around Jackson's neck, drawing him closer, her fingers tangling in his hair as she kissed him with growing fervour. His arms tightened around her, his hands firm yet tender as they held her securely, grounding her in the intensity of the moment.

Their kisses grew more passionate, a cascade of longing, affection, and desire. Every press of their lips, every touch, was a testament to the emotions that had been building between them.

Jackson guided her to the sofa, sitting down and gently pulling her onto his lap. The move brought them even closer, their bodies fitting together as though they were made to be this way. His hands rested on her back and hip, holding her as their kisses deepened, unhurried but undeniably intense.

Jessica felt her heart racing, every sensation heightened as she settled against him. The warmth of his embrace, the strength of his arms around her, and the way his lips moved against hers—everything about this moment felt right.

The room seemed to melt away, leaving only the two of them, their connection a cocoon that shut out the rest of the world.

Jackson's hand slowly and cautiously slid from her hip to her thigh, his touch gentle and exploratory. As his hand moved, he maintained a careful respect for her boundaries, aware of the intimacy of the moment. The atmosphere between them remained charged with the mutual affection and trust they had built.

Jessica, her voice soft and filled with a mix of vulnerability and desire, asked him to touch her. Her eyes were filled with a longing that matched the warmth of the embrace.

Jackson's hand, guided by a mix of tenderness and intent, glided carefully from her thigh, over her stomach to her breast. His touch was gentle, exploring with a softness that matched the intimacy of the moment. She responded to his touch with a mixture of anticipation and pleasure, her breath catching slightly as their connection grew more profound.

Jessica moaned softly with pleasure as his touch continued, her body responding to the gentle caress. His breath was warm against her lips as he whispered her name, "Jessica," with a deep, husky tone. The intimate sound of his voice only heightened the sensations between them.

Jessica instinctively pressed herself closer into his hand, her desire for deeper contact evident in the way she moved. Her body responded to his touch with a heightened sense of urgency, seeking more from the intimate connection they were sharing.

Jackson carefully pulled her blouse out from the waist of her skirt, his fingers tracing a path up her bare stomach. He slid his hand beneath her bra, his touch exploring the soft, warm skin as he gently cupped her breast.

Jessica moaned softly, her voice trembling with pleasure as she whispered, "Jackson." She followed it with a breathy, "Yes," expressing her eagerness and desire.

She could feel the evidence of his arousal pushing into her thigh, which was just making her more desperate for his touch.

Jackson gently pulled back, he looked into Jessica's eyes and, with a deep breath, murmured, "I want you so much." His voice was full of emotion, reflecting the intensity of the moment.

He gently lifted her from his lap, cradling her in his arms. He carried her with a tender urgency to his bedroom, his eyes locked on hers as he moved with careful deliberation.

Jackson gently set Jessica on her feet beside the large bed. He slowly began unbuttoning her blouse, his movements deliberate and tender. Jessica reciprocated, her fingers working on buttons of his shirt. They both eased their garments off each other's shoulders, the clothes slipping away to the floor.

Jackson reached around Jessica and unfastened her bra, letting it fall to the floor. In the dim light of the room, he looked at her, her creamy, velvety breasts that his fingers ache to touch, and said softly, "You're so beautiful."

Jackson slid his hand into her hair, tangling in the soft curls as he tipped her head back to expose her throat and rained kisses on it. His other hand was at her breast, teasing and tantalising artfully, evoking little gasps of pleasure from Jessica. Slowly his lips moved lower, into the white valley between her perfect breasts and then with a groan of desire he closed his mouth hotly over one taut nipple.

A jolt of fire exploded through her as his tongue rasp over her nipple in a caress that robbed her of nearly all sense. She gasped, writhing against him in ecstasy, arching her body pleading for more.

Jackson unfastened her skirt, letting it fall to the floor, as Jessica's hands reached for his trousers, undoing them and slid them off his hips.

At that moment, she sank to her knees, her fingers wrapping firmly around his arousal. Holding his gaze, she ran her tongue slowly over the bead of moisture at the tip, savouring the taste. Jackson let out a low, guttural groan, his breath hitching in pleasure.

He called out her name as she took him into her hot, eager mouth.

"Jessica," he groaned, his voice rough with desire. His fingers tangled in her hair, guiding her as she moved, her tongue swirling over him with deliberate, torturous slowness. Heat coiled low in his stomach, his muscles tensing as she hollowed her cheeks, drawing him deeper. A curse slipped from his lips as pleasure surged through him, his grip tightening, desperate to hold on as she unravelled him with every intoxicating stroke of her tongue.

Then, with a ragged breath, he muttered, "You need to stop."

His hands gripped her shoulders, gently but firmly pulling her up. Jessica blinked up at him, her lips swollen, her breath warm against his skin. His jaw was clenched, his eyes dark with restraint, fighting against the pleasure she had been so willing to give.

"Why?" she whispered, her voice husky, teasing.

Jackson exhaled sharply, brushing his thumb over her cheek. "Because if you don't, I won't be able to."

Jackson lifted Jessica into his arms, cradling her as though she were the most precious thing in the world, and gently laid her on the bed. His gaze roamed over her, dark with unspoken hunger, as he shed the last of his clothing and settled beside her.

Holding her captive with his smouldering eyes, he traced slow, deliberate circles over her stomach, teasing, tormenting, his fingers drifting lower until they hovered just above the edge of her panties. A knowing smirk played on his lips as he leaned down, capturing her mouth in a kiss that was sweet at first—slow and unhurried—before deepening into something far more demanding.

As his fingers slipped between her thighs, a sharp gasp escaped her lips, her breath catching in anticipation. Jackson swallowed her moan, his tongue plundering her mouth with the same relentless hunger his fingers explored her, sliding through the slick heat of her most intimate depths.

Jessica sobbed against his lips, her body arching into him, seeking more, needing more. His touch was torturous in its expertise, stroking, circling, coaxing her higher and higher until the pressure became unbearable.

"Jackson," she whimpered, her voice a plea, a prayer.

He answered her with a wicked grin, increasing the pressure, his movements deliberate, knowing. Until—

The pleasure crashed over her like a tidal wave, stealing her breath, sending shudders through her trembling frame. She cried out his name, her fingers gripping his shoulders as ecstasy consumed her.

Jackson watched her come undone, a look of pure satisfaction on his face, before pressing hot, open-mouthed kisses down the column of her throat. He moved lower, his mouth worshipping her skin, taking his time savouring every inch of her. He lingered at her breasts, drawing a taut peak between his lips, his tongue teasing and flicking until she gasped, then moved to the other, giving it the same reverence.

His hands were everywhere, kneading, stroking, igniting.

Jessica's head spun, her senses overloaded, but Jackson wasn't finished. His mouth travelled lower, lower, his lips pressing reverent kisses over the softness of her stomach before he slowly peeled her panties down her thighs.

And then, his mouth replaced them.

A broken cry tore from her throat as his tongue found her most sensitive place, licking, teasing, drawing her back to the edge with ruthless precision. Her hips lifted instinctively, chasing the friction, her fingers threading through his hair as he sucked the aching nub into his mouth.

"Jackson… please!" she sobbed, barely coherent.

He groaned against her, the sound vibrating through her core, sending another shudder of pleasure through her. He didn't stop, didn't slow, licking and sucking with practiced ease until the pressure inside her coiled unbearably tight and then—

Another wave of pleasure crashed through her, more intense than the first, her body convulsing beneath his mouth as she shattered again.

Only when the tremors subsided did Jackson move, kissing his way back up her trembling body, his mouth finding her breasts once more, lavishing them with the same attention, his tongue rasping over her sensitive peaks.

Jessica barely had time to catch her breath before she felt him settle between her parted thighs, the hard, heavy length of him pressing intimately against her softness.

Jackson kissed her neck, his breath hot against her ear as he whispered, "Jessica, you're so beautiful, you're driving me crazy. I need you. I want to take you."

His voice was rough, desperate.

And Jessica, already lost in him, could do nothing but whisper, "Yes."

Jackson hovered at her entrance, the thick, rigid length of him pressing against her slick heat. With a slow, deliberate motion, he pushed forward, inch by inch, stretching her, filling her. She was impossibly tight, her body gripping him in a molten vice, her warmth drawing him deeper.

Jessica gasped, her fingers digging into his back as she clung to him. He stilled, his breath ragged, giving her a moment to adjust, to soften around him, but the effort to hold back was excruciating. Every muscle in his body tensed with restraint as he fought against the primal urge to take her, to claim her completely.

Then, with one powerful thrust, he buried himself to the hilt.

Her eyes flew open, and she screamed his name. "Jackson!"

A guttural groan tore from his throat as pleasure crashed over him like a tidal wave. He began to move, slowly at first, savouring the feel of her wrapped around him, so hot, so wet, so perfect.

She met each of his movements with desperate urgency, her body rising to meet his in a rhythm that quickly turned wild, unrestrained. Jackson captured her lips in a searing kiss, his tongue mirroring the deep, relentless thrusts of his hips, tasting her moans, drinking in her pleasure.

The tension coiled between them, tight and electric. His pace grew harder, faster, driving into her honeyed warmth with fierce, unrelenting need.

Jessica's nails raked down his back, her breath coming in ragged gasps as she shattered beneath him, her release overtaking her in a blinding rush of ecstasy. She cried out his name, her body pulsing around him, gripping him like a vice.

Jackson's control snapped.

With a low, primal growl, he drove into her one final time, burying himself deep as pleasure exploded through him, raw and consuming. His body stiffened, his fingers tangled in her hair, his breath hot against her skin as he spilled into her, lost in the overwhelming sensation of her.

For a long moment, neither of them moved, their bodies locked together in the aftershocks of their release. Their breaths mingled, their hearts pounding in sync.

Finally, Jackson shifted, rolling onto his back and pulling Jessica with him. She fit against him perfectly, her soft curves moulding to the hard lines of his body. He held her close, one arm wrapped securely around her waist, the other tracing lazy circles along her spine.

She sighed contentedly, her breathing slowing, her body melting into him. The steady rise and fall of his chest lulled her, and within minutes, she drifted into a peaceful sleep.

Jackson lay awake, his gaze fixed on the ceiling as the morning sunlight filtered through the penthouse windows, casting a golden glow across the room. He glanced down at the woman in his arms, and his breath caught.

Jessica was breathtaking—not just in her beauty, but in her very presence. She had a lightness about her, a quiet strength that filled the space around her, settling deep into him in a way he hadn't expected.

His fingers traced the curve of her hip absently as he watched her sleep. She looked so peaceful, so utterly at ease in his arms. And for the first time in years, he felt something stir inside him—something unfamiliar, something terrifying in its intensity.

It wasn't just attraction. It wasn't just desire.

It was something more.

His pulse quickened as realisation crashed over him like a bolt of lightning.

I'm in love with her.

The thought struck him with the force of a tidal wave, knocking the breath from his lungs.

For years, he had kept his relationships light, effortless, free of entanglements. Love was a complication he had never wanted—a risk he had never been willing to take. But Jessica had unravelled him, stripping away the carefully constructed walls he had built around himself.

The more time he spent with her, the more he craved her—not just her body, but her mind, her laughter, the quiet strength in her eyes. She challenged him in ways no one ever had, met him stride for stride, unafraid to push back, to stand her ground.

His desire for her surged again, but this time, it wasn't just physical.

It was something deeper. More profound.

And it terrified him.

Because now that he had her, the thought of losing her was unbearable.

This wasn't fleeting admiration or simple infatuation—it was love. A deep, soul-shaking love that left him breathless. He loved her for her fire and her resilience, for the way she met the world with quiet confidence and unwavering determination. He loved her for the softness she tried to hide, for the way she looked at him like he was more than just a man who had everything—like he was someone who mattered.

Instinctively, Jackson's grip tightened, pulling her closer.

Jessica stirred, her lashes fluttering open, and when her gaze met his, a sleepy smile curved her lips.

"What is it?" she murmured, her voice a gentle caress.

Jackson swallowed, his heart pounding as warmth flooded his chest. He didn't say it—not yet. He wanted the moment to be perfect when he finally told her. Instead, he cupped her cheek, his thumb brushing over her silky skin with aching tenderness.

"Nothing," he said, his voice rough with emotion. "I'm just… happy you're here with me."

Jessica's smile deepened, her eyes shining with trust as she nestled closer, savouring his touch.

And Jackson knew, with unwavering certainty, that this was different.

This was real.

This was forever.

Chapter Nineteen

The day of the wedding rehearsal and rehearsal dinner had arrived, bringing with it a flurry of activity and excitement. From the moment Jessica awoke, Jackson had been by her side, his every action a testament to how deeply he cared for her. Whether it was stealing a quick kiss over breakfast or placing a guiding hand on her back as they moved through the day, he was proving to be a thoughtful and affectionate partner.

Jessica couldn't help but feel her heart swell as they prepared for the rehearsal. She had never experienced this level of closeness or care in a relationship before, and Jackson's attention felt both thrilling and grounding.

As they got ready to leave for the venue, Jackson paused and took her hand, pulling her gently toward him.

"Before we go, there's something I need to ask you," he said, his tone serious but his eyes warm.

Jessica tilted her head, curious. "What is it?"

Jackson took a deep breath, his thumb brushing over her knuckles. "After the wedding… would you consider moving in with me?"

Her eyes widened in surprise, and she instinctively pulled back slightly. "Jackson, I… I don't know," she stammered, the unexpectedness of the question catching her off guard. "That's a big step. I don't want to rush into anything."

For a moment, Jackson's confident demeanour faltered. He looked at her with an earnestness that made her chest tighten. "I know it's a lot, but it feels right to me. I just want us to be together, Jess. Please… just think about it. Please."

Jessica's heart ached at the vulnerability in his voice. She nodded slowly, wanting to reassure him even if she wasn't ready to commit to such a big change. "I'll think about it, Jackson. I promise."

Relief flickered across his face, and he smiled softly, pulling her into his arms. "That's all I ask."

The afternoon sun bathed the garden in a golden glow as Jessica stepped out of the house, smoothing the soft fabric of her floral dress. The wedding rehearsal was set on the expansive lawn of Phyllis's family estate, where rows of white chairs were neatly arranged, facing an ornate floral arch that framed the perfect backdrop of manicure gardens. Jessica felt a flutter of anticipation as she spotted Phyllis, the bride-to-be, standing near the arch and directing a small group of people.

"Jessica, over here!" Phyllis waved enthusiastically, her smile brighter than the sun.

Jessica made her way over, greeted by the familiar buzz of pre-wedding excitement. The bridal party had already started to assemble, and Jackson was standing with Nathan as his best man, looking effortlessly handsome in a crisp white shirt and tailored trousers. He caught her eye and gave her a subtle wink that made her heart skip a beat.

The wedding planner clapped her hands for attention. "Alright, everyone! Let's walk through this step by step."

Nathan and Jackson stood at the makeshift alter waiting for the bride. Jessica being the maid of honour found her place in the lineup after the flower girl and before the bride. As they walked down the imaginary aisle during the first run-through, Jackson couldn't take his eyes off her.

The rehearsal continued with the expected mix of laughter and minor missteps. Phyllis fussed over every detail, while Nathan tried—and failed—to calm her nerves. Jessica admired the way Jackson stayed relaxed through it all, effortlessly charming everyone around him.

By the time they finished, the group was more at ease, their confidence growing for the big day. The wedding planner dismissed everyone, urging them to get ready for the rehearsal dinner.

The rehearsal dinner was held at an elegant waterfront restaurant, the private dining area decked out with soft string lights and floral centrepieces that mirrored the wedding theme. Jessica arrived with Jackson, his hand resting lightly on the small of her back as they entered the room.

Phyllis and Nathan were already there, glowing with happiness as they greeted their guests. Family and close friends filled the space, their laughter and chatter creating a warm, celebratory atmosphere. Jessica found herself seated between Jackson and Mary, who immediately pulled her into conversation about her dress that she would wear tomorrow and how much she was looking forward to the wedding.

As the evening progressed, glasses clinked, and heartfelt toasts began. Jackson as Nathan's best man delivered a humorous speech, recounting their college adventures and offering heartfelt wishes for the couple's future. Jessica couldn't help but glance at him during the toasts.

When it was Phyllis's turn to speak, she stood with a glass of champagne, her voice trembling slightly with emotion.

"I just want to thank all of you for being here," she said, her eyes glistening. "Nathan and I are so lucky to have such wonderful friends and family supporting us. And to my maid of honour Jessica and my brother and best man Jackson—thank you for putting up with all my chaos. I couldn't do this without you."

Jessica noticed Jackson's faint smirk and nudged him playfully, earning a chuckle in return.

After dinner, the group moved to the outdoor terrace, where the view of the moonlit water added to the evening's charm. Jessica found herself standing by the railing, enjoying the fresh breeze, the sounds of laughter and celebration fading into the background. The soft breeze carried the scent of the ocean, and Jessica felt a calm she hadn't expected.

Jackson appeared beside her, two glasses of wine in hand. "For you," he said, offering one to her.

"Thank you." She smiled, taking the glass. "It's been such a lovely night."

He nodded, leaning against the railing. "It has. But tomorrow will be even better."

"I'm glad I'm here," she said softly.

Jackson met her gaze, his expression serious but warm. "I am too. More than you know."

His words lingered in the air, sparking a flicker of hope in Jessica's heart.

As the night deepened, Jessica's mind kept circling back to the way he'd asked her to move in with him. It wasn't just the request; it was the way he'd looked at her, like she was his entire world.

She loved him. She had loved him for years, though she had only recently allowed herself to admit it. But could she take that leap now? After all, they had spent so much time apart. Was two weeks enough to erase the years of uncertainty?

Jessica glanced at Jackson, who was watching her with a quiet intensity. Her heart ached with the weight of her decision. She wanted to trust this new version of him, the one who saw more than her outward transformation. The question wasn't just about moving in together—it was about whether she could trust him with all of her, flaws, and all.

As they returned to the warmth of the celebration, Jessica resolved to think hard. She needed to be sure—for both their sakes.

The big day had arrived, and the back garden had been transformed into a romantic haven, ready to witness the beginning of a beautiful new chapter for Phyllis and Nathan. The space had undergone a magical makeover, with soft drapes of white and blush cascading over a grand floral arch where the couple would exchange their vows. Rows of white chairs adorned with delicate floral arrangements lined the aisle, and the scent of fresh roses and lilies filled the crisp morning air.

A large marquee had been erected for the reception, complete with a polished wooden dance floor and a stage for the live band and wedding singer. Twinkling fairy lights hung overhead, giving the space a dreamlike quality. Jessica had wandered through the setup that morning, marvelling at the effort and care poured into every detail. It felt like stepping into a wonderland, and she couldn't help but think how thrilled Phyllis would be with the result.

Nathan and Jackson had left the estate the night before to spend the night at Jackson's penthouse, ensuring the bride and groom wouldn't cross paths until the ceremony. Meanwhile, the Phyllis's bedroom buzzed with activity as Phyllis and Jessica prepared for the big event.

When Phyllis finally woke up, the preparations kicked into high gear. Hair stylists and makeup artists fluttered around the room, transforming them into picture-perfect visions. Phyllis's hair was styled into an elegant chignon, delicate tendrils framing her radiant face. Her lace bridal gown hung nearby, waiting for its moment in the spotlight.

Jessica, ever the supportive maid of honour, ensured Phyllis was relaxed and pampered while getting ready. Her own look was nothing short of stunning. Her hair was left down, but artfully swept to one side, cascading in loose waves over her bare shoulder. Her dress was a masterpiece of emerald-green shining silk, hugging her figure in all the right places. The design featured a wide shoulder strap on one side, leaving the other shoulder elegantly bare—the side her hair was swept to.

The gown's slim fit extended all the way to the floor, accentuating her graceful silhouette. A delicate gathering of fabric on one side, adorned with a row of sparkling crystals, caught the light with every movement, mimicking the brilliance of diamonds. On the opposite side, a high slit ran up her thigh, offering just a glimpse of her toned leg when she walked. Completing the ensemble were matching three-inch emerald heels that added height and poise to her already striking appearance.

As Jessica glanced at her reflection in the mirror, she couldn't help but feel a mix of excitement and nerves. The day wasn't about her, but she knew all eyes would be on the bridal party as they made their way down the aisle.

"You look incredible," Phyllis said, turning to her with a warm smile. Despite her own pre-wedding jitters, she couldn't hide her admiration.

Jessica laughed softly. "Not as incredible as you will in that gown."

Phyllis beamed, reaching out to squeeze Jessica's hand. "Thank you—for everything. I couldn't have done this without you."

"You deserve the perfect day, and you're going to get it," Jessica replied, her voice filled with conviction.

As the clock ticked closer to the ceremony, the bedroom was filled with laughter, last-minute touch-ups, and a shared sense of anticipation. The garden outside awaited, brimming with love and beauty, ready to welcome the couple into their new life together. And Jessica couldn't shake the thought of Jackson— how he would look seeing her walk down the aisle, even if only as a maid of honour. Her heart quickened at the idea, and she quickly shook the thought away, focusing on the task at hand.

The day had only just begun, and it promised to be unforgettable.

Jessica gently eased the lace wedding gown over Phyllis's head, carefully smoothing the intricate fabric to ensure every detail fell into place. The gown was a vision of elegance—delicate floral lace overlaying a fitted silhouette that flared out into a soft, flowing train. Phyllis's eyes sparkled as she caught her reflection in the mirror, her hands trembling slightly with excitement.

"You look absolutely breathtaking," Jessica said sincerely, her voice filled with warmth.

Phyllis smiled, her cheeks flushing. "Do you think Nathan will like it?"

Jessica chuckled, stepping behind her to start fastening the row of tiny buttons running down the back. "Phyllis, Nathan is going to lose his mind. Though, I have to say… these buttons are a bit of a mission. Poor guy's going to have a time undoing all of these later tonight."

Phyllis burst out laughing, her nervous energy momentarily replaced with joy. "Well, that's his problem, isn't it?"

Jessica joined in the laughter, her hands working deftly to finish securing the gown. Just as she was about to step back and admire her handiwork, the door to the bedroom opened, and Phyllis's mother stepped in.

"Oh, my goodness," she gasped, her hand flying to her chest as she took in the sight of her daughter. "Phyllis, you look absolutely stunning!"

Phyllis's smile softened, and her eyes glistened with unshed tears. "Mum…"

Jessica, standing behind Phyllis, adjusted the veil, securing it gently over the intricate chignon. She looked up and met the gaze of Phyllis's mother, who now turned her attention to her.

"And Jessica," her voice brimmed with emotion, "you look beautiful too. Both of you do."

Jessica smiled warmly. "Thank you, Mary. But today is all about Phyllis—she's the real star."

Mary stepped closer, her eyes scanning every detail of Phyllis's gown and veil. "You're both stars in my eyes. I can't believe my little girl is getting married." She reached out to adjust a strand of Phyllis's hair, her touch gentle and affectionate.

Jessica stepped back, giving the mother and daughter a moment. Watching them, she felt a pang of longing, wishing her own parents could be here to see her in this role, to share in the joy of the day. But she quickly pushed the thought aside, focusing instead on the happiness surrounding her.

"Alright," Jessica said after a moment, clapping her hands softly to lighten the mood. "Let's finish up and get you ready to walk down that aisle. You've got a groom waiting who's going to be absolutely floored when he sees you."

Phyllis turned to Jessica, her smile wide and grateful. "Thank you for everything, Jess. I couldn't do this without you."

Jessica grinned. "What are best friends for?"

With the veil in place and final touches complete, Phyllis looked every bit the glowing bride. As they headed out of the bedroom, Jessica couldn't help but feel a swell of pride. This was Phyllis's moment, and she was honoured to stand by her side through it all.

They descended the grand staircase, the soft rustle of Phyllis's lace gown accompanying each step. At the bottom, Phyllis's father, John, stood waiting with an expression of awe and pride.

"Oh, sweetheart," he said, his voice thick with emotion. "You look… amazing." He glanced at Jessica and added with equal warmth, "You both do."

Phyllis's eyes shimmered with unshed tears as she leaned in to kiss her father's cheek. "Thank you, Dad. I'm ready."

Jessica offered an encouraging smile and took her place at the front of the small procession. She joined the flower girl, who clutched her basket of petals with a determined look. Behind her, Phyllis took John's arm, and together they waited for their cue.

The soft strains of the string quartet began to fill the garden, signalling the start of the ceremony. Jessica's heart raced as she stepped forward, leading the way down the aisle.

The flower girl walked ahead, carefully scattering rose petals with every step. The guests watched with warm smiles as the little girl performed her role beautifully. Then it was Jessica's turn.

Taking a steadying breath, she began her slow walk down the aisle, her emerald-green dress shimmering under the soft light. Her stomach fluttered with nervous excitement as her gaze shifted forward. Nathan, standing at the altar, looked dashing in his tailored suit, his smile wide as he caught sight of Phyllis behind her.

But it wasn't Nathan who held her attention.

Her eyes found Jackson, and for a moment, the world seemed to fade. He was devastatingly handsome in his black suit, the crisp white shirt beneath accentuating his broad shoulders and lean frame. His hair was perfectly styled, but it was the look in his eyes that nearly made her stumble.

Jackson's gaze was locked on her, filled with admiration and something deeper, something that sent a shiver down her spine. The intensity in his expression was almost overwhelming, as if she were the only person in the room.

Jessica's pulse quickened, her stomach tightening with a mix of nerves and exhilaration. She couldn't help but notice the subtle clench of Jackson's jaw as his eyes flicked to the slit in her dress, where her toned leg occasionally peeked through.

At the altar, Jackson stood beside Nathan, who shifted slightly, his nervous energy apparent. But Jackson barely noticed. His focus was entirely on Jessica as she moved closer.

She was a vision in emerald-green, the dress hugging her curves in all the right places, the crystals catching the light with every step. Her hair, swept to one side, framed her radiant face perfectly. Jackson's chest tightened as his admiration deepened, his breath catching in his throat.

When her leg appeared through the slit in her dress, it nearly did him in. There was something effortlessly graceful and alluring about her, and he found himself fighting the urge to break into a smile.

As Jessica reached the altar and took her place, Jackson's gaze lingered on her for a moment longer before he forced himself to focus on Nathan. His best friend was grinning like a man ready to burst with happiness, his eyes fixed on Phyllis as she and John made their way down the aisle.

The music swelled, and all eyes turned to the bride. But Jackson's thoughts lingered on Jessica, his heart pounding as he realised just how deeply she had captivated him.

Chapter Twenty

The ceremony went off without a hitch, filled with love, emotion, and just a touch of laughter when Nathan stumbled over a few of his vows, earning a round of chuckles from the guests and a playful eyeroll from Phyllis. When the officiant declared them husband and wife, Nathan's grin could have lit up the entire garden. He pulled Phyllis into a kiss so full of joy and passion that the crowd erupted into applause and cheers.

Hand in hand, the newlyweds walked back down the aisle, glowing with happiness. Jessica couldn't help but smile at the sight, her heart swelling for her best friend.

As tradition dictated, Jackson extended his arm to Jessica, his eyes warm as they met hers. She slipped her hand into the crook of his elbow, the touch sending a familiar spark through her.

"You look stunning," he murmured, his voice low and intimate as he leaned closer to her ear.

Jessica felt heat rise to her cheeks. "You look very handsome," she replied softly, glancing up at him with a smile that betrayed just how much she meant it.

Their moment was brief but electric, and then they were walking together, following the newlyweds down the aisle amidst a sea of congratulatory smiles and scattered rose petals.

On the other side of the garden, the wedding photographer waited with a list of shots to capture. The space had been transformed into a picturesque backdrop, with soft greenery, climbing roses, and a canopy of fairy lights that twinkled in the late afternoon sun.

The bridal party assembled, the laughter and chatter creating a lively atmosphere. Nathan and Phyllis stood at the centre; their joy palpable as the photographer directed them into poses. Jessica found herself standing beside Jackson once again, the two of them paired for a series of shots.

The photographer asked them to stand close, and Jackson didn't hesitate. He wrapped an arm around her waist, his touch warm and steady. Jessica's heart fluttered as she leaned slightly into him, her hand resting lightly on his chest.

"Smile," the photographer called out, and Jackson's lips curved into an effortless grin. Jessica followed suit, her smile radiant and natural.

"You're stealing the show," Jackson said under his breath, his voice teasing but filled with genuine admiration.

Jessica rolled her eyes playfully, though her cheeks flushed with colour. "It's a wedding, Jackson. I think the bride and groom are the stars today."

"They are," he agreed, his gaze lingering on her a beat too long. "But you're hard to ignore."

Jessica glanced away, pretending to adjust her dress as she tried to calm her racing heart.

The photographer moved them into a new arrangement, instructing Jackson to stand behind Jessica and rest his hands on her shoulders. His touch was light but grounding, and Jessica felt an unexpected wave of comfort.

"You're doing great," he murmured near her ear, his tone reassuring.

Jessica turned her head slightly, meeting his eyes with a small, grateful smile. "Thanks."

As the session continued, the group dynamic made the experience lively and fun. Phyllis couldn't stop giggling when Nathan dipped her for a dramatic pose, and Jackson surprised everyone by cracking a joke that had the entire bridal party in stitches.

When the formal photos were done, the photographer announced it was time for candid shots. Jessica found herself standing near Jackson once more, the two of them caught in easy conversation as the camera clicked away.

"Ready for the reception?" Jackson asked, his tone light but curious.

Jessica nodded. "I think it's going to be amazing. Phyllis deserves the perfect evening."

"And you?" he pressed, his voice softening. "Do you think you'll enjoy yourself?"

She tilted her head, studying him with a small smile. "I think I will, as long as I have good company."

Jackson's grin widened; his expression filled with unmistakable warmth. "You'll have the best company, I promise."

The way he said it made Jessica's heart skip a beat, and as the photographer called the group together for one last shot, she couldn't help but wonder what the rest of the night might hold.

After everyone was seated in the beautifully decorated marquee, with its elegant floral arrangements and soft string lights, the waitstaff began serving the meal. The guests enjoyed a delectable menu, each course met with murmurs of approval and appreciation. Laughter and conversation filled the air as friends and family celebrated Phyllis and Nathan's love.

Once the plates were cleared, the room quieted as it was time for the speeches. Nathan stood first, thanking everyone for coming and expressing his love and gratitude for Phyllis. He recounted their journey together with humour and tenderness, earning both laughs and teary smiles from the crowd.

Next, Jackson rose from his seat, his tall frame drawing everyone's attention as he held a glass of champagne. He cleared his throat, his charming grin already earning a ripple of anticipation from the room.

"When Nathan told me he was proposing to Phyllis, my first thought was, 'Finally, someone's brave enough to deal with my sister.'" The crowd erupted in laughter, including Phyllis, who gave Jackson a playful glare.

Jackson continued, his tone shifting to something more heartfelt. "In all seriousness, Nathan, you've always been my best mate, and I couldn't ask for a better guy to join our family. And Phyllis, I think we all know you might've been just a little jealous of my friendship with Nathan. So, naturally, you had to steal him for yourself."

The guests laughed again, and even Nathan shook his head with a grin. Jackson's expression softened as he looked between his sister and her new husband.

"But honestly, I've never seen two people who complement each other so perfectly. You both bring out the best in one another, and it's been an honour to stand by your side today. Here's to a lifetime of happiness, love, and hopefully, no more sibling rivalry!"

The crowd erupted into applause as Jackson raised his glass. Jessica clapped enthusiastically; her chest warm with admiration for him.

Then it was Jessica's turn. She stood gracefully, her emerald-green dress catching the soft light as she held her champagne flute. She glanced at Phyllis, her smile tender.

"Phyllis," she began, her voice steady but filled with emotion, "you've been my best friend for as long as I can remember. You've seen me at my worst, supported me at my lowest, and celebrated with me at my best. Today, I get to celebrate you."

Her gaze turned to Nathan. "Nathan, you're one of the good ones. You make Phyllis so happy, and for that, I'll always be grateful. She's lucky to have found someone as kind, patient, and funny as you. But Nathan… so are you. Phyllis deserves all the happiness in the world, and I'm glad she found it with you."

Jessica lifted her glass, her voice brightening. "To Phyllis and Nathan—may your life together be as beautiful as this day."

The applause that followed was warm and genuine, and Jessica returned to her seat feeling a mix of pride and joy.

Finally, John, Phyllis's father, stood up. His strong presence immediately drew everyone's attention, but there was a visible softness in his demeanour. He held his glass high, his voice steady as he began.

"I want to thank everyone for being here today to celebrate my daughter and her new husband." His eyes moved to Nathan, a warm smile tugging at his lips. "Nathan, welcome to the family. From the moment I met you, I knew you were the one for my little girl. You've got a good heart, and I couldn't be prouder to call you, my son-in-law."

John's voice hitched slightly as he turned to Phyllis. "Sweetheart, seeing you today… you've taken my breath away. You've grown into an incredible woman, and I'm so proud of you. I've always wanted the best for you, and looking at you and Nathan, I know you've found it."

His voice wavered as emotion threatened to overwhelm him. He paused, gathering himself, before raising his glass higher. "To Phyllis and Nathan—may your marriage be filled with love, laughter, and all the things that make life beautiful."

The room erupted into cheers, the applause echoing off the marquee walls as guests clinked glasses and celebrated the couple.

Jessica glanced at Jackson, who caught her gaze and smiled. For a moment, it felt like the world had narrowed down to just the two of them amidst the celebration, and Jessica felt a sense of belonging she hadn't experienced in years.

As soon as the music began, the crowd hushed, all eyes turning to the newlyweds. Nathan took Phyllis's hand, guiding her to the centre of the dance floor. The soft melody of a romantic ballad floated through the air as they began their first dance as husband and wife.

They moved together effortlessly, their gazes locked, their love evident in every step. Phyllis's dress swirled elegantly as Nathan spun her gently, eliciting murmurs of admiration from the crowd. Jessica watched them with a warm smile, her heart swelling with happiness for her best friend.

When the song shifted to a livelier tune, both sets of parents joined the couple on the dance floor. Phyllis's father, John, beamed with pride as he led her mother into a graceful waltz, while Nathan's parents danced with a natural ease that spoke of years of love and partnership. The sight was heartwarming, and the crowd cheered them on.

Moments later, Jackson appeared at Jessica's side, his hand outstretched, his smile inviting. "May I have this dance?"

Jessica hesitated for only a second before placing her hand in his. "Of course."

Jackson led her to the floor, his confidence and natural grace making her feel instantly at ease. As he pulled her close, one hand resting gently on her waist, Jessica's breath hitched. The warmth of his touch, the way he looked at her— it was intoxicating.

"You look stunning," he murmured, his voice low and intimate, meant only for her.

Jessica tilted her head up to meet his gaze. "You already said that," she replied with a teasing smile, though her heart was racing.

They moved together as if they'd done this a hundred times before, their steps perfectly in sync. The emerald-green of Jessica's dress shimmered under the soft lights, and the high slit revealed glimpses of her toned leg as they danced, a detail that hadn't gone unnoticed by Jackson.

"You're stealing the spotlight," he whispered, his tone playful but filled with admiration.

Jessica laughed softly, feeling a warmth spread through her chest. "I think that's supposed to be Phyllis's job tonight."

The music flowed around them, and for a moment, it felt as if they were the only two people in the room. Jackson's hand tightened slightly on her waist, drawing her closer, and Jessica couldn't help but let herself melt into him.

As the song came to an end, the guests erupted into applause, cheering for all the couples on the dance floor. Jackson dipped Jessica slightly, his eyes never leaving hers, and when he brought her back up, the intensity of his gaze left her breathless.

"Thank you for the dance," he said, his voice filled with a warmth that made Jessica's heart skip a beat.

"It was my pleasure," she replied, her cheeks flushed, though whether it was from the dancing or from being so close to Jackson, she wasn't entirely sure.

John and Phyllis moved gracefully across the dance floor, father and daughter sharing a moment that brought tears to more than a few eyes. The pride in John's face was unmistakable as he spun Phyllis gently, the two laughing as the music swelled. Nearby, Nathan danced with Mary, the two sharing an easy rhythm, their smiles bright as they chatted and swayed to the music.

As the song transitioned into a more upbeat tune, more couples joined in, filling the dance floor with energy and joy. Jackson stood near the edge of the floor, deep in conversation with Nathan's parents. His relaxed posture and warm smile reflected how much he enjoyed the evening, even as he occasionally glanced toward Jessica, as if drawn to her presence.

Jessica, seated at the table and soaking in the lively atmosphere, felt a light tap on her shoulder. She turned, surprised to see Terry standing there, his charming smile firmly in place.

"Terry," she said warmly, though caught off guard, "how are you?"

"I'm good," Terry replied, his smile broadening. "I was hoping I could have this dance."

Jessica hesitated briefly, glancing at the dance floor, then nodded with a polite smile. "Of course, I'd love to."

As they made their way to the floor, Jessica caught Jackson's gaze from across the room. His conversation faltered as his eyes followed them, a flicker of something unreadable crossing his face.

Terry took Jessica into his arms, holding her just a touch closer than was comfortable, though she chose not to comment.

"You look breathtaking tonight, Jess," Terry said, his tone low and earnest. "I think you outshine the bride."

Jessica laughed lightly, trying to keep the mood friendly. "Please don't say that. I'd never want to take any attention away from Phyllis—it's her day."

Terry shrugged, his grip firm on her waist. "Maybe so, but it's impossible not to notice you. I've missed spending time with you."

Jessica offered a polite but sincere smile. "I enjoyed our time together too."

Terry leaned in slightly, his voice softening. "If Jackson ever messes up, you know where to find me, Jess. I mean it. You're the one that got away."

Jessica's smile faltered as she tried to gently deflect. "That's kind of you to say, Terry, but—"

Before she could finish, she felt a familiar presence at her side.

"Mind if I cut in?" Jackson's voice was calm but carried an edge, his expression unreadable as he addressed Terry.

Terry hesitated, reluctant, but finally stepped back with a forced smile. "Of course. Enjoy the dance."

Jackson stepped into the space Terry had vacated, sliding an arm around Jessica's waist and pulling her close. "You looked like you were having an interesting conversation," he murmured, his tone quiet and for her ears only.

Jessica let out a breathy laugh, some of her tension easing. "You have no idea."

Jackson's grip on her waist tightened slightly, his eyes locked onto hers with a steady intensity. "I think I do. I've seen the way he looks at you." His voice dropped further. "He told you he's waiting for me to mess up, didn't he?"

Jessica blinked in surprise. "How did you know?"

Jackson's jaw tightened briefly before he spoke. "He told me to my face at the barbecue."

Jessica's eyes widened. "Oh."

Jackson exhaled, softening as he looked at her. "Jess, I'm not going to mess this up. I know what I have in you, and I'm not going to throw it away."

Jessica didn't respond immediately, her thoughts swirling. She wasn't sure what she could say, or even what she wanted to say, as they continued to sway to the music.

Instead, she let herself relax in his arms, the tension melting away as she laid her head lightly against his chest. For now, his presence, his warmth, and the unspoken promise in his words were enough.

Chapter Twenty-One

The next morning, there was a collective sense of relief as the whirlwind of the wedding finally came to an end. The lawn, once transformed into a romantic haven for the ceremony, was now being dismantled. Workmen moved swiftly, packing up the marquees and floral decorations, returning the garden to its usual state. House guests trickled out, bidding their farewells, some offering hugs and congratulations, while others murmured their own words of parting. The house was gradually emptying, leaving behind only the memory of the celebration.

Phyllis and Nathan had left early, their bags packed for their honeymoon. They had slipped away quietly, hand in hand, already lost in their new life as husband and wife. The air was lighter now that the tension and anticipation of the wedding day were behind them. Even the house, still filled with remnants of the festivities, seemed to exhale a sigh of contentment.

Jessica, however, didn't feel entirely at ease. She stood by the window, watching as the last of the guests departed, a strange emptiness settling over her. The excitement of the wedding was behind her, but with it came the realisation that everything was shifting—again.

Tomorrow, she would start her new job. It was a fresh beginning, a new chapter in her life that she had eagerly anticipated. She had been waiting for this moment for months, but now, the prospect felt almost overwhelming. The thought of diving into the work ahead, of finding her rhythm in a new environment, made her heart race with both excitement and anxiety. It was a good step for her, professionally, but it felt like another piece of her world was being rearranged.

And then there was Jackson. He would return to his apartment tomorrow, his life resuming its usual pace. Jessica tried to be logical about it, but as she gazed out the window at the now quiet garden, she felt a pang of loss. Their time together had been intense, and while they had only recently begun to explore the depth of their relationship, it already felt like he had become an integral part of her life.

The thought of him leaving, of returning to his routine without her in it, left a bitter taste in her mouth. She didn't want to be dramatic, but a small part of her wondered what this would mean for them. Would the distance create a gap between them, or would it make the moments they did share even more meaningful?

She tried to shake off the feeling, but it lingered.

Jessica sat down on the couch, absentmindedly smoothing her dress as she watched the workmen finish their tasks. It was then that Jackson appeared, stepping into the room with a look on his face that mirrored her own quiet contemplation.

"Hey," he said softly, his voice warm but laced with a touch of sadness, "you okay?"

Jessica nodded, but her smile didn't reach her eyes. "Yeah… just thinking."

Jackson sat down beside her, his presence solid and comforting. He didn't press her for more, but the silence between them spoke volumes.

"I'll miss you," he said after a beat, his voice low but sincere. "I know it's not forever, but it still feels… strange."

Jessica glanced up at him, her heart swelling. "I'll miss you too," she whispered, her fingers brushing against his.

They sat there for a while, neither of them saying much. The house had settled into a peaceful quiet, but it felt like the calm before something more.

"Have you thought about moving in with me?" Jackson asked, his voice gentle but carrying a hopeful undertone.

Jessica met his gaze, a mix of emotions swirling inside her. She took a breath before responding, choosing her words carefully. "I have," she said softly. "I think I need to get settled into my new job before I make any more changes. But once I do that, if you still want me to, I will move in with you."

Jackson's expression softened, his eyes lighting up with warmth at her words. He reached for her hand, holding it tenderly. "Of course I want you to. I want you with me. I understand that things need time to settle, and I don't want to rush you. We can take it at your pace."

Jessica smiled, feeling a rush of affection for him. She squeezed his hand, feeling the reassurance in his touch. "I just need to find my rhythm, Jackson. Once I feel like I've got things in place, I'll be ready. But I want to make sure it's the right time for both of us."

He nodded, his thumb gently brushing the back of her hand. "Whenever that is, I'll be here. There's no rush, Jess. Just take the time you need. I'll be patient."

The sincerity in his words eased the knot of uncertainty she had felt in her chest. She felt safe with him, knowing he was willing to wait, to support her, no matter how long it took.

"Is this all you have?" Jackson asked, raising an eyebrow as he picked up her suitcases and placed them in the trunk of his car.

Jessica nodded, a smile tugging at her lips. "Yes, that's all I need."

It had been a month since she'd started her new job, and she had settled in quickly, feeling as though she had been there for years. Her colleagues were welcoming, and the work was fulfilling. Each day had felt like a new adventure, and she was finally starting to feel like she was carving out her place in this new chapter of her life.

The transition to moving in with Jackson had been gradual, but smooth. They had grown even closer over the past few weeks. Jackson called her every night, eager to hear about her day, and Jessica stayed over at his place every Friday and Saturday night. It had become a routine they both enjoyed, each weekend filled with cozy moments and shared laughter.

At first, Jackson had tried to come over to see Jessica during the week, but she noticed the strain on him—his job was demanding, and he was often exhausted. She didn't want to put any pressure on him, so she gently told him to focus on his work and they would spend the weekends together.

They had made peace with it, knowing that their bond would only grow stronger with the time they spent together, no matter how often they saw each other. The important part was that they had both committed to making this relationship work, and now, as she stood on the threshold of this new phase, she couldn't help but feel excited and grateful.

As she slid into the passenger seat beside Jackson, she glanced at him, her heart swelling with affection. "Are you sure you're okay with this? With me moving in?"

Jackson gave her a reassuring smile as he started the engine. "I've never been surer of anything in my life." His gaze softened as he reached over to take her hand, giving it a gentle squeeze. "I'm just happy it's finally happening, Jess."

She smiled, feeling the warmth of his words sink in. "Are Phyllis and Nathan coming over for dinner tomorrow night?"

"Yes, and my parents will be there as well. Phyllis wants us all to see the honeymoon photos."

Jessica nodded, feeling a mixture of excitement and nerves. "I hope I don't disappoint everyone at being a hostess."

Jackson chuckled, his tone full of affection. "You couldn't fail at anything you do. I'll be there with you."

Her heart lightened at his words. She had always worried about not measuring up, but with him by her side, the weight of those insecurities felt a little easier to bear. "Thanks, Jackson," she said softly. "I'm looking forward to seeing Phyllis and Nathan."

His smile widened. "So am I."

As the car drove down the road, Jessica rested her head back against the seat. Jackson and she had been together for six weeks now, and she still hadn't told him that she loved him. Every time she thought about saying those three words, a wave of uncertainty would rise within her. She was sure he loved her by the way he looked at her, the gentle way he cared for her, and how he treated her like she was the only woman in the world. Yet, she couldn't shake the feeling that saying it out loud would make it all too real, too vulnerable.

Her heart fluttered at the thought of it, but she stayed silent, content to feel his hand gently resting on hers. It wasn't that she didn't want to say it—she did. She just wanted to make sure she was ready, and more importantly, that the time was right.

Jackson glanced over at Jessica, noticing the thoughtful expression on her face. "You okay?" he asked, his voice gentle with concern.

Jessica offered a small smile, nodding, but her mind was still racing with thoughts she hadn't yet voiced. "Yeah, just thinking."

"About what?" he asked, squeezing her hand.

She met his gaze for a brief moment, her heart pounding in her chest as the words tumbled out before she could stop them. "About how much I love you."

Jackson's eyes widened slightly, then without a word, he pulled the car over to the side of the road. The sudden stillness in the car made Jessica's heart race, her stomach twisting with anxiety. She felt as if she'd just blurted out something too soon, too much.

As the car came to a stop, Jackson unbuckled their seatbelts and, to her shock, gently tugged her onto his lap. Before she could react, his lips were on hers, warm and tender. The kiss was everything she'd hoped for—passion, tenderness, a silent confession in every move.

When they finally broke apart, both of them breathless, Jackson held her close, his eyes full of sincerity.

"I love you too," he whispered, his voice thick with emotion.

A weight lifted from Jessica's shoulders, her heart swelling with the answer she'd hoped for. She smiled, feeling like everything had just fallen perfectly into place.

The family dinner at Jackson's penthouse was a complete success. The spacious dining room buzzed with the soft hum of conversation, the glow of candlelight reflecting off the polished glass surfaces. Jessica's meal was a hit—each dish more delicious than the last, her careful attention to detail evident in every bite. Jackson sat back in his chair, watching her as she moved around the room, her laughter blending perfectly with the conversations, her natural warmth filling the space.

Phyllis and Nathan, now settled into their new home, were relaxed and at ease. They exchanged soft smiles as they discussed their honeymoon and the subtle joys of married life. Phyllis, ever the storyteller, regaled the table with amusing anecdotes from their trip, while Nathan chimed in with his own playful comments. Their happiness was infectious, and it was clear they were both enjoying this phase of their life, content in each other's company.

John and Mary, on the other hand, shared a few grumbles about Jackson taking Jessica away from them, but their complaints were softened by the smile on Jackson's face and the way he kept his hand on Jessica's, showing just how much, he cherished her. They were happy, too, in their own way—relieved to see their son so in love, even if it meant a bit of distance from their lives.

As dinner wound down, Jackson never missed an opportunity to remind Jessica how much she meant to him. He leaned in close, his voice soft but full of sincerity, "I'm so proud of you, Jess. You've made this whole evening perfect."

Jessica smiled, her heart-warming at the words. "I'm just glad everyone's enjoying themselves," she said, brushing her hand over his.

"I meant what I said earlier," Jackson continued, his gaze fixed on her with a tenderness that made her chest tighten. "I love you."

The words felt so natural, so right now. She leaned in to kiss him, savouring the moment, knowing that with every passing day, their love was growing stronger. It was as if the whole world had faded away, leaving just the two of them, in their little bubble of happiness.

The evening wrapped up with more laughter and promises to get together soon. As the last of the guests trickled out, Jessica lingered for a moment, glancing around the penthouse, her heart full of contentment. This had been a good night—a night of family, love, and warmth. And as she looked over at Jackson, the man she had come to love more with each passing day, she knew that this was just the beginning of something even more beautiful.

Later that night, after the last of the guests had left, the penthouse grew quiet. The soft hum of the city echoed below as Jackson led Jessica out onto the balcony. The night air was cool and crisp, and the view of the harbour spread out before them, sparkling under the moonlight. The soft breeze ruffled her hair as she leaned against the railing, taking in the beauty of the scene. It felt like the world had slowed down, leaving just the two of them standing in the quiet, the weight of the evening still lingering in the air.

Jackson stood behind her for a moment, wrapping his arms around her waist and pulling her close. She leaned into him, savouring the comfort of his presence, when she felt him shift slightly. She turned her head, meeting his gaze, and noticed the seriousness in his eyes.

Jackson's hand moved to his pocket, and with a calm motion, he pulled out a small velvet box. The light from the balcony glinted off the surface of the box, and for a moment, Jessica felt her breath catch. Her heart started to race, but she couldn't quite make sense of the moment.

She looked at him with confusion, unsure of what was happening. "Jackson?" she asked softly, her voice trembling slightly.

He didn't say anything at first. Instead, he opened the box to reveal a simple yet elegant diamond ring, the stone sparkling softly in the dim light. Jackson took a deep breath, his gaze never leaving hers, and said the words that made Jessica's pulse quicken with both surprise and overwhelming emotion.

"Marry me, Jess."

Her breath caught in her throat, and for a long moment, the world seemed to stop. She didn't know what to say. The man she loved was standing there, asking her to share her life with him in the most profound way. Her chest tightened with a mixture of joy, disbelief, and love. It was everything she had ever dreamed of and more, but in that moment, she couldn't quite process the enormity of the question.

Slowly, she reached for the ring, her fingers brushing against the cool metal as she whispered, "Jackson…" Her heart was in her throat, and her eyes welled with tears.

He smiled gently, a reassuring smile that made her feel safe in his arms. "You don't have to answer right now," he said, his voice tender, "but I want you to know, I love you. I've never been surer of anything."

Jessica stood there, looking down at the ring, then back up at the man she had come to love with all of her heart. In that moment, everything felt right. The world had led her to this point, and she knew, deep down, that this was just the beginning of their forever.

With a shaky breath, she finally spoke, her voice thick with emotion. "Yes, Jackson. I will marry you."

A smile broke across his face, and without another word, he pulled her into his arms, kissing her with all the love and promise that the moment held. The city stretched out before them, but in that instant, nothing else mattered. They had found each other, and that was all they needed.

Epilogue

It was Jackson and Jessica's wedding day, a day they had dreamed of and planned for with love and anticipation. The sun was shining brightly, casting a golden glow over Jackson's parents' estate, where the ceremony would take place. The lush gardens and rolling hills had been carefully prepared for this special occasion, a celebration of not only their love but also the journey they had taken together over the past year.

Jessica's heart raced as she stood in the bedroom, taking one last look at herself in the full-length mirror. The silk and lace of her wedding dress clung perfectly to her frame, the elegant design a reflection of her personality—timeless and graceful. The dress was a slim fit that flared slightly at the knees, showcasing her natural beauty. The delicate lace overlay added a touch of vintage charm, while the simple, yet stunning, pearl details on the bodice made it feel even more magical. Her hair was styled in soft waves, pinned back with a delicate pearl tiara, and her makeup was understated, highlighting her glowing skin and the sparkle in her eyes.

Phyllis stood beside her, looking radiant in her long red maid of honour dress, her smile wide and proud. They had been through so much together, and now, as Jessica stood on the cusp of this new chapter, Phyllis couldn't help but feel overjoyed for her best friend. "You look stunning," Phyllis whispered, giving Jessica a quick hug before stepping back.

"Thank you," Jessica whispered back, her voice trembling slightly. She was overwhelmed with emotion. After all the uncertainty, the ups and downs, they had arrived at this beautiful moment—together. The day was perfect in every way, but it felt almost surreal to her that this was happening. She had found her forever.

Meanwhile, Nathan and Jackson were waiting at the altar, standing in front of a sea of loved ones. Nathan, ever the jokester, teased Jackson, but he could see the genuine joy and excitement in his friend's eyes. Jackson stood tall and proud in his tailored black suit, looking dashing as ever. But as he stood there, waiting for his bride, his thoughts were only on one thing—Jessica.

When the music began, the guests turned to watch as Phyllis made her way down the aisle, looking every bit the vision of grace. Then, just as the music swelled to its crescendo, Jessica appeared at the top of the aisle, arm linked with his father's. The crowd gasped, and Jackson's heart skipped a beat.

He was stunned by how breathtaking she looked. It wasn't just the dress, though it was undeniably beautiful—it was her. Her radiant smile, the way she walked toward him with grace, the sparkle in her eyes that seemed to light up the entire world around her. She was the woman he had dreamed of for so long, the one who had captured his heart in ways he never thought possible. As she drew closer, he couldn't help but marvel at how he had once thought she was 'unattractive'. Now, all he saw was pure beauty—inside and out—a beauty beyond words.

His breath caught in his throat as their eyes locked, and for a moment, the entire world seemed to fade away. All he could see was Jessica—his future, his everything.

As she reached him at the altar, his father kissed her cheek and gave Jackson a proud look, before stepping back to his seat. Jackson took her hands in his, his heart racing, not from nervousness but from sheer joy.

"You're stunning," he whispered, his voice thick with emotion.

Jessica smiled, her eyes shining with love. "You're not so bad yourself," she teased softly.

The ceremony was a blur of beautiful vows, heartfelt promises, and laughter. Jackson couldn't help but steal glances at Jessica throughout, his heart swelling with pride. They had come so far, and now, they were here—committed to a lifetime together.

When it came time for the vows, Jackson squeezed Jessica's hands tightly. "I vow to always love you, to stand by your side through whatever life brings, to never take you for granted, and to always cherish you, just as I do today. I love you, Jessica."

Jessica's voice shook as she responded, "I vow to love you with all that I am, to be your partner, your best friend, and your confidante. I will support you, trust you, and always make a home with you, no matter where we are. I love you, Jackson."

With a smile, the officiant declared, "By the power vested in me, I now pronounce you husband and wife. Jackson, you may kiss your bride."

Jackson didn't need to be told twice. He leaned in, lifting her chin gently, and kissed her softly, sealing their vows with a kiss that promised forever.

As they pulled away, they were met with a chorus of applause and cheers from their friends and family. The celebration that followed was filled with love, laughter, and happy tears. Phyllis and Nathan gave heartfelt speeches, and even Jackson's parents, couldn't help but beam with pride as they watched their son marry the woman of his dreams.

The reception was full of joy, the dance floor alive with energy as everyone celebrated the newlyweds. Jackson and Jessica shared their first dance as husband and wife, lost in each other's arms, the world fading away as they moved together to the music.

"I'm so glad we're here," Jackson whispered into her ear as they danced. "With you. Forever."

Jessica smiled, her heart full, as she looked into his eyes. "Me too. I've never been surer of anything in my life."

And with that, surrounded by the people who loved them, Jackson and Jessica knew that this was only the beginning of their beautiful journey together. Forever had started, and it was even more beautiful than they could have ever imagined.

The End

Still Yours

Alison Reid

A complete standalone romance

Previously published individually

Chapter One

"I won't! *I will not!* Do you understand me, Sienna?"

Kiera's voice shook with fury as she stood rigid in her living room, glaring at her mobile phone like it might burst into flames. If only Sienna could see the rage blazing in her eyes. If only she cared enough to be affected by it.

"I can hardly fail to understand," came Sienna Scott's cool, clipped reply. Her tone was precise, too calm—intentionally calm. "Your words are quite specific. However, I feel you owe this to your father. It's a small request, Kiera—just a couple of weeks. After all the years of love and care he's given you—"

"Don't," Kiera snapped, her voice rising to a pitch that made her flinch. "Don't stand there and pretend this is about him. You're the one asking. If my father truly wanted me there, he'd call me himself instead of sending his perfect puppet to do his bidding."

There was a pause, taut with the kind of silence that screamed.

"As for all that love and care," she continued, her voice dropping to a bitter undertone, "that was long before you ever came along. You wouldn't know the difference. So maybe you should cancel your little getaway to Paris and repay some of that supposed care—especially considering how much money he's thrown at you over the years."

The words hung in the air like shards of glass, and for a moment, Kiera almost regretted them. Almost.

Her hand trembled as she ended the call with a final, defiant tap and hurled the phone onto the table. It clattered across the wood, skidding to a stop at the edge. She collapsed into a nearby chair, her legs buckling beneath her, breath shallow and uneven.

Confrontations drained her. Especially this kind.

Dealing with Sienna was like stepping into a cage with a snake—cold, calculating, always coiled and ready. And no matter how calm she tried to stay, Sienna always found a way to strike beneath the skin.

But not this time.

Kiera curled her fingers into fists, grounding herself. This time, I didn't retreat. This time, I stood my ground.

Because she wasn't that frightened teenager anymore, wilting beneath Sienna's sharp smile and smooth control. She was twenty-three now. Grown. Capable. Successful, even, in her own quiet way. And no longer powerless.

Still, the argument left her shaken, a molten frustration burning in her chest like acid.

She stood abruptly, heading into the kitchen and flipping on the kettle. She needed something to steady her. A cup of tea—extra sweet, the way her mother used to make it. It was a childhood ritual she hadn't managed to outgrow, and the very fact that she still needed it—still craved comfort like that—infuriated her all over again.

How could one woman still have such a grip on her?

And worse—how could Sienna think she didn't know? As if the trip to Paris was just another social jaunt, another indulgent escape. But the truth wasn't nearly so innocent.

Kiera's jaw clenched as she reached for the sugar jar, spooning two heaping teaspoons into her mug.

She knew exactly who Sienna would be meeting in Paris.

The so-called secret was no secret at all.

She could see it now, the image rising unbidden: Sienna's elegant blonde head turned slightly toward a darker one—raven-black hair, slate-grey eyes, and that crooked, devastating smile that haunted far too many of Kiera's memories.

Andrew Foster.

Tall. Charming. And utterly treacherous.

They wouldn't meet at the airport—not with Andrew's name and reputation splashed across financial headlines and glossy business profiles. No, he was too careful for that. Too practiced at deception. Just like Sienna.

If her father ever discovered the affair, it would destroy him. But he wouldn't. They were too meticulous. Too discreet. Their little charade had been running like clockwork for six years now.

And Kiera—angry, watching, powerless—had kept their secret the whole time.

She took her mug and descended the polished wooden stairs into her gallery, trying to shed the storm of emotion, though the image of Sienna and Andrew still clung to her mind like a stain. Thankfully, the space was empty. She didn't need an audience while she wrestled with the past.

As always, the sight of the gallery soothed her. Its clean lines, warm lighting, and soft gleam of oils on canvas reminded her that she had built something of her own. Something good.

Animals filled her walls—graceful horses, playful dogs, serene cats—all captured in vivid, glowing oils. She had carved out a niche, and people traveled far and wide for her pieces. Even among the bigger galleries, hers had a reputation.

Her latest American client was collecting setters. Just last week, Kiera had found her another—a rare Old English setter—at an obscure sale, the auctioneer's raised brows betraying his surprise when she kept bidding. He had known its worth, and that she'd turn a tidy profit. Most of them knew her now. Her gallery's fame was spreading, fast.

Not bad for someone who'd abandoned college at nineteen, too miserable to stay.

Sally came in from the back, buttoning her coat. Her gaze sharpened the moment it landed on Kiera's face.

"Trouble?" she asked.

Kiera shook her head with a tight smile. "Not really. I just… might need to go home for a bit. A couple of weeks, maybe."

Sally had worked with her for a long time and had become something close to a friend. But some things weren't meant to be shared—not even with a friend.

The smile faded from Kiera's lips as she checked the time. "You head off, Sally. I'll lock up."

"Anything you need, just say." Another perceptive glance, then Sally was gone.

Kiera closed the blinds and locked the doors, wishing she'd accepted Gary's invitation tonight. At the time, she'd looked forward to a quiet evening alone. Now, all she had was bitterness for company.

Back in her apartment, she tried to distract herself—television, a light meal—but the gnawing sense of dread wouldn't leave. The idea of returning home turned her stomach. She hadn't been back since she was nineteen. Her father still visited her—he was even commissioning her to collect shire horse paintings—but going home was different. Not with Sienna there. Not with the shadow of Andrew Foster looming.

Their secret had poisoned everything. Even now, it clung to her like a second skin. In her childhood home, she wouldn't be able to pretend anymore. The pressure might finally make her burst—and then what? Tell her father the truth? Destroy what was left of his peace?

Andrew wasn't even living there anymore. He had his own grand place now—her father had told her proudly. Still adored him. They both had, once.

But Kiera had seen the truth. She'd wanted to scream it years ago, to tear the smug smile off Sienna's perfect face. But her love for her father—and Andrew's haunting grey eyes—had silenced her.

Hadn't Andrew all but admitted it?

She leaned back, eyes on the flickering screen but seeing none of it, memory dragging her relentlessly toward the moment everything had changed.

She had always been a shy child, but her early life had been filled with happiness. Her father, a successful businessman, had provided a secure, loving home. Each school day, she was dropped off and picked up by her mother. They were inseparable, alike in manner and spirit, their bond radiant with mutual delight. David Scott devoted every spare moment to his family, and Kiera's earliest memories were of racing to meet him at the door each evening—her mother close behind—followed by laughter, hugs, and the warm comfort of being together again.

That beautiful world shattered the day her mother died in a car accident. Kiera had been just eleven—grief-stricken and vulnerable—trying desperately to comfort her devastated father while struggling with her own pain. Nothing was ever the same, but slowly, over the next two years, they settled into a quiet, numb kind of healing.

It was during that time she first met Andrew Foster.

Fresh out of university and already building a name for himself, Andrew had just joined her father's firm. Kiera had heard bits of conversation that painted him as brilliant, a rising star in the business world. She was thirteen and still at the local private school, and Andrew's weekend visits added a quiet excitement to her life. Her father, deeply impressed by Andrew's intellect, often invited him to lunch, and the two would walk for hours in the garden, talking in low, serious tones.

Kiera never felt excluded. There was something about Andrew—his blue-black hair, his slate-grey eyes—that saw too much, understood too deeply. Somehow, she felt he knew how much she still hurt. He always returned her hesitant smiles with warmth, and gradually, he became simply "Andrew." She missed him when he wasn't around. Slowly, life began to take shape again. Her recovery had begun.

Then came the shock.

Her father announced he was remarrying.

Kiera couldn't reconcile her emotions. If she was allowed to recover, why shouldn't he? But the thought of another woman replacing her mother was unbearable. On the day he told her, she fled to the river that bordered the grounds of Wickham Hall, unable to face lunch—or Andrew. She didn't want to spoil her father's joy, but she couldn't pretend.

It was Andrew who had found her.

Even now, years later, the memory played in her mind like a reel of film— sunlight rippling on the water, the hush of reeds swaying in the breeze, and the sound of his footsteps on the soft riverbank. She'd been curled beneath the old willow tree, her knees drawn to her chest, her arms wrapped around them like a shield. Grief clung to her skin like a second, suffocating layer.

He came toward her without saying a word at first, just lowered himself onto the grass beside her, close but not touching. The silence between them wasn't awkward. It was deliberate, respectful. He always had a way of giving her space before reaching into the dark.

Finally, he spoke, his voice low and measured. "He's only forty-four, Kiera. Still a young man. You can't expect him to live like a hermit forever."

She didn't turn to face him. "I thought he loved my mother," she said hoarsely, her voice brittle with grief, each word dredged from the hollow ache in her chest.

He shifted slightly, and when she finally met his gaze, his grey eyes were narrowed against the sunlight—but softened with something she almost didn't recognise. Compassion.

He reached out, gently turning her tear-streaked face toward him. His touch was warm, steady. "Never doubt that," he murmured. "His whole life was wrapped up in you and your mother. Everything he did—every decision—was for you. But it's been two years, Kiera. People mourn… and then they move on. You're moving on."

She swallowed hard, the words pressing against her chest like a stone. She couldn't argue—not completely. Healing wasn't linear, but she was healing. Slowly. Painfully. But there were mornings when she could breathe again without crying. Nights when she could fall asleep without hearing her mother's last words echoing in her ears.

Still. "He was married to her," she whispered, as if that vow should have granted eternal loyalty.

Andrew nodded solemnly. "And you loved her too. Just as deeply. Just… in a different way."

She closed her eyes and let the ache swell. When he drew her into a quiet embrace, she didn't resist. His arms were solid, grounding, his chin resting briefly against the top of her head. There was nothing romantic in the gesture— it was something else. Protective. Reassuring.

"You'll survive, Kiera Scott," he said quietly.

And because it was Andrew, she believed him.

She had tried. God knew she had.

But Sienna made everything harder.

With her cinematic beauty and razor-sharp ambition, Sienna had swept into their lives like a thunderstorm—luminous and cold and utterly unstoppable. There was no room in her world for the inconvenient weight of a grieving, awkward teenager. Kiera had been thirteen: all sharp elbows, puffy eyes, and desperate longing. She didn't stand a chance.

Sienna hadn't shouted or slammed doors. That wasn't her way. Instead, she played the long game—tight smiles, veiled barbs, carefully curated moments that chipped away at Kiera's sense of belonging. The house that had once been filled with her mother's laughter slowly shifted, repainted in neutral tones and silences. Her bedroom redecorated without warning. Her mother's piano closed and covered with expensive books no one read.

David, her father, had tried. But he was tired. Worn down by grief and, later, by Sienna's quiet insistence on peace.

Kiera's protests—her cries for attention, for truth—were dismissed as adolescent tantrums.

And before the year was out, she was gone. Tucked away in a pristine boarding school with polished staircases and manicured lawns, hundreds of miles from home.

Sienna had won.

Boarding school was lonely and miserable. Kiera, too shy and wounded to make friends easily, became isolated. The only light in her life was Andrew. He stayed close, visiting during holidays, taking her on outings, defying Sienna's disapproval with quiet defiance. Sometimes he'd show up at school to take her to dinner, and by the time she was fifteen, he had become her anchor—her very best friend.

Despite the ten-year age gap, she felt safe with Andrew. He was her stability, her constant, the one person she could count on. As her relationship with her father grew more strained, her bond with Andrew deepened. He was her rock in a world she no longer understood. In her heart, he had become her knight in shining armour—and she clung to that belief with everything she had.

Kiera would never forget the summer everything changed.

For the first time, she invited a friend home with her. Harper Miller, the daughter of an army officer, had been facing a lonely summer—either stuck at school or visiting distant relatives she couldn't stand. Kiera brought her home not because she wanted to, but because she couldn't bear the thought of Harper spending the holiday alone. She told herself it was the right thing to do, even if the truth was more complicated: she didn't want to share Andrew with anyone.

Andrew was surprised, too. He had long since become more than a family friend—closer to her than her own father. And now that she was seventeen, Kiera saw him through different eyes. The angles of his face, the way his slow smile transformed him, how those slate-grey eyes could catch hers and send a warm, unfamiliar flush to her cheeks. She had never felt quite like this before. The innocence of childhood had faded, replaced by something far more fragile, far more thrilling.

That first morning back, Kiera rose early—too early for Harper, who was still fast asleep—and wandered into the gardens. Andrew found her there, just as he always seemed to, his presence as familiar and comforting as the sound of her name on his lips.

"You brought reinforcements," he teased gently, falling into step beside her. "It never occurred to me I'd have to share you this holiday."

She blushed and looked away, unsure if he was joking—or if there was something else behind his words.

"Harper had nowhere else to go," she explained. "I couldn't leave her at school. I didn't think you'd mind."

"I don't mind, angel," he said, smiling. He reached out and took her hand, his fingers brushing hers with casual intimacy. His eyes lingered on her flushed cheeks. "It was probably a good idea. Safety in numbers."

"I'm safe with you," Kiera said softly.

His gaze held hers longer than usual. Then, almost reluctantly, he turned her back toward the garden path.

"You always have been," he murmured.

They walked on in silence, the air between them thick with something unspoken. Her heartbeat slowed, but she was aware of every brush of his arm, every glance he gave her from the corner of his eye.

It wasn't until they neared the house that he spoke again, his voice rougher than before.

"How much longer do you have at that damned school?"

"School?" she repeated, caught off guard. "Another year."

He stopped, frowning. "Another year? Hell."

She looked up at him, anxious. His jaw was tense, his mood suddenly darkened. Then, as though remembering himself, he reached for her hand again, turning it gently in his. When he looked up, his expression had softened.

"Does it seem like a long time to you, Kiera?" he asked. "Or am I just being impatient?"

She hesitated, then whispered, "It seems like a long time."

He smiled and touched her cheek with the back of his fingers. For a moment he was so close—too close—and her breath caught. Then he grinned, the old familiar Andrew breaking through.

"When we go out this holiday, we'll take Harper," he said softly. "Sharing the time with her might be a very good idea."

And she understood exactly what he meant.

Harper was a buffer. A cover. A distraction.

Things had changed—not just for her, but for him. And though no one said it aloud, the shift shimmered between them, delicate and exhilarating. She hugged the knowledge to herself, glowing with it.

It was a wistful, beautiful summer—one she would remember for the rest of her life. Not even Sienna could ruin it. Not even Harper, who remained oblivious to the undercurrent that ran between Kiera and Andrew. She didn't notice the way Andrew looked at Kiera when he thought no one was watching. She didn't see how often his hand found Kiera's arm, or how gently he lifted her down from a stile, his touch lingering just a moment too long.

And Kiera lingered, too. Every glance, every shared smile felt like a secret. A promise. She drank in every moment, knowing Andrew was just as aware as she was.

Harper, unknowingly, had become their chaperone.

Chapter Two

Toward the end of the holiday, her father made an announcement that changed everything.

He waited until the final moments of dinner, casually topping off everyone's wine before dropping the news like a stone into still water.

"Andrew is joining the firm as a full partner," her father declared. "I can't risk letting a financial wizard like him get away. A few firms have already tried to poach him. This way, he stays—safe and sound."

Andrew, of course, had already known. He offered a quiet, composed smile. But Kiera was overwhelmed with joy. It meant he would never leave. He was part of them now. She would never have to be parted from him.

And then she looked up—and saw the truth.

Andrew wasn't looking at her. His gaze was fixed on Sienna; their eyes locked in silent communication. Kiera's smile faded. Something passed between them—something unspoken, unmistakable—and her skin went cold.

She glanced at her father, but he was too busy pouring more wine, oblivious to the sudden shift in atmosphere. When she looked back, Sienna had composed herself, expression as guarded as ever. But it was too late. Kiera had seen it: the flicker of triumph in Andrew's eyes and something almost smug in Sienna's.

Andrew finally turned toward her, but Kiera couldn't meet his gaze. It felt like the floor had vanished beneath her—like she was plummeting, fast, into something dark and irreversible.

That night, she couldn't sleep.

She stood on the veranda outside her room, wrapped in moonlight and warm night air. A breeze stirred the trees gently. Everything was quiet—until she heard voices below.

Sienna's, unmistakably cool and edged with satisfaction: "So, you've finally got what you wanted?"

Kiera froze. She didn't need to hear the second voice to know it would be Andrew's.

"Not entirely," he said. "But I'm close. I've always known what I wanted."

"As long as David's alive, things will stay as they are," Sienna replied, her voice low, laced with amusement.

"I don't see why they should," Andrew countered. "They haven't stayed as they're supposed to, so far, have they? David hasn't the faintest clue what's happening around him. He's far too trusting."

"Lucky for both of us," Sienna murmured. "So? Are you going to do anything about it?"

"Not yet. I can wait. I've waited three years already."

"Still playing me along?" Sienna asked, her tone mock soft.

Andrew laughed—a sound that chilled Kiera to the bone. "You like being played along, Sienna. You love the game. You want to see how far this can go without David ever finding out."

Kiera slipped back into her room and shut the windows, gently but firmly. She'd heard enough. More than enough.

It was true. No matter how many times she told herself there had to be another explanation, that what she'd overheard, what she knew in her bones couldn't possibly be real—there was no escaping the truth.

Andrew Foster—her Andrew—was having an affair with her stepmother.

And now, as if that betrayal weren't enough, her father had handed him power on a silver platter: a full partnership in the firm. Trust, authority, influence—all of it gifted to Andrew with a proud handshake and a speech about legacy and loyalty.

If Andrew and Sienna decided to walk away together—hand in hand, lovers and business partners—there would be nothing her father could do to stop them. He'd given them everything. He'd handed over the keys to his kingdom. And he didn't even realise it.

Kiera's world, already fragile, began to crack at the seams.

All of her secret hopes—all the daydreams she'd tucked away in the quiet corners of her heart—shattered. Every lingering glance, every kind word, every whispered moment she'd cherished had been nothing but dust. A fantasy spun by a lonely girl desperate for connection.

She was seventeen.

Too young. Too naïve. Too irrelevant.

And to Andrew—who had once held her hand, who had called her angel, who had looked at her like she was something fragile and precious—she was nothing. Not when there was Sienna. Not when there was a woman like that—beautiful, ruthless, and fully grown.

It had all been in her head.

Everything she had imagined between them had been just that: imagination. A girl's foolish illusion dressed up as love.

The next morning brought confirmation. Harper looked pale and distracted as she came down to breakfast and wasted no time pulling Kiera aside.

"You won't believe it," she whispered. "Last night, your stepmother and Andrew were—well, practically flirting in stereo."

"Don't be ridiculous," Kiera snapped, instinctively defensive. But she didn't doubt Harper for a second.

"Believe it or not," Harper said stiffly. "I had my window open. I heard them. Couldn't see, but I didn't need to, did I?" She gave Kiera a pitying look, then changed the subject and never mentioned it again.

After that night, Kiera cut Andrew off entirely.

There were no confrontations, no tearful explanations, no dramatic parting words. Just silence—a cold, deliberate shutting of the door. If she hadn't known better, she might have believed he was hurt by it. Sometimes, when she caught him watching her across a room, his expression unreadable, she thought she saw confusion… maybe even regret. But it didn't matter. Whatever flickers of feeling he allowed himself were irrelevant now.

He had made his choice.

He had never truly belonged to her—not in the way she had once hoped. He was always working, always traveling, always orbiting in the gravitational pull of her father's empire. Not hers. Not theirs.

And what an empire it had become.

What had begun as her grandfather's modest contracting firm had evolved into something sprawling and untouchable—airports, defence contracts, smart cities. The very skeleton of modern civilisation. And at the centre of it all was Andrew Foster: brilliant, ambitious, and utterly relentless. He held the reins now, and he was not the kind of man to ever let go.

Once, she had admired that. Once, she'd thought he was building it all for them—for the family. For her, maybe, in some quiet, unspoken way.

But now, when he looked at her, she looked away. When he entered a room, she found a reason to leave. The avoidance became a ritual—a quiet armour forged from pain. It hurt, of course it did. But not as much as the realisation that she had never truly mattered. Not beyond being David Scott's daughter. Not beyond being a child he could easily cast aside.

Back at school, she made sure to memorise his travel schedule. She arranged her life around the gaps—joining clubs she didn't care about, volunteering for late study sessions, saying yes to every invitation. Anything to avoid the man who had so effortlessly broken her heart. Anything to keep from being near the one person whose presence still made her stomach knot with the bitter ache of everything she'd lost.

And she had lost something.

Not just a first love, not just trust.

She had lost the version of herself who had believed she could be seen—and chosen.

Andrew had taken everything in stride over the past year—her newfound independence, her silences, her deliberate distance. He never pushed, never demanded explanations. He simply absorbed her absence with that maddening patience of his, as if it were a phase she'd grow out of.

But when Kiera turned down a university placement and chose art school instead, everything changed.

She didn't consult anyone. She secured a place at a small but reputable art institute in London, rented a cramped studio apartment in a half-renovated building, and stopped going home altogether. She thought, perhaps foolishly, that by creating a new life, she could outrun the shadow of the old one.

Then, on the morning of her nineteenth birthday, he came.

No call. No warning. He was just there, standing in the doorway of her apartment like a storm she couldn't escape. There was no time to prepare, no time to pretend. She had no choice but to let him in.

He walked into her tiny space like he owned it, his gaze cool and sweeping. The frown he wore wasn't loud, but it promised trouble. He stood in the centre of her living room—such as it was—surrounded by half-unpacked boxes, mismatched chairs, paint-stained floors, and canvases stacked haphazardly against every wall.

"So," he said, voice calm but laced with something sharp. "This is how you plan to live?"

Kiera folded her arms across her chest, suddenly aware of how small her world looked through his eyes. "It's temporary. I'm still settling in."

He looked around, unimpressed. "Frittering your days away at art school and your nights in this squalor? That's the grand plan?"

"I'm not living in a squalor," she said, but the conviction in her voice wavered. "I just moved in."

"When will you be settled, then? When you're thirty? Still trying to prove a point no one asked you to make?" His voice tightened. "You're smart, Kiera. You're not some wandering dreamer. God knows how they even let you into that program."

"I can draw!" she snapped, flushed with indignation.

"So can half the bloody population," he bit back. "That doesn't mean they can build a life with it. Or be happy trying."

Her fists clenched. "You don't get to tell me what happiness looks like."

He turned from her in frustration, dragging a hand through his hair. "You should've gone to university. You had options. A future."

"It's none of your business!"

The words hit the air harder than she meant. His head snapped around. In two strides, he was in front of her, his hands gripping her arms—not hard, but firm. Anchoring.

"It's never been my business," he said, his voice rough. "Not really. But you used to want my opinion. You used to listen to me. Now you won't even look at me. What the hell changed?"

"I grew up," she said, the words trembling on her lips.

"Did you?" he asked, his mouth twisting. "Because you seemed more mature at thirteen. Back then, you weren't a petulant girl with a martyr complex. You used to think."

Her anger flared like a match. "Well, I've done some thinking. And I see you for what you are now. I'm not a naïve child anymore."

He froze.

His grip didn't tighten—but it didn't release either. His eyes searched hers, and for one suspended second, she thought he'd ask. Thought he might explain.

But instead, his voice dropped, low and dangerous. "What am I, Kiera? What dark revelation have you uncovered that justifies all of this? What's the great sin I've committed?"

She opened her mouth.

But the words wouldn't come. I know about you and Sienna. It pulsed like a wound behind her eyes, but her lips couldn't form the syllables. To say it aloud would make it real. Would force her to shatter the last of what little remained.

"I just don't like you anymore," she said quietly.

It was cowardly. It was cruel.

But it was the only thing she could say without falling apart.

The shift in his eyes was instant. The warmth she'd always found in them—infuriating, grounding, familiar—vanished. The soft grey turned to slate.

He let go of her and turned toward the window, the angles of his face suddenly unfamiliar, sculpted in shadows.

"Maybe you have grown up," he said after a long silence. "Little girls are easy to impress. They adore anyone who's kind to them. It was foolish of me to think that kind of loyalty could last."

He turned to leave.

"I hope everything works out for you," he added, pausing at the door.

But she could tell—he didn't believe it. Not really.

When the door shut behind him, the silence he left behind was unbearable. Kiera wandered her small apartment in restless circles, too raw to cry, too shaken to sit still. She had sketches to finish, an essay due, readings to complete—but all of it felt meaningless.

She should have told him. Should have told someone. But she couldn't.

Instead, she carried the knowledge like contraband. Andrew and Sienna. But how could she tell her father that the man he trusted with his business—his legacy—had betrayed him with his wife?

She couldn't. So, she did what she always did.

She bore the weight of their guilt like it was her own.

Coming back to the present with a sharp jolt, Kiera got up and turned off the television. The screen had gone black long ago. Now there was only silence.

She felt tired. Bone-deep tired—and angry.

She had moved on. She'd built a good life, made something of herself despite Andrew's doubts. But every time she saw her father, it came rushing back. The lie. The daily deception. Three people entangled in something toxic—two of them willing, one of them blissfully unaware.

And she couldn't do a damned thing about it without breaking the heart of the only person she still loved without reservation.

Her father called the next morning, before Kiera had even opened the gallery. She'd half expected it. When Sienna wanted something, she was relentless.

"Kiera, could you find it in your heart to come home for a while?" he asked immediately, his voice weary.

Kiera's lips curved wryly. There it was—Sienna's victory. Still, the fatigue in her father's voice struck a chord. She couldn't say no.

"Sienna called," she said flatly. "I hear she's off to Paris?"

"One of her endless buying trips," her father confirmed. "I wouldn't trouble you, but I've got a few people coming next week. It's too late to cancel."

Kiera considered asking whether Sienna had given the guests any thought but decided against it. What was the point? In a way, returning might be a blessing. It had been years since she'd walked the grounds without the shadow of Sienna—or Andrew—lurking nearby.

Her stomach tightened. Andrew Foster might be among the guests. Her father often held meetings at the house, and if it was business, Andrew would almost certainly be there.

"I'm not catering for hordes," she warned.

Her father chuckled, clearly sensing she was softening. "No need. I just need a hostess. The usual staff will handle everything. And of course, there's Mrs. Williams."

Ah yes—Mrs. Williams.

Kiera's brows drew together at the thought of the stern housekeeper who had ruled Wickham Hall since Sienna took over. When her mother was alive, a pair of village women had done perfectly well. But Sienna had insisted on a "proper housekeeper" and hired one to suit her taste.

The woman had been a daily torment to Kiera during her school years, aligning herself quickly with the new mistress of the house and treating Kiera with a chilly disdain. It would almost be fun to return now—older, independent, and successful. Let Mrs. Williams try to brush her aside now.

"When do you want me?" she asked, surprising even herself with her readiness.

"I'd say now, but I suppose you have things to organise?" His voice was lighter already.

"You could say that." She smiled. There was a sale coming up the day after tomorrow, one she'd already previewed. Coincidentally, it was only ten miles from her hometown.

"I'll be there tomorrow afternoon," she said. "There's a sale nearby the next day, so it works out. I'll get Sally to cover while I'm gone."

"Tomorrow it is, then," her father said cheerfully. "You've got this gallery business running like clockwork. I'm impressed."

Kiera laughed and ended the call. She was impressed herself—mainly by the fact that she hadn't even asked who the guests were. Her mind had immediately jumped to Mrs. Williams instead, that old ghost of her past.

But now her smile faded. What if Andrew wasn't among the visitors? What if he was in Paris—with Sienna?

She caught her reflection in the nearby mirror and grimaced. Just the thought of him was enough to summon memories—sharp, vivid, and unwelcome. Perhaps going home was the right idea. Time to shake off old ghosts and sweep out the mental cobwebs. Time to face the past.

And perhaps, she thought with a touch of wickedness, time to rattle a few skeletons—starting with Mrs. Williams. She wondered how the formidable housekeeper would react when given orders by the "child" she'd once dismissed.

With a new sense of resolve, Kiera headed downstairs to the gallery, already rehearsing how she'd persuade Sally to extend her hours. Only then did it strike her—she hadn't asked how long her father needed her. No matter. She'd take it day by day. And if necessary, she'd make a quick trip back to London… to twist Sally's arm just a little further.

Chapter Three

As Kiera drove between the towering stone pillars that marked the entrance to Wickham Hall, a familiar ache stirred within her—an echo of the joy she'd once felt here, back when her mother was alive, and every day had felt like a celebration.

She glanced up at the stone spheres crowning the gateposts and smiled faintly. As a child, she'd begged her father to replace them with griffins, convinced that mythical guardians would suit the grandeur of the estate better. Now, older and wiser, she recognised the symmetry—how those same stone spheres were mirrored on the balustrades that descended from the grand front windows to the sweeping lawn.

Despite the sunlight and blooming azaleas, a flutter of dread touched her heart. What if things had changed? What if the image she'd carried in her heart all these years had been distorted by time? This place had become a symbol of perfection in her memory, and now she was afraid to find the cracks.

The lodge by the gate caught her eye—curtains now framed the windows. That startled her. No one had lived there in years. It had always been meticulously maintained, of course—just like the Hall itself—but never occupied. A passing thought made her grin. Perhaps her father had finally come to his senses and banished Mrs. Williams to the lodge. No such luck. More likely, someone from the village was renting it. Though that, too, seemed unlikely. Sienna had always been possessive of every square inch of Wickham. Still, she'd find out soon enough.

As she rounded the final curve in the long drive, Wickham Hall came into view—its stately façade rising against the backdrop of tall trees. The sunlight bathed the azaleas in gold and pink, and relief washed over her. It looked just the same. For a moment, it was like stepping into a dream.

Her father appeared almost instantly, emerging from the house with a beaming smile and outstretched arms.

"Kiera! You don't know how good it is to have you back home!"

She fell into his embrace, burying her face against his shoulder, blinking away the sudden tears. It was good to be back. But it was only temporary—and only possible because Sienna was away. Sienna had made it clear long ago that Kiera's presence wasn't welcome.

Anger stirred with grief. Sienna had succeeded in her quiet campaign to drive her out. But Kiera wasn't a child anymore. She wasn't here to cry over what had been lost. Her mother was gone, and no amount of mourning could bring back the days when Andrew had been her champion and Wickham had felt like a true home.

"Come inside," her father said gruffly. "I won't believe you're really here until I see you under this roof."

They both laughed, but Kiera felt the weight of truth in his words. This was no longer her home. That right had been quietly taken from her, one cold day at a time.

As they stepped into the grand hallway, Mrs. Williams appeared—unyielding as ever. Kiera felt her spine straighten. She was in no mood for pleasantries.

"Good afternoon, Miss Scott," the woman said with a clipped tone.

Kiera gave her a frosty smile in return. The years had not softened that face— it still reminded her of a particularly grim thundercloud.

"Good afternoon," she said coolly. "My luggage is in the car. Please have it brought up. I trust my old room is ready?"

Turning away without waiting for a reply, she slipped her arm through her father's and led him toward the sunny sitting room, where golden light warmed the furniture and softened the past.

She caught a glimpse of Mrs. Williams' flushed face before the door shut behind them and felt a twinge of satisfaction.

"Starting as you mean to go on?" her father chuckled.

"She is the housekeeper," Kiera replied lightly. "Perfect for a Victorian melodrama. We wouldn't want to confuse her with joy or warmth."

"I wouldn't count on her being confused by anything," he said with a grin. "I expect she'll storm in here any moment to hand in her notice."

"If she does, I'll be happy to take her place temporarily," Kiera replied, sinking onto the couch. "Strictly out of familial duty, of course."

He laughed and brought over a silver tea tray. "Serve us, will you?" he asked, settling in beside her.

She reached for the teapot, her curiosity already piqued. "By the way, I noticed curtains in the lodge windows. Have you let it out?"

"Not exactly," her father replied. "Andrew's staying there for a couple of weeks while his apartment is being redecorated. He moved in last week. He'll be joining us for dinner tonight. We usually eat together—it's companionable, and it saves the cook the trouble of preparing two meals."

Kiera froze, the porcelain teapot trembling in her hand. For a long moment, her thoughts scattered. Andrew? Here? The words that rose to her lips nearly escaped before she caught them: But why isn't he in Paris with Sienna?

It was only as she regained control that Kiera realised how close she'd come to actually saying the words aloud. Her father's continued calm suggested he hadn't noticed her reaction, and she gratefully busied herself with the tea tray, relieved that he expected no comment on his bombshell.

Why should he? She was the one who'd stayed away. Andrew had never altered his habits—he had been coming to Wickham Hall for years. There was no reason for her to assume anything had changed.

If anything, staying in the lodge was a convenient excuse to remain close to Sienna. Her father's trusting nature would never suspect anything, no matter how often they were together. He had always taken Kiera's past camaraderie with Andrew at face value, content to believe everything was as it appeared. Astute in business, perhaps—but blind when it came to those closest to him.

This was going to be harder than she had imagined. She couldn't face Andrew with any semblance of friendliness or even polite detachment. The last time she had seen him was seared into her memory, despite the three years that had passed. Nothing could erase that. And Andrew, she was sure, remembered too.

A ripple of panic began to rise, and she forced it down. She had thought herself safe here—at least for a while. But she had been wrong. Facing Sienna would have been easier; at least with her, the battle lines were clear. Andrew was far too subtle for open warfare. Worse, he was close to her father.

Later, alone in her room, Kiera stood at the window, staring out over the manicured lawn with its bright banks of azaleas. The lodge wasn't visible from here—the trees lining the winding drive hid it from view—but in her mind, she could see it perfectly. And she could see Andrew too. Whether he was already there or not, he would be soon.

The situation had been thrust upon her without warning, and she wasn't sure she could handle it. Just the three of them for dinner, no one else to steer the conversation. She could already picture the sardonic curve of Andrew's mouth as he greeted her, feel the weight of his cool grey eyes as they met hers.

She turned from the window with a jolt of impatience. There was no escaping it. He would be at dinner, and she would have to face him. But why wasn't he with Sienna? They must have worked out some plan—maybe he was joining her later. Her stepmother hadn't said how long she'd be gone, and her father hadn't mentioned her at all. But Sienna wouldn't leave things to chance. She always had a strategy.

It was only then that Kiera noticed how little the room had changed. The white walls, the delicate floral bedspread, the matching curtains—all as she remembered. The room had been updated over the years, of course, but the essence remained. That would be her father's doing. Left to herself, Sienna would've turned it into a linen cupboard.

Her luggage had been brought up, as she'd asked, and she smiled faintly to herself. This panic was childish. She wasn't the same girl who had last seen Andrew. She was older, stronger. It was just the past, clinging on, whispering memories she no longer had time for. Determined to shake it off, she unpacked methodically, sliding clothes into drawers and hanging dresses in the wardrobe, trying to keep her mind blank.

A hot bath would help. She was glad to find the bathroom untouched as well— everything as it had been. She ran the water, added a generous dose of her favourite bath oil, and sank into the tub, letting the heat draw out the tension of the long drive—and the shock of learning that Andrew was near.

He was too entwined in her past to separate from the present, even now. He had been everywhere—at holidays, at dinners, at her father's side. Even in her own home, she could hardly think of her childhood without his shadow in it. She snorted softly at herself and slid deeper into the water. Ridiculous. She was successful, independent, running a thriving business. Her life was perfectly in order.

But Wickham Hall wasn't just a house. It was a capsule of memory. And in that memory, Sienna still loomed.

That perfect face. The golden hair. The ice-blue eyes. Sienna Scott was the picture of elegance and charm, and nothing ever seemed to go wrong for her. Kiera could be proud of her small but flourishing business, but Sienna had succeeded too—of course she had. Clothes had always been her passion, and once she'd convinced her husband to back her boutique, it had taken off. Now she had several, and the launch of the latest one—three years ago—was what had finally ended everything for Kiera.

She had been foolish to attend. But her father had persuaded her, coaxed her, taken her out to dinner for her birthday and softened her resolve. He had even given her the stunning red silk dress she wore that night—a bribe disguised as a gift.

And that night had been the last time she saw Andrew, which changed everything.

Sienna knew how to stage an event. The boutique launch had been dazzling, glittering with guests and flashing cameras. Kiera, forewarned, had made sure she looked dazzling too. She was only twenty, and not ready for what the evening would bring.

Harper Miller had arrived early at her apartment, still a good friend then.

"You look stunning!" Harper had breathed, circling her in admiration. "Red is your colour."

She'd grimaced playfully. "Correction—every colour is your colour."

It was true enough. Kiera's nut-brown hair, softly waved and glossy, framed her wide green eyes perfectly. She could wear almost anything and look remarkable. But tonight, red had felt like armour.

"Gosh! It's like a first night," Harper muttered as their taxi pulled up in the West End. "People arriving in busloads!"

Not quite—but it felt that way. Once inside, the atmosphere was charged, and Kiera had felt it immediately: the subtle competition, the laughter that was just a bit too polished. The event was supposed to be a fashion preview, but it was really just a party. A very expensive, very glamorous party. One hosted by Sienna, designed to showcase more than just clothes.

It was also the night that everything finally broke between her and Andrew Foster.

Presumably, all the other boutique launches had been just as lavish, but Kiera wouldn't know—she'd never attended any of them. She glanced at her watch, already wondering how soon she could make a dignified exit. She would have to stay, at least for a while. Her father was present, and the moment he spotted her, he made a beeline in her direction. With Harper practically swooning over the whole event, Kiera knew she was trapped.

Sienna shot her a cold, assessing look before turning away without a word. Kiera wondered what her father made of the silent snub, though he said nothing. She felt as excluded as she had always felt. Time had done nothing to change that.

Still, she managed well enough—until she glanced up and saw Andrew deep in conversation with Sienna. The sight of the two of them together brought the past crashing over her in a wave so sharp it left her breathless. Nothing had changed. She didn't belong here. She was still on the outside—of this world, of their lives.

Without thinking, she turned toward the door, scanning the room for Harper, but instead found herself face-to-face with her father again.

"Darling where are you off to?" he asked, concerned. "You've gone quite pale."

"I've got a headache," she said, the lie making her stomach turn. She hated deceiving him, but somehow the truth—any truth—felt even more impossible. "I was looking for Harper. When I get one of these, I really have to go. You know how it is."

He did. She'd suffered from migraines as a teenager—ones that had mysteriously vanished after Sienna was no longer a fixture in her life. He didn't know that part, of course. The excuse had come too easily, and the fact that he believed it only made her feel worse.

"I'll find Harper," he said quickly. "You stay put, love."

At least she wouldn't have to argue with him about leaving. Kiera leaned against the wall, eyes cast down. Just a little longer and she'd be out of this awful place. She didn't know anyone here—and she didn't want to. Seeing Andrew again had cracked something open inside her she thought was long buried.

Her father returned with Harper just as Andrew approached. The moment his gaze landed on Kiera, something in the air shifted.

"Leaving so soon?" His voice was dry, faintly amused.

Chapter Four

Kiera's head snapped up, her eyes colliding with his. He thought she was running—from him. She wasn't about to correct him. Not when her insides had already gone numb from the shock of seeing him again—up close—was more than she could process.

He had changed. Sharpened. The angles of his face were more defined now, his grey eyes cooler, harder. They glittered with something unreadable — mockery? Disdain? Whatever it was, it pinned her in place. He looked every inch the man she remembered—and yet nothing like him at all.

"She's got one of her migraines coming on," her father explained, stepping in when she couldn't speak.

Kiera tore her eyes from Andrew's and forced herself to refocus. This had nothing to do with him.

"I'll get a taxi," she said, voice brittle. "Sorry, Harper."

"Don't worry about me," Harper replied with a grin. "This whole thing's been an experience. A bit more of it and I might start feeling important."

Unfortunately, the moment Kiera opened the boutique door, she was met with a downpour. Her father frowned at her pale face.

"Forget the taxi. I'll drive you both home."

"Oh darling!" Sienna breezed in, slipping her arm through her husband's. "Don't leave me now. I can't possibly manage on my own." It was clear she had no intention of being upstaged—or ignored.

Before Kiera could object, Andrew stepped forward. "Don't worry, David. I'll take them. You stay here and look after your wife."

"You think I need looking after, Andrew?" Sienna purred.

Kiera's lips tightened. If she stayed any longer, the headache would become real.

"We'll get a taxi," she said quickly.

But Andrew had already taken her arm, ignoring Sienna and pushing the door open again. "I'll take you," he said flatly. "Wait here. My car's just up the road."

And just like that, she was standing under the boutique's awning, rain slashing the pavement just inches away, caught up in a whirlwind of Andrew's making once again.

"Come inside, darling," Sienna cooed, clinging to her father. "Kiera's not a child. She proved that when she walked away. She doesn't need you—but I do."

"I'll call you later," her father promised distractedly, before being pulled back into the boutique. Kiera felt nothing but relief. He would call—but Sienna wouldn't let him talk for long.

A soaking would have been better than being trapped in a car with Andrew Foster.

"Andrew Foster's a very forceful man," Harper observed, drawing back from the edge of the awning.

Kiera wasn't sure if it was admiration or a warning in her tone. Maybe both. But she didn't care. She just wanted to get out.

And she wouldn't be alone in the car with him.

Except she was.

"I'll drop you off first," Andrew said as they pulled away from the curb. He didn't look wet at all—how had he managed that? His Mercedes was warm, sleek, and luxurious, and Kiera was absurdly grateful for the comfort. She had gotten wet just moving from the awning to the car, and he'd all but thrown her into the front seat, giving her no chance to argue. Harper was in the back. That had not been the plan.

"Don't bother," Harper said lightly. "I'll grab a cab from Kiera's place. I live well out of your way."

"It's no trouble," Andrew replied. "The rain's coming down hard, and you might have trouble finding one. Just give me the address."

That was that. Kiera could practically feel Harper's eyebrows raise in the back seat. Yes, Andrew Foster was indeed a forceful man.

He hadn't always been hard—but he certainly was now.

Kiera shivered.

Andrew glanced at her. "Cold?"

She hadn't remembered his voice being so deep. It unnerved her more than she cared to admit.

"Not really. Just damp," she murmured. Her voice sounded thin, even to her own ears. He looked at her again but said nothing.

By the time they dropped Harper off, Kiera was still shivering. Without a word, Andrew took off his jacket and draped it around her shoulders.

"I don't want—" she started, but he settled it around her anyway.

"You don't want to be wrapped in anything that reminds you of me?" he asked coolly. "Then think of it as an object. Purely functional. Forget who it belongs to."

She didn't answer. There was no point. She wouldn't forget—it still carried his scent, faint and familiar, and it wrapped around her like a memory she didn't want to have.

At this rate, she really would need that headache tablet before they got back.

She didn't speak—mostly because Andrew didn't. The silence held between them all the way to her apartment, only breaking as the car eased to a stop and the night opened up into a fresh downpour. Rain hammered the pavement now, relentless and heavy.

Andrew glanced at the flood outside, reached into the side pocket of the car, and retrieved an umbrella.

"Be prepared," he said dryly, catching the surprise on her face. "I'm not the type to stroll around with a furled umbrella, but this one's compact and opens wide. Wait here."

Before she could protest, he was out—umbrella up, striding through the storm with quiet determination. He appeared at her door a moment later, water already beading on his jacket.

"Your coat," she said weakly, unsettled by the gesture, but he took her arm firmly and guided her toward the stairs.

"When we're inside," he said smoothly.

That was when Kiera stiffened. He wasn't coming inside. That wasn't part of the plan.

"Give me the umbrella," she insisted, tugging back. "You keep the jacket." He gave her a look—sardonic, unreadable. "No chance. I've got plenty of jackets—

but only one umbrella. And I'm not letting you walk into that downpour alone."

There was no dignified way to argue. The apartment's front door opened straight onto the street, and trying to swap items would leave them both soaked. She had the uncomfortable feeling he knew that too.

Inside, the jacket was off her shoulders in seconds, and she handed it back as if it were radioactive. Andrew took it without a word, his gaze unreadable.

"Coffee?" he asked, faint amusement curling in his voice.

She hesitated. He had left the party to bring her home, dropped Harper off, shielded her from the rain. Telling him to leave now felt petty—even rude. And if she was honest, she didn't have the courage. He wasn't the Andrew she remembered. This man was colder, controlled. A stranger.

"I'll put the kettle on," she muttered, avoiding his gaze. "It's only instant."

"That'll do," he said. Then, more quietly, "You should change out of that beautiful dress before you catch your death."

"I'm warm enough," she replied, a little too fast. The truth was, she could still feel the residual warmth of his jacket—disturbingly so.

"You'd be warmer in a nice, thick robe," he said in a tone that sent a flush creeping up her neck.

What was wrong with her? He was an old friend. An enemy, even. His opinion shouldn't matter. She looked up sharply—and froze. His eyes were on her, cool and assessing, moving over her face, lingering on the cling of silk at her breasts.

"I'll make the coffee," she said, brittle and flustered, and fled into the kitchen.

Her heart thudded like a war drum.

It hadn't beaten like this since she was seventeen—since the summer everything fell apart. He'd looked at her then too, but not like this. This wasn't wistful. This was something else. Something harder. Something frightening.

Behind her, she could hear him moving about the apartment. She wasn't sure whether to hurry back in and face him or stay hidden and hope he'd leave. She doubted he'd leave.

He appeared in the doorway, leaning against the frame with infuriating ease.

"You've made the place nice," he said.

Her cheeks flared again—this time with remembered hurt.

"You expected I'd stay in squalor?"

"Ouch," he murmured. "Forget I said that. I was angry. Frustrated."

"I still don't see why my life frustrated you," she replied, handing him a mug of coffee.

He took it without comment and wandered back into the living room.

"I was afraid you'd lose your way," he said over his shoulder. "You were my little angel, gone very sadly astray."

"I was never an angel," she snapped, stung by the condescension.

He turned to look at her, and the weight in his gaze made her stomach twist.

"That's how I thought of you once. A long time ago." A pause. "I hear you left art school."

The jab caught her off guard. For a second, she couldn't reply.

She had been too miserable to paint, too hollow to create. For the past few months, she'd lived off her mother's inheritance, retreating from the world. But now, quietly, she had a plan. Her own gallery. A place to hide and maybe heal. She'd spoken to her father about it. She only hoped he hadn't told Andrew.

"Yes," she said at last.

She considered leaving it there. But his gaze—steady, invasive—compelled her to explain.

"I did have talent, as it turned out," she said, lifting her chin. "But I walked away."

"Why?"

She shifted irritably. "I wasn't happy."

If he asked why again, she might scream. But he didn't. He simply sipped his coffee and stared at her as if cataloguing every change, every secret she thought she'd buried.

"Don't you have somewhere to be?" she snapped.

"Such as?"

"Back at the boutique opening. You're missing the glitter."

"You're glittering enough for me." His eyes drifted over her again. "What happened to the headache?"

Her cheeks burned. She had forgotten all about the excuse she'd used to leave the party.

"It went away."

"Then let's go back. Together."

She stared at him, jaw tight, arms folded like armour. "Thank you, no. I can do without that kind of company."

A beat passed.

"Mine?" His voice dropped slightly, edged with ice. "Or Sienna's?"

The question wasn't innocent. He knew what he was doing—testing the fault lines, pressing on an old bruise. She felt it. But she was done playing nice.

"Both," she said, her tone cool and sharp enough to cut. "There's not much to choose between you."

For a second, he didn't move. Then he rose slowly from the chair, setting down the mug he hadn't touched. The air shifted. Darkened. His expression had gone unreadable, but something in his posture coiled tight.

"You're twenty, Kiera," he said. "Old enough to stand by your words. So go ahead—say what you mean."

"Oh, stop pretending!" Her voice cracked like lightning. Three years of silence broke all at once, fury pouring out like a flood. "You can fool my father, Andrew, but not me. And probably not anyone else. Anyone looking can see it. The way you are with her—" Her voice trembled. "You don't even try to hide it anymore."

His jaw clenched, and when he spoke again, his voice was low, dangerous. "Be specific."

But she wasn't listening. Couldn't. The pain had lived inside her too long, growing teeth. She was shaking now, too full of it to stop.

"You're sleeping with my father's wife," she said, each word landing like a blow. "How's that for specific?"

She could see the flare in his eyes, like a fuse had been lit.

"Don't deny it," she pressed on, voice raw. "I heard you. The night he made you partner. You and Sienna, laughing like lovers. Whispering."

Her voice broke. "Harper was in the next room. She heard it too. We both did. We just didn't understand it then. But I do now."

The words felt wild in her mouth—too heavy, too bitter. But they had lived inside her for years, poisoning her inch by inch. Now they were out.

Andrew stepped forward, slow and controlled, but something violent simmered beneath the surface. His face was pale; the edges of his expression honed to steel.

"You believed that?" he asked, voice tight. "For three years?"

"I know it," she shot back. "You've taken everything. The business. My father's trust. Her. And now you stand there acting like none of it matters?"

She tried to pull away when he reached for her, but his grip was iron. His hands closed around her arms, not hurting her—but firm enough to stop her from running again.

"Then why haven't you told him?" he demanded. "If you were so sure? Why keep it a secret, Kiera?"

"Because it would destroy him!" she hissed. "And you know it."

Her chest was heaving now, rage and panic tangling in her breath.

"I hate you, Andrew Foster," she whispered, voice shaking. "One day I'll make you pay."

For a moment, he went utterly still.

Then, without warning, he moved.

In two steps, he closed the distance between them and drove her back against the door. His body pinned hers—not brutally, but with force enough to make her gasp. His heat bled through her clothes. Her fists flew up, beating against his chest in a blind rush of panic and fury.

"Let me go!"

But he didn't.

One hand slid up, cupping the back of her neck, firm and unrelenting. He tilted her head toward him until their faces were inches apart, his breath ghosting over her lips.

"You want to pay me back?" he growled. "Go ahead. Pay me back for every damn second I cared. For every night I lost sleep wondering if you were okay. For every time I wanted to protect you, and you looked at me like I was enemy."

His voice cracked, just barely. "Do that, and we'll be even. Because you, Kiera—you weren't worth a moment of it."

Chapter Five

Kiera had no chance to process his words.

One heartbeat—and then his mouth was on hers.

It wasn't gentle. It wasn't hesitant. His kiss came hard and hungry, like a dam breaking after years of restraint. The shock of it jolted through her, leaving her breathless. She went still, not from fear, but from the dizzying heat of it—the sheer, unexpected force behind his desire. She hadn't braced for this. She hadn't braced for him.

Her instincts kicked in fast. She clenched her teeth, turned her head, her hands pressing against his chest in protest. "Andrew—"

But he didn't retreat. His body remained taut with purpose, holding steady rather than pinning. One hand lifted—not cruelly, but firmly—to guide her face back toward his. His touch demanded, not dominated, and his mouth never strayed far, hovering just close enough to steal her breath.

The door at her back left her nowhere to go. His body was all around her—shoulders, chest, hips—heat pouring from him like fire through her thin dress. The scent of him wrapped around her: spice, sweat, something darker. Her senses reeled. He was too close. Too much.

She opened her eyes, searching for escape—but he was already there, staring back at her with storm-grey intensity. Not cold. Not calculating. Determined.

She shut her eyes again. It didn't help.

His hand slipped from her jaw and drifted downward, tracing her spine in a maddeningly slow caress. Each vertebra his fingers passed made her shudder. Her back arched in response—unbidden, unwanted—and her breath caught in her throat.

A sound escaped her—a soft, helpless thing. She hated it. Hated the way her body reacted, the way heat pooled low and heavy despite the battle raging in her mind. But she couldn't stop it.

He shifted slightly, adjusting the angle between them, and the slide of their bodies stole what was left of her breath. His other hand came to rest at her hip, anchoring her, steadying her. His mouth returned—gentler now, coaxing instead of demanding. He brushed kisses across her sealed lips, teasing, tempting, tasting her resistance with the patience of a man who already knew she was slipping.

And when she faltered—just for a moment—he took it.

His tongue swept into her mouth in a slow, claiming stroke that shattered her control.

A strangled sound rose from her chest, half fury, half want, and still, she didn't pull away.

She couldn't.

No one had ever kissed her like this.

No one had ever undone her like this.

Desire surged—hot, reckless, and terrifying. Her hands betrayed her first, sliding into his hair, gripping the hard line of his jaw. She kissed him back—fiercely, brokenly, as if punishing him for all the years she'd spent pretending she didn't still want him.

He groaned low against her mouth, deepening the kiss, pulling her tighter, until she could feel every inch of him pressed against her.

Her thoughts splintered. Her pride burned away in the heat. There was only him—his hands, his mouth, the deep, dark pull of everything she swore she didn't need.

And then—

He tore himself away.

The absence hit her like a slap. She staggered, dazed, breathless, her hands still fisted in his shirt.

Her lips were swollen. Her body trembled.

She looked up at him.

And froze.

His eyes were cold now. Shuttered. There was no heat, no emotion—just the calculated distance of someone who had gotten exactly what he wanted.

It hit her like a blow to the gut.

He had humiliated her.

Deliberately. Completely.

Her face flushed, shame flooding her so fast she thought she might be sick. She opened her mouth to speak—but no words came. Just the echo of his kiss, still burning on her lips, and the awful realisation that he'd done it to prove a point.

To remind her of the power he held.

"I hate you," she choked, her voice trembling. "You're disgusting."

He didn't flinch. Not a flicker of remorse touched his face.

"Probably," he said, his tone emotionless. "Still, for a moment there, you seemed very eager to take your stepmother's place in my bed."

He stepped back, freeing her. Instinct took over. She struck him across the face, her palm stinging with the force of her fury. He didn't try to stop her. He even smiled, a dark, amused curl of his lips that chilled her to the bone.

"Was that disgust for me or disgust for yourself?" he asked dryly.

He turned to the door, his gaze drifting over her, dismissive and lingering. She could feel the angry flush on her cheeks, the heave of her chest, the humiliating awareness of how swollen her lips felt, how sensitive her breasts were beneath the silk of her dress.

"Very nice," he murmured, sardonic. "But don't pretend to be an angel, Kiera."

He left, closing the door behind him with infuriating calm.

Kiera sank to the floor where she stood, her knees giving out. She was shaking—humiliated, stunned, and deeply ashamed. He had played her body like an instrument, taught her the unbearable ache of desire, and left her raw with confusion. Worse still, she had responded—hungrily, shamelessly.

He had stolen her control, shredded her dignity, and exposed a side of herself she hadn't even known existed. And the thought of facing him again made her shudder with revulsion—not just for him, but for herself.

Well, she would be seeing him tonight, after three years of silence.

Kiera shook herself free of the misty thoughts clouding her mind and sat up in the bath. She had been lying there far too long, lost in memory, and the water had grown cold. Enough. She would face Andrew without flinching. If there was any guilt to carry, it belonged to him—he hadn't come out of that last encounter with a shred of honour.

It had been three years ago. A lifetime, in some ways. She was no longer that impulsive, emotionally fragile girl. She had Gary now. Her life was balanced, her feelings contained. Andrew had dragged her into that blazing, chaotic world, but she had climbed out—and stayed out. She was in control now. Always.

Their encounter had been a convergence of too many things—confusion, youth, vulnerability. But mostly, it had been immaturity. And that was behind her.

She stepped out of the tub and wrapped herself in a towel, her movements brisk. At the mirror, she dried herself and studied her reflection with a steady, clinical gaze. Tall, poised, nearly eye-level with Gary—which was oddly comforting. She was still slender, still carried herself with the same upright confidence, her breasts high and tilted, her legs long and graceful. Damp curls framed her face, her hair a rich, glowing brown that caught the light. Her eyes—green and clear—met her own without hesitation.

Annoyance flickered across her face. Not at Andrew this time, but at herself— for wasting even a moment brooding over the past. That wasn't who she was anymore. For the next few weeks, she was her father's hostess, and she intended to play the part flawlessly.

She glanced at the clock. Six-thirty. There would be no flustered, last-minute scramble down the stairs tonight. Not for anything.

She dressed with care, choosing a soft chiffon gown in cream, streaked with autumnal swirls of brown and orange. The fabric moved around her like breath, the colours warming her skin, drawing out the deep green in her eyes and the golden undertones in her hair. When she stepped back from the mirror, satisfaction settled over her like a cloak. Yes—like this, she could face anyone. Even Andrew.

She had gained what she lacked three years ago: composure, grace, the kind of calm confidence that couldn't be shaken by an old ghost.

Her father was in the drawing room when she entered, and the first thing her eyes found—inevitably—was the portrait above the fireplace. Her mother's portrait. It had always been there.

But now, it didn't hurt to look.

Kiera stood still, gazing up at the familiar face. The resemblance was uncanny—people always said so—but tonight she saw it as something else. A legacy.

"She was beautiful," she murmured, almost to herself, as her father joined her.

"She was," he replied quietly. Then added, with a flicker of dry humour, "But I wouldn't go around saying that, if I were you. You're exactly like her. Some might call it boasting."

His voice held a note of warmth she hadn't heard in a long time, and it comforted her. He, too, could stand before that portrait now without flinching. The ache had dulled. The wound had, perhaps, begun to heal.

She opened her mouth, hesitated, then asked the question anyway. "Why…?"

But she didn't need to finish.

"Why is it still there?" he echoed, as though reading her mind. "It's always been there. It belongs there."

There was something almost fierce in his tone, a thread of emotion she couldn't quite decipher. Kiera glanced at him, sensing there was more beneath the surface. But then he smiled and stepped away, reaching for the decanter.

"A drink before dinner?" he offered lightly.

And just like that, the moment passed.

Kiera nodded, but as she turned to follow her father across the room, she stopped abruptly, her whole body tensing in shock.

Andrew was standing in the doorway.

Silent. Watching.

She had no idea how long he'd been there. His gaze was cool, unreadable—like she was something distant and enclosed behind glass. He didn't move, didn't speak, and only when her father noticed him did the faintest flicker of expression pass across his face.

The years had changed him.

She recognised him—of course—but the familiarity ended there. His features were sharper now, more refined, but colder, too. Harder. The man she had once known was gone. What stood before her was a stranger with Andrew's face, hollowed of warmth, carved by cynicism.

"The prodigal daughter," he said at last; the words dry as dust. His tone made it clear—there would be trouble between them. He hadn't forgotten. Not even close. The last time they'd seen each other still lingered in the ice of his grey eyes.

"She's stepping into Sienna's shoes for a while," her father said with a smile, slipping an arm around Kiera's shoulders. His cheerful tone tried to bridge the tension, but Andrew remained unmoved. He stepped fully into the room, his posture relaxed, his eyes anything but.

"Is she capable?" he asked, voice deceptively lazy.

Kiera held herself still, refusing to let the words bite. Her composure was already frayed—thinking of him in the bath had left her rawer than she'd admitted—and now here he was, unsettling her without even trying.

Her father chuckled, brushing the comment off. "She's grown up, Andrew. You'll have to find a new approach. She's not your little pet anymore."

"Obviously," Andrew murmured, his gaze never leaving Kiera's face. "Don't worry. I'll treat her very differently this time."

He turned his eyes to the portrait above the mantel. "A striking likeness. What about the character?"

"Kiera's more spirited—" David began.

Andrew cut in with dry amusement. "So, you're excusing her bad temper in advance?"

"She's sparky," her father replied with a grin.

"And standing right here," Kiera said sharply, her voice edged with anger now. She forced a smile and extended her hand, her earlier shock now buried under a layer of frost. "Good evening, Andrew. How are you?"

"Humbled by the sight of you," he said smoothly, taking her hand without hesitation. His smile didn't reach his eyes. "I'm sorry if my presence at the lodge complicates your time here. Still, I'm only one more guest to manage. And you've always handled me… rather well."

She met his gaze evenly, unwilling to flinch, though the coldness in his eyes made her skin prickle.

At that moment, Mrs. Williams appeared in the doorway.

"I'm about to serve dinner. Sir," she said brusquely, not even glancing Kiera's way.

Kiera didn't hesitate. "Thank you, Mrs. Williams. We'll join you shortly. We're not quite ready yet."

There was a flicker of surprise in Andrew's eyes—subtle, but there. Her father's mouth twitched with amusement.

"Round two, Kiera," he murmured under his breath. "Keep going. With any luck, we'll be rid of her before Sienna gets back."

Kiera gave a tight smile. She doubted it. Even if Mrs. Williams were dismissed, Sienna would waste no time reinstating her. And if Andrew was going to be a regular presence in this house again, then she would be keeping her visit as brief as possible.

She hadn't missed the sharp edge of anger beneath his casual voice, or the way he had walked into the room—slow, deliberate. There had been something almost predatory in his movement. A stalking animal, cloaked in civility.

Standing beside him as her father poured the drinks, Kiera became acutely aware of Andrew's height. Just hours ago, she'd been thinking how comforting it was that Gary didn't tower over her. Andrew did. He always had, but she'd never noticed it quite like this before.

There was something about him now, that made her feel unnervingly fragile, and she told herself it was just his physicality. But perhaps it was also his intellect—he'd always had plenty of that, too. Whatever it was, the air between them felt charged, and she sensed he was just as aware of her as she was of him.

He turned and looked down at her, catching her green-eyed scrutiny.

"Almost like old times," he said dryly, just as her father stepped away to answer the phone.

"Not at all like old times," Kiera replied, her voice clipped. "I see the world differently now."

His gaze swept over her face, and then that sardonic smile curved his mouth— the same one she remembered all too well.

"I'm sure you'll endure your time here. Then you can scuttle back to your little shop."

The derision stung. Her eyes flashed. She couldn't speak her mind with her father in the next room, but her anger was obvious.

"It's a gallery," she hissed under her breath. "And I'm very well known."

"Really? I must drop by. I need new art for my place."

"I specialise in animals," Kiera snapped, her pride bristling.

His brows lifted mockingly. "And why would I not know that? David and I spend hours discussing you." His voice was pure irony. "As for animals, it's fitting, don't you think? You've always considered me something straight from the jungle."

"I don't consider you at all!" she shot back. "And I don't do snakes."

He laughed, low and pleased. She'd walked right into it.

Polite indifference would have disarmed him, but it was too late for that. The tone had been set for her entire stay, and she had no one to blame but herself.

"One of the larger predators, then?" he mused just as her father returned.

"We're talking about Kiera's gallery," Andrew announced smoothly. "I've commissioned her. She's going to find me a large cat."

"A cat?" David looked surprised. "I didn't know you had a soft spot for felines."

"Only the dangerous kind," Andrew murmured. "She's promised to find one that suits my lifestyle—and my nature. Isn't that right, Kiera?"

Her father laughed, but Kiera felt the chill of something more serious beneath Andrew's words. She was sure he intended to stay close, to watch her. He hadn't forgotten—or forgiven.

Chapter Six

The next morning, Kiera was up early for the auction. She was just leaving the house when her father called from the study.

"Drop in at the lodge on your way, will you, Kiera? I need a word with Andrew, but he's not answering. Something must be wrong with his phone."

"Maybe he's out," she suggested quickly. She had no desire to see Andrew again—last night had been more than enough. The housekeeper had seated her directly opposite him at dinner, and every time she looked up, he was watching her.

Worse, she'd caught herself looking at him when he wasn't watching. The way the light caught the blue-black sheen of his hair... how maddening it was that she still noticed such things.

"He's working from the lodge today—it's Saturday," her father replied. "Just remind him to bring the Eastbourne papers up later. There's a good girl."

"Sure," she said with a grimace. *There's a good girl.* Her father still thought she was twelve.

She reached the lodge and gave a sharp blast of the horn. No response. She tried again. Nothing.

The front door stood ajar, and Kiera scowled. Was he ignoring her on purpose? If he thought she was too timid to come to the door, he was wrong.

Marching up the path, she banged loudly on the door. Still nothing. Annoyed now, she pushed it open.

"Andrew!" she called out, sharp and impatient. "Andrew!"

He sauntered in, towel in hand, water gleaming on his skin, another towel knotted low around his waist.

"You bellowed?" he said, voice rich with irony, as he slung the smaller towel over his neck.

"I honked the horn. I knocked! Why didn't you answer like a normal person?"

"I was in the shower," he said with exaggerated patience. "I don't usually parade around like this, but if I'd known you were dropping in, I might've skipped the towels entirely."

"You're disgusting," she snapped, cheeks flaming.

"I know," he purred. "You told me three years ago. So—what's this? A social call or a fresh threat?"

She choked on a retort. Threaten him? He could break her in half with those arms. Her gaze refused to look away from the bronzed expanse of his chest, the definition of his torso. This was humiliating.

"Daddy wants you to bring the Eastbourne papers up to the house," she managed stiffly.

"Message received." He didn't move. Neither did she.

His eyes slid slowly over her—cream pleated skirt, slim hips, the cinnamon blouse softly fitted at the waist. When his gaze rested on her breasts, she felt like she'd burst into flame.

"Anything else?" he asked. "Something I can do for you… personally?"

"Yes," she spat. "You can drop dead."

She turned and stormed out, his laughter following her all the way to the car. She'd played right into his hands—again.

For a moment in there, she'd been completely undone. No wonder Sienna clung to him. He'd stood there like some smug, dripping Greek god and stunned her senseless. He was vile.

By the time she reached the main road, she was furious with herself. She even said aloud, "I will not think about Andrew." The ridiculousness of it made her snort—until she imagined his echoing laugh and clamped her mouth shut.

The sale was a welcome distraction. She had to stay sharp—especially for the husky she wanted, beautifully framed and slightly over budget. Worth it, though. The Irish setter was a bargain, and she was about to settle up when the auctioneer announced a few late additions.

The final piece stopped her cold.

A large painting—easily twice the size of the others. A panther. Magnificent. She leaned forward, pulse quickening. Not a jungle scene. No. The panther stalked a silent city, with lit windows glinting off its coat like black velvet. Power and menace in every line of its body.

A predator in a world of men.

Hardly anyone seemed interested. She might not have been either—if Andrew hadn't made his mocking comment about commissioning a big cat. Imagine the look on his face when she unveiled this. It was everything he'd asked for. And more.

Even if he didn't want it, she'd be proud to have it in her gallery. But the thought of wiping the smirk off his face tipped her hand.

She bid—and won it for far less than she'd expected. The auctioneer glared. Kiera just grinned.

Let Andrew try to out sneer that.

Driving back to the hall, Kiera felt immensely pleased with her morning's efforts. Wild plans churned in her mind about how she would confront Andrew Foster in a blaze of triumph. But as she turned through the gates, her certainty began to waver.

She could already picture him laughing, paying an outrageous price, and then donating the panther to charity when her back was turned. It would be patronising, and she'd feel like a child. Maybe she had been childish. By the time she pulled up at the hall, her confidence had cooled. She left the panther in the car.

Her father was in the sitting room and came over to inspect the other two pictures as she propped them against the couch and knelt down beside them.

"They're beauties!" he said with enthusiasm. "Just what my study needs. I'll buy them both."

"Sorry," Kiera replied, looking up with a laugh, her face glowing with satisfaction. "They're already sold. The husky's a rare find—one of my clients has been waiting ages for one like it. And the setter's heading to New York next week. You'll have to tell me what you want. I rarely have pieces like this to spare, and I never break up a collection."

"Too damned professional," her father grumbled with affection. "What do you think, Andrew?"

Kiera startled. She hadn't realised Andrew was in the room. She'd assumed he'd left, but there he was—leaning in the doorway, just as he had the night before. His eyes moved over her: the soft fall of her skirt as she knelt, the way her hair brushed her cheek, and finally, met hers—wide and startled, green with confusion.

For a fleeting second, she thought she saw something soften in his expression—something like the old Andrew. There was even the beginning of a smile that didn't seem sardonic. But she knew she was wrong the moment he spoke.

"Hard as nails," he said dryly, moving closer to examine the fruits of her morning.

"What a shame," he murmured. "No big cat. I suppose that would've been too much to hope for in such a small gallery."

Kiera rose smoothly to her feet, determined not to let him see her irritation.

"I was going to put it on display," she said briskly, a smile fixed on her lips, though her eyes flashed. "But if you're really that set on a big cat—wait here."

She strode out of the room before he could respond, seething inside. So, this was his plan—mockery at every turn, constant jabs to undermine her. He thought she couldn't find anything difficult or rare. He should meet her Japanese clients—or her discerning American collectors. Andrew Foster was the only person who ever sneered at her. Well, Sienna did too. No wonder they got on so well. They deserved each other.

She pulled the panther from the car, hauling it inside with a burst of fury-fed strength. When she returned to the sitting room, Andrew was laughing with her father. If she hadn't known her father so well, she'd have thought they were laughing at her. Andrew was already getting under her skin.

"The cat," she announced crisply, placing the painting by the door so they had a perfect view. "One predator, as requested. Beautiful condition. Excellent framing. Dramatic composition. I want a thousand for it. No haggling."

"My God." Andrew stepped forward, his eyes on the painting. A slow smile spread across his face—genuine this time, and purely appreciative. "You're a miracle, Miss Scott. It's as if you pulled it straight from my imagination."

"You mean you actually want it?" Kiera stared at him, stunned. She'd paid five hundred and had doubled the price out of sheer spite. Andrew Foster—the sharpest man she knew—looked utterly captivated.

"Try to back out now and I'll strangle you," he growled, glancing up at her. "I know exactly where this belongs."

"It's... very large," Kiera said uncertainly. "Not ideal for an ordinary room."

"I don't have ordinary rooms," he replied absently, crouching to inspect it more closely.

She made one last effort. "It's modern. It's unlikely to appreciate in value. I just think—"

"You can stop wriggling." Andrew stood, pulling out his phone. "I ordered it. You delivered. It's mine. Case closed." He got her bank details and transferred the money instantly.

Kiera looked at him in a daze. "Shall I wrap it?" she asked, her voice almost a whisper.

He tilted her chin with firm fingers. "Do you get this reluctant with all your clients?" he asked, dry amusement in his voice. "If you try to talk them out of a deal, warn them against the purchase, and then look stunned when they pay— it's a miracle your business is thriving."

"How do you know it is?" she asked, still a little dazed.

"Finance is my business," he said, all irony now. "I seem to recall you telling me, years ago, that even your father wouldn't know where to turn without me."

It hit her like a slap. In one sentence, he'd dragged her back to that terrible argument three years ago. She'd been raging. Hurt. But for a moment just now, she'd forgotten why she'd hated him. Remembering it twisted something in her.

His hand lingered, eyes dipping briefly to her lips. He was reminding her of that night—how easily she'd burned for him. She couldn't stand it. She turned and walked out.

"Kiera?" Her father's voice followed her. Then Andrew's, dry and unconcerned.

"Let her go, David. I've offended her again. As usual."

"I don't understand it," her father muttered. "There was a time I thought she loved you more than she loved me."

"She grew up," Andrew said flatly.

Kiera heard no more. But she knew she needed air. She needed distance. She called Gary to take her out to dinner.

Let Andrew entertain her father. Let him mock her all he liked. She would not give him the satisfaction of falling apart. When the guests arrived next week, she'd invite Gary down. He was kind. Safe. A good man to help prop up her crumbling self-esteem.

Her father was disappointed she was heading back to town, but when she explained she needed to prepare the gallery and check in on Sally, he accepted it. She also made sure to find out when the meeting at the house was scheduled—Gary would need to know.

Relief washed over her when she saw Gary enter the restaurant. He was unthreatening, solid, and wonderfully ordinary. A broker, through and through. No dangerous edges. No smirking smiles. No past.

"If absence makes the heart grow fonder, then stay away a little longer," he teased as she embraced him warmly.

"How long are you staying away, anyway?" he added.

Kiera admitted she didn't know. There was no real reason to stay at the hall anymore. If Andrew hadn't been there, she might have stayed until Sienna returned—but he cast a long shadow.

Only Andrew made her doubt herself. Only he made her remember.

She invited Gary to dinner the night the guests were due. By the time she pointed her car back toward the hall, Kiera felt ready—prepared, at last, to face whatever game Andrew Foster intended to play.

Chapter Seven

To Kiera's irritation, Andrew hadn't left.

When Kiera poked her head around the study door to say goodnight to her father, she found them both knee-deep in papers. Her father looked exhausted; even Andrew seemed faintly worn.

"It's time you stopped," she said firmly, eyes on her father's pale face. "Nothing can be so urgent that it keeps you working past midnight on a Saturday."

"We got carried away," her father admitted, standing and rubbing his eyes. "I'm worn out. Lucky you came to order me off to bed."

Andrew reached for his jacket, never once glancing in her direction—a fact that immediately roused Kiera's suspicion.

"Did you have a good evening?" her father asked.

"Yes. We had dinner, then I drove straight back." She paused, then added casually, "I invited Gary down to dinner on Tuesday."

It was mostly for Andrew's benefit, to make it clear that she had someone in her life. "Once you two are deep in conversation, I'll finally get some time alone with him. I doubt I'll see much of him while I'm here."

When she glanced at Andrew, he was frowning, his dark eyes locked on her face. The disapproval in them only fuelled her annoyance.

"You have a problem with that?" she asked sharply.

But Andrew just shrugged. "Is it my business? If I look displeased, it's probably just because I realised how late it is. I walked up from the lodge. Now I have to walk back."

"Stay here for the night," her father offered, yawning.

Kiera felt a jolt of panic. Before she could think, she blurted, "My car's out front. I'll drive you down—it's no trouble."

Andrew looked up, startled. Her father kissed her cheek.

"Kind girl," he murmured, then left the room, swaying a little with fatigue.

Andrew stared at her. "Is this kindness going to kill me?"

"It was a charitable gesture. If you'd rather walk—"

"Not at this hour. I'll take the gesture at face value—and analyse it when I'm more awake."

In the car, Kiera realised the gesture might just kill her.

Offering him a ride had been reckless. Foolish. But panic had made the words spill from her mouth before she could stop them—panic at the thought of him spending the night under the same roof again, of walking past her door, of existing so close.

She could have handed him the car keys, told him to take it himself.

She should have.

Instead, here they were—trapped in the heavy silence of the car, his presence a suffocating weight in the confined space.

The silence between them wasn't empty. It throbbed with everything unsaid, with years of pain, misunderstanding, and the ache of what might have been.

By the time they reached the lodge, her grip on the steering wheel had gone white-knuckled. Every nerve in her body screamed for release, for distance, for escape.

She pulled up and shifted into park.

"Goodnight," she said, her voice clipped and cold. Her fingers hovered over the ignition.

But he didn't move.

She turned to him in frustration—only to find him watching her, his gaze steady and unreadable.

"Right," he said softly, his tone edged with something dangerous. "I've figured it out. You panicked. Thought if I stayed the night, I'd creep into your room in the dark."

Her heart jumped. "I don't like this conversation. Please go."

But he kept going, like a blade sliding under the skin.

"Let me remind you—if I'd ever had that inclination, I had my chance three years ago. You clung to me like ivy, Kiera. You kissed me back like it meant something."

She recoiled as though slapped. "Get out of my car!" she snapped, grateful for the darkness that concealed her flaming cheeks. "Or I will!"

"You won't walk back. And you know I won't let you."

She reached blindly for the door handle, but his hand caught her arm—not to restrain, but to stop her gently. The contact was almost tender.

"I'm going," he said quietly, his grip loosening.

Still, he didn't move.

His voice was lower now, almost broken. "How did we get here, Kiera? Like this—two strangers with a shared history?"

Her throat tightened. She turned her face away and restarted the engine, willing herself to silence.

"What did you expect?" she murmured bitterly. "That I'd go on following you around like a lost dog? Even after you took up with Sienna?"

He exhaled a breath that might have been a sigh or a laugh. "Ah. Sienna. I forget sometimes that you found out about that... through a bit of schoolgirl snooping."

"I wasn't snooping!" she snapped, spinning toward him. "It was a mistake. Something I never wanted to know."

He leaned back, eyes dark and unreadable. "Because you worshipped me?"

She didn't answer.

The pause stretched, weighted and still.

"Yes," she whispered at last. "I did. You were everything. And then, suddenly... you were nothing. Everything I believed in—gone overnight."

He nodded once, solemnly. "So, you turned down university. Quit art school. It hurt that much?"

"I wasn't hurt. It was shock," she said, voice shaking. "When an idol falls, the backlash is yours to carry. I carried it. Alone."

Still, he said nothing. No denial. No apology. No excuse.

Just silence.

And then he spoke, soft as a memory. "Goodnight, angel face."

The nickname. Like a ghost from another life.

He opened the door, stepped out, and disappeared into the dark.

Kiera stared straight ahead, blinking furiously. Her throat burned. She shoved the car into gear and began to drive back toward the hall, her hands trembling, her breath coming fast.

The tears caught her off guard.

Hot, silent, furious.

She brushed them away with the back of her hand, then again, more frantically, but they kept coming—faster, harder.

Her father had once said she loved Andrew more than she loved him.

He'd been right.

She had loved Andrew Foster—utterly, foolishly, blindly. He had been the centre of her world, the spark behind every dream, the ache behind every heartbreak.

And now, with a handful of words and a name she hadn't heard in years, he had shattered everything she'd so carefully buried.

She had hated him.

She had raged and blamed and hardened herself like stone.

But she had never grieved him.

Not truly.

Not until now.

And as she drove alone into the night, the last of her defences crumbled.

She had loved him.

And he was quite, quite gone.

The day of the dinner party dawned clear, and with it came a sense of quiet resolve. Kiera had already made it abundantly clear to Mrs. Williams that she was in charge, and she anticipated no trouble. And, of course, Gary would be there. Not that she felt the same desperate need for his protection anymore.

Andrew's cold politeness no longer posed a threat. Her only concern now was ensuring the evening ran smoothly.

By the time the first guest arrived, Kiera allowed herself a breath of relief. The caterers had been punctual, Mrs. Williams was being frostily efficient, and Kiera had spent considerable time getting ready. It was her first time acting as hostess on behalf of her father, and instinct alone would have to carry her through. She lacked Sienna's polished charm, but she could give it her best.

There were ten men. No women. That, at least, was a blessing. Making small talk over coffee with a group of unfamiliar women would have been far worse. Once the business discussions began, she planned to slip into the sitting room with Gary and catch her breath.

Everything moved at a blur. Though she was introduced to each guest as they arrived, she couldn't remember a single name. Andrew hadn't shown up yet, and her father was managing the room alone—not that it seemed to matter. Drinks were being served in the drawing room, and already the conversation had turned to finance.

When Gary was shown in, she all but rushed to him. Without him, she would have been adrift at the dinner table, surrounded by talk of mergers and assets. A language she didn't speak.

"You look gorgeous," Gary murmured, grounding her with his steady presence, as she hugged him. He kissed her cheek and stepped back, his gaze sweeping over her. "Fit to eat," he said approvingly.

Kiera flushed, pleased. She had made an effort tonight. Her nut-brown hair was swept into an elegant knot, the closest she could get to sophistication. Her gown—soft, lilac silk—flowed from a halter neckline in gentle folds. She wore no jewellery, relying on simplicity for impact. It worked. She felt confident— until she saw Andrew.

He entered only moments after Gary, and she noticed him instantly. He saw her too, though perhaps that was inevitable. She was, after all, the only woman in the room. His eyes swept over her, cool and assessing, and the indifference in his expression stung.

It actually hurt—the absence of even a flicker of admiration. Every other man had given her a look of polite approval, at least. But Andrew? Nothing. She turned quickly and introduced the two men.

"This is Andrew Foster, my father's partner," she said with bright politeness. "And this is Gary Peterson."

The handshake was brief. Andrew barely looked at Gary. His gaze was already moving around the room as if none of it interested him.

"I see the gang's all here," he said drily. "Kiera, get me a drink, would you? If I walk over there, I'll be knee-deep in numbers before I even touch the soup."

She had no choice. She was the hostess, after all. But it meant leaving Gary with Andrew, and something in her tightened with unease. There was a quiet menace about Andrew tonight that hadn't been there in days. Her hands shook slightly as she poured the drink.

"Perfect," Andrew said, taking the glass from her. "You always did know exactly what I wanted."

He smiled down at her, his presence suddenly overwhelming, eclipsing even Gary. She looked up at him suspicious—and unsettled. His tone was deliberate. Possessive.

"Have you told your friend how far back we go, angel?"

"Er… Andrew's an old family friend," she said quickly. The unease was morphing into fear. She couldn't read him. Everything about him tonight felt charged, unpredictable.

"Kiera, come and do your duty," her father called, beckoning her to join the larger group.

Relieved, she stepped away—but couldn't stop herself from glancing over her shoulder. Andrew was still watching her. Smiling. Like a tiger waiting for the right moment to pounce.

Throughout dinner, the tension only deepened. Every time she glanced up, Andrew's eyes were on her. He seemed to be conducting two conversations at once yet never stopped watching. She cursed herself for letting her guard down. She'd known from the beginning that Andrew would be dangerous. But she had let herself forget.

When the men finally settled into business discussions after dinner, Kiera nearly fled to the smaller sitting room with Gary. But by then, her head was buzzing too much to make conversation.

Chapter Eight

"He's a clever man," Gary remarked as he settled back with his coffee. "Alarming, almost. I've met people like him before, but never quite like… him."

"Who?" she asked, though she already knew.

"Foster." Gary gave her a curious look. "He said he's known you since you were a child. You never mentioned him."

"I… hadn't seen him in years. Until recently. I didn't think it mattered."

"I imagine he'd be hard to forget," Gary said, eyes narrowing slightly. "He watches you like a hawk."

"There's nothing between us," Kiera said, too quickly. "Except old animosity."

"He never took his eyes off you. From the moment he walked in."

Kiera rubbed her temple. She was tired. Too tired for this conversation. She liked Gary—he was kind, attentive. He held her hand and kissed her gently. But suddenly, she knew with stark clarity that she didn't want anything more. Not with him.

This was her battle. Hers and Andrew's.

Even now, after all these years, bitterness still bound them together. Just as affection once had. She wasn't free of Andrew. That realisation hollowed her out.

"Andrew and I go back a long way," she said wearily. "There are… family matters between us. Just don't get the wrong idea."

"He sounds possessive when he talks about you."

"What did he say?" Kiera sat up, dread prickling across her skin. The tension coiled tight inside her.

"Not much," Gary said. "Just… little things. But the way he spoke—it was like he was warning me off. Very polite, but unmistakable."

"You're imagining things."

"He called you angel."

"I've known him most of my life. It's just a nickname. From the past." A deliberate echo, she realised. He'd wanted her to hear it. And now something else from the past was catching up with her.

The pain behind her eyes flared—sharp and familiar.

"What is it?" Gary asked, suddenly alert. "You've gone pale. Did I say something wrong?"

"It's a migraine," Kiera whispered. "I haven't had one in years. I… I'm not cut out for this hostess business."

"What do you need? Tell me."

"Nothing you can do," she gasped. "I just need to lie down. Oh, Gary, I'm so sorry. This evening's been awful for you."

"I think it's been worse for you," he murmured. "And I've only made it worse with all my jealous questions."

"No, honestly—"

"If anyone caused it," she said without thinking, "it was Andrew."

"You love him, don't you?" he asked gently.

"I did once. When I was a child." She looked at him through a haze of pain. "Now I hate him. And he hates me. He's just… trouble. After these two weeks, I'll never see him again."

But even as she said it, she knew it was a lie.

She followed Gary into the hallway, the guilt gnawing at her making everything feel worse. She couldn't even bring herself to go in and see her father, let alone explain why she was leaving. All she could do was slip away like a coward. Even now, she longed to cling to Gary's arm for support.

They were nearly at the front door when Andrew appeared. His sharp gaze swept past Gary and landed on her.

"What's wrong?" He was beside her in an instant, and Gary answered before she could find her voice.

"Migraine," he said curtly, shooting Andrew a look full of disdain that Andrew completely ignored.

"Damn. I thought you'd shaken that," Andrew muttered, tilting her pale face toward the light. She winced, and he gently guided her head back down, his hand warm at the nape of her neck. "Well, at least you're not faking it this time."

"She has to go to bed," he added, eyes flicking back to Gary. "You can see yourself out."

"I'm not a child," Kiera whispered, trying to summon some dignity. But she heard the possessiveness in Andrew's voice—so had Gary. Andrew's fingers continued to lightly massage her neck, the warmth and care undoing her composure. She wanted to lean into him.

"Just a nuisance," Andrew muttered, holding her firmly as she moved slightly toward Gary.

"It's alright, Kiera," Gary said gently. "I'll phone you."

"You don't understand…" Her voice trembled. She knew how it looked, knew Andrew was punishing her for knowing too much about Sienna.

"Forget it, love," Gary said softly, brushing a kiss against her cheek and ignoring Andrew's presence. "Get some rest. I'll call."

He left, and Kiera pulled away from Andrew and turned to the stairs, but everything felt like too much. Her body ached to stay pressed against his, to sink into the comfort he grudgingly offered.

"I let everyone down," she whispered. "A disaster as a hostess, and I practically threw Gary out after inviting him. Now I'm sneaking away like a coward."

"You were bright and beautiful," Andrew said behind her, firm and certain. "You set the tone for the evening just by being there. That was enough. Your father will manage without you—and your friend overstayed his welcome anyway."

"He is my boyfriend," Kiera murmured, needing to assert it, even if it wasn't true. Andrew's warm hand urged her forward.

"Fancy that," he said dryly. "Could've fooled me. Now get upstairs. He's safely out of reach."

She wanted to argue, but she couldn't. She needed to lie down, but the stairs loomed too tall, too steep. Halfway up the first step, she stopped, her head bowing in defeat.

"I can't," she breathed. "The stairs are too much. I'll fall."

"You little fool," Andrew growled, scooping her into his arms. "What were you trying to prove? You should've called me."

"It hit me all at once…" she shivered, and he pulled her closer, carrying her up with steady strength. It had been so long since he held her like this. The comfort pierced her with a grief she didn't expect—something long lost, aching to be found again.

"I can't see you, Andrew," she whispered. Her vision blurred and dimmed.

"Then imagine me," he said softly. "I haven't changed. I got over my adolescent traumas long before I met you. You're the only one still clinging to ghosts."

"All I have is a migraine."

"And a stubborn need to see me in hell. That's what's giving you the migraine. You're out of your depth."

He sounded detached again. Kiera gave up fighting. She let her head fall to his shoulder, exhausted. If he kept walking forever, she might have been content to go with him.

In her room, he laid her on the bed, glancing around with faint disdain.

"A pale girl in a pale room," he murmured. "Virginal simplicity."

"It's just the room," she protested weakly. "I've changed."

Andrew looked down at her, his gaze cold. "An experienced woman of the world," he sneered. "No wonder your boyfriend didn't mind leaving—you've probably trained him to wait."

She'd invited that remark, but she didn't have the strength to argue.

"Thank you for bringing me up," she murmured. "I can manage now."

"You're not getting the chance. Where are your tablets?"

"I haven't had any for years. Maybe the bathroom cabinet… if they haven't been tossed."

"If they're still any good," he muttered, stalking to the bathroom. "You're never prepared for anything."

Especially not for him, she thought. She heard him rummaging as she lay back, the light stabbing her eyes. When he returned, he was reading a label.

"These will do," he said gruffly. "I'll get water."

He returned and handed her the glass. She swallowed the pills and collapsed back.

"Get undressed," he ordered.

"Just go away," she cried. "You raging at me is making everything worse."

"I'm not raging, I just want you settled."

"Well, you're snarling," she snapped, the tears finally escaping.

Andrew cursed under his breath, then knelt beside her. "It's self-defence. When an animal is confused and under attack, it snarls." His voice softened. "Come on, you poor little thing. Let's get you out of this fabulous dress."

"Did… did you think it was fabulous?" she asked, her voice trembling.

"You're rambling," he warned. "Say nothing else—you'll regret it and blame me."

He removed the pins from her hair, letting it fall softly. His touch slowed.

"Yes," he added quietly. "You looked fabulous. I noticed."

He unfastened her halter, and suddenly she realised—there was nothing beneath.

"Stop!" she gasped. "I'll do it myself."

His gaze swept over her. He hesitated, then turned away.

"Fine. But I'm not leaving until you're in bed. Tell me when."

She struggled into her nightie, barely finishing before the door opened without warning.

Mrs. Williams stood there with towels. She froze. So did Kiera.

"I brought fresh towels, Miss Scott. I didn't realise you were up here…"

Kiera flushed, but Andrew stepped in.

"Do you usually barge into bedrooms without knocking?" he snapped. "Or is this a special occasion?"

"There's a gathering downstairs. The guests usually stay downstairs," Mrs. Williams began, reddening.

"And still," Andrew interrupted icily, "bedroom doors should be knocked on. Miss Scott is home. This is her room."

Mrs. Williams placed the towels down and retreated. Andrew closed the door, face thunderous.

"Get rid of her," he muttered. "She's a menace."

"She'll tell Sienna…" Kiera started, then yelped as Andrew yanked her up and pulled her hard against him.

"Shut up," he growled. "One more word and I'll forget how pathetic you are right now."

He kissed her—fiercely, furiously—until her lips parted under the force of it. Then he let her go, and she crumpled, trembling.

He tucked her into bed, covering her with the sheets.

"Now sleep," he said roughly. "Be grateful you're in this state—otherwise, I'd be teaching you a lesson, virginal room or not."

He slung her dress over a chair, turned off the lights, and marched to the door. She could barely see him now, the migraine clouding everything. He turned and glared.

"One of these days," he rasped, "I'm going to lose my self-control and either kill or cure you, Kiera."

He slammed the door.

She lay there, lips stinging, vision swimming. The tablets were finally working. Tomorrow, she could think. Andrew would be gone. She could find her strength again.

But for now… she was just glad it had been Andrew looking after her.

It was two days before Kiera felt fully well again. During that time, Andrew kept completely away. According to her father, he'd returned to London to inspect the renovations at his own place and would soon be heading down to Eastbourne.

At least his absence gave Kiera time to gather her scattered thoughts and brace herself for seeing him again. No doubt the Eastbourne trip would stretch long enough for a detour to Paris—and to Sienna. The thought bit deep, and she tasted the bitterness of it.

"When is Sienna coming back?" she asked her father one evening.

He shrugged, his interest barely stirred. "No idea. She hasn't even called. Typical. Once she gets to those places, she thinks of nothing but clothes. I just pick up the bills."

His amused indifference struck Kiera like a splash of cold water. How distant she'd become from him over the years. Sienna's boutiques might be doing well, but he was still footing the bill. He'd helped Kiera start the gallery, backing her until she found her footing—but she'd insisted on repaying every penny. Sienna, by contrast, had never hesitated to take. And somehow, she still got everything she wanted.

Still, it was good to have these quiet days with her father—to walk the estate without worrying about running into Andrew. Her father had sheepishly admitted that the meeting held at the house had been the only one planned. He'd just wanted her home.

Well, she would stay. Sally was managing the gallery just fine. Kiera would need to check in during the week, but until Sienna returned, she was content here.

A few days later, she drove down to London, spending a pleasant morning rearranging paintings, chatting with Sally, and going over the books. The setter was en route to America, and the husky had already been collected. According to Sally, the customer had been thrilled.

She was nearly ready to leave when the bell above the door tinkled and someone stepped in. Sally moved forward to help, but as soon as the man spoke, Kiera froze. She knew that voice—it was Andrew, and he was asking for her.

There was no escape. She took a steadying breath and descended the steps from her apartment. He stood watching her, eyes scanning her face. She knew she'd lost a few pounds during the migraine spell, but did he have to examine her like she was a specimen?

"Buying or browsing?" she asked, her tone light and edged with false cheer.

He smiled—a real one, almost—and answered, "Looking for help. David told me you were here when I rang. I need advice on the panther."

"What have you done with it?" she demanded. "You haven't damaged it, have you? That painting's a gem, and even if you don't want it—"

"Hold on," Andrew interrupted. "No need to panic. The panther is fine. I just want your opinion on where to hang it."

"I sell paintings," she said stiffly, suspicion prickling.

"And you place them to perfection," he added wryly, glancing around the gallery. "Look, I paid a thousand pounds for that panther. You can spare me five minutes to help pick the right spot."

Over his shoulder, Kiera caught sight of Sally's expression—eyes wide, eyebrows high, silently mouthing 'thousand? pounds?' It was almost too much. Kiera felt her lips twitch despite herself.

"You're in a good mood," Andrew said, watching her. "I couldn't have timed it better. Take pity on me."

His grey eyes had darkened to smoky silver. The sight pierced her, a vivid reminder of how deeply she had once loved him. It wasn't fair. Even now, he had the power to unravel her with a look.

"Alright," she said, her voice low. "I'll come. But I'm not staying long. I'm going back home."

"I'll drive you," Andrew offered gently, eyes alert to her downcast gaze.

But she lifted her chin. "I drove down. Naturally, I'll drive myself back."

He nodded. "Fair enough. We'll go in convoy. I'm eager to get back anyway. That lodge is starting to feel like home—and there's still magic in the estate."

She understood what he meant. Wickham Hall had a magic all its own—the sprawling grounds, the river, the trees. It was something she had given up for Sienna. Just as she had given up Andrew.

She turned to say a quick word to Sally. Andrew waited at the door, his expression thoughtful. When she joined him, he said nothing, simply walked to his car.

Kiera followed, a storm of misgivings churning inside her. She should never have let him talk her into this. It was madness. She didn't want to know where or how he lived. She wanted no part of his world.

Because she could not—would not—let him hurt her again.

Chapter Nine

Andrew lived in a sleek, ultra-modern block right in the heart of the city, and Kiera was caught off guard. Only minutes ago, he had spoken wistfully about the magic of Wickham Hall—and now he was leading her into the penthouse of a towering steel and glass monolith.

"I thought you liked being at Wickham," she said as the lift shot upward with unnerving speed. "Skyscrapers don't seem very magical."

"If I can't have the magic I want, I'll settle for clean lines and steel," Andrew said curtly. "The idea of a quaint townhouse with roses around the door doesn't appeal."

At the top, he unlocked the door and stepped aside to let her in. The interior hit her like a gust of cold air. It was pristine, stark—almost severe. The entry hall was vast, but impersonal. It felt more like a gallery than a home.

"We're not even in the living area yet," he said, nodding to a staircase. "I like living above it all. There's a strange satisfaction in looking down on the city."

"I thought you already did that," Kiera murmured, eyeing the clean white walls and sharp lines. "No elevation needed."

He cast her a sideways glance. "Is that a compliment or a warning?"

"Take it how you like," she said, following him up the stairs.

The living room was enormous, dominated by floor-to-ceiling windows that offered a sweeping, cinematic view of London. The skyline stretched in every direction, dizzyingly beautiful—but Kiera barely glanced at it. Her focus was on the room itself. White walls, white leather sofas, dark lacquered side tables, and cutting-edge audio equipment. Minimalist. Clinical. Immaculate.

"And you called my room virginal?" she muttered, half to herself.

Andrew's brow lifted. "At the time, I thought it suited you. Then you displaced that idea very quickly."

He glanced around the space. "This... is the opposite of Wickham. It's deliberate, I suppose. A kind of rebellion."

"An efficient purge of anything resembling magic," Kiera said softly. "And yet... it could be beautiful."

He looked at her then, eyes unreadable. "Are you going to make it beautiful for me?"

The question made her pulse jump. She turned away sharply, swallowing any softening that might have crept into her thoughts.

"It's nothing to do with me," she said briskly. "This visit is professional. That's all."

"Then I'll make us coffee while you choose the panther's resting place."

He disappeared into another room, and Kiera clenched her jaw, annoyed at herself. He still had the power to disarm her with a few words. Worse, she almost pitied him—for losing something he clearly still longed for. She shoved her hands into her pockets and wandered the space.

It definitely needed artwork. The emptiness felt deliberate, like something done in reaction, not design. She had the oddest sense that the room had been redecorated not for aesthetics, but out of frustration—maybe even anger.

She was still staring at one bare wall when Andrew returned, two mugs in hand. She took one without thinking, leaning casually against the railing that overlooked the drop to the hall below.

"What was it like before you redecorated?" she asked, her tone light, almost teasing.

He paused, then gave her a guarded look. "What makes you think it wasn't always like this?"

She gestured vaguely around the room. "I don't know. Instinct? There's a mood here. A tension. Like it was wiped clean in a fit of… I don't know. Rage? Grief? Maybe it's just me being fanciful."

She gave a soft, self-conscious laugh and took a sip of her coffee. "Forget it. I'm probably imagining things."

Andrew sat on the white couch opposite her, his gaze tracing the tension in her face. Kiera caught herself, suddenly aware of how easily she'd slipped into something too close to intimacy. It was a mistake. She straightened, tore her gaze from his, and resumed her pacing, searching for the perfect place.

"There," she said at last, nodding toward the wall behind him. "Dead centre. That's where it should go."

She grimaced, then shot him a wry look. "It would take every piece I have in the gallery to soften this place."

"Then collect things—for me," he said quietly.

She turned to face him, half-expecting sarcasm, but his expression was sincere. Unsettlingly so.

"Not a collection, exactly," she said, wary now. "This space needs variety. Layers. Something with… soul."

She broke off and turned away, placing her coffee down without drinking. The tension inside her had returned—tight and urgent.

"You shouldn't be here," she said, more to the room than to him. "It doesn't suit you. It's not even… happy."

She looked back at him, frustration pulling her brow into a frown. "Why are you doing this to yourself?"

Andrew rose slowly and walked toward her, his expression unreadable.

"You've become very astute," he said softly. "Why am I doing this? Maybe rebellion, like I said. Or maybe… sheer bloody-mindedness. If I can't have the magic I want, I don't want any magic at all."

"Then go after it," she urged. "Find your magic again."

But he only smiled, slow and bittersweet. "It's gone, Kiera. Somewhere along the way, it slipped through my fingers."

There was such finality in his voice, such quiet sorrow, that it struck something deep inside her. Her green eyes searched his face.

"Don't stay here, Andrew," she said gently. "Eventually… it'll break you."

His lips quirked in a twisted smile. He lifted a hand and brushed her cheek with a feather-light touch.

"For now, it's perfect. You and I, high above the world, in a room with no past—and no future. What could be better?"

His eyes held hers—stormy, steel-grey, unreadable—and Kiera felt the pull of him again.

It was dangerous. It was familiar. It was everything she didn't trust and everything her body remembered.

She moved without thinking. A breath. A heartbeat. And then she was in his arms, drawn by a gravity neither of them could deny nor name. His hold was firm, steady—like the world had shifted beneath her feet and only he could anchor her now.

His chest rose and fell beneath her palms. He smelled of wind and woodsmoke and the echo of memories that refused to die. The steel in his gaze darkened to smoke, and she stared up at him, pulse hammering.

"Angel face," he murmured—his voice low and reverent—and then his mouth was on hers.

Soft, at first. A brush of lips like a question. A taste of a beginning. But the kiss deepened in the next breath, igniting something wild, something reckless and real that had never stopped burning.

He kissed her like he was remembering. Like he was claiming. Like he hadn't spent the last three years regretting every moment they'd lost.

Kiera didn't want to be soothed. She didn't want gentle. She wanted to feel—everything. The pain, the want, the years of longing wound so tightly inside her they threatened to snap.

She wrapped her arms around his neck, pulled him closer, and he responded with a growl low in his throat, gathering her into his body like a man starved of light.

Just like before, the spark between them caught, flared, and turned to flame.

His hands framed her face, then slid into her hair as he kissed her deeper. Her sweater bunched under his fingers as he drew her to the couch. She followed blindly, breathless, aching, alive.

When her back met the cushions, he didn't stop—didn't ask. He just kept kissing her like she was the air he needed, like stopping would kill him.

He trailed his mouth along her jaw, down the slope of her neck, each press of his lips dragging a gasp from her throat. She arched into him as his hand found her breast through the fabric, and he held her there, steady, until she gasped his name.

"Andrew…"

He groaned, then claimed her mouth again—hot, open, consuming.

Her hands fumbled with the buttons of his shirt, half-crazed with need, while his fingers slid under her sweater and over bare skin, slow and reverent, like a man touching something sacred.

When he finally tugged her sweater over her head, he paused—just for a breath—and looked down at her. And in his eyes was awe. Raw, wordless awe.

"Kiera…"

She silenced him with a kiss, her fingers working the last buttons loose. When he stripped his shirt and tossed it aside, she felt the scratch of his chest hair against her bare skin and shuddered, her breath catching in her throat.

"I want you," he said hoarsely. "You're driving me insane."

She felt it too—the madness, the heat, the hunger that had never gone cold. When he pulled down the zip of her skirt and let it fall, his hands moved over her thighs with aching slowness, as if he were memorising the shape of her all over again.

She moved beneath him, desperate for more, and he crushed her to him, whispering against her skin, "You're mine, Kiera. You always were."

Her eyes flew open, dazed and glassy.

"Look at me," he growled. "Let me see those green eyes."

She met his gaze—hot, intense, burning—and saw in him a man barely holding on to control. A man who'd lost her once and didn't know how to let her go again.

She reached for him, pulled him down, her mouth seeking his with trembling urgency. He kissed her hard, deeply, like he could devour the distance between them.

His hands were everywhere—mapping her, moulding her, learning her again. When he cupped her breasts, she arched into him, gasping. He slid lower, fingers skimming the silk between her thighs.

"Andrew… please…"

The thin lace did nothing to shield her, and his touch pressed through it, slow and knowing, until she cried out. He growled something guttural against her throat—some sound of possession, of need so fierce it made her tremble.

And just when she was falling—just when the world had narrowed to the heat between them—

The sharp, insistent ring of his phone shattered the moment.

Once.

Twice.

A third time.

Relentless. Jarring. Real.

He swore under his breath, resting his forehead against hers, his body still heavy and hot over hers. "Ignore it," he rasped.

She did. Tried to. But it rang again.

Andrew growled in frustration and rolled away, reaching into his pocket. The moment his warmth left her, Kiera curled into herself, shivering, her body still burning. She watched him sit up, silhouetted by the faint light, the phone pressed to his ear.

Everything inside her ached.

The loss of him—the loss of that moment—was unbearable. She hadn't realised how deeply she'd needed it. Needed him.

Panic clawed at her chest. She wanted to reach for him, knock the phone from his hand, beg him to take them back to where they'd just been—together, unthinking, perfect.

But everything had changed.

"Hello?" Andrew's voice was curt, sharp-edged. His face hardened as he listened. Kiera didn't need to hear the other end of the conversation to know. Trouble. She could feel it.

"I'm busy," he snapped. "And Paris is a long way off. Not remotely important right now."

She blinked, heart still pounding, and saw her sweater on the floor. The chill hit her skin—and then she realised who he was talking to. His tone was ice. Still, it didn't comfort her. She could almost write the rest of the conversation herself—Sienna demanding he come, asking where he was, wanting answers. And Andrew brushing her off. For now.

"Maybe you do, but that's your problem. Call David. See what he thinks."

That was all Kiera needed. She was already on her feet, pulling on her skirt, dragging her sweater over her head. By the time Andrew ended the call, she was halfway across the room.

"Kiera!" His voice was disoriented, wounded. But she didn't stop.

She spun around, fire in her eyes. "Don't come near me!"

He froze, looking stunned. Pale. She was shaking too, but she wasn't going to let him see it.

"You bastard!" she hissed, the words like venom. "Phone her back! Go to Paris! It's a short flight, isn't it?"

"Kiera, it's not what you—"

"I understand just fine!" she cut in, her voice cracking. "Don't ever touch me again. Come near me and I swear, I'll tell my father everything I should have told him years ago."

And with that, she bolted down the stairs, half-blinded by rage and shame. She slammed the door behind her, took the lift, and fled to her car. Only when she was close to home did the truth crash down on her.

She pulled over, trembling, and let her forehead rest against the steering wheel.

What had she been doing? She had never behaved like that. Not with anyone. But with Andrew… just a look, a touch, and she had surrendered everything.

And worse—she wanted him still.

The ache in her chest was unbearable. Regret burned hot inside her, but it was twisted up with something else: longing.

Things couldn't go back. Not now.

She had to leave the Hall. The promise she made her father—she'd have to break it. There was no way she could sit across from Andrew every night, pretending nothing had happened. She'd think of a reason. Something plausible. Anything.

But fate, it seemed, was one step ahead.

As she stepped through the door, her father was waiting in the hallway.

"Andrew won't be around for a while," he said cheerfully. "He's flying out to Portugal. There's a big contract there going off the rails—he thinks the team's asleep at the wheel. He'll whip them into shape. You should see him in action. Feathers fly."

Kiera forced a smile.

"A dangerous hunter," she murmured, bitterly.

Her father chuckled. "That's him. Quiet as a shadow, but people trip over themselves trying to explain things. I don't know how I managed before Andrew came on board." He squeezed her shoulder gently. "He's like a son to me now. You know that don't you?"

She nearly broke down.

If he only knew. If he knew what Andrew had done. If he knew about Sienna. If he ever found out how close Kiera had come to making a terrible mistake…

She excused herself and went to her room.

Portugal. That wasn't the destination. She knew it. He might have snapped at Sienna, but he'd go to her all the same. That call had changed everything. If his phone hadn't rung…

She closed her eyes, pressing her face into her pillow. If it hadn't rung, she would have given herself to Andrew completely. Body and soul.

And she wasn't sure if she was grateful it rang—or shattered.

All she knew was that she must never see him again. Never come back to this place that still smelled like him.

It was over.

Chapter Ten

Over the next few days, Kiera divided her time between Wickham Hall and the gallery. With nothing to occupy her while her father was at the office, she had more important things to do than loiter around, enduring Mrs. Williams's frosty presence. Since Andrew's confrontation with the housekeeper, Mrs. Williams had become icily polite, clearly biding her time until Sienna returned. She was a thorn in Kiera's side, a constant, unwanted reminder.

Each morning, after consulting with Mrs. Williams about dinner, Kiera left shortly after her father. It was always a relief to escape to the stillness of her gallery or the quiet of her apartment—anywhere that wasn't Wickham Hall, where every corner seemed to echo with thoughts of Andrew.

She was home each evening for her father's sake, but during the day she met Gary for lunch on several occasions. To his credit, he had the good sense not to mention the disastrous dinner party. She wasn't sure what she would have done if he had brought it up. Andrew's face still haunted her thoughts—no longer the image of arrogant scorn, but the wounded fury of a man deeply hurt. Something had changed between them, and she couldn't deny it.

By the time Friday arrived, she had almost convinced herself that life had returned to normal. She'd spent the morning at a sale and, in a moment of impulsive distraction, had purchased two landscapes and a surrealist painting. It was a thoughtless act—almost hypnotic—and only later did she realise the truth: she'd bought them for Andrew's apartment. She had no use for them herself, but the stark emptiness of his place had lingered in her mind. She'd mentally rearranged the space more times than she cared to admit, all in an effort to think about anything but him.

Back at the gallery, she left the paintings in her car, suppressing the instinct to bring them inside. It was ridiculous—this urge to provide for him. What Andrew needed was Sienna, and Kiera was furious with herself for forgetting it, even momentarily. She grabbed her more typical acquisitions and joined Sally to discuss them, forcing herself into business mode.

The shopping had made her late, and she barely had time to change clothes and touch up her makeup before hurrying off to lunch with Gary. Since she wouldn't be in London over the weekend, it would be the last time they'd see each other until next week.

When she arrived at the restaurant, Gary was already there, standing to greet her with an admiring smile. Kiera responded with one of her own—brilliant, warm—but it faltered almost immediately. She felt it before she saw him, as if someone were willing her to look. The sensation was so strong it couldn't be ignored. She turned her head slightly, and her smile vanished completely.

Andrew.

He sat just a few feet away, deep in conversation with two men—clearly a business lunch. Of all the restaurants in the city, the coincidence was almost cruel. Gary had taken her somewhere different every day. That they would end up here today, of all days, felt like fate twisting the knife.

For a moment she froze, wide-eyed and stricken, but Andrew didn't acknowledge her. His cool grey gaze swept over her as if she were a stranger. Only Gary's gentle hand on her arm brought her back to herself.

"Sit down, Kiera," he urged quietly. "Whatever it is, don't just stand there."

"Sorry," she said faintly, allowing him to guide her to her chair. Thankfully, once seated, she couldn't see Andrew—though she could still feel him. His presence pressed against her like static, igniting her nerves.

"I take it things haven't improved between you two," Gary murmured dryly, eyeing her pale face. "We can go elsewhere if you'd prefer."

"No." She straightened, her voice fiercer than she intended. "He's not driving me out. I'm fine."

"Then let's eat and ignore him," Gary replied comfortably, and she was grateful for his ease.

"You're one of the good ones," she said softly.

He gave her a quizzical smile. "But not the one. I'm not an idiot, Kiera. That man's got you—hook, line, and sinker. I don't know how he's keeping it together. Frankly, I'm amazed he hasn't come over here to punch me."

"He wouldn't," she murmured. "He's… very sophisticated."

"Is he?" Gary grunted. "Well, his sophisticated façade is cracking. If his jaw gets any tighter, it'll snap. If he weren't such a 'civilised' man, he'd have turned every table over by now."

That didn't help. Kiera's hands trembled, and she couldn't even hold the menu. Gary sighed and took it from her, ordering for both of them. If he hadn't been so easy to be with, she might have bolted.

The last time she'd seen Andrew, they'd nearly made love. She hadn't recovered—not really. She'd pretended, but the second she'd seen him, her stomach had clenched with sickening longing. He had a hold on her, and what terrified her most was the fact that she didn't want to let go.

Gary kept talking, drawing her out of her spiral, and slowly she calmed. She was halfway through a meal she hadn't tasted when she finally began to feel safe.

He won't come over, she told herself. He'll leave when his meeting ends. He won't say a word.

And then Gary leaned forward, eyes locked on something behind her.

"They're going," he murmured. "Now pull yourself together. He's coming over."

Her stomach lurched, butterflies turning vicious.

Andrew appeared at her side, looking down at her and ignoring Gary entirely.

"So—you've deserted ship," he said in an icy tone.

Kiera met his gaze coolly. "If you mean Wickham Hall, I haven't. I'm still there. I work, remember? I'll be back tonight."

She forced a calm expression, determined not to let him draw blood first. "How was Portugal? You don't look very tanned. Or did you get… sidetracked?"

"Oh, I went," he replied smoothly, but there was a glint in his eye that made her uneasy. "I'll be returning tomorrow. Business called me home early." His gaze held hers, unflinching. "I know I'm interrupting your lunch, but before I leave again, I had to ask—have you given any thought to the last time we saw each other?"

Her face drained of colour. He knew exactly what he was doing, dragging her back to that vulnerable moment.

"You mentioned I needed more artwork. Keep an eye out for some, will you? Money's no object."

"I already have three," she snapped, furious at his manipulation. "Two landscapes and a modern canvas. You can collect them from the gallery. They'll cost you."

"You've already cost me," he said softly, tossing a set of keys onto the table. "Hang them for me. Charge extra."

"I'll never go to—" she began, but he cut her off with a look.

"I'll be out of the country by four. You'll have the place to yourself."

His arrogance grounded her. She met his gaze with fury.

"How long is this 'safe window' then?" she asked. "If I'm doing it, I want the place to myself. And yes—I'll charge you for every minute."

"I'll be gone a week," he said curtly.

She could guess where. Paris. Sienna.

"Then I'll do it while you're away… in Paris," she said sharply.

His expression darkened, but before he could reply, she looked sweetly at Gary. "You can come help me, Gary."

He didn't even have time to respond.

"Don't," Andrew said, his voice low and dangerous. "I've been known to attack intruders. If you'd prefer to keep your face intact, stay out of this."

And with that, he stalked off.

Kiera stared after him, guilt rising.

"I'm sorry," she said shakily. "I shouldn't have dragged you into it. I just… wanted to get the better of him."

Gary exhaled through his nose, tight with anger. "It's fine. He only came to provoke you. I'm shocked by my own restraint—I nearly decked him."

Kiera felt like a rabbit caught between two wolves. No one could truly go up against Andrew—six-foot-two, all steel and strength. She'd felt that power firsthand. And she was quietly grateful this confrontation had happened somewhere public.

When Kiera returned to the gallery, she found it impossible to settle. Her mind refused to focus, her hands moved restlessly, and long before closing time, she gave up and went home.

She had the keys in her bag and the paintings in the car, but stepping through his door felt unthinkable—too intimate, too real. She doubted she'd ever find the courage.

At home, her father was already back—unusually early—and he looked so drawn that worry flared in her chest.

"You must be overworking," she said anxiously. "I've never seen you look this tired. Not even the other night when you were still at it at midnight."

"I've always worked like that," he muttered, rubbing his eyes. "Can't think what's wrong with me these days."

After dinner, Kiera persuaded him to go to bed early. But she lay awake most of the night, unease gnawing at her. He insisted he wasn't ill, yet his pallor and weariness told a different story.

Had he found out about Sienna and Andrew? She couldn't be sure. If he had, he wouldn't necessarily tell her. It was just like him to keep that sort of thing to himself. She couldn't exactly ask.

If only Mrs. Williams had been at all normal. She might have noticed a change in him before now, might have offered some insight. But with Mrs. Williams as she was—and no one else to confide in—Kiera kept her worries to herself.

By the next morning, he seemed better. After a quiet weekend of rest, he looked almost like his old self again. He insisted on going into the office, and Kiera left for work shortly after he did.

But she never made it.

Somewhere along the drive, a decision took root in her chest, stubborn and sudden. Before she could talk herself out of it, she found herself parked outside Andrew's building. Paintings in tow, she stepped into the lift, her heart pounding.

She would not let him think she was scared. Or hurt. This wasn't about emotions—this was just another job, another commission. She'd do what she came to do and leave without a fuss. No drama, no vulnerability. He'd see that it meant nothing to her.

She might even leave him a generously padded invoice—for her time and her trouble.

The silence inside the apartment unnerved her at first. She walked through the rooms slowly, studying everything, letting the starkness of the space wash over her. Her first impression hadn't changed—it was cold, impersonal. A place to hide, not to live. It felt as if Andrew had deliberately retreated from the world, surrounded himself with emptiness.

The atmosphere clung to her skin. She couldn't ignore it. She had to either act or leave.

And she couldn't leave.

Foolish as it was, the thought of Andrew returning to this barren place made her ache.

She shut down every emotion and began. Once she started, she couldn't stop. The task consumed her. It would take far more effort than she'd expected, and before lunchtime she was out again, placing orders, ignoring the boundaries of what she'd been hired to do.

Hanging the paintings as-is would only make things worse—it would be like applying bright makeup to a lifeless face. No. The place needed transformation. She threw herself into it, spending freely, neglecting her own work, swept up in a purpose she couldn't explain.

In her mind, she heard his quiet voice: *"Are you going to make it beautiful for me?"*

She was. More than that—she was making it his.

As the apartment evolved, so did her excitement. She even missed a sale, too caught up in her mission to care.

His bedroom was the hardest. That felt like a true intrusion. But it was as bleak as the rest, and she couldn't leave it untouched. She forced herself to work through it, ignoring the thoughts of Andrew sleeping there.

By the end of the week, it was done.

Kiera stood in the middle of the transformed space, breathless with quiet satisfaction. The heavy drapes softened the light pouring in from the vast windows. Bright cushions dotted the white couches. Carefully chosen paintings brightened the walls. Mirrors reflected light and space, and three lush plants filled the corners like anchors.

Her final touch came from the boot of her car—a tall, elegant vase, filled with vibrant lilies. She placed it on the coffee table she'd purchased to match the rest of the room. It was perfect—sophisticated, bold, alive.

She chewed her lip as she considered the bill. It hadn't been cheap—not even close. And truthfully, Andrew had never actually asked her to do all this. His only mention of it had come when he was trying to charm her.

The memory irritated her.

Good. Let him be shocked.

She left the invoice—itemised and eye-watering—on the coffee table, right beside the lilies. Then she walked out, smiling to herself.

He'd be back in a week. If not, the lilies would die. That wasn't her concern.

She returned to the gallery and threw herself into her work, determined to make up for lost time.

Chapter Eleven

Andrew arrived just before closing. Sally was on her way out as he stepped into the gallery, and Kiera was upstairs, hurriedly packing a small bag with clothes for the next few days. Living between the gallery apartment and Wickham Hall was a constant shuffle—always taking something to the hall, always bringing something back.

"A visitor," Sally called. "See you tomorrow, Kiera." Kiera barely heard her add, "She's upstairs," before the door clicked shut behind her.

Assuming it was Harper, who sometimes dropped by for coffee and a chat, Kiera didn't think much of it—until she heard the distinct sound of heavy, male footsteps on the stairs. She froze. Then she stepped out of the bedroom just as Andrew entered the living room.

A flicker of alarm shot through her. All she could think about was that enormous bill. His past offences—Sienna, the argument—vanished under the weight of her own guilt. She stared at him, unsure, while he looked back, silent and unreadable.

"I'm going," she said at last.

He nodded, still without a word.

"Was there something you needed?" she asked, her voice tighter than she intended.

He stepped forward and placed a cheque on the table. She glanced at it—too many zeroes. It made her dizzy just thinking about it. Where he'd been, what he'd done—it didn't cross her mind. All she could focus on was how much she'd spent without permission. And the last time they'd spoken, he'd walked out of a restaurant in fury.

"It's… a lot," she said cautiously.

He smiled—slowly, warmly—the kind of smile she hadn't seen in years.

"You made it beautiful," he said simply. "The cost doesn't matter. It was almost too beautiful to leave. But I thought I might catch you before you left." His gaze held hers. "Thank you, Kiera."

"I enjoyed it," she murmured, relieved more than she cared to admit. "Maybe I'll expand into interiors. A new sideline."

"I hope not," he said. "I want to believe you did it just for me."

His smile lingered. "I even thought about staying the night. I could still smell your perfume when I walked in. The whole place—it was… unexpected."

"Did you get to Paris?" she asked abruptly, thrown by his tone, trying to regain her footing.

"No. I went back to Portugal. That was the plan, remember?"

"I wasn't really listening," she muttered, turning away. But he caught her shoulder and gently turned her back to face him.

"So… you never really stopped worshipping, even when the idol fell?" he said softly.

Kiera laughed thinly. "Don't flatter yourself. It was a job. You paid me. I got carried away, maybe—but it wasn't personal. I didn't mean to go that far. Sorry if I overstepped."

He didn't respond to her deflection.

"There was care in every choice you made. That was for me, Kiera."

"You've got an overactive imagination," she said, but her voice faltered when he tilted her chin, his eyes searching hers.

"No," he said quietly. "Just a long memory."

She pulled away sharply. "So have I. Maybe I felt sorry for you, but you don't need pity—and you definitely don't deserve it."

"I couldn't be angry with you right now," he said softly. "One day, though, you'll laugh about Sienna. One day, you'll beg me never to mention her again."

"Don't hold your breath!" she snapped, fury rising at the name alone. The spell was broken. "There's nothing about her I'll ever laugh at. And as for 'one day'—there won't be one. I'm only in contact with you because I had to come home. You were just… there."

But he only smiled again. That maddening, knowing smile.

"Time will tell. I know more now than I did before." He turned toward the door. "I'll see you at home. Tell the cuddly Mrs. Williams I'll be there for dinner."

"You can't—you know I can't—"

"I could stay in that beautiful apartment," he said casually, "and breathe in the last trace of your perfume. But I'm going to the hall instead."

"Why?" she demanded.

He looked her in the eye. "Because I've managed without what I need for a long time. I'm not willing to anymore."

And then he was gone.

Kiera stood frozen. What did he mean? What was he planning? Was this some scheme he and Sienna had concocted? No matter what he said, she still believed he had gone to Paris. Yet Sienna hadn't returned. She hadn't even called. The silence was unnerving.

Her thoughts turned to her father—how tired he had looked lately, how pale. Any shock might undo him. If he discovered the truth about Andrew and Sienna…

It could break him.

She had to get there first—before Andrew. If anything happened, she had to be the one to absorb the impact, to protect him.

She shoved her belongings into her case, flew down the stairs, and left the massive cheque untouched on the table.

Only one thing mattered now: getting home.

Impatience made the journey feel twice as long, but Kiera turned in through the lodge gates just as Andrew was unloading his car. She couldn't have been more than a few minutes behind him, but inside, she was already spiralling, the dread of what might be coming playing like a reel in her mind.

Without thinking, she pulled up behind his Mercedes and leapt out, striding toward him, her nerves frayed to the edge.

"Just be careful what you say to my father," she snapped before he could speak. "I've been worried about him while you were off wherever, and if you're planning to bring up you and Sienna, it can wait. It's waited this long already—he doesn't need any kind of upset right now."

Her voice was sharp, urgent, and loud enough to echo slightly in the cool air. Andrew's eyes locked on hers, dark with something raw—rage, regret, maybe even longing. His jaw was clenched so tightly a muscle jumped in his cheek. For a second, she thought he might turn and leave. But then he stepped toward her, every movement tightly controlled, like a man on the edge of losing it.

"I warned you once that I'd either kill or cure you, Kiera," he bit out, voice low and savage, striding toward her and gripping her shoulders. "And right now, the killing option's looking pretty damned attractive. Come into the lodge—I'm going to throw you over my knee and pound some bloody sense into you. I should've done it years ago."

She gasped, struggling wildly as he made a move to steer her inside.

"Listen to me!" she shouted, fighting him off. "I'm not accusing you of anything right now. I'm just telling you—my father's not well, and if you start something, if you bring Sienna into this, I'll never forgive you."

Andrew let her go with a frustrated snarl, breathing heavily. His narrowed eyes locked on hers. "What's wrong with David?"

"I don't know," she admitted, rubbing her sore shoulder where his fingers had gripped too hard. "He won't see a doctor, but something isn't right. You'll see for yourself. He's been pretending he's fine, but he isn't."

Andrew exhaled slowly, reigning in his temper. "Alright. I'll be up shortly." His gaze darkened. "But if you want peace, try behaving like a rational adult for once. I know it's not your strong suit—you haven't used your head since you were fifteen—but try. Just this once, keep your wild side hidden."

"I'm never wild," Kiera said stiffly.

Andrew raised a skeptical brow as he turned back to his car. "Selective memory must be a gift. Me, I remember everything. Especially the wild parts." His eyes flicked over her, lingering, and Kiera felt the heat rise under her skin. "If I could forget everything but that, I probably would. But don't worry—I won't let it affect me."

She didn't dignify that with an answer. Instead, she stalked back to her car, cheeks burning, and drove past him without looking back. He stood watching her with a smug little smile, and it infuriated her that he had once again come out on top.

But none of that mattered. All that mattered was her father, and keeping the atmosphere light for his sake. If Andrew could manage charm, then so could she. He wasn't the only one capable of putting on a façade.

Later that night, Kiera sat on the edge of her bed, fuming. The whole evening had gone smoothly—frustratingly so. Andrew had been charming, polite, even affectionate in a disarming, infuriating way. Not once had he mentioned the apartment, nor Sienna, nor the enormous cheque still sitting untouched in her apartment. He had laughed with her father, discussed business as if he'd never been away, and nodded along with casual interest while her father explained the plans for Portugal.

Kiera had barely made it through the meal without snapping. He had completely disarmed her with civility—and she hated him for it. He always knew how to throw her off balance, always had the upper hand. And now, somehow, it was worse than ever. He had a grip on her she couldn't shake, even when she tried.

She went to bed muttering angrily and woke the next morning in no better mood.

Staying at the hall was out of the question—it was Saturday, and Andrew had made it clear he had no intention of going anywhere. When she came down to breakfast and saw him already seated with her father, smiling pleasantly over his coffee, she bristled.

"I'm going into the gallery," she announced abruptly. At her father's disappointed look, she softened. "I've been neglecting it lately. I really ought to put in a few extra hours."

"We'll try to manage without you," her father said with a gentle smile. "Back for dinner, darling?"

"I don't know," she replied quickly, deliberately avoiding Andrew's gaze.

He was far too pleased with himself, and she knew why—he knew exactly where she'd been spending her time. "I'll probably have dinner with Gary. Don't wait for me."

That wiped the smile off Andrew's face, and Kiera and felt a fleeting sense of victory as she drove away. But it was hollow. She didn't want to be at the gallery. She didn't want dinner with Gary. What she wanted—absurd as it was—was to stay at the hall, to watch her father, and, worse still, to watch Andrew when he wasn't watching her.

She gave an angry snort. There was no future in that kind of thinking. No honour in it, either. She had known the truth about Andrew for years—known what he was—but now, unreasonably, she didn't want it to be true.

Wishing wouldn't change facts. She pushed all thoughts of him away, buried herself in work, skipped lunch, and eventually called her father to say she'd be late.

She made a light supper in her apartment and kept working, trying to ignore the quiet ache beneath her frustration.

Andrew was in her life again. And just like before, he was forcing her out—only this time, without saying a single cruel word.

Her phone rang much later, just as Kiera was about to leave for home. She paused, debating whether to ignore it—she was tired, her apartment was already locked, and she'd had enough of the day. But it wasn't in her nature to walk away from anything unfinished. With a sigh, she turned back and picked up the receiver.

"Kiera?"

Andrew's voice. No derision, no chill—just that steady tone she remembered from long ago. Her heart sank. Something was wrong.

"Yes."

Even before he spoke again, fear prickled at her skin. Andrew wouldn't be calling her here unless it was serious. Deep down, she already knew.

"Your father is in hospital," he said carefully. "Don't panic. I was with him when it happened. I acted immediately—I'm at the hospital now. I think you should come."

"Is… is it the local one?" Her lips felt numb. All she could think was that she had deliberately stayed away all afternoon and evening, avoiding Andrew, and now her father—

"Yes, the local," he said steadily. "Do you want me to fetch you, or can you manage?"

"I'll manage. Stay with him, please."

She stared at the phone, panic rising despite his steadying voice. "Andrew!" Her fear cracked in her throat.

"Calm down," he said sharply. "He's all right for now. Come slowly, drive carefully. Do you hear me?"

"Yes," she whispered, unable to say more.

She hung up with a trembling hand, the dial tone humming against her ear like a warning bell. For one stunned heartbeat, she stood frozen—anger, suspicion, defiance still crackling through her like static. And then, in a single breath, it all collapsed.

The weight of their arguments, the lingering sting of Sienna's betrayal, Andrew's maddening smugness—it all disintegrated under the crushing fear blooming in her chest.

Her father was in the hospital. And Andrew—Andrew was there, steady and calm, already doing what she should have done.

She reached for her coat with shaking hands, guilt rising like a tide.

I wasn't there. I stayed away.

For the first time in days, she didn't care what he'd done, said, or meant. She just needed to get to her father—and Andrew was suddenly the only solid ground beneath her feet.

Chapter Twelve

He saw her as soon as she stepped into the lit entrance. The hospital was small, familiar. Andrew rose from his seat in the corridor and met her halfway.

"Is it his heart?" she asked, rushing toward him. He took her cold hands in his.

"I thought so at first, but I might be wrong. The doctor's with him now. They've run several tests. Don't assume the worst."

Kiera nodded numbly and sank into a chair. Andrew went to the vending machine and returned with a steaming cup, pressing it into her hands.

"It's hot, if nothing else," he said wryly. "I figured you'd need it."

Kiera stared down at the drink. "My antidote," she murmured. "You remembered."

He didn't smile. Just looked at her with the kind of quiet grief that made her chest ache.

"I remember everything about you," he said quietly. "Too many years to forget."

He glanced at his watch. "We should hear something soon."

"What happened?" she asked, resting her head back. She felt bone tired. This was the final blow after weeks of emotional exhaustion. And the more time she spent with Andrew, the more the past refused to stay buried.

"After dinner, your father looked off. Said he was tired, but then he just collapsed. I got him here as fast as I could."

"Maybe I should've done something sooner," she murmured miserably.

Andrew placed his hand over hers. "No guilt, Kiera. If he hadn't collapsed, I would've believed him too. You can't force someone to admit they're ill. This is going to be hard enough without beating yourself up."

The words landed deeper than they should have. Maybe because she was so tired. Maybe because, for the first time in weeks, someone was looking out for her. She felt a swell of warmth toward him. His hand stayed over hers, and she didn't pull away. She had always needed him.

The doctor approached. Andrew's arm slipped around her waist, steadying her as they stood.

She didn't want to admit it—not even to herself—but having Andrew here steadied her. As if the past hadn't fractured everything beyond repair.

"It's not his heart," the doctor said firmly. "We're still unsure, though it may be exhaustion. His schedule is ridiculous."

"It is," Andrew said grimly. "There's no stopping him."

"Well, this has stopped him," the doctor replied. "His body forced the issue. We'll keep testing, but for now, bed rest is best."

Kiera started to ask something, but the doctor cut her off gently. "We'll know more before he's discharged. For now, no need to worry yourself sick. In fact, you look like you could use a good night's rest."

"She'll get it," Andrew said flatly. "Can we see him?"

"Briefly. He'd want to see his daughter."

Inside the room, her father looked pale and fragile against the hospital-white sheets. The sight hit her hard. She took his hand and held it tightly. Guilt swelled in her chest—she had stayed away for too long, let pain and pride rob her of time with him.

He was too tired to speak much, but just before they left, he looked up at Andrew.

"Take care of her," he said gruffly. Then, with a rueful smile: "Not that I need to ask. You always did a better job than I did."

Kiera tried to protest, but the nurse returned and gently ushered them out.

"Call in the morning," she offered kindly. "We'll be with him all night."

Outside, Kiera turned to Andrew, her voice trembling. "Do you think—?"

"I don't speculate," he said, gripping her shoulders. "The doctor said it's not his heart. He's in the best place now. My instincts say we stop panicking—and I get you home and into bed."

She nodded and turned toward her car, but he caught her arm.

"Right behind me, all the way," he said. "I'll be watching."

She managed a small smile. "Thank you."

"For what? As David said—I've always taken care of you. You just slipped away for a while. It's not hard to pick up the reins."

She drove behind him, thoughtful. He had picked up the reins, and she had leaned into him as if no time had passed. He was her safety, her steady place. And for a moment, it felt as if nothing had come between them. Not even Sienna.

But Sienna did exist. She would have to be told. David was her husband. And Andrew—Andrew belonged to her, not Kiera.

At the house, Andrew showed no sign of leaving. That was fine—Kiera had something she needed to say. Something he wouldn't like.

Mrs. Williams met them in the hallway, asking after Mr. Scott. Andrew answered smoothly, but Kiera bristled as the housekeeper tried to take charge.

"No—I'll see to his things," Kiera said firmly. "Anything he needs, I'll bring it tomorrow."

"As you wish," Mrs. Williams replied coolly and walked off. Kiera opened her mouth to argue further, but Andrew laid a calming hand on her arm.

"Not tonight," he said. "Fight her when you're rested."

She bit back her reply and walked into the sitting room. But she wasn't done yet—not with Andrew.

"We have to let Sienna know," she said quietly. "She's his wife, whether we like it or not."

Andrew tensed instantly. "You're right. No comment."

"I'll need her number. If you have it, I'll make the call."

Andrew froze by the door, his expression hardening. "And why do you assume I'd have that?"

"I'm not judging," she said, weariness thick in her voice. "I just need to reach her."

"And of course I must know," he bit out. "Do I beam over to Paris every night and return in time for breakfast?"

"I know you're not there regularly," Kiera shot back, "but you have been. She called you. I heard her."

Andrew took a step back, as if putting space between them might keep the fury in check. But it didn't.

"Think what you like." His hands clenched. "Your body grew up, but your mind—God, Kiera. Making love to you would have been a tragedy. At least Sienna saved me from that."

"How can I contact her?" she demanded, shaking. "Just give me the number."

But Andrew was already at the door.

"Try your father," he said coldly. "She married him, remember?"

It appeared to have been Andrew's final word on any subject, because from that moment on, Kiera was left entirely alone. If she'd hoped that her father's hospitalisation might prompt Andrew to look out for her, she'd been sorely mistaken. He never once came by the house. And each time she visited the hospital, she found he had already been and gone.

At least there was no grave diagnosis. Her father's heart was strong, and though he was growing increasingly restless, he agreed to stay on for additional tests and the rest his doctors insisted he needed. A slightly elevated blood pressure had convinced him to take their advice. Kiera was grateful for the excuse to bring him books and newspapers, especially since Andrew had flatly refused to bring work from the office—something that surprised her more than she cared to admit.

It was with some hesitation that she raised the subject of Sienna.

"We ought to let her know you're in hospital," Kiera said one afternoon, when he was feeling considerably better.

"I don't see the point," her father replied. "It's nothing serious. Let her be, Kiera."

"But she's been away so long," Kiera protested gently.

He made a wry face. "That's hardly unusual. Between skiing holidays, trips to the sun, and shopping sprees in Paris, Sienna's away more than she's here. Her boutiques are in London. I hardly see her at all."

Kiera was stunned. She hadn't considered this. Her thoughts flew instantly to Andrew—his apartment in London, his constant travel. Was that how they'd sustained the illusion for so long? Had the secrecy been unnecessary simply because there was nothing to hide?

"You must be alone a lot," she said softly. "I'm sorry. I didn't realise."

"You've got your own life," he said, a little too quickly. "And I'm not really alone. There's always Mrs. Williams."

Kiera made a face, and he chuckled.

"Just joking," he added. "There's always Andrew."

"Andrew?" She looked at him, puzzled. "What do you mean?"

"You know exactly what I mean," her father said. "Andrew still haunts Wickham Hall. Perhaps not as much as he did when you lived there, but he's around more than you'd expect."

It gave her a great deal to think about, and when she left the hospital, she drove away with a heart full of questions. Was it Wickham he couldn't leave—or her? Was that what he'd meant when he said the magic had slipped through his fingers? And what about Sienna? He flared with anger every time her name was brought up. Did he resent being caught between loyalty to her father and whatever tangle still bound him to Sienna?

Kiera shook her head as she drove on. It was a mess—too many secrets, too much hurt. She kept telling herself it would all be easier when it was over. But in her heart, she wasn't so sure it ever would be. Andrew's hold on her hadn't weakened. If anything, it had deepened. What existed between them now was far more consuming than anything her girlish heart had once imagined.

On her way to the gallery from the hospital, she made the mistake of stopping by the Hall to retrieve something she'd forgotten—and found herself face-to-face with Mrs. Williams, a confrontation she could have done without.

"Mrs Scott should be informed of Mr Scott's illness," the housekeeper said stiffly, stepping directly into Kiera's path at the front door. "She has every right to know."

"And what makes you think she hasn't been told?" Kiera asked coldly, her patience fraying at the woman's officious tone.

"She'd have returned by now," Mrs. Williams said with a self-satisfied look, folding her hands before her as if her opinion were law. Kiera's temper flared.

"My father tells me she spends most of her time away," she snapped. "If I'd known that, I'd have come home a lot sooner—and perhaps spared you the trouble of lingering on here."

"If you're so keen for her to know," she added icily, "why don't you inform her yourself?"

"I've no idea where she is," Mrs. Williams huffed.

Kiera met her stare with one of her own. "Then clearly, she doesn't think much of you either. That puts you in the same boat as the rest of us, doesn't it? Now, unless you're planning to fly to Paris yourself, I suggest you stick to your duties—and hope she comes back before you're replaced."

She stormed out, seething. The woman knew something—Kiera was certain of it. She had the smug, puffed-up air of someone Sienna would confide in. People like Sienna always needed an audience for their vanity.

Let her call Paris, then. Let her bring Sienna back. Maybe then this could all be over. Andrew could pick up where he left off—if he'd ever left off—and Kiera could return to the gallery and her quiet, predictable apartment.

Far from magic. But safe—if she could convince herself that was enough.

Chapter Thirteen

Kiera returned to the gallery with a strange sense of gratitude. This place—her place—was solid, dependable, hers alone. She had built her life here, brick by emotional brick, carving out a quiet security that no one could touch. If not for her father, she might never have had to see Andrew or Sienna again. Their world was separate now. She had tried for years to keep it that way. But her father had always been the thread that connected her to the past—and now the past had caught up with her.

And Andrew… he wasn't so easy to shrug off anymore.

Despite everything, too many things about him still stirred memories of what she used to feel. And sometimes, without even realising it, she found herself walking straight back into the ache she had once fled.

She worked alongside Sally until closing time, grateful for the distraction. Then she climbed the stairs to her apartment. It looked neglected and stale—plants drooping, a fine film of dust dulling the once-polished surfaces. A flare of irritation burst through her. Who was she kidding? When this was over, she'd be right back here. Nothing would change. Andrew's life would carry on without a ripple, and hers would fold back into its quiet routine.

There was no going back to Wickham Hall—not permanently. She had left it behind for good reason. This apartment, this gallery, this independent life—this was her reality, and she would do well to remember it.

Fuelled by frustration, she changed into old clothes and began to clean. She ate standing in the kitchen, too keyed up to sit, scrubbing and dusting with a restless energy. Slowly, the bitterness dulled. She moved from one task to the next, losing track of time—driven by nothing more than the need to put her small world back in order.

It was late when she finally set out again for Wickham Hall. Rain had just begun to fall in fine, steady threads. Normally, she would have stayed put at this hour, but she couldn't risk being too far from her father. The hospital was only a few miles from the hall, and while he was there, she needed to be nearby.

The drizzle soon thickened into a downpour, the road slick and glinting under her headlights. The night was ink-dark, the glare of oncoming cars blinding. Her wipers strained to keep up. And then came the first unsettling stutter from the engine.

She frowned, glancing at the dashboard. Once or twice the headlights flickered. Anxiety prickled beneath her ribs. The car might be small, but it had always been reliable. She checked the time—it was well past eleven. The roads were deserted except for the occasional car, and she was uneasy about flagging down strangers in the dark.

Come on, she urged silently. Just a little farther.

The countryside stretched emptily around her, no sign of life or shelter. But then—at last—the gates of Wickham Hall loomed through the downpour. Relief swept through her.

And then the car gave one final shudder and died.

Every light went out. The engine, silent. No coaxing brought it back to life.

Kiera sat motionless for a beat, listening to the hammering rain on the roof. She was smack in the middle of the entrance. If another vehicle came along, it could plow right into her. The thought of the early milk delivery pushed her into action.

She stepped out—and was instantly drenched. The rain was relentless, a curtain of water that clung to her like a second skin. Still, she had no choice. The nearest help was the lodge. With any luck, Andrew would be there. Though after their last exchange, she doubted it.

Still, she had to try.

The short walk to the lodge felt endless. She had no umbrella, no torch. Just the dark and the storm and her own stumbling footsteps. She almost missed the building entirely, spotting it only because a faint glow seeped around the edges of the curtains.

He was home.

The tight coil in her chest finally eased.

She raised her fist and banged on the door; the same way she had the last time she'd come to see him at the lodge. She had half a mind to call his name—again. Rain slid down her neck, her hair plastered to her face. She was frozen, soaked, miserable.

And completely unbothered by pride.

She needed him. Why wasn't he answering?

Kiera nearly stumbled inside when the door swung open and Andrew stood in the doorway, staring at her in stunned disbelief.

"Good God." He caught her arm, hauling her out of the torrential rain and into the warmth of the room. "What happened to you?"

He didn't move at first, just stood there, eyes scanning her as if checking for injuries rather than springing into action. The intensity of his gaze only made her more irritable.

"I broke down," she said, breathless and wet and rapidly losing patience. "I got this far, but now I'm stuck. And obviously, I'm soaked." She glanced down as water streamed from her clothes, puddling at her feet.

"I worked that part out," he said dryly. "You'd better get out of those wet clothes before you catch pneumonia. Or, if that doesn't appeal, I'll drive you up to the Hall like this."

"It's not that simple." She wrapped her arms around herself, teeth chattering. "I broke down right between the gates. The car's blocking the entrance—it's dangerous. You'll have to move it."

Andrew stared at her for a long beat, then exhaled sharply, jaw tightening. "You are the most maddening woman I've ever met."

"Oh, don't start," Kiera muttered.

"No, seriously. Why is it that every time you're in trouble, I end up being the one to sort it out? Where's Peterson when you need him? I assume you've been with him all evening. Maybe you two should've just made a night of it."

"I have not been with Gary," she snapped, seething. "For your information, I've been at my apartment. Alone. Cleaning. Not that it's any of your concern. If you're so put out, I'll walk up to the Hall and call for a breakdown truck from the village."

"Oh, they'll love that," he muttered. "Midnight, pouring rain. Just the kind of emergency they dream of." He slammed the door behind her and gestured toward the fire. "Stand there. I'll find you something dry to wear. And try not to drip on the rug—God knows I'm close to losing my temper."

Kiera stood stiffly. "I'll stay here. Though a more civilised host might offer the use of a bathroom. I'm fairly certain this place has running water and not a pump out back."

Andrew's lips twitched in reluctant amusement. "Touché. Help yourself, Miss Scott. Towels are in the bathroom cupboard. I'll get my torch and see what damage your deathtrap has done to the driveway. With any luck, I'll survive this latest encounter with you."

His eyes ran over her again, and despite the sarcasm, there was a flicker of concern there. "You're hopeless," he muttered. "Get warm. Or you'll be in the hospital wing next to your father."

He turned away and began gathering things—an oilskin, a heavy-duty flashlight, gumboots—and Kiera scowled. Of course he had everything ready, even in the middle of the night during a monsoon. Typical Andrew. Always prepared, always competent. Unlike her.

He caught her look and smirked. "Don't wait for an engraved invitation," he said, pulling on his coat. "The bathroom's easy to find. And if I come back soaked through, I'm claiming the hot shower for myself."

She glared at him as he yanked the door open and vanished into the storm, the wind hurling one last wet gust into the room before it slammed shut behind him.

Kiera stood there bristling. Before Andrew reentered her life, she'd felt competent. Capable. Now, she needed him more than she cared to admit—and he never let her forget it.

With a sigh, she wandered down the narrow hallway in search of the bathroom, glancing into the other rooms as she passed. The lodge had been modernised years ago, back when she was still living at Wickham Hall, but it looked more lived-in now. Warmer. There was a cozy sitting room that opened onto the main entrance, a sleek little kitchen, a single bedroom, and a compact but clean bathroom.

The furnishings were clearly Andrew's. The space had never been properly furnished before. She paused at the sight of the curtains—soft grey linen—and her stomach twisted. Had Sienna helped him choose those? Had she been here with him?

Just a mile from her husband's estate.

The thought turned her cold all over again.

She pushed the thought away and stepped under the hot spray, letting it thaw the chill from her bones. The warmth soaked into her skin, chasing away the sting of the rain. After drying off, Kiera reached for the white bathrobe hanging behind the door. It was clearly Andrew's—far too large, brushing her ankles and swamping her arms—but it was warm, and it wrapped around her completely. Her own clothes were drenched, hopelessly so, and there wasn't a radiator in sight.

In the kitchen, she found a plastic bag and stuffed the wet clothes into it. Then, with nothing else to do, she wandered back into the living room. She peered through the curtains—no sign of Andrew. The rain still came down in sheets, the darkness outside absolute. He'd be soaked by now. Likely furious, too.

Oddly, she didn't care as much as she should. The lodge was warm and quiet, and the fire crackled invitingly. She added a few logs, then drifted back to the bathroom to tidy up. Andrew's things were scattered around—talc, aftershave— and before she could stop herself, she uncapped the bottle. The scent was the same as it had always been, instantly familiar. It transported her to another summer—years ago, by the river. That was the first time she had noticed him not just as her friend, but as a man. She had wanted to lean in then, to breathe in that scent from his skin.

Even now, it stirred something unexpected—something warm, something dangerous. Flustered, she screwed the cap back on quickly and returned to the fire, cheeks tingling with heat not entirely from the shower. She stood there awkwardly, as if she'd been caught in something indecent.

Then the door opened.

Andrew stepped inside, rain streaming off his oilskin. Even with it on, he was drenched. His dark hair was plastered to his head. He shrugged off the coat and kicked off his boots before fixing her with a sharp look.

"You really do need a garage," he said curtly. "It's beyond me. I moved the car onto the grass."

"You had to get your car? A towrope?" she asked, guilty now.

"I wasn't planning to haul it with my teeth," he muttered, casting another irritable glance her way. "It'll have to stay there until morning. Someone will have to phone the garage. No doubt, that'll be me."

"I can do that," Kiera said quickly, stung by his continued annoyance. "You don't have to do everything for me."

"Well, thank God," he snapped. "I was about to resign and take on the full-time job of managing your life."

"I'll make some tea," she offered, trying to defuse the moment.

"Brilliant," he said dryly. "Just don't scald yourself. My good deed quota is full for today."

He disappeared toward the bathroom, and Kiera sighed, nibbling her lip. She hadn't expected him to be so… sharp. He'd always handled her crises with calm—exasperation, yes, but never this edge. He was taking longer than usual to cool off.

She put the kettle on, moving carefully in the borrowed robe, and tried not to feel awkward about the fact that she was completely at his mercy—no clothes, no transport, no dignity left to speak of.

Chapter Fourteen

By the time Andrew returned, showered and dressed in jeans and a sweater, she had two mugs of tea ready. He took one with a silent nod and sank into the small sofa. He didn't speak. Just stared into the fire, the flickering light carving out the stern lines of his face.

She sat gingerly on the edge of the armchair, her nerves fraying.

He was unsettling her—and he knew it. Since they'd reunited, he'd been alternately scathing and kind. He had comforted her, taken care of her—but also wounded her with a look, a word. It was exhausting.

"I should probably go back," she said softly, breaking the silence. "To the hall."

"Later," he replied, eyes unmoving from the flames.

It was all he said. And all she was apparently going to get.

She bit back a sigh and cast around for anything to say that might thaw him. "The furniture—it's yours?"

He glanced at her without interest. "From my apartment. The rest I gave away."

"It's lovely," she said cautiously, her eyes roaming the fire-lit room. The wood gleamed. It was elegant, masculine. She remembered his old place—sleek, impersonal—and wondered what had changed. What made him throw it all out and start over?

She looked up and found him watching her intently. The firelight made his eyes startlingly clear, and her stomach fluttered. She dropped her gaze and set her mug down quickly.

"Who made the curtains?" she asked, too quickly.

"Why?" His tone was unreadable.

"No reason. I just… wondered. They look like they were a pain to hang."

"A woman in the village made them," he said at last. "I put them up myself."

"Oh," she murmured, heart thudding too loudly in her ears. "I thought… maybe Sienna helped."

She hadn't meant to say it. The words slipped out, traitorous, born of the ache in her chest. The lodge felt too much like home, too warm, too intimate. And Sienna haunted every corner of it. How often had she been here, not a mile from her husband's home?

Kiera wanted to bite the words back, but it was too late.

Andrew's gaze didn't waver.

And the silence stretched, heavy with everything unspoken.

Andrew looked at her steadily, his expression masked, and Kiera felt a flush bloom beneath her skin. He'd come out on a night like this—just to help her. She was wearing his bathrobe, for heaven's sake. And still she couldn't stop herself from prying into the one thing that tormented her thoughts.

"I'm sorry," she whispered, throat tight. "I don't mean to say these things. I just… can't seem to stop."

When she glanced up again, his gaze hadn't shifted—but something in his expression had. His eyes narrowed slightly, speculative. A faint smile curved his lips.

"Come here, Kiera," he said softly, the command wrapped in velvet.

She didn't mean to move. She shouldn't have. But he kept looking at her— calm, unwavering—and something in her responded. Her tongue swept nervously across dry lips as she stood, drawn to him by a will that didn't feel like her own.

"Don't, Andrew," she said in a shaken voice.

He didn't answer—just waited, watching her.

"Come here," he repeated, low and dark.

Her feet obeyed before her mind caught up. She crossed to him, eyes caught in his, until he reached for her hand and pulled her gently into his lap. When she tried to rise, murmuring a protest, he silenced her with the strength of his arms, tucking her head against his shoulder.

"I… I should go home," she breathed, though she knew the trembling urgency inside her had nothing to do with prudence. The rest of the world faded beside the nearness of him—his scent, his warmth, the memory of a moment long past and never forgotten.

"You are home." He tipped her chin upward, and his gaze swept slowly over her face. "I've never seen you look so at home in your life."

She closed her eyes against the pull of those smoky grey eyes, her pulse racing wildly. Memories collided with desire. He hadn't held her this close since apartment. She'd never recovered. That raw intimacy lingered like an ache— and now, it lured her again, holding her breathless, helpless.

What kind of woman was she to let this happen, knowing what he did? Knowing about Sienna?

"No." The word escaped in a pained moan, tears gathering under her lashes.

His hand cradled her cheek, turning her face to his.

"Yes," he said simply. "Wherever I am—that's where you belong. You've always belonged to me. And I'm done waiting."

Her eyes flew open, shimmering with tears.

"You're going to force me to—?" she faltered, heartbreak in her voice.

His mouth curved, amused and tender, as he brushed back a lock of her hair.

"I've never hurt you in my life, angel-face."

"You have," she whispered. "Not just me. My father—what happens when he finds out about Sienna?"

She'd hoped the name would push him away—anger him into letting her go. But he didn't flinch. He only kept looking at her, and suddenly she knew the terrible truth: she didn't want him to let her go.

"Right now," he murmured, "you're not thinking about your father. You're thinking about us. You're jealous—and it's such a waste."

His lips brushed hers—just a whisper of contact—and yet it sent a violent tremor through her. She was acutely aware of his arms, the fire, the warmth of the room, the silence between them.

"There is no Sienna," he said, voice husky. "Only us. And everything we want."

"You don't know what I want," she cried, even as her head tipped back, inviting his lips to the curve of her throat.

But he knew. God, he knew. His mouth traced a scorching path along her skin, searching for the parting of her robe with devastating urgency, as though each second without her was agony.

"I do," he rasped against her throat. "You want me. You're soft, warm, and desperate—and I'm burning for you."

His hands slid beneath the bathrobe, bold now, claiming her as though he'd been waiting a lifetime for permission. She cried out into his mouth, arching into the heat of his touch, undone by the feel of him.

"I've waited years for this," he breathed, voice raw. "For you."

Her hands, trembling and eager, reached for him blindly, tugging at his sweater with an aching sound that barely qualified as a whimper. He pulled it over his head and tossed it aside without a glance, his chest rising and falling, hard and sculpted under her fingertips. She ran her hands across him like she was memorising, discovering, worshiping.

But he stopped her, gently but firmly, taking her hands in his and drawing them lower. His gaze burned into hers.

"If you want to touch me," he said hoarsely. "Really touch me."

The flare of his response nearly shattered her. She obeyed, trailing her fingers across the ridges of his abdomen, down the V of muscle that led into the waistband of his jeans, and he groaned—a low, guttural sound that lit her veins on fire. He kissed her with bruising intensity, grinding them together in a frenzy of longing.

Then, like a storm breaking through the heat, his voice broke through in a tormented growl. "Does Peterson touch you like this?"

"No! Never!" Her eyes flew wide, wild with emotion. "I wouldn't let anyone—"

"I'd kill him," Andrew ground out. "If anyone but me ever laid a hand on you—"

His eyes roved over her face, fierce and claiming, and softened for a heartbeat. "You look seventeen again," he said quietly. "How could I have believed you'd ever let someone else near you? Jealousy's a cruel thing, isn't it?"

His hand stroked her, slow and reverent, and she gasped, twisting beneath him.

"I lost you," she choked.

"No." He kissed the tears as they slipped down her cheeks. "You didn't, I'm still yours. I've wanted you since you were seventeen. And now—" he cupped her face, voice thick with emotion "—we're here."

He gathered her in his arms like she was weightless and carried her to the bedroom. Her mind gave in completely. There was no past, no future—only the burning present. Only Andrew.

In the soft glow of lamplight, he laid her down gently, slipping the robe from her shoulders, watching it fall like a whisper to the floor. She watched him undress, breathless, as if the very sight of him could burn her alive. When he joined her in the bed, the first full contact of skin against skin sent a cry spilling from her lips. She arched into him, need coiling low and tight, silent in its insistence.

"Not yet," he murmured against her mouth, his restraint barely holding. "Go too fast, and you could get hurt. Your first time… it can be painful."

She hesitated, a flicker of fear dancing in her eyes. But he cupped her face in his hands and kissed her tenderly. "Relax, sweetheart," he whispered. "I'll take it slow. I'll take care of you."

And he did.

His mouth worshiped her, tracing every inch of skin—her breasts, her belly, her hips. He kissed the hollow beneath her ribs like it was sacred, like she was something precious. When he moved between her thighs and began to taste her, her body bucked in helpless pleasure.

He lifted his head just long enough to say, "You taste like heaven. Just like I thought you would."

His tongue returned to its slow torment, building her up, wave after wave, until her body shattered with a cry that echoed through the room. He didn't stop until the tremors stilled, and then he kissed his way back up her body, lingering at her breasts, sucking gently until she moaned again.

When he finally rose above her, she looked up at him with wide, trusting eyes, her heart thundering.

"I need you," she whispered.

His gaze held something raw—like he was memorising her, starved for every inch.

He positioned himself at her entrance, the head of his shaft teasing her slick folds, and she could feel the heat, the tension in him.

He pushed forward slowly, carefully, and a sharp cry tore from her lips—pain and pleasure, mingled in a dizzying rush. He stilled immediately, brushing his lips across her face, whispering soft comforts.

"I've got you," he murmured. "I'm here. You're mine, Kiera. At last."

She couldn't speak—could only feel. She moved her hips gently, encouraging him, and he began to thrust, each motion more fluid, more claiming. The pain faded, replaced by an intense, growing heat. She wrapped her legs around him, pulling him deeper, grounding herself in the weight and rhythm of him.

Her climax built again, fiercer this time, and when it hit, she cried out—loud, uncontrolled, lost in the storm of sensation. Andrew followed her with a shout of his own, collapsing against her, his breath ragged against her neck.

"Kiera," he gasped. "Sweetheart. You're incredible."

She floated in the aftermath, limbs heavy, skin slick with sweat, and soul utterly undone. He gathered her into his arms and pulled the sheet over them both, kissing the crown of her head, breathing her in like she was life itself.

"Andrew…"

"Shh…I'm not going anywhere," he whispered. "I'll be here."

She pressed her cheek to his chest, the steady beat of his heart lulling her. Her eyes fluttered closed, her body boneless with contentment. The last thought she had before slipping into sleep was pure and certain:

It had always been Andrew. Through every lost year, every ache and unanswered longing—he had been the one. And now, at last… she was his.

Chapter Fifteen

When Kiera woke, daylight filtered softly through the closed curtains, and for a moment, disoriented, she couldn't remember where she was. And then she remembered, she had spent the night here—in Andrew's bed, wrapped in his arms, her body curled intimately against his.

And with that memory came the full weight of what had happened.

She had made love to him—with wild, aching hunger, matching him need for need. That memory alone made her stomach turn.

She had been wild, insistent, swept away by need and the fierce relief of having him close again. The shame that washed over her now was unbearable. She couldn't blame Andrew—he was a man, older, experienced, probably no stranger to nights like last night. There was Sienna, too. God, Sienna.

No—this was her fault as much as his. She'd chosen to surrender, had wanted to belong to him, even for a moment. But now came the reckoning. Facing herself was hard enough. Facing him—those unreadable grey eyes—felt impossible.

She could hear him in the kitchen. The sound only increased her dread. She needed to get up, to go out there and face him. But her nakedness now made her flush with shame. The robe—white, soft—was folded neatly on the chair. He must have placed it there after he got up. Had he looked at her body with satisfaction? Pity? She didn't even know if she'd been decently covered.

Drawing the robe around her tightly, she forced herself out of bed.

The bathroom offered a moment's sanctuary. She slipped inside unseen and locked the door. In the mirror, a pale, haunted face stared back at her. Her hair was a tangled mess—Andrew's fingers had been there, she remembered—and her eyes were heavy, shadowed, unfamiliar.

One night. That's all it had taken to undo her.

She splashed cold water on her face, ran her fingers through her hair, trying to bring some order to the chaos. Her bag—where was it? Still in the car, maybe. She didn't even have a lip-gloss to hide behind. But she couldn't stay in the bathroom all day.

With a final breath, she opened the door and stepped into the small kitchen.

Andrew turned from the stove. His gaze swept her face, his eyes narrowing.

"Sit down," he said quietly. "Breakfast's almost ready."

"I don't want anything," Kiera whispered. "I… I feel sick."

He turned to her fully, taking in her pale cheeks, trembling lips, the haunted desperation in her eyes. His jaw tightened, and for a moment, something like anger flickered across his face.

"Tea," he said shortly, guiding her to a chair. Moments later, a steaming mug was in her hands. "Drink it."

She tried, but her hands shook too badly. Her teeth chattered against the rim. She put it down, unable to lift it again. His nearness only heightened her unease.

Andrew watched her for a long moment, then switched off the stove and came to stand before her. Without warning, he pulled her to her feet.

"Talk to me," he said, his voice low but firm.

"I want to go home." Her voice was small, her cheeks colouring. She tried to explain. "Last night… I don't know why I let it happen. I must've been mad to—"

"To let me seduce you?" he interrupted coolly. "Is that what you've decided? That I seduced you and now you regret it?"

"What do you expect me to feel?" she snapped, anger rising to cover her shame. "Of course I regret it. I was stupid. I let myself be lured in, and all the time I knew I was just… someone convenient, a replacement, for Sienna."

She was goading him, hoping he'd lash out, hoping his anger would make hers feel justified. But he didn't rise to it. His expression went flat. He released her and stepped back.

"So. You were there, you were soft and desperate in my robe, and I—what? Lost all self-control and ravished you?"

"I never said that!" she cried, horrified.

"You said you were vulnerable," he said, calm and unforgiving. "And I took advantage."

She dropped her gaze. "I'm ashamed," she whispered.

"You weren't ashamed last night," he said quietly. "You weren't reluctant. You were passionate. You didn't beg me to stop—you wanted more. And don't pretend otherwise. It happened. You felt it, too. That changes things."

Kiera turned away, her cheeks flaming.

"It was a mistake…" Her voice faltered. "We should never have—"

But when she glanced back, he was watching her with a slow, infuriating smile.

"Don't lie to me," he said softly. "I know what we felt. I know the way you responded to me. That's not something I'll forget."

Her panic rose again. "I want to go home," she said, barely above a whisper.

He shrugged. "Fine. I'll take you. I already called the garage—your car might be ready by lunchtime. If not, you can borrow your father's. Or Sienna's."

The name hit its mark like a blade. She stiffened but said nothing, forcing herself toward the door. She had to get out—away from him, away from this.

She needed space to breathe. To think. To piece herself back together.

It wasn't until she reached the door that Kiera realised, she had no shoes. Hers were still somewhere in the kitchen—soggy and abandoned beside the plastic bag of wet clothes. She turned back awkwardly, only to find him behind her, a faintly amused smile playing on his lips. He held the bag and her ruined shoes in one hand; her handbag tucked under his arm like a courier delivering an unfortunate parcel.

The shoes were still damp when Kiera slipped her feet into them, squelching uncomfortably as she tried to walk. They were likely beyond saving, like whatever fantasy she clung to last night.

Hobbling to the car, she was too proud to ask for help. He didn't offer any. He simply dropped her belongings at her feet once she was seated, then circled the car without a word, settling behind the wheel like a disinterested taxi driver who had never seen her before in his life.

The drive felt interminable.

Andrew stared ahead, focused solely on the road, and said nothing. Kiera sat beside him in aching silence, her throat tight, tears stinging her eyes. How could he be so detached? Just last night, he had whispered into her ear like she was the centre of his world, his touch branding her skin, his words unravelling everything she thought she knew. But this morning, she was nothing to him. No one special. Just another girl foolish enough to believe in stolen moments.

"How can you be like this?" she choked, as the car slowed in front of the house. "How can you treat me so… so coldly, when last night—?"

"When last night I was enjoying the delights of your body?" he interrupted smoothly, finally turning toward her. His expression was unreadable. "You've already answered that, Kiera. I seduced you. You made it easy. Unless you'd like me to drive back to the lodge and do it again, I don't see that anything's changed."

"Last night, I forgot about Sienna!" she cried, her voice cracking with pain.

He nodded slowly, eyes darkening. "So did I," he said. "And I'll forget about her again. The next time I make love to you."

"There won't be a next time!" she blurted, eyes wide with something close to panic.

His gaze swept over her; his smile laced with mockery. "Not until we're alone again," he said quietly. "But when that happens, you'll come the moment I say your name."

She shook her head violently, lips parting to deny it—but no words came. Deep down, she knew the terrifying truth: she would. She had always been vulnerable to Andrew, even as a teenager. And now she was hopelessly lost. If she didn't belong to him, she didn't know who she was anymore. The only answer was to stay far, far away.

She grabbed the handle and opened the door, desperate to escape the humiliating conversation. But as the cool morning air touched her bare legs, reality set in with a slap.

"I can't go in like this!" she said frantically, glancing at him without hesitation, panic overriding pride. "Please, Andrew—help me!"

"Why?" he murmured. "Tell Mrs. Williams you went for a dip in the river and a vagrant stole your clothes."

She stared at him, horrified. Was he serious?

His expression remained impassive, eyes glinting.

"Please!" she whispered. "The longer I sit here, the more curious she'll become."

He considered her, then offered another suggestion with a maddening calm. "Then tell her to mind her own business. Or better yet, go in dancing and tell her you're wearing my bathrobe because you slept with me. That should shut her up."

Tears of humiliation stung her eyes. He reached out, brushed a finger along her cheek with surprising gentleness.

"Forget her," he said quietly. "Walk in there like she doesn't matter. Because she doesn't."

"Will… will you come with me?" she asked, her voice barely a whisper.

He leaned back and shook his head slowly. "No. I'm no longer your saviour, Kiera. Or your protector. Every time I see you now, I'll want you. You need to understand that."

"You're forgetting about Sienna," she said through clenched teeth as she stepped out of the car.

He held her gaze. "Not really," he said softly. "But she's gone most of the time, as you know. That leaves us."

Kiera snatched up her things and ran toward the house, his gaze following her like a tether she couldn't quite sever. There was something in his eyes—pity, maybe, or reluctant longing. She looked like a girl again in that moment, wild-haired and wounded, the same green-eyed girl who had stirred something reckless in him.

Mrs. Williams was waiting just inside, as Kiera had dreaded. Her sharp eyes flicked to the oversized robe and wild hair, taking in every incriminating detail.

"I didn't know you were back," she said coolly, which was clearly a lie.

"Only just," Kiera replied lightly. "My car broke down during the storm last night, so I stayed at the lodge. Let me know if the garage calls, won't you?"

She swept past, every step measured, though her heart was hammering. She knew Mrs. Williams would report everything to Sienna the moment she returned. The thought made Kiera's stomach churn. She reached her room and shut the door making her way straight to her bathroom.

One day soon, Sienna would be back. But Kiera knew she couldn't wait around for that confrontation. Seeing Andrew again was impossible. He'd made himself clear.

Under the warm spray of the shower, she spotted faint bruises along her skin—fingerprints from last night. They made her stomach twist, and her breath catch.

The memory rolled over her, vivid and sensual, and despite everything, it still thrilled her. If he called her name, she would come. That had to stop.

She had never imagined herself as Andrew's mistress. He already had one: polished, sharp-edged, and worthy of him.

But she couldn't leave yet. Her father still needed her. That dilemma—the pull between love and duty—held her prisoner.

When the garage returned her car earlier than expected, she went straight to the hospital. Her father looked brighter, more alert. Just before she entered his room, the doctor stopped her in the hall.

"We're discharging him tomorrow," he said. "He'll need to rest for a week. I've spoken with his partner already—your presence will help him take it seriously."

Kiera smiled and thanked him, though her chest felt tight.

Andrew had been there again. Always ahead of her. Always stepping in. And now, she would have to see him again—work beside him—for her father's sake.

It was more than she knew how to handle. She went to the gallery but spent the rest of the day pretending to work, her mind circling the same agonising truth: she might still love him, but she couldn't survive him.

Chapter Sixteen

When Gary called, Kiera declined as gently as she could. That part of her life was over. She wasn't the same woman anymore, and she felt certain people would see it just by looking at her. She saw it every time she caught her reflection—something in her expression had shifted. Andrew had left a mark on her, not physical, but soul deep. There was a wistful pull to her mouth now, a sadness lingering in her eyes. She felt altered, and even if no one else noticed, she couldn't unsee it.

Gary wasn't easily discouraged. Just before the gallery closed, he arrived with a warm smile and a bouquet in hand. Her heart sank with regret. Gary was everything a woman might hope for—steady, kind, endlessly patient—but beside Andrew, every other man seemed to fade. And now, seeing Gary again felt like deception.

"You sounded down," he said as she greeted him. "I figured you'd want to get home, but I brought these. Thought they might help."

"You're sweet, Gary." She offered a soft smile. "My father's coming home from the hospital tomorrow. I have to drop off some things for him tonight, but I can make you a coffee if you like."

His face lit up, pleased by the offer. She led him upstairs to her apartment, heart heavy with the weight of the goodbye she knew she had to say. It wasn't fair to string him along when her heart was tied to someone else.

While she made the coffee, he watched her with gentle curiosity. When she sat across from him and handed him a cup, he smiled again.

"Nice and cosy," he said warmly, glancing around.

The words hit her like a blow. Cosy—that's what she'd thought last night too, wrapped in Andrew's robe at the lodge. Her face tensed involuntarily, the memories rushing in like a storm.

"Another migraine?" Gary asked, concerned.

She shook her head, unable to speak for a moment.

"Hit a nerve then," he said quietly. "It's Foster, isn't it?"

"Yes," she whispered, dropping her gaze before meeting his again. "I can't see you anymore, Gary. I'm sorry. We've known each other a long time, but there's no future in it. Not now."

"Because you love him," he said, without judgment.

She nodded. She always had. There had never been anyone but Andrew. And now, it hurt more than ever.

"I never meant to hurt you," she murmured.

"Is he hurting you?" Gary asked gently.

"It can't be helped," she said, her voice tight. "It's always been like this. Since I was barely more than a girl."

"Would it help if I bashed him up?" he offered with a wry smile.

Despite everything, she laughed softly.

They left together, locking up the gallery, and paused on the quiet street.

"Goodbye feels too final," he said. "Can we just… leave it open for now?"

"I'd like that," she said honestly, her hand resting on his arm. "But it would be dishonest. I care about you too much to lie."

"I won't vanish," he told her. "If you need me—or change your mind—you know where I am."

He leaned in to kiss her cheek but, at the last second, gently pulled her into a full embrace, brushing his lips across hers with quiet affection.

"Keep fighting," he murmured against her hair. Then he stepped back and left with a wave, his car disappearing down the street.

She watched until his car vanished around the bend, and though she'd said goodbye with words, it felt like her heart whispered a quieter, more permanent farewell. She wouldn't see Gary again—not like this.

The regret on Kiera's face hadn't faded before Andrew appeared.

He was striding toward her, his expression thunderous, eyes stormy with rage. The urge to run surged through her, but it was too late. He was in front of her before she could move.

"So," he growled, "you're keeping the boyfriend. Have you updated him on your latest developments?"

"I was saying goodbye," she said defensively, but he cut her off.

"Of course. I saw the whole thing—his flowers, his smile, your welcome." His voice was thick with jealousy.

"You were watching me? You've no right—"

"I've every right," he snapped, catching her arm. "If he'd stayed in that apartment one more minute, I'd have dragged him out. I'm not one to share, Kiera. Tell him to keep his distance—if you care about his safety."

His grip wasn't bruising, but the old fear flared in her chest—fear not of violence, but of losing control again, of spiralling back into his orbit. Her temper flared. She wrenched her arm free and glared at him.

"My father's coming home tomorrow. As soon as he's well enough, I'll be back here, living my life. Gary is part of that life. What happened between you and me was one night—nothing more."

"I'll be here every day," Andrew shot back. "I'll haunt you."

"You'll be too busy with Sienna," she hissed, her eyes sharp with fury. "I've been ashamed of what happened, how easily I let you use me. But shame is wasted on you. You should carry enough for both of us."

"I've got enough determination for both of us," he said through clenched teeth.

She turned on her heel. "Leave me alone," she snapped. "You still make me feel the same way I did for years—sick at the sight of you!"

For a moment, she thought he might stop her. But he didn't. She managed to drive away, only to pull over minutes later, trembling so badly she couldn't continue. Why had he come? What did he expect—that she'd be waiting, eager for his command?

And when Sienna returned, what then? Andrew had no problem warning her off Gary, even knowing their relationship had never been physical—yet he had no shame in his long-standing affair with Sienna. The hypocrisy made her stomach churn.

The next morning, Kiera collected her father from the hospital alone. She half expected Andrew to be there, as he so often was when least wanted, and found herself glancing over her shoulder more than once. He haunted her even in absence, and she feared that wouldn't change any time soon.

Her father was delighted to be home at Wickham Hall after his forced stay in hospital—but Kiera no longer shared his joy.

Andrew was everywhere. Every room, every shadowed corner echoed with memories of him. And though she had said all she meant to say to him—fiercely, even cruelly—there remained a hollow ache inside her. A sadness so vast, it made her want to leave and never return.

Admitting, even to herself and to Gary, that she loved Andrew had stripped away her last defence. Now, the bitterness she felt toward Sienna ran deeper than ever. Sienna would come through this unscathed—she always did. She always won. And Kiera? She had never been able to fight her. She couldn't even begin to fight for Andrew. He didn't love her.

Restless and hurting, Kiera fussed over her father until he finally had to draw a line.

"I'm not in a wheelchair, Kiera," he said sharply before dinner. "Another week and I'll be back at work. No one is turning me into an invalid—not even you."

"I just want to take care of you," she protested, her voice tight. "You scared me when you were ill. I'm going away again soon, and I want to make sure you're fully well before I do."

Her father looked at her, serious. "Why are you going away? This is your home. I want you here. You don't know how much happiness it's given me to have you back."

"I can't come back." Her voice broke. She sank to the carpet, resting her head against his knees. "I don't belong here—not when Sienna's around. I never have. I can't fight her now, any more than I could before." She glanced up at him, suddenly regretful. "I'm sorry. I shouldn't have said that. She's your wife."

"Listen, love—" he began, reaching for her hand.

But the sound of a voice from the doorway froze them both.

"Well, you're back, David. Am I interrupting a touching father-daughter moment?"

Andrew stood in the open doorway.

Her father beamed at him. Kiera scrambled to her feet, heart pounding, every instinct screaming at her to flee. She'd unleashed all her fury on him last night, but his face held no trace of anger. Just quiet resolve—which, somehow, felt more threatening.

"I'll go check on dinner," she said quickly, sidestepping toward the door.

"There's something I need to tell you, Kiera," her father called after her.

"Later," she muttered, not meeting Andrew's eyes as she brushed past him.

She had known—deep down—that he'd come tonight. But that didn't make it any easier. Dinner loomed. She glanced down at her trembling hands, willing them to be still. Whatever her father had been about to say, she could guess: a plea to live in peace with Sienna.

Impossible.

Sienna would return and reclaim Andrew with a flick of her fingers. She always knew where he was, how to reel him back. Her only escape was to leave Wickham and forget everything. If only Sienna would stay gone—but no, she was likely on her way now.

Uneasy, Kiera turned to Mrs. Williams, her concern driving her bluntness.

"Have you heard from my stepmother?"

"As I told you before, Miss Scott," came the cool reply, "I've no idea where she is." Mrs. Williams didn't even glance up from the stove.

Kiera's fists clenched. No other household would tolerate this insolence. If her father were ever alone and ill, this woman would run the place like a tyrant.

Still seething, Kiera returned to the drawing room. Andrew was speaking quietly with her father, but their conversation ceased when she entered. Her father studied her flushed face.

"What's wrong?"

"Oh, just temper," Kiera said lightly, trying to smile. "Good thing I'm heading back to London soon. Much longer here and I'll either sack that woman or dunk her head under the cold tap."

Andrew's lips twitched. Her father chuckled.

"You might get the chance sooner than you think—" he began, but Andrew shot him a sharp look and swiftly changed the subject.

Kiera blinked in surprise. Andrew's manners were usually faultless. Tonight, however, he was different—calculated, controlled. All through dinner, he steered the conversation away from her, keeping it centred on work. Every time her father turned to include her, Andrew jumped in, shifting the focus again.

By the end of the meal, Kiera felt completely shut out. As soon as she could, she excused herself and left the table. But she couldn't settle. Restless, she grabbed a jacket and slipped into the moonlit garden.

She wandered through the shadows, memorising everything. She would have to leave for good now. Her feelings for Andrew ensured that. It was over.

As she returned toward the house, the front door opened. Andrew stepped out. They both froze.

"I didn't expect you to leave so soon," she said, startled.

"And I thought you were in bed. I realise I bored you out of the room."

He didn't sound sorry. Kiera's eyes narrowed. Normally, Andrew was the kind of dinner guest who could charm a room. Tonight, he had deliberately dominated the conversation—and twice stopped her father from speaking.

"I'll go check on my father," she said uneasily.

"No need. I persuaded him to go to bed."

Her suspicions flared. She turned to face him. "He knows, doesn't he? He's found out."

Andrew didn't flinch. "He knows."

"And it doesn't bother him?" she demanded. "You're saying he knows about you and Sienna—and he's fine with it?"

Andrew's smile was faint, ironic. "I think he's secretly relieved. Sienna's a walking liability. He probably feels like he's stopped banging his head against a wall."

Kiera stared at him, horrified.

"You can't mean that. He loves you like a son."

"He does," Andrew said lightly.

She tried to speak, to make sense of this awful betrayal, but Andrew just laughed. Clearly, her expression amused him.

"You're so naïve, Kiera," he said, catching her hand. "You haven't changed."

"You mean I'm a fool," she snapped. "I must be. To fall for your tricks. You don't care about anyone—not even my father. I thought at least you cared about him, even while you were stealing his wife!"

"Maybe he was ready to pass her on," Andrew said with a shrug, still grinning.

Kiera wrenched away, storming toward the house—but he grabbed her arm and pulled her back into his arms.

"You don't understand," he said quietly, his smile gone. "But whether you're outraged or not, don't talk to your father about this."

"Because he's devastated by your duplicity?" she spat.

Andrew's gaze darkened. "Duplicity?" he repeated. "Depends, whether you mean treachery or strategy. Let's just say he's surprised—and he doesn't need more surprises right now."

He hesitated, then added, "Sienna's coming back tomorrow."

The words struck like a blow. Kiera had expected it. Dreaded it. But it still hurt like nothing else.

"So, you contacted her?" she asked bitterly.

He shook his head. "She called my office this afternoon."

"Then why didn't she call my father?" Kiera whispered. The answer was plain—and unbearable. "She called you to make sure she still had a future."

Andrew didn't deny it.

Kiera pulled away. He let her go.

She walked inside and closed the door behind her, leaning against it for a long, trembling moment.

Everything she'd believed about Andrew, every fragile hope she'd let herself cling to, cracked under the weight of his smirk. Her stomach twisted with shame. She'd let him in again, only to be played like everyone else.

She had loved him. Against her better judgment, against all reason—she had loved him.

But Andrew wasn't who she thought he was. Behind the charm and the easy laugh, he was as calculating as Sienna.

And now, they had their future.

Without her.

Chapter Seventeen

When Kiera woke the next morning, her first instinct was to flee. She couldn't bear to be here when Sienna arrived. She didn't want to hear the words spoken aloud—the confirmation that from now on, Sienna belonged to Andrew. But escape wasn't an option. Her father still needed her. No matter how composed he appeared, Kiera knew he must be grieving. Andrew hadn't just betrayed her—he'd betrayed her father as well. So, she stayed, determined to be there for him and just as determined to keep her own grief buried deep.

At breakfast, she kept silent about what was to come. Her father looked strained, barely able to speak, and soon excused himself, disappearing into his study. Kiera watched him go, anxiety curling in her chest. He looked older this morning, more shaken than he had since her mother's death. Andrew might believe her father was handling things well, but Kiera saw the truth. He was suffering. And that alone gave her the strength to see this through.

The morning passed in a haze of wasted hours. Kiera kept watch on the drive, waiting for Sienna. Andrew would be the one to fetch her, and sooner or later they'd return—together. The image of them stepping out of his car side by side would etch itself into her memory, a cruel preview of the future.

Just after lunch, Andrew's silver Mercedes pulled up the drive. Kiera moved to leave the window, to spare herself the sight—but something stopped her. A miserable compulsion rooted her in place. She needed to see it. Needed to feel it. As Andrew stepped out of the car, sunlight caught in his dark, blue-black hair. The sharp lines of his face were lit with that familiar golden light. A soft sound escaped her lips. She was memorising him, knowing—almost certainly—this would be the last time she saw him.

But Sienna wasn't with him.

For a moment, Kiera couldn't make sense of it. Andrew walked into the house alone. She peered anxiously down at the car, half-expecting to see Sienna waiting inside. But there was no one. It didn't make sense. Andrew had been so sure Sienna would arrive today.

Driven by confusion, she went downstairs. She could hear voices coming from the study—Andrew and her father talking. Andrew's tone was firm, almost authoritative. She waited for raised voices, for an argument. None came.

Then, unable to stay away any longer, she stepped inside—ready to defend her father, to fight Andrew if she had to.

But what met her wasn't conflict. It was her father's sharp, impatient look.

"Give us a minute, Kiera," he said brusquely, clearly expecting her to go.

Before she could move, Andrew cut in.

"We don't need a minute. We need coffee." His voice was clipped, resolute. "The discussion's over, David. Stick to what I told you—and leave the rest to me. This is my field of expertise, after all."

"More than I can reasonably expect you to do," her father muttered, and Kiera watched them both, baffled.

"It's a pleasure," Andrew replied grimly. He turned to her with the same grim expression. "Get us some coffee, will you? And don't take too long. We don't want Mrs. Williams hovering around. Sienna will be here soon."

Kiera left without a word, too stunned to even feel hurt. What was wrong with her? Was she missing something? The two men had spoken about Sienna like it was a business arrangement—her father practically handing over his wife to Andrew. No bitterness. Not even surprise. Just polite, detached planning. The only irritation had been directed at her, as if she was too naive to grasp the sophistication of their arrangement.

Maybe they were right. She didn't understand. She had seen more passion at estate auctions.

She didn't see Mrs. Williams. She fetched the coffee herself, though what she really needed was a brandy. By the time she returned, she could no longer picture the ordeal ahead—couldn't even imagine how it might unfold. The way these two men thought was beyond her comprehension. The arrangement they'd settled on left her cold.

Ten minutes later, Sienna arrived.

Kiera's nerves were taut, stretched thin. The silence between the three of them since she returned with the coffee had been unbearable. She'd expected at any moment to be dismissed. But neither man had said a word. Occasionally, she looked up to find Andrew watching her—his gaze unreadable, shadowed.

Then a car engine sounded on the drive. A door slammed.

Andrew rose and crossed to the window.

"Sienna," he announced flatly, a cold satisfaction in his voice. "Now we can finally sort out our lives."

Kiera stood abruptly, ready to leave them to their grotesque arrangements. But Andrew's voice stopped her mid-step.

"Where are you going?" His tone was sharp, commanding.

"This has nothing to do with me," she managed. "I can't bear—"

"Kiera, love—" her father began, but Andrew cut him off.

"You stay, Kiera," he said, his voice like steel. "If you walk out, I'll come after you. Nothing gets said unless you're here. You hear every word."

She stared at him, stricken. Was this cruelty? Did he want to make her suffer by forcing her to listen to him commit to Sienna?

"I can't," she whispered, turning away. But she hadn't taken more than two steps before Andrew was beside her, his hand closing firmly around her arm.

"You can," he said quietly. His eyes met hers—dark, brooding, intense. "You owe me this, Kiera."

And that was the moment she couldn't fight. Because despite everything— whatever he had done, whatever he might still do—she loved him.

"All right," she whispered, brokenly.

His hand slid down her arm, fingers curling around hers in a fleeting, tender grasp.

"Sit with your father," he said softly. "And keep your nerve. He might need you—for the next few minutes."

Kiera didn't know how she managed to make her legs carry her back toward her father. The sharp staccato of Sienna's heels echoed on the parquet floor in the entrance hall—each step like a countdown to the end of everything Kiera had hoped for with Andrew.

Then Sienna entered. Beautiful as ever. Impeccably made up, not a hair out of place, dressed in a deep sapphire suit that made her eyes blaze like ice. Kiera felt like a windswept schoolgirl in comparison—crumpled, insignificant.

Sienna was older than Andrew by five years yet somehow looked younger. She radiated power, poise. One glance told Kiera she'd never stood a chance. Not really. She couldn't compete with that.

She placed her hand on her father's shoulder, and he covered it with his own. He didn't rise as Sienna came in—too drained, too broken. Her fingers tightened under his, a small gesture of comfort. Andrew had been right—her father did need her. Not just because of his recent illness. He was dreading this confrontation, but not nearly as much as she was.

"Surely we're not having this discussion in front of everyone?" Sienna said sharply, stopping in the doorway. Her gaze landed on Kiera with disdain, then flicked to Andrew. "What is this, a committee?"

"Deeply interested parties," Andrew replied, his voice cool, unreadable.

Kiera glanced at him, hoping to catch some glimmer of warmth, some recognition of Sienna's presence. All she saw was cold, quiet triumph.

"Very well," Sienna said with a flick of her hand, stepping further into the room. "I suppose she had to know eventually. Doesn't bother me." She sat, crossing her elegant legs, eyes fixed on her husband. "I assume Andrew told you—I want a divorce?"

"He did," David said simply.

Kiera's hand gripped tighter on his shoulder, bracing him, bracing herself.

"Well?" Sienna demanded. "Do you agree? No need for mess, is there? I'll disappear quietly. I'm sure you'd prefer that."

"You're very considerate," David murmured. "Andrew and I have discussed it. He has the details."

Sienna's eyes narrowed. Suspicion bloomed. "Surely your lawyer—?"

"We'll get to lawyers," Andrew interrupted smoothly. "But I imagine what matters most to you right now is money. Since I handle David's finances, he left this to me."

Kiera blinked. Something in his tone unnerved her. He wasn't acting the way she had expected. His gaze on Sienna was ice, without even a flicker of admiration. He perched on the edge of an antique desk—relaxed, confident, as if savouring this moment.

"This isn't proper," Sienna snapped, visibly rattled. "This is between David and me. Or at the very least, a discreet solicitor."

"Oh, I'm discreet," Andrew said silkily. "In fact, I've been discreet for ten years. Astonishingly so."

Sienna's face paled under her flawless makeup. "That has nothing to do with me."

"It has everything to do with you," Andrew said quietly. "But let's move on. You won't be divorcing David. He'll be divorcing you."

"I refuse," Sienna said sharply.

"You have no choice." Andrew's voice dropped, dangerous now. "The grounds will be adultery. The proof is in my safe."

Her face crumpled in the subtlest way.

"But David," Andrew continued, "is willing to be generous. He'll file for incompatibility. No scandal. But there's a catch. You get nothing."

Sienna shot to her feet. "You can't do that. I can claim a substantial settlement—"

"You won't," Andrew cut in flatly. "If you try, the grounds change. To adultery. Ten years of it, with a very married, very public man. I imagine the press coverage alone would be… devastating."

"You're vile," she hissed, sinking back into her chair.

Andrew gave her a razor-edged smile. "Brilliant, actually. I've had this in hand for years. You thought I suspected. I knew. I waited until David was ready to know the truth. Now he is."

Kiera sat frozen, the foundations of everything she had believed collapsing beneath her. She had blamed Andrew—loathed him—for something he had never done. And now… she didn't know how to face him.

The guilt hit her like a blow. Every furious word she'd thrown at him in London now felt cruel and unwarranted. She had misunderstood everything.

"So… I get nothing?" Sienna said, her voice flat, defeated for the first time.

Andrew shrugged. "David's offering you the boutiques."

"They're mine already!"

"Not even on paper. David funded them. I arranged the transactions. You've repaid none of it. Legally, he owns it all. Stock included."

He turned, eyes meeting Kiera's. "His daughter, on the other hand, repaid every penny. She owns her thriving business. David owns yours."

Sienna's expression twisted. "This can't be legal!"

"It is," Andrew said calmly. "You can fight, but you'll lose. Badly. Or you can walk away with the boutiques as a parting gift. Your choice."

"This is blackmail!"

"It's an arrangement," Andrew corrected. "A concept you understand very well."

Sienna jumped up and began to storm out of the room, but Andrew's voice stopped her, his tone like a steel whip.

"Well?" he bit out. "We want an answer now!"

"Do I have any choice?" she asked bitterly.

He looked at her with a very bland expression on his face before he said quietly, "No. You don't. You ran out of luck years ago, soon after you met me, in fact."

"I underestimated you," Sienna sneered. "I imagined you just disapproved of what you thought was my occasional fling. In fact, I actually thought you were too wrapped up in Kiera to notice. Of course, I should have known better. You're a clever, sophisticated man, and there's not much to interest you in a girl like that."

"Be careful, Sienna," Andrew warned softly. "It would be very easy to talk yourself out of your boutiques. David loves his daughter and I'm not at all generous. The gift of the boutiques is his idea, not mine. Left to me, you would have had your moment on television."

"I'll pack," she spat. "I can't wait to get out of here."

As she stormed out, Andrew watched the door, his face unreadable—but when he turned back, Kiera saw the barely restrained rage simmering beneath the surface.

"You made it through," he told David quietly. "Don't weaken. She'll fight to the end."

"I won't," David said, gripping Kiera's hand. "I want her gone. And I want Kiera back. I should've seen through her sooner. But I let my pride blind me."

Andrew's gaze swung to Kiera, cold and hard.

"There's no reason for her not to live here now," he said. "Unless she prefers London… and her life there."

Kiera flinched. He was reminding her of Gary—of the awful things she'd said outside her apartment. But the man she'd accused had never deserved it. She had been wrong. Terribly wrong. And it might be too late to make it right.

"Pour us a drink, Kiera," her father said, trying to lighten the moment. "We should be celebrating."

She was glad for the task. Andrew didn't look at her. The satisfaction he had shown earlier was gone now, replaced by something far colder.

Mrs. Williams entered then, looking uncertain for the first time.

"Mrs. Scott says she's leaving, sir," she said awkwardly. "She wants me to go with her."

"Then go," David said flatly. "It's for the best."

"It'll look like desertion—"

"You're free to choose," he said. "But I have my daughter now. We'll manage."

Mrs. Williams hesitated, then nodded and left. The old world order had ended.

"Is that all right, Kiera?" Her father asked gently.

"It's perfect," she said with a forced smile. "We'll find someone new. I'll manage in the meantime."

"And you'll stay?"

She nodded. "I can commute. Maybe even turn the apartment into a showroom."

Andrew said nothing, just watched with that closed-off, forbidding look that sliced her to pieces.

"I'll go start dinner," Kiera murmured, desperate to escape.

"I'll take you both out," Andrew offered, his tone cool.

"I like to cook," she muttered, not looking back.

Kiera fled toward the kitchen, hoping for a moment of escape, but Sienna was already descending the stairs with her first load of suitcases. Kiera froze as their eyes met.

"So, back with Daddy, are we?" Sienna said with a poisonous smile. "Flying home to the nest like a dreary little bird. Don't expect things to be like they were when you were seventeen. I knew Andrew fancied you back then—men always chase after the youngest thing in the room. But he's not the same man now, and you're hardly alluring."

"Just go, Sienna," Kiera said coldly. "You've done your damage. There's no one left to ruin. But you never knew Andrew—not really. His contempt for you was a mile wide. I seem to recall he warned you once to watch your tongue."

"Why?" Sienna sneered. "Are you going to run and tattle that I've been horrid to you?"

Kiera summoned a cool, mocking smile. "Horrid things didn't happen to me, Sienna. You were on the receiving end of all that. As Andrew pointed out, I own my business. Yours still seems to be floating in the lap of the gods."

She turned and walked into the kitchen, leaving Sienna staring after her, smile faded. But Kiera's triumph was short-lived. Sienna couldn't hurt her anymore— but the damage had already been done, long ago. And if Kiera had only trusted her own heart, maybe none of it would have happened at all.

Moments later, Andrew walked in. She glanced over her shoulder, saw it was him, and turned quickly back to the sink, slicing potatoes with studied calm.

"We're going out to dinner," he said, voice flat. "Your father wants to celebrate."

"I can cook something—" she began, not looking up.

"Your father wants to go out," Andrew interrupted sharply. "He feels guilty having you stuck here working."

"I never seem to have much of a choice, do I?" she murmured, dropping the knife and bowing her head. "I don't feel like celebrating."

When she finally turned to face him, his expression was unreadable, his eyes hard. He studied her a moment, then shrugged.

"I'm just the messenger. Take it up with your father. Or better yet, invite Peterson to join us. Maybe that'll brighten your mood."

He left before she could reply.

She went to her room and began getting ready, feeling numb. She should've been relieved—Sienna was gone, Mrs. Williams too. But the house felt unbearably quiet. Her father didn't seem to notice the shift at all, too buoyed by Sienna's departure to care that Andrew would move on.

Chapter Eighteen

The next day, Andrew left the lodge and returned to his London apartment. Her father grumbled about seeing less of him but consoled himself that work would bring them back together soon enough. Kiera wasn't so hopeful. She doubted she'd see Andrew again.

Of course, she could have apologised. She could've picked up the phone, sent a message, driven across the city—anything to close the distance between them. But her mistake felt too raw, too rooted in pride and pain, for simple words to fix. And Andrew? He had shown no sign of softening. No late-night call. No message asking if she was okay. No knock at the door. Just silence.

She hadn't had the courage to reach out—not when the one thing she feared more than anything was hearing him say it was truly over. And she loved him. God, how she loved him. With a heart that hadn't stopped aching for him, not once in all those years.

But the longer she sat with the pain, the more it twisted. Hardened. Transformed into something hotter.

Kiera rose abruptly and began to pace the room. Her steps quiet in the rug, but her mind screamed.

Anger—first at herself. For not trusting him. For walking away without asking for the truth. But then it turned on him.

Because what about her?

Yes, she hadn't told him why she disappeared. She was young and didn't know how to confront him with her suspicions. She'd just vanished, and that had been her fault. But it had been three years since he found out the truth. Three years since he learned why she walked away. And in all that time, he'd said nothing. Not once had he come to her with the truth in his hands. Not once had he said, "You were wrong, Kiera. I was never with Sienna. That was never real."

Instead, he'd let her believe the worst. Let her drown in guilt. Let her carry the shame of not telling her father about what she suspected. Why? Why had he let her think that?

Why the careful half-truths? The silences? The vague allusions that kept her wondering, doubting, hurting? Did he want her to suffer? Was this his way of making her pay for the pain she caused him when she disappeared?

And then, inevitably, her thoughts drifted to that night.

The night he made love to her.

He had been furious. Because she inconvenienced him with her car breaking down. He had helped her, like he always did. But his words had sliced through her. Hopeless, he'd called her. Like she was a burden. A disappointment.

It wasn't the first time he'd made her feel that way.

Since she came home, he'd treated her like someone unsteady. Fragile. A mess. As if she was a storm, he couldn't quite weather anymore. And yet, somewhere in that storm—he kissed her. He undressed her. He laid her down like she still belonged to him.

And he'd been gentle. Tender. He'd said things no one had ever said to her. That he'd waited years. That she was his. That he'd kill any man who dared touch her.

But was that love?

Or possession?

Was it passion—or punishment?

The doubt crept in like a shadow. Had he used her body to make a point? To take back something he thought she'd stolen. Had he wanted to make her feel powerless—to remind her of what she gave up?

It hadn't felt like that in the moment. It had felt like breathing again. Like coming home.

But maybe that was the cruelest part.

And the next morning—when she'd again dared to bring up Sienna—he hadn't denied it. He hadn't ended her torment. He'd let the suspicion hang in the air like it might still be true. Like she had been right all along.

He could've told her then. After holding her, loving her—he could've ended it.

But he didn't.

And that choice… after everything they'd shared that choice felt like betrayal.

She had stayed away from her family home for six years because of that belief. Because she thought she couldn't face Andrew everyday loving him the way she did and thinking he belonged to someone else. And for three of those years, Andrew had known the truth. He could have given her peace. Given her father back to her. But instead, he kept her in the dark.

Yes, she had run. Yes, she had been wrong not to trust him.

But Andrew had let her suffer.

She owed him an apology. She could admit that now.

But damn it… he owed her one too.

She returned to the gallery, throwing herself into work. With the help of Sally and a warm-hearted housekeeper, life began to settle into a quiet rhythm.

Andrew stayed away.

When she asked after him, her father only said there was a mountain of work at the office and a couple of overseas trips on the horizon.

Two weeks later, Sienna strolled into the gallery while Kiera was there alone.

Kiera tensed immediately, her voice clipped. "What do you want?"

"Just browsing," Sienna said lightly, her eyes roaming the walls. "I've never been here before. Thought I might buy something."

"You'll need a place of your own now that you're out of Wickham Hall," Kiera replied coolly. She wasn't about to be rattled.

"True," Sienna murmured, inspecting a nearby canvas. "Of course, I wouldn't normally come all the way out here, but I heard how well you decorated Andrew's apartment. Do you do that professionally, or was it just a little something special for him?"

"It was a favour," Kiera said evenly. "I'm glad you liked it, but I deal in art, not interiors."

Sienna raised her brows, as if surprised. "Oh, I haven't seen it myself. I doubt Andrew would invite me over. Can't imagine a world where he'd even speak to me again. No, I just heard about it. From the woman who lives there now."

Kiera's chest tightened, but she said nothing.

"She says it's delightful now," Sienna continued with feigned sweetness. "Apparently, she hated the vibe before you worked your magic. She's planning to redo a few more things—insists on using you. Andrew, of course, lets her do whatever she wants. He's always been generous with his women. Gives them everything—until he doesn't."

"I'm sure she'll be in touch," Kiera muttered.

Inside, her thoughts spun, tumbling over each other in disbelief. So, there was someone else. Someone living in the home she had shaped with love. Someone enjoying the very space she had poured her heart into making it beautiful for him.

It was one thing to imagine Andrew might move on. That cruel, quiet ache had always lingered in the back of her mind. But hearing it out loud—spoken with barbed politeness and casual finality—cut deeper than she was prepared for.

He'd told her to get rid of Gary. Made it clear that her connection to another man was unacceptable. But he was living with someone?

How was that fair?

Why was it okay for him to move on, to build something new, while she was expected to remain stuck in the past? Still tethered to guilt. Still accountable. Still in love.

The hypocrisy stung more than she wanted to admit.

Sienna lingered a moment longer, clearly savouring the damage she'd dealt, then finally swept out.

Kiera managed to hold herself together until the door closed behind her. Then she flipped the sign to "Closed," even though it was barely afternoon. She was just grateful Sally had the day off.

Back upstairs in her apartment, she wept. And when the tears were done, she quietly packed her things. Little by little, she'd been moving her personal belongings back to Wickham. But now the joy of returning there was gone. The magic had left with Andrew.

He would rarely visit now—he had someone to come home to in London. And even if he did, she doubted she could meet him without betraying everything she still felt. She had prayed for Sienna to be gone, and now she was. But the victory felt hollow.

She had lost Andrew.

This wasn't some petty argument. It wasn't about one mistake. It had started years ago—when she let doubt creep in, when she hadn't trusted the love, he offered her with both hands. That had been her failure. But his came after.

He had known the truth. And he had chosen not to tell her.

That was the crueller wound.

Not a lie, but a silence. Not an absence of love, but an absence of mercy.

He had punished her—with distance, with silence, with the unbearable weight of not knowing the truth. And worst of all, it had worked. She had suffered exactly the way he must have intended—alone, ashamed, and believing he belonged to Sienna.

Chapter Nineteen

A few days later, Gary appeared at the gallery again—right as Kiera was preparing to head home. She looked at him with mild reproach, but he only grinned and began wandering among the paintings.

"I'm buying," he declared. "Or at the very least, placing an order."

"You don't have to, Gary," Kiera said softly. "I told you how things stand because I wanted to be honest. It doesn't mean I'll shriek and faint if I see you."

"I know," he laughed. "Honestly, this isn't just about pestering you. There's a movement in the boardroom to 'beautify' the place. Too cautious to invest in expensive art that might increase in value, they've decided to collect modestly and hope for the best."

"The very long-term investment strategy," Kiera said, amused at such logic from supposed high-flyers. "What are you thinking?"

"Believe it or not, I have a free hand," Gary replied wryly. "That being the case, I thought—friends first. And since you're constantly on my mind, I figured I'd ask your advice."

"I can collect for you," Kiera said thoughtfully. "If you approach other galleries and get them to do the same, you could build a small portfolio that might grow in value."

"Dinner to discuss it?" he asked hopefully.

She studied him for a long moment before nodding. Why not? She'd been upfront with him—he knew how she felt about Andrew. But Andrew was gone, and there was no point wallowing in pain.

"All right," she agreed. "Not tonight. Early next week. Come prepared. I'll want to know how much you're willing to spend—and exactly what you expect."

"You'll also want to be sure this isn't a ploy to sneak back into your life," he said dryly.

She smiled brightly. "That too. It's Friday. By Monday, you should have a solid idea."

Gary stayed for a while longer, keeping the conversation strictly professional. He seemed genuinely interested in her insights. They didn't leave the showroom, and when she locked up for the evening, he walked out with her. But this time, he simply waved goodbye and drove off. It left Kiera with a warm feeling—comforted by the knowledge that, to at least one man, she still mattered. That she wasn't despised… not like Andrew surely despised her.

And thinking of Andrew seemed to summon him.

As she almost reached her car, a cold jolt of shock ran through her. Across the street, a dark Mercedes was parked, its driver leaning casually against the hood. When she looked, he straightened slowly.

Andrew.

It had been weeks.

For a split second, Kiera thought she was imagining him—just a flicker of memory conjured by exhaustion and too many sleepless nights. But no. He was real. Standing across the street, watching her. Intent. Focused. Determined.

Her chest tightened—and then anger surged.

Was he here to start another argument about Gary? To flaunt the woman he was living with? Whatever it was, Kiera didn't want to hear it. Her patience was gone, her heart scraped raw. She moved toward her car, the keys clenched tight in her hand, her only intention to leave.

But then—he stepped into the road, directly in her path, blocking her escape.

"Kiera, we need to talk," he said, his voice urgent, like it mattered.

She stopped, arms folding tightly across her chest. "About what?"

He hesitated—just long enough for her to see the uncertainty flicker in his eyes. Clearly, he hadn't expected the ice in her voice.

"About us," he said finally.

She let out a dry, humourless laugh—sharp and cold. "There is no us, Andrew. Not anymore." Her voice wavered just enough to betray the crack beneath her armour, but she straightened her spine. She couldn't let him see her break. Not again.

If he had moved on, then so would she. She had to. No more waiting. No more hoping.

"I see it clearly now," she went on, her tone clipped. "And yes, I owe you an apology. I was wrong—six years ago. I believed something I shouldn't have. I judged you unfairly, and I'm sorry for that."

He opened his mouth, a reply already forming—but she lifted her hand and cut him off before he could speak.

"But you owe me one too."

His brows drew together. "For what?"

Her eyes blazed, the fire in them barely contained. "For keeping the truth from me. You knew. For three years, you knew exactly why I disappeared. You knew what I believed—and you let me sit in it. You let me carry that guilt like it was mine alone. Do you have any idea what that did to me?"

His voice was low, but it couldn't soften the blow of what he said. "I was angry. And hurt."

"Hurt?" Her voice broke, raw and shaking. "You think you were the only one in pain? I stayed away from my father because I thought I was betraying him— because I believed you were having an affair with his wife. And when I finally came home, when you had the chance to tell me the truth—you still didn't. You just kept feeding my assumption with your silence, your innuendo."

"I didn't mean to—"

"No?" she interrupted. "Then what did you mean, Andrew? Because the night you made love to me, you didn't treat me like someone you forgave. You treated me like someone you wanted to punish."

"That's not true," he said, stepping closer.

She shook her head, voice trembling. "Then explain it. Explain why the next morning, you were so cold. And when I brought up Sienna, you didn't just tell me the truth. Why you still let me believe you were both lovers. Why you looked me in the eye and let me drown in it."

He looked away, jaw clenched.

She turned, reaching for her car door, hands trembling with a storm of fury and heartbreak. Her voice cracked as she spat, "Why are you even here, Andrew? Sienna told me you're living with someone. Congratulations. I hope she makes you very happy."

"Kiera, wait—"

"No." She yanked the door open, her breath catching in her throat. "You don't get to show up now. Not when I've finally stopped hoping. Not when I've finally accepted that you and I have no future."

He reached out instinctively. "Kiera, please—"

She jerked away from his touch, slipping into the driver's seat before he could stop her. The door slammed shut behind her, the sound sharp and final, cutting through the quiet street like a gunshot. He flinched.

"Kiera, stop! You don't understand—" He reached for the handle, but she'd already locked the doors.

She refused to look at him. Her hands gripped the steering wheel as she blinked back hot tears.

"Go away, Andrew," she said, her voice low, hollow, and fraying at the edges. "You're free now. You don't have to worry about me ever again."

"Kiera, please—!"

She turned the key. The engine roared to life, drowning out the rest of his words. With one last glance at the man who had once been her everything, Kiera pulled away from the curb—leaving him standing alone in the silence he'd helped create, watching her go… again.

She didn't think he would follow her.

But as she merged onto the junction where the motorway ended and the road to Wickham began, her stomach dropped. In the rearview mirror, his car glided in behind hers—smooth, deliberate, unshakable. A shadow she hadn't escaped after all.

Her pulse spiked. No. She couldn't face him again—not like this. Not when she was barely holding herself together.

Kiera downshifted, darting around two cars, slipping back into her lane just before a truck thundered past in the opposite direction. Normally, the close call would've shaken her. But not now. Now, only one instinct remained: flee.

In the miles that followed, she drove with a recklessness that didn't feel like her at all.

But Andrew wasn't giving up.

When she finally turned into the long drive, she thought—hoped—she'd lost him. Her heart pounded as her tyres crunched over gravel.

Then, behind her, his car surged through the gates.

She had barely thrown hers into park before his Mercedes skidded to a stop behind her. The moment she reached for the door handle, he was there—wrenching it open before she could react.

"You maniac," he barked, his face pale with fury. "I saw you nearly kill yourself five times in the last ten miles. It's a miracle you're in one piece!"

"I don't want to talk to you," she said, her voice shaking. She tried to sound calm, composed—but her legs felt like water, and the reckless drive had left her raw. Andrew's nearness only made it worse.

"Oh, well done then," he snapped. "Driving like a lunatic just to shut me up. That's safer, is it?"

She flinched but turned away. "Goodbye," she said stiffly, stepping toward the house.

She didn't get far. His hand caught her arm and pulled her back, spinning her to face him.

"Oh no, you don't," he said, his voice cold and low. "You scared the hell out of me—and now you think you can just walk away? Not this time. We're going to talk."

"There's nothing left to say." Her voice cracked. "I know I owe you an apology. I misjudged you. I didn't even have the courage to talk to you about it. So yes, I'm sorry, Andrew. But that's it. That's all I've got."

"Really?" he said, disbelief thick in his voice. "You think I followed you all the way out here just to hear that?"

"If not, I don't know why you're here," she whispered, exhausted. "You don't come here anymore. You see my father at the office; there is no reason for you to be here, I don't need to be involved."

"You think you're not involved with me?" he said roughly.

"Not anymore," she murmured. "You've moved on. I'm glad your girlfriend likes the apartment—It was something I could do for you. If she wants changes, have her call me."

His grip slackened, his breath catching.

Kiera took her chance and turned toward the steps.

"Kiera," he said, almost reverently. She didn't stop. Couldn't.

But when he caught her again—gently this time—and pulled her back against his chest, the warmth of him undid her. She began to struggle.

"Let me go, Andrew," she said, voice breaking. "You've made a new life. I'm not part of it. I need to start over too. Just… please, let me go."

But his arms only tightened.

"Kiera," he whispered into her hair. His voice cracked, and when she looked up at him, his expression was raw—bare stripped of pride. "Forgive me."

She froze. "Forgive you?" she whispered, disbelieving.

"Please," he said, voice raw. "I was trying to make you feel what I felt. I wanted you to wait like I did. I wanted you to ache. But I never meant for it to go this far. Not enough to make you drive like that. Not enough to make you risk your life to get away from me."

Kiera slumped against him, her body limp with exhaustion. The fight had left her, drained every last bit of energy she had.

"Please, Kiera… can we just talk?" His voice was gentler now, rough with emotion. He turned her carefully in his arms. "Come to the lodge. Let's talk properly. No shouting. No running."

She looked up at him, hesitant. But then she nodded, too tired to argue, too heartsick to resist.

Chapter Twenty

He guided her toward his car. The drive was quiet, tense, but not hostile. At the lodge, he unlocked the door and stood aside, letting her step in first. She walked in slowly, like her feet didn't quite trust the ground, and sank onto the couch without a word.

Andrew followed, then sat beside her, close—but not too close. He reached for her hands, and this time, she didn't pull away.

"First, you need to know—Sienna was lying. There is no other woman. You're the only one I want."

Kiera blinked, startled. "But why would she—?"

"Why does Sienna do anything? To stir chaos." He gave a tentative smile. "That was the last time she'll ever be in a position to hurt you."

Relief softened Kiera's expression.

"I'm sorry," he said quietly, his thumbs brushing gently over her knuckles. "You were right—about everything you said this afternoon. I should've told you the truth from the beginning. I should've told you there was nothing between me and Sienna. Not then. Not ever."

Kiera met his gaze but said nothing. Her silence held weight—wary, uncertain—but her hands didn't pull away.

"For first three years, I thought you just didn't want me anymore. That you just didn't like me anymore. I didn't understand. I thought you'd changed your mind… or outgrown whatever we had. Then, after the boutique opening, when you finally told me you thought I was having an affair with Sienna—" He swallowed hard. "I lost it. I was so angry. I didn't even try to explain. I wanted you to feel what I'd felt—years of silence, years of not knowing."

Her gaze dropped, but he held on gently.

"I told myself I didn't care anymore," he went on, voice lower now. "I tried to move on. God knows I tried. But it didn't work. I couldn't stop thinking about you, wondering how it went so wrong. And somewhere in the middle of all that bitterness and silence… I realised I could never stop loving you."

Kiera's breath caught. Her eyes lifted slowly to his. "You… loved me?"

His gaze didn't waver. "Of course I did," he said quietly. "I still do."

Her brows lifted, stunned—hope flickering like a candle in a storm. "You do?"

He nodded slowly. "When I saw you at the boutique opening, you looked… so beautiful. But still you avoided me. Then you finally told me why you left, and I was furious. Blindsided. But once the anger passed, all I could think about was you. I couldn't stop. That's when your father mentioned Peterson."

"Gary?" she blinked, confused. "But there was nothing to tell, we only dated casually. It was never serious."

"Your father made it sound like you were in love with him," Andrew said, his voice tight with restrained emotion. "That's when I lost it. I stripped the apartment bare—if I couldn't have the magic I wanted, I didn't want any of it. Honestly, I didn't want to live anywhere. It all felt hollow without you."

He looked away for a beat, jaw clenched. "Wickham Hall became torture. Every corner, every damn room reminded me of you. I was lashing out—angry, wounded. I thought I'd lost you for good."

Kiera looked away, her throat tightening. "I never meant to make you think that."

"You didn't have to. When you finally came home, you looked at me with such scorn. Like I disgusted you. And the worst part?" He let out a bitter breath. "I finally had the chance to tell your father the truth about Sienna—about what she was doing. But I waited. I knew if I told him too soon, before he was ready to hear it, it would destroy him."

Her voice was low, tentative. "So… you had proof? Of her cheating?"

"No," he said. "Not at first. I saw it with my own eyes."

Kiera's lips parted. "Then why didn't you tell anyone?"

"Because no one would've believed me. Not without making it look like I had something to gain. And maybe I did. But I never wanted it to cost me you."

She looked down, eyes full of the hurt she'd carried for years. "I heard you, you know. When I was seventeen. You and Sienna. You sounded like lovers."

He flinched. "I don't know what you heard… but whatever it was, it wasn't what you think. Sienna knew how I felt about you. She told me David would never approve of a grown man looking at his teenage daughter the way I did."

Kiera's head snapped up, eyes wide. "What do you mean—what way did you look at me?"

He gave a soft, broken laugh. "Like I was already in love with you—and too terrified to admit it."

Her voice trembled. "I was in love with you, Andrew. And when I thought you loved Sienna instead of me… it shattered me." Tears welled up, spilling down her cheeks.

He reached out, his touch tender as he brushed a tear away with his thumb. "I know it hurt. I'm so sorry you ever felt that way."

She placed her hand over his, pressing it to her cheek. "When I saw your apartment… I felt your pain, Andrew. I don't know how, but I did. And I didn't want you to feel that way. So, I redecorated it—for you."

His eyes softened. "When I came back from Portugal and walked in and saw it changed… I knew. You still cared. You wouldn't have put so much of yourself into it if you didn't."

"I love you," she whispered, her voice barely audible.

His breath hitched. "God, Kiera… I love you more than I'll ever be able to say. I can't do this anymore—can't be away from you. Please… tell me you want this too. Tell me you're still mine."

"I will always be yours," she breathed. "I could never be with anyone else."

He pulled her into his arms and kissed her—slowly, deeply—like a man anchoring himself to everything he'd nearly lost.

When he drew back, his voice was raw, unsteady. "Marry me, Kiera. Please… just say yes."

Her breath caught. Tears shimmered in her eyes as she whispered, "Yes, Andrew. I'll marry you; I love you."

He exhaled a shaky breath, then gathered her effortlessly into his lap, cradling her like something precious. "Finally," he murmured into her hair. "I've loved you since you were seventeen."

She closed her eyes, her voice thick. "And I… I threw it away. I was so foolish. I'm sorry."

He cupped her face, tender and unyielding. "No more blame. We have to forgive ourselves. You were too young. But you grew into this incredible woman—brilliant, strong. You built a life, a business, all on your own. You're not the innocent I was afraid to touch back then."

She reached up and touched his cheek, her thumb brushing lightly over the stubble along his jaw. "I've never wanted anything more than I want this—with you," she whispered. "Is this real?"

His smile was soft, almost awed. "God, I hope so. Because if it's a dream… I don't ever want to wake up." He tilted her face up, threading his fingers gently through her hair and kissed her—slow and reverent at first, then deeper, fiercer, as though years of longing were finally catching fire.

She responded without hesitation, kissing him back with everything she had. Time blurred. Breathless, aching, they clung to each other until Andrew pulled away just enough to rest his forehead against hers, his breathing ragged.

"We should stop," he said hoarsely. "If we don't… we won't be leaving this place tonight."

Kiera's gaze flicked to his, shy but certain. "Would that really be so bad?"

"Your father's probably wondering where you are," Andrew said reluctantly, his thumb brushing softly over her swollen lips.

Kiera sighed. "You're right."

"Come on, let's go tell your father the good news." He kissed her once more, lingering and tender. "That we finally came to our senses."

She laughed softly, and together they walked to the door. Andrew drove them back to the house, the silence between them warm, full of everything that had finally been said.

When they stepped out of the car, he tucked her close against his side, his arm secure around her waist as he guided her up the steps.

Just as they stepped into the entrance hall, her father was crossing from the library. He paused mid-step, eyes narrowing slightly at their slightly disheveled appearance—and the unmistakable shift in the air between them.

"What happened to you two?" he asked, trying for casual, though his brow was arched with interest.

Andrew chuckled quietly, the sound tinged with satisfaction. "Nothing serious. But we need to talk."

David studied them for a beat, then gave a small nod and followed them toward the sitting room.

Once inside, Andrew didn't let go of Kiera's hand. In fact, he tightened his grip, as if anchoring himself to her presence. Then he turned to David with a calm, unshakable resolve.

"I'm not here to ask your permission—because honestly, I couldn't bear to hear 'no.' I'm here to tell you: I'm going to marry Kiera. As soon as it can be arranged. I'll be waiting at the altar, and you'll be the one giving her away. I've waited long enough."

David blinked, then gave a dry smile. "Who's arguing? I've been wondering for years why you two didn't do this sooner."

"So have I," Andrew said with a quiet laugh, his fingers threading more tightly through Kiera's.

"I know I was slow too," David admitted with a wry grin. "Well, I guess that settles what we're talking about at dinner."

"I'll go let Mrs.—Mrs. What's-her-name—know to set another plate," Kiera said, flustered and blusteringly happy, already retreating toward the hallway.

Andrew's smile widened as he watched her go, his thumb lazily tracing circles against her palm before she pulled away. She was still blushing.

"It's Jones," her father called after her. "Mrs. Jones. Easy name to remember."

Kiera gave a quick nod and practically danced her way toward the kitchen, her heart pounding and her steps light. Andrew loved her. He'd always loved her. And now, he was hers.

She gave Mrs. Jones the dinner update in a rush of breathless joy, then hurried back toward the sitting room—because being apart from him, even for a moment, suddenly felt like time wasted.

During dinner, her father leaned back and asked casually, "You'll stay the night?"

Andrew glanced at Kiera, catching the hopeful light in her eyes.

"Anything to have more time with Kiera," he said softly, his voice like velvet. Her father smiled and instructed the housekeeper to ready the guest room Andrew always used.

They wanted to be alone, but neither could deny her father this happiness— not tonight.

"I've prayed for this for years," he said, raising his glass. "It always felt inevitable. I just couldn't understand why you two parted in the first place."

"She was young," Andrew said, his eyes resting on Kiera with a quiet intensity. "But none of that matters now. We've found our way back."

A silence fell over the table—warm, full of unspoken things.

Then David cleared his throat. "There's something I'd like to ask. I know it's selfish, and I'll understand if the answer's no."

"What is it, Daddy?" Kiera asked gently, covering his hand with hers.

"It's about Wickham Hall," he said. "I know it was my fault for letting Sienna drive you away. But now that you're home… I'd like it if you stayed. When you're married, would you live here? We could rework the west wing, give you your own space. I'd still get to see you."

Kiera looked at Andrew, but she didn't need to speak. Everything she felt was already mirrored in his eyes.

"There is no need to rework the west wing. This place is part of us," he said quietly. "There's no reason we can't all be happy here. And if we ever need a getaway, we've got our apartment in London. But Wickham… this is home."

"And I've got years to make up for," Kiera added warmly. "Besides, who's going to keep you in line if I leave?"

David beamed. "Then that's the last of my worries gone. Now, let's talk wedding plans."

Later, when her father stepped out to take a call, Andrew gently pulled Kiera down beside him on the couch. He turned toward her, tilting her chin with his fingers, his voice a low murmur wrapped in tenderness.

"How does it feel," he asked, "to be asked to share a house?"

She gave him a playful smile. "With you? Like the best kind of dream."

He chuckled, the sound deep and warm. "Newlyweds usually want privacy."

Kiera leaned her shoulder into his. "It's a big house. We can disappear if we want to."

His eyes darkened with affection, and he brushed a slow kiss along her temple. "I used to dream about that when you were seventeen," he admitted. "I was already gone for you. Hopelessly."

Her breath hitched. "And I ruined everything. I walked away and threw it all away."

He touched her cheek, his thumb gentle. "No regrets," he whispered, then kissed her—slow and full of promise. "If anything, the wait made it burn hotter. And this time, Kiera, I'm never letting you go."

Later, when the house had fallen silent, Kiera lingered in a warm, scented bath, the evening playing over in her mind like a dream. Andrew was here—in this house—and he loved her. That truth shimmered through every moment they'd shared. It had been clear all evening how much he longed to be alone with her, yet he never once tried to draw her away. Her father had been happy, and Andrew would never risk spoiling that.

She stepped from the bath, dried herself, and slipped into her nightie, her emotions too heightened for sleep. It was past midnight, and Kiera was sure she'd still be wide awake when the sun rose. She was too restless, too alive. Her thoughts drifted to another midnight—the night at the lodge—when she had surrendered to him completely. Was he remembering that too? Or was he lying in bed now, waiting for morning, as she was?

Without allowing herself time to second-guess, Kiera reached for her silk negligee, slid it over her arms, and stepped quietly into the softly lit corridor that led to the room Andrew always used in the old house.

It was the first time she had ever taken the initiative. But she needed to be near him, needed it so badly that morning felt impossibly far away. She didn't even know if he'd be awake, but when she reached his door, she knocked gently— and turned the knob.

The lights were still on. Andrew was pacing, his steps restless, agitated—until he saw her.

He froze.

His eyes locked on her, sweeping over her with a raw, hungry intensity that made her breath catch. She closed the door softly behind her, leaning against it like she needed its support.

"I couldn't sleep," she whispered, her voice trembling. Her eyes shimmered with emotion.

"Kiera..." His voice cracked on her name.

In two strides, he was across the room, gathering her into his arms. His mouth found hers in a rush—fierce, searing kisses that stole the breath from her lungs. He kissed her like a man starved, like he was afraid she'd vanish if he let her go. Then he buried his face in the curve of her neck, clinging to her.

"If you hadn't come, I would've paced all night," he said against her skin. "I can't stand being away from you anymore."

He drew back just enough to cup her face, his thumbs brushing tears she hadn't realised had fallen.

"I still can't believe this. That you're here. That we're together."

"I… I probably shouldn't be," she whispered, voice catching. "But I wanted to be with you."

"Did you?" His hands slid down her arms, skimming her sides, reverent and possessive. "Did you come because you want to sleep beside me? Wake up in my arms? Be mine again?"

She moaned softly, her head tipping back as his lips grazed the sensitive skin of her throat. Her body leaned into his, pliant and aching.

"Oh God, I want you," he groaned, his voice rough and reverent. "I'll never have enough of you. You're never close enough."

His hands found the edges of her negligee, baring her shoulders with aching slowness. "Let me undress you," he murmured, kissing every inch he uncovered. "Let me see you… touch you."

Her fingers were no gentler, tugging open the buttons of his shirt with urgency. He shrugged it off, his skin warm beneath her palms. Her negligee slid to the floor like water, leaving her bare before him. His gaze darkened as he drank her in, then lifted her effortlessly into his arms.

"You're mine," he whispered against her ear as he laid her gently on the bed. "You've always been mine."

He stripped away the last of his clothes and joined her, every inch of his body desperate for hers. When he sank into her, they both gasped—every breath ragged, every movement a confession of the years they'd lost.

Their lovemaking was not soft. It was raw and hungry, a collision of need and memory, of forgiveness and surrender. They moved together like they'd been waiting their whole lives to belong again—mouths searching, hands clutching, hearts open.

When they finally stilled, tangled in the sheets and each other, it was with the quiet knowing that everything had changed. The past was behind them. Their future just beginning.

A long moment passed before Andrew moved. He tucked her against his chest, her cheek resting on his damp skin.

"I'm sorry," he whispered hoarsely. "I didn't mean for it to be like that. I feel like a barbarian." He stroked her flushed skin, voice rough with emotion. "Did I hurt you?"

She lifted her head, her green eyes luminous, a teasing smile curving her lips.

"I think I was fairly barbaric myself," she murmured, noticing the red marks on his shoulders. "Oh no—I scratched you!"

Andrew glanced down at the damage, then chuckled, slow and deep.

"Just remember that next time you claim you're not wild," he said. "And don't think you're escaping now. Not after looking at me like that. Until we're married, your father will just have to accept you live with me."

"I'll tell Mrs. Jones in the morning," she replied demurely. Their smiles met as they lay wrapped around each other. Andrew's hand skimmed over her body again, warm and possessive, finding the soft curves he loved. His touch quieted every wild edge of her.

"If you knew how much I want you," he breathed, voice shaking, "you'd be afraid."

"The only thing that scares me is the thought of you not loving me," she said seriously.

His gaze softened, and he kissed her with aching tenderness—slow, reverent, like he was memorising the feel of her all over again.

"I never stopped loving you," he said quietly. "I tried to… when it felt hopeless. But you never really left me—not for a single day."

Her eyes shimmered. "Is it real?" she whispered.

"It's real," Andrew said, his voice thick with feeling. "It's always been real. You made me wait, angel face… and now we've got a lifetime to make up for."

He brushed a strand of hair from her cheek, then gently rolled over her, his body covering hers like a promise. They made love again—slowly this time, deeply, like they were sealing something sacred between them.

Later, as their breathing slowed and the room settled into quiet, Kiera curled closer to him, her head tucked beneath his chin.

"I love you," she whispered.

Andrew pressed a kiss to the top of her head, his arms tightening around her. "I love you too," he murmured. "Always."

Epilogue

Andrew never imagined he'd feel nervous walking down the back terrace of Wickham Hall. He'd spent ten years on these grounds—first as a guest, then as something more. He could still remember that first visit: twenty-three, fresh out of university, invited by David. Kiera had been thirteen then—a whirlwind of laughter and curiosity.

This was where it started. This place was in his blood now. And yet today, his hands fidgeted with his cufflink like a schoolboy about to take a leap into the unknown.

Not because he was uncertain—God, he'd never been surer of anything in his life—but because it still felt surreal. After everything they'd been through—the misunderstandings, the years apart, the aching weight of what might've been— he was finally here. Waiting for her.

The ceremony was set in her mother's rose garden, just beyond the old stone fountain where he'd once stolen glances at her, trying to mask feelings too dangerous to name. Now, rows of chairs lined the lawn, white ribbons dancing in the breeze. The music swelled—a string quartet playing something soft and full of promise—and laughter drifted from the seated guests. But Andrew barely heard it.

He was standing at the edge of everything—heart pounding, hands clasped— ready to begin.

And then she stepped into view, and the world stopped.

Kiera.

She looked like a dream, spun into daylight. Her veil fluttered behind her like mist, her gown a whisper of elegance that clung to her curves and shimmered in the late afternoon sun. But it wasn't the dress or the setting that undid him— it was her face. That smile. Soft, steady, radiant with love. The kind of smile a man might spend his entire life chasing—and never quite believe he's earned.

David walked beside her, pride and emotion etched in every line of his face. As they reached the front, he gave Andrew a steady look—one filled with both warning and warmth—then gently placed Kiera's hand in his.

"You take care of her," he said, his voice gruff with unshed tears.

"I will," Andrew promised, gripping her hand like a lifeline.

The ceremony blurred after that, not because it lacked meaning, but because every moment felt like an out-of-body experience. He remembered the hush as Kiera repeated her vows, the tremble in her voice when she said, "I do," and the way her fingers curled tightly into his like she never intended to let go again.

And when he kissed her—when she became his wife beneath the sun-dappled sky and ancient oak trees—it felt like the past, present, and future folding into one perfect, breathless second.

Later, as champagne flowed beneath the marquee and laughter swirled like petals on the breeze, Andrew stood back and watched her. She danced with her father, hugged her friends, and seemed to light up every inch of the garden just by being there. He couldn't stop looking at her. Couldn't believe she was his.

"You've been staring at your wife for ten straight minutes," his best man teased, slapping him on the back.

Andrew just grinned. "She's worth it."

When Kiera finally slipped her hand into his and tugged him gently down the old orchard path, he followed without question. Wickham Hall hadn't changed much. The magic was still all around them—but they had.

She turned to him beneath the great oak where she'd once carved her initials, her expression lit with quiet wonder. "We're really here," she murmured. "Getting married at Wickham Hall… where it all started."

He cupped her face, brushing his thumb over her cheekbone. "It's full circle."

She nodded, emotion shimmering in her eyes. "I still can't believe it's real."

"It is," he whispered. "You're my wife now."

A tear slipped down her cheek, and he caught it with his lips. "I used to think I didn't deserve this," he said quietly. "Didn't deserve you."

"You were always mine, Andrew," she whispered. "Even when we were both too scared to admit it."

He kissed her—slow and deep, like a vow all over again. And when she breathed, "I love you," into the space between them, he felt his whole soul settle.

"I know," he whispered back, brushing her hair behind her ear. "You always did."

And now, at last, he could love her the way he'd always wanted to—without fear, without hesitation.

Forever.

The End

Before You Go...

If you fell for these characters and want more love stories filled with emotion, passion, and second chances, my newsletter is where I share them first.

You'll receive:

💕 Early access to new releases

💕 Exclusive reader-only content and extras

👉 **Join my reader list here:** https://alisonreidauthor.com

I'd love to welcome you.

Alison Reid

Thank you for reading Love After Regret!

If you enjoyed this collection of emotionally charged romances, keep an eye out for more upcoming romance collections by Alison Reid, including:

Accidental Heirs - *A Billionaire Legacy Romance Collection*

Alpha Kings - *A Billionaire Alpha Male Romance Collection*

Cautious Hearts - *A Trust-After-Heartbreak Romance Collection*

Dark & Dangerous - *Brooding Heroes Romance Collection*

Final Surrender - *Alpha Heroes Yielding to Love Collection*

Forbidden Hearts - *A Forbidden Love Romance Collection*

Forever Mine - *A Longing-for-Love Romance Collection*

Guarded Hearts - *A Surrender to Love Romance Collection*

Hearts & Secrets - *Small Town Romance Collection*

Hearts in Peril - *A Suspenseful Romance Collection*

Hidden Truths - *A Secret Identity Romance Collection*

Lies & Hearts - *A Lies, Secrets & Betrayal Romance Collection*

Misjudged Hearts - *A Love After Judgement Romance Collection*

Torn Between Hearts - *A Love Triangle Romance Collection*

All of Alison Reid's books feature standalone stories, swoon-worthy heroes, and guaranteed happily-ever-afters.

Books by Alison Reid

A Billionaire for Christmas

A Heart in Florence

After The Storm

Always You

Before I Fell

Before the Thaw

Beneath the Lies

Billionaire Bodyguard

Billionaire Rancher

Blueprints of the Heart

Branlow

Collide

Echoes of Deception

Falling for the Billionaire

Forever Yours

Heart of the Outback

Hearts on the Line

Hidden Gem

Kept Promises

Mended Hearts

Mistaken Hearts

New Year's Eve Kiss

Quiet Danger

Reckless Hearts

Reflections of Deception

Second Glance

Shadows of the Past

Shattered Dreams

Shattered Hope, Stolen Kisses

Still Yours

The Billionaire's Accidental Legacy

The Billionaire's Bargain

The Billionaire's Mistake

The Billionaire's Regret

The Billionaire's Return

The Billionaire's Secret Baby

The Billionaire's Unexpected Heir

The Blood Debt

The Playboy's Surrender

The Wrong Sister

Trust in Time

Undercover Billionaire

Until you Loved Me

Vows of Vengeance

Wife in Name Only

Find all my books on Amazon:

About the Author

Alison Reid writes contemporary and small-town romance filled with heart, passion, and second-chance love stories. Her novels feature strong heroines, irresistible heroes, and the happily-ever-afters readers adore.

Before turning her love of storytelling into a publishing career, Alison spent thirty-five years working as an engineer—proof that happily-ever-afters can be built as carefully as any blueprint. She began writing as a hobby during the COVID lockdowns and quickly discovered a passion she couldn't ignore.

Alison is happily married, has two grown children, and shares her home with two beautiful dogs who are convinced they deserve to be her main characters. When she's not writing, she enjoys reading, spending time with her family, and imagining new love stories. She hopes her books give readers a few hours of escape, joy, and swoon-worthy romance they won't soon forget.